SUNSET
OF THE
GODS

Baen Books
by Steve White

The Prometheus Project
Demon's Gate
Forge of the Titans
Eagle Against the Stars
Wolf Among the Stars
Prince of Sunset
The Disinherited
Legacy
Debt of Ages
St. Antony's Fire

The Starfire Series:
by David Weber & Steve White
Crusade
In Death Ground
The Stars at War
Insurrection
The Shiva Option
The Stars at War II

by Steve White & Shirley Meier
Exodus

by Steve White & Charles E. Gannon
Extremis

The Jason Thanou Series:
Blood of the Heroes
Sunset of the Gods
Pirates of the Timestream (forthcoming)

SUNSET
OF THE
GODS

STEVE WHITE

SUNSET OF THE GODS

A Baen Books Original

Baen Publishing Enterprises
P.O. Box 1403
Riverdale, NY 10471
www.baen.com

ISBN: 978-1-4516-3846-2

Cover art by Kurt Miller

Map by Randy Asplund

First Baen printing, January 2013

Distributed by Simon & Schuster
1230 Avenue of the Americas
New York, NY 10020

Library of Congress Cataloging-in-Publication Data

White, Steve, 1946-
  Sunset of the gods / by Steve White.
      p. cm.
  ISBN 978-1-4516-3846-2 (trade pb)
  1. Gods, Greek--Fiction. 2. Time travel--Fiction. 3. Fantasy fiction. I.
Title.
  PS3573.H474777S86 2013
  813'.54--dc23
                              2012035231

Printed in the United States of America

10 9 8 7 6 5 4 3 2 1

SUNSET
OF THE
GODS

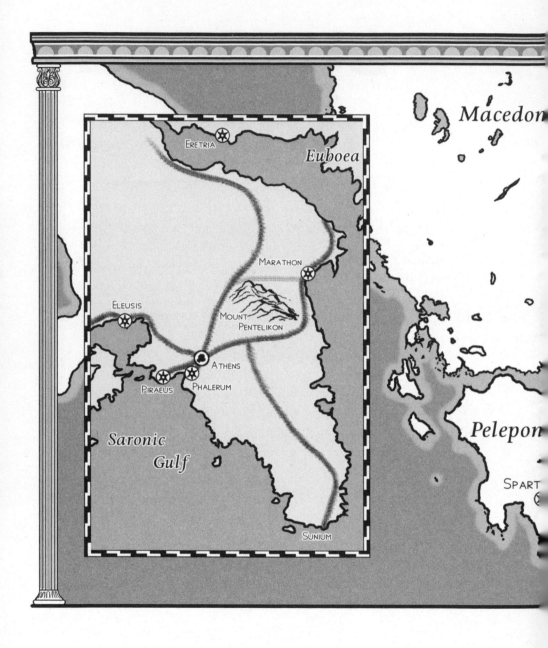

Macedon

Eretria

Euboea

Marathon

Mount
Pentelikon

Eleusis

Athens

Piraeus Phalerum

*Saronic
Gulf*

Pelepon

Spart

Sunium

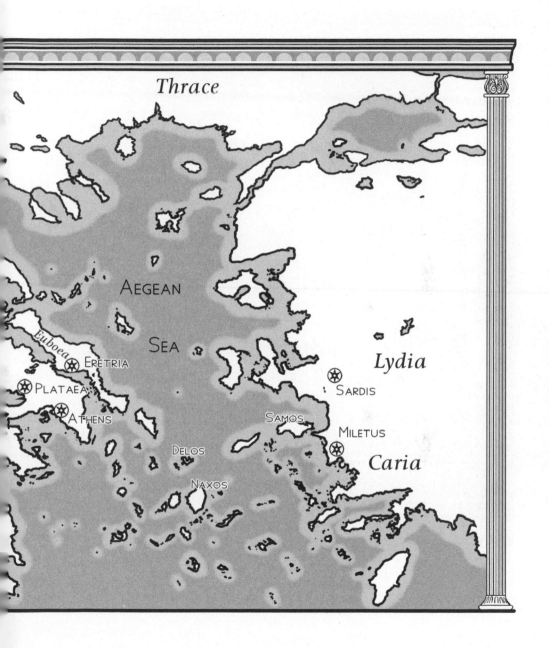

Thrace

Aegean

Sea

Euboea

Eretria

Plataea

Athens

Delos

Naxos

Samos

Lydia

Sardis

Miletus

Caria

CHAPTER ONE

EVEN ON OLD EARTH, nothing was forever unchanging, as Jason Thanou had better reason than most to know—not even on the island of Corfu, however much it might seem to drift down the centuries in a bubble of suspended time, lost in its own placid beauty.

For example, the Paliokastritsa Monastery had long ago ceased to be a monastery, and the golden and silver vessels were no longer brought there every August from the village Strinillas for the festival of the Transfiguration of Jesus Christ, by a road which had led laboriously up the monastery's hill between tall oak trees and through the smell of sage and rosemary. Now aircars swooped up to the summit, and the monastery had been converted into a resort, bringing visitors from all around Earth and far beyond it, who stared at the ancient chambers, a few of those visitors at least trying to comprehend what must have been felt by the cenobites who had lived out their lives of total commitment under the mosaic gaze of Christ Pantocrator.

They came, of course, for the incomparable location. From the monastery balcony, one could look out on the endlessness of Homer's wine-dark sea. Northward and southward stretched the coast, its beaches broken into a succession of coves by ridges clothed in olive and cypress trees and culminating in gigantic steep rocks like the one that the local people would still tell you was the petrified ship the Phaecians, once rulers of this island, had sent to bear Odysseus home to Ithaca and his faithful Penelope.

Now Jason stood on that balcony and wondered, not for the first time, what he was doing here.

He could have taken his richly deserved R&R in Australia, where the Temporal Regulatory Authority's great displacer stage was located . . . or, for that matter, anywhere on Earth. Or he could have gone directly back to his homeworld of Hesperia—his fondest desire, as he had been telling everyone who would listen. Instead he had come back to Greece . . . but only to this northwesternmost fringe of it, as though hesitating at the threshold of sights he had seen mere weeks ago. Weeks, that is, in terms of his own stream of consciousness, but four thousand years ago as the rest of the universe measured the passage of time.

There were places in Greece to which he was not yet prepared to go, and things on which he was not yet prepared to look. Not Crete, for example, and the ruins of Knossos, whose original grandeur he had seen before the frescoes had been painted. Not Athens, with its archaeological museum which held the golden death-mask Heinrich Schliemann had called the Mask of Agamemnon, although Jason knew whose face it *really* was, for he had known that face when it was young and beardless. Certainly not Santorini, whose cataclysmic volcanic death he had witnessed in 1628 B.C. And most assuredly not Mycenae with its grave circles, for he knew to whom some of those bones belonged—and one female skeleton in particular. . . .

Unconsciously, his hand strayed as it so often did to his pocket and withdrew a small plastic case. As always, his guts clenched with apprehension as he opened it. Yes, the tiny metallic sphere, no larger than a small pea, was still there. He closed the case with an annoyed snap. He had seen the curious glances the compulsive habit had drawn from his fellow resort guests. The general curiosity had intensified when word had spread that he was a time traveler, around whose latest expedition into the past clustered some very odd rumors.

"Is it still there?" asked a familiar voice from behind him, speaking with the precise, consciously archaic diction Earth's intelligentsia liked to affect.

A sigh escaped Jason. "Yes, as you already know," he said before turning around to confront a gaunt, elderly man, darkly clad in a style of expensive fustiness—the uniform of Earth's academic establishment. "And what brings the Grand High Muckety-Muck of the Temporal Regulatory Authority here?"

Kyle Rutherford smiled and stroked his gray Vandyke. "What kind of attitude is that? I'd hoped to catch you before your departure for. . . . Oh, you know: that home planet of yours."

"Hesperia," Jason said through clenched teeth. "Psi 5 Aurigae III. As you are perfectly well aware," he added, although he knew better than to expect anyone of Rutherford's ilk to admit to being able to tell one colonial system from another. Knowledge of that sort was just so inexpressibly, crashingly vulgar in their rarefied world of arcane erudition. "And now that you've gotten all the irritating affectations out of your system, answer the question. *Why* were you so eager to catch me?"

"Well," said Rutherford, all innocence, "I naturally wanted to know if your convalescence is complete. I gather it is."

Jason gave a grudgingly civil nod. In earlier eras, what he had been through—breaking a foot, then being forced to walk on it for miles over Crete's mountainous terrain, and then having it traumatized anew—would have left him with a permanent limp at least. Nowadays, it was a matter of removing the affected portions and regenerating them. It had taken a certain amount of practice to break in the new segments, but no one seeing Jason now would have guessed he had ever been injured, much less that he had received that injury struggling ashore on the ruined shores of Crete after riding a tsunami.

The scars to his soul were something else.

"So," he heard Rutherford saying, "I imagine you plan to be returning to, ah, Hesperia without too much more ado, and resume your commission with the Colonial Rangers there."

"That's right. Those 'special circumstances' you invoked don't exactly apply any longer, do they?" Rutherford's expression told Jason that he was correct. He was free of the reactivation clause that had brought him unwillingly out of his early retirement from the Temporal Service, the Authority's enforcement arm. He excelled himself (so he thought) by not rubbing it in. Feeling indulgent, he even made an effort to be conciliatory. "Anyway, you're not going to need me—or anybody else—again for any expeditions into the remote past in this part of the world, are you?"

"Well . . . that's not altogether true."

"What?" Jason took a deep breath. "Look, Kyle, I'm only too well aware that the governing council of the Authority consists of snobbish, pompous, fatheaded old pedants." (*Like you*, he sternly commanded himself not to add.) "But surely not even they can be so stupid! Our expedition revealed that the Teloi aliens were active—dominant, in fact—on Earth in proto-historical times, when they had established themselves as 'gods' with the help of their advanced technology. The sights and sounds on my recorder implant corroborate my testimony beyond any possibility of a doubt. And even without that. . . ." Jason's hand strayed involuntarily toward his pocket before he could halt it.

"Rest assured that no one questions your findings, and that there are no plans to send any expeditions back to periods earlier than the Santorini explosion." Rutherford pursed his mouth. "The expense of such remote temporal displacements is ruinous anyway, given the energy expenditure required. You have no idea—"

"Actually, I do," Jason cut in rudely.

"Ahem! Yes, of course I realize you are not entirely unacquainted with these matters. Well, at any rate the council, despite your lack of respect for its members—which you've never made any attempt to conceal—is quite capable of seeing the potential hazards of any extratemporal intervention that might come in conflict with the Teloi. The consequences are incalculable, in fact."

"Then what *are* you talking about?"

"We are intensely interested in the role played in subsequent history by those Teloi who were *not* trapped in their artificial pocket universe when its dimensional interface device was destroyed—or 'imprisoned in Tartarus' as the later Greeks had it. The 'New Gods,' as I believe they were called."

"Also known as the Olympians," Jason nodded, remembering the face of Zeus.

"And by various other names elsewhere, all across the Indo-European zone," added Rutherford with a nod of his own. "They were worshiped, under their various names, for a very long time, well into recorded history, although naturally their actual manifestations grew less frequent. And as you learned, the Teloi had very long lifespans, although they could of course die from violence."

"So you want to look in on times when those 'manifestations' were believed to have taken place? Like the gods fighting for the two sides in the Trojan War?"

"The Trojan War. . . ." For a moment, Rutherford's face glowed with a fervor little less ecstatic than that which had once raised the stones of the monastery. Then the glow died and he shook his head sadly. "No. We cannot send an expedition back to observe an historic event unless we can pinpoint exactly when it took place. Dendrochronology and the distribution of wind-blown volcanic ash enabled us to narrow the Santorini explosion to autumn of 1628 B.C. But after all these centuries there is still no consensus as to the date of the Trojan War. It is pretty generally agreed that Eratosthenes' dating of 1184 B.C. is worthless, based as it was on an arbitrary length assigned to the generations in the genealogies of the Dorian royal families of Sparta. On the other hand—"

"Kyle. . . ."

"—the Parian Marble gave a precise date of June 5, 1209 B.C. for the sack, but it was based on astronomical computations which were even more questionable. Other calculations—"

"*Kyle.*"

"—were as early as 1334 B.C. in Doulis of Samos, or as late as 1135 B.C. in Ephorus, whereas—"

"*KYLE!*"

"Oh . . . yes, where was I? Well, suffice it to say that even the Classical Greeks couldn't agree on the date, and modern scholarship has done no better. Estimates range from 1250 to 1180 B.C., and are therefore effectively useless for our purposes. The same problem applies to the voyage of the Argonauts, the war of the Seven against Thebes, and other events remembered in the Greek myths. And, to repeat, the gods tended not to put in appearances in the full light of history. There is one exception, however." Rutherford paused portentously. "The Battle of Marathon."

"Huh?" All at once, Jason's interest awoke. It momentarily took his mind off the irritation he felt, as usual, around Rutherford. "You mean the one where the Athenians defeated the Persians? But that was much later—490 B.C., wasn't it?"

"August or September of 490 B.C., most probably the former," Rutherford nodded approvingly. The faint note of surprise underlying the approval made it less than altogether flattering. "By that period, it is difficult to know just how widespread *literal* belief in the Olympian gods was. And yet contemporary Greeks seem to have been firmly convinced that Pan—a minor god whose name is the root of the English 'panic'—intervened actively on behalf of the Athenians."

"I never encountered, or heard of, a Teloi who went by that name," said Jason dubiously.

"I know. Another difficulty is that Pan—unlike most Greek gods, who were visualized as idealized humans—was a hybrid figure with the legs and horns of a goat and exceptionally large . . . er, male sexual equipment."

"That doesn't sound like the Teloi," said Jason, recalling seven-to-eight-foot-tall humanoids with hair like a shimmering alloy of gold and silver, their pale-skinned faces long, narrow, and sharp-featured, with huge oblique eyes under brows which, like their high cheekbones, tilted upward. Those eyes' strangely opaque blue irises seemed to leak their color into the pale-blue "whites." The overall impression hovered uneasily between exotic beauty and disturbing alienness.

"Nevertheless," said Rutherford, "the matter is unquestionably worth looking into. And, aside from the definite timeframe involved, there are numerous other benefits. For one thing, the more recent date will result in a lesser energy requirement for the displacement."

"Well, yes. 490 B.C. is only—" (Jason did the mental arithmetic without the help of his computer implant) "—twenty-eight hundred and seventy years ago. Still, that's one hell of an 'only!' Compared to any expedition you'd ever sent out before ours—"

"Too true. But the importance of investigating Teloi involvement in historical times is such that we have been able to obtain authorization. It also helped that the Battle of Marathon is so inherently interesting. It was, after all, crucial to the survival of Western civilization. And there are a number of unanswered questions about it, quite aside from the Teloi. So we can kill two birds with one stone, as people say."

"Still, I don't imagine you'll be able to send a very large party." The titanic energy expenditure required for displacement was tied to two factors: the mass to be displaced, and the temporal "distance" it was to be sent into the past. This was why Jason had taken only two companions with him to the Bronze Age, by far the longest displacement ever attempted. Since the trade-off was inescapable, the Authority was constantly looking into ways to reduce the total energy requirement, and the researchers were ceaselessly holding out hope of eventual success, but to date the problem remained intractable. This, aside from sheer caution, was why no large items of equipment were ever sent back in time. Sending human bodies—with their clothing, and any items they could wear or carry on their persons, for reasons related to the esoteric physics of time travel—was expensive enough.

"True, the party will have to be a small one. But the appropriation is comparable to that for your last expedition. So we can send four people." Rutherford took on the aspect of one bestowing a great gift. "We want you—"

"—To be the mission leader," Jason finished for him. "Even though this time you have to *ask* me to do it," he couldn't resist adding, for all his growing interest.

Rutherford spoke with what was clearly a great, if not supreme, effort. "I am aware that we have had our differences. And I own that I may have been a trifle high-handed on the last occasion. But surely you of all people, as discoverer of the Teloi element in the human past, can see the importance of investigating it further."

"Maybe. But why do you need me, specifically, to investigate it?"

"I should think it would be obvious. You are the nearest thing we have to a surviving Teloi expert." Jason was silent, as this was undeniable. Rutherford pressed his advantage. "Also, there is the perennial problem of inconspicuousness." Rutherford gazed at Jason, who knew he was gazing at wavy brown-black hair, dark brown eyes, light olive skin, and straight features.

Jason, despite his name, was no more "ethnically pure" than any other inhabitant of Hesperia or any other colony world. But by some fluke, the Hellenic contribution to his genes had reemerged to such an extent that he could pass as a Greek in any era of history. It also helped that he stood less than six feet, and therefore was not freakishly tall by most historical standards. It had always made him valuable to the Temporal Regulatory Authority, which was legally interdicted from using genetic nanoviruses to tailor its agents' appearance to fit various milieus in Earth's less-cosmopolitan past. The nightmare rule of the Transhuman movement had placed that sort of thing as far beyond the pale of acceptability as the Nazis had once placed anti-Semitism.

"If we were sending an expedition to northern Europe," Rutherford persisted, "I'd use Lundberg. Or to pre-Columbian America, Cardones. But for this part of Earth, you are the only suitable choice currently available, or at least the only one with your—" (another risibly obvious effort at being ingratiating) "—undeniable talents."

Jason turned around, leaned on the parapet, and looked out over the breathtaking panorama once again. "Are you sure you really want me? After my latest display of those 'talents.'"

Rutherford's face took on a compassionate expression he would never have permitted himself if Jason had been looking. "I understand. Up till now, you have taken understandable pride in never having lost a single member of any expedition you have led. And this time you returned from the past alone. But that was due to extraordinary and utterly unforeseeable circumstances. No one dreamed you would encounter what you did in the remote past. And no one blames you."

"But aside from that, aren't you afraid I might be just a little too . . . close to this?" Once again, Jason clenched his fist to prevent his hand from straying to his pocket.

Rutherford smiled, noticing the gesture. "If anything, I should think that what you know of Dr. Sadaka-Ramirez's fate would make you even *more* interested."

Deirdre, thought Jason, recalling his last glimpse of those green eyes as she had faded into the past. *Deirdre, from whom it is practically a statistical certainty that I myself am descended.*

He turned back to face Rutherford. "Well, I don't suppose it can do any harm to meet the other people you have lined up."

CHAPTER TWO

SEVEN DECADES EARLIER, Aaron Weintraub had held the key.

Before that, time travel had been merely a fictional device. That it could *never* be anything more than that had been as certain as any negative can ever be. Over and above its seemingly preposterous physics, the concept self-evidently violated the very logic of causality. The classic statement was the "Grandfather Paradox": what was to prevent a time traveler from killing his own young, childless grandfather? In which case, how could the time traveler have been born? And who, therefore, had killed the grandfather? No; this was one case in which the dread word *impossible* was pronounced without hesitation or doubt. Physicists and philosophers were at one about that. Reality protected itself.

Then Weintraub had embarked on a series of experiments to verify the existence of the temporal energy potential which he had postulated (to the near-unanimous hoots of his colleagues) as a necessary anchor to hold matter in time. If it existed, theory predicted that it could be manipulated. And Weintraub had proceeded to do precisely that. Subatomic particles had appeared in his device a few microseconds *before* the power was turned on and remained for a certain number of nanoseconds, and then vanished for the same number of nanoseconds *after* the switch was thrown. And nothing would ever be the same again.

But temporal energy potential had proven to be very resistant to manipulation. Subatomic particles sent back microseconds in time were the limit—and they only tolerated such unnatural treatment for nanoseconds before indignantly snapping back to their proper time. The physicists had heaved a qualified sigh of relief, the philosophers an unqualified one; Weintraub's discovery, however revolutionary in theory, was clearly devoid of practical applications, including the murder of grandfathers-to-be. Reality still protected itself.

Or so it had seemed for twenty years. Then Mariko Fujiwara had persuaded the by-then aged Weintraub that he had been traveling a dead-end road. Their joint experiments had confirmed her intuition: no energy expenditure could manipulate temporal energy potential to any significant degree; but a tremendous yet finite one, properly applied, could *cancel* it altogether, breaking the anchor chain, as it were, and setting an object adrift in time. That terrific energy surge sent the object three hundred years into the past before it became controllable. But beyond that it *was* controllable, and the object, living or otherwise, could be sent to a predetermined temporal point in the past. (*Not* the future, for temporal energy potential was in an absolute sense nonexistent beyond the constantly advancing wave-front known as "the present.") There the object would remain until its temporal energy potential was restored—very easy to do, for reasons relating to its already-known stubbornness. A temporal retrieval device that could be so miniaturized as to be easily surgically implantable, and that drew an insignificant amount of energy, sufficed to bring the object back to the location (relative to the planetary gravity field in question) from which it had been displaced, after a total elapsed time identical to that which it had spent in the past.

Neither Weintraub nor Fujiwara had been the kind of sociopath common in the fiction of the twentieth century, when science had first become scary: the "mad scientist" who would pursue his reckless experiments to the bitter end with fanatical if not suicidal perseverance, heedless of the consequences to himself or the world. They had recognized, and been duly terrified by, the mind-numbing potentialities of what they were doing. Moreover, they had been products of a society which had recoiled from the Transhumanist madness just as Europe had once recoiled from the seventeenth century's savage religious wars into the eighteenth century's mannered *ancien regime.* True to the twenty-fourth century's almost Confucian-like ethos, they had concluded that if reality no longer protected itself, someone else had to—preferably the bureaucratized intellectual elite committed to safeguarding the integrity of the human heritage that had almost been lost.

Thus the Temporal Regulatory Authority had been born. The safest course would have been not to use the Fujiwara-Weintraub Temporal Displacer at all, but the temptation to settle history's controversies and resolve its mysteries by direct observation had been irresistible. So the Authority had been given exclusive jurisdiction of all extratemporal activity. Its legal monopoly had been confirmed by its possession of the only displacer in existence—an exclusiveness that hardly needed to be legislated, given the installation's colossal expense and power requirements, which placed it beyond the reach of any private individual or group. And even if some other organization *had* been able to build and operate such a thing, it could never have done so unnoticed, barring some as-yet-elusive breakthrough.

Then, as experience in time travel had accumulated, two realizations had dawned—the first one staggering in its implications, and the second one seeming to contradict the first.

The first was that the past could be changed.

The second was that reality still protected itself.

"There are no paradoxes," Jason stated firmly to his new team members. "There are no alternate worlds or branches of time either."

They sat in a briefing room deep in the Authority's town-sized installation in Western Australia's Great Sandy Desert, northwest of Lake Mackay—as far from population centers as it had been possible to put the displacer and its dedicated power plant, lest the latter's multiply redundant failsafe systems should ever prove inadequate. (As some wag had put it centuries earlier, "Mister Antimatter is *not* your friend.") Rutherford was also there, although he had thus far been uncharacteristically laconic, letting Jason conduct the orientation.

"But I don't understand," said Dr. Bryan Landry, with the thoughtfully perplexed look that came naturally to his mild, rather broad face. That face was gray-eyed and fairly light complexioned, and his straight hair was a prematurely graying brown. In short, he was not going to blend as well as the Authority—and Jason—preferred. But there was no help for it; all the available Mediterranean-looking experts in Classical Greek studies were disqualified by reason of age or health. The Authority sent no one back in time who was not up to the rigors of an extended stay under primitive conditions. Would-be time travelers had to be reasonably young and physically fit, and to pass a course in low-technology survival . . . and, for certain particularly blood-drenched milieus, a course in self-defense. It was a winnowing process that continued to elicit howls of "Discrimination!" from the groves of academe, but the Authority was adamant. When necessary, a cover story would be crafted around a team member's incongruous appearance. In the present case, their group would supposedly be from Macedon, where coloring and features like Landry's were less uncommon.

"You're not the only one who doesn't understand," Jason assured him. "Over the last half century, physicists and philosophers have joined the ranks of occupational groups—lawyers, for example—noted for drinking to excess."

Landry refused to be put off—Jason had already learned he could be stubborn in his mild-mannered professorial fashion. "Let me put it this way," he said, while reloading his briar pipe with his favorite brand of gengineered non-carcinogenic tobacco. (It was an indulgence he was going to have to do without in Classical Greece.) "I've done some background reading on the Authority's operations, and I know about your 'message drops.'"

"Yes," Jason nodded. "Putting a message on some very durable medium and concealing it in a prearranged place is the only way time travelers can communicate with the present."

"But if what I've read is true, such a message *isn't there* in its prearranged place before a period of time has passed in the present equal to the elapsed time the time travelers have spent in the past before placing it there."

"The 'linear present,' we call it," Jason interjected helpfully.

Landry looked even more perplexed. He puffed the pipe to life as though fueling his thought processes with tobacco. "Well then, suppose a time traveller, a day after his arrival in the early twentieth century, shot Hitler? By analogy, it would seem that those of us in the present day would continue for a day, until that point in the, uh, linear present, to live in a world whose history included Hitler and World War II and everything that flowed from them, and then suddenly, after that point . . ." He trailed to a bewildered halt.

Jason smiled. "Here's why your example doesn't apply. Those locations we use for our message drops are obscure ones where nothing is ever known to have happened. Hitler and World War II *did* happen. You can't go back and shoot Hitler—a favorite bit of time travel wish-fulfillment, by the way—for the simple reason that *we know he didn't get shot*. The past can be changed, but observed history can't."

"But *why* can't it?"

"No one knows. In fact, the question appears to be meaningless. All we do know is that something will prevent you from doing anything that creates any paradoxes."

Alexandre Mondrago spoke up. "This makes it seem like you have an awful lot of freedom when you're in the past, Commander." (He used Jason's rank in the Hesperian Colonial Rangers. The Temporal Service had no structured system of rank titles, and seniority was on an ad hoc basis; Jason was simply designated mission leader.) "Do anything you damned well want to do, because as long as you *can* do it, you know it won't do any harm." A white-toothed grin split his swarthy face. "Sounds like it could be a lot of fun."

Rutherford gave a pre-expostulation splutter. Jason waved him to silence while studying the Service man he wished he'd had more time to get to know.

Mondrago was shorter than Jason, lean but wide-shouldered and long-armed, with a nose that belonged on a larger face. People often wondered whether he was French or Italian. In fact, as Jason knew from his file, he was of Corsican descent—heir to a long and violent tradition. He had served as a professional soldier in a variety of capacities, but there was less and less use for his talents on today's Earth. So he had made himself a master of various styles of low-tech combat, eventually becoming so good that the Temporal Service had accepted his application despite certain reservations. This was to be his first extratemporal expedition. He was on it because what they were going into—while not quite bad enough to require the entire team to be combat trained—might involve a little more than Jason alone could handle, especially given the possibility of Teloi involvement. So, to assure the safety of the academics, Jason had been assigned a second Service man.

As a theoretical question of detached, intellectual interest, Jason wondered if he could take him.

"That's an attitude we don't encourage," Jason said. "And I'll tell you why. Before my last expedition, one of the team members asked me the same kind of question about shooting the young Hitler that Dr. Landry just did." *Deirdre*, flashed through his mind, and he stopped himself before he could reach for the little plastic case in his pocket. "I told her that if you tried it, the gun might jam. Or you might find out later that you'd shot the *wrong* little tramp. But here's a third possibility: maybe one of the hydrocarbon-burning ground cars they were starting to use in the early twentieth century would run you over while you were drawing a bead on him. You've heard that old saw about reality protecting itself? Well, reality doesn't give a damn *how* it protects itself. You might not want to be standing nearby when it's doing so. Clear?"

"Perfectly, sir." Mondrago's tone was more serious, but his eyes met Jason's unflinchingly.

"Furthermore," said Rutherford, no longer to be restrained, "there is the matter of elementary caution. Half a century's experience of time travel leads us to believe that what Commander Thanou has been telling you is true. But in the absence of absolute proof, we prefer to behave as though it is our responsibility to *make* it true. One example is the course of treatments you will soon be undergoing to cleanse your bodies of evolved disease microorganisms to which the people of the fifth century B.C. would have no more resistance than the Polynesians did to smallpox. We believe that reality helps those who help themselves. Or, at least, we dare not assume otherwise."

Chantal Frey spoke in the diffident, almost timid way Jason had learned was usual for her. "Is that why you've ruled out any expeditions to study the Teloi before 1628 B.C.?"

Jason studied her. The xenologist was a fellow colonial, from Arcadia, Zeta Draconis A II. He recalled that a tidelocked world of that binary system's red-dwarf secondary component held the enigmatic ruins of a long-dead race, which might help explain her interest in aliens. She was a youngish woman, certainly not a spectacular looker like Deirdre Sadaka-Ramirez (again he stopped his hand short of his pocket) but not altogether unattractive in a slender, intellectual-appearing way, with narrow, regular features and smooth dark-brown hair. Jason viewed her presence with a certain skepticism, doubting her ability to stand up under the various stresses of time travel. Granted, the Authority had certified her as up to it, but there was something about her—something besides her seeming physical fragility, a kind of weakness that went beyond that—that bothered him. He also wished she had some secondary skill to contribute, for if they did *not* encounter the Teloi, and the "Pan" legend proved to be just that, then an expert in alien life forms was going to be fairly useless.

At least, he thought (although he had no intention of sharing the thought with her), her quiet personality should make her inconspicuous in the profoundly sexist society of Classical Athens, where the only assertive, articulate women were the *hetairai*—high-end whores/geishas whose unconventionality must have been a tinglingly irresistible turn-on for men accustomed to, and doubtless bored to distraction by, the "respectable" female products of the prevailing purdah.

"That certainly has something to do with it," Rutherford acknowledged. "That, and the ruinous expense of sending an expedition of useful size into the really distant past."

Landry looked troubled. "We've all heard something of these Teloi, and the rumors have been rather sensational, but it's all been awfully vague."

"We have been releasing the information with great caution, because of its revolutionary if not explosive nature. However, the three of you have a legitimate need to know more than the general public. As you recall, the Articles of Agreement you signed contain a clause requiring you to abide by all confidentiality restrictions applicable to information imparted to you. I trust you are clear on this—and on the legal penalties for violation." Rutherford paused. Jason reflected that Mondrago would be no problem—he understood security classifications. He sensed a hesitancy in the other two, and he understood why: they were academics, committed to the free flow of knowledge, and the whole concept of official secrecy was repugnant to them. But all three heads nodded.

"Very well. On that understanding, I'll ask Commander Thanou to give a brief summation of what he learned on his expedition to study the Santorini explosion."

"The Teloi," Jason began without preamble, "were an alien race of unknown origin. I say 'were' because we've found no trace of them in our present-day interstellar explorations. They were a very ancient race which had sought to genetically engineer itself into gods. They succeeded in making themselves effectively immortal, although not literally so, of course, and they could certainly die by violence. A side effect was a mentality incomprehensible to us—insane by our standards. Their chief drive became a need to find something to fill the eons of their empty, meaningless lives. About a hundred thousand years ago, one group arranged to maroon themselves on Earth, where they had discovered a species—*Homo erectus*—which by sheer coincidence was of a general physical form that could be molded by genetic engineering into a kind of sub-Teloi, useful as worshipers and as slaves."

Jason saw in their eyes that they knew where he was headed.

"Yes," he said, as gently as possible. "The Teloi created us. *Homo erectus* evolved by the natural course into *Homo neanderthalensis* in northern Eurasia, but the Teloi gengineered it into *Homo sapiens* in an area to the south, where northeastern Africa and southwestern Asia were then joined, in societies that were vast slave-pens."

"Now you understand why we have been reluctant to make this general knowledge," said Rutherford into the silence.

"We can be proud of our ancestors," Jason said firmly. "The Teloi didn't know what they'd created. The humans soon began to break free of their control, spreading across the planet, wiping out the Neanderthals and differentiating into the various racial stocks we know."

"How did you learn all this?" demanded Landry, puffing furiously.

"We learned it from Oannes, a member of another alien race. The Nagommo were hermaphroditic amphibians, extremely long-lived by our standards, who had been at war with the Teloi for a long time. One of their warships crash-landed in the Persian Gulf in the early fourth millennium B.C. The survivors, with a perseverance foreign to human psychology, continued to follow their basic mission statement, which was to fight the Teloi wherever possible, in any way possible. Stranded on Earth, this meant helping the humans in the area rebel, and teaching them the rudiments of civilization."

Landry almost choked on his pipe-smoke. "Oannes! Wasn't that the name, in Sumerian mythology, of a—"

"—Supernatural being, half fish and half man," Jason finished for him. "As rebellions spread, the Teloi tried to create a kind of super-stock of humans, using women as surrogate mothers of artificial embryos, to serve as proxy rulers. This was the origin of our legends of semi-divine Heroes." *One of whom I got to know*, he thought, remembering Perseus. "Once again, the Teloi blundered; their tame demigods were even less amenable to control than the general run of humans, and led still more rebellions.

"Eventually, the Teloi withdrew in disgust from the original civilized areas. By 1628 B.C., their area of activity stretched from western Europe to northern India, with a special focus in the Aegean."

"The Indo-European pantheon!" Landry blurted, scattering hot ashes on his shirt-front, which looked as though this had happened to it once or twice before.

Jason nodded. "Yes. We know them by many names from many places. In Greek mythology the older ones were the Titans, the first generation of gods—Cronus, Hyperion and the rest. The younger ones were the Olympians."

"But," Landry persisted, brushing off his shirt, "what happened to them? As I said, one hears some rather remarkable rumors about your expedition."

"Some rather remarkable things happened," said Jason mildly. "You see, the Teloi had an absolutely invulnerable refuge: an artificially generated 'pocket universe' with only one access interface, which was portable. We arranged for that interface to be obliterated in the Santorini explosion. The 'Titans' were permanently trapped in the pocket universe with most of their high-technology paraphernalia."

"Imprisoned in Tartarus by Zeus," Landry breathed.

"So the later Greeks thought. But it wasn't Zeus who did it. Oannes gave his life to make it possible." *The last of his race*, Jason recalled. *Not just on Earth but in the universe. Their war with the Teloi had proceeded to mutual annihilation. The Nagommo evidently won, but to do so they gengineered themselves into overspecialized subspecies . . . unsuccessfully, in the long run.*

I knew that, having seen the horror show that is the Nagommo home planet in our era, an endless vista of ruins inhabited by none but degenerate, deformed, sub-sentient travesties of what was once a great race—the race that unknowingly died to give us a future free of the Teloi. But I never told him I knew it. I thought I was being merciful. Was I?

"One of my team members also gave his life," Jason continued. "A Dr. Sidney Nagel." *A conceited, opinionated, socially inept little twit . . . who taught me what courage is.*

"Wasn't there a third member of your expedition?" Mondrago asked.

Jason's features went immobile. "Dr. Deirdre Sadaka-Ramirez," he said expressionlessly. "She remained in the seventeenth century B.C."

They waited attentively for an explanation. None was forthcoming.

"Thank you, Commander Thanou," said Rutherford briskly. "Now you all know the background in general terms. During the next few days, you will be given more in-depth presentations, including video and auditory recordings of both the Teloi and the Nagommo."

Chantal Frey's eyes lit up with enthusiasm, which was immediately banked down by puzzlement. "But. . . . If you don't mind my asking, how were such recordings obtained? The Articles of Agreement were very explicit: we aren't allowed to carry any out-of-period equipment into the past."

"Good question," Mondrago nodded. "I'm new to the Service, but even I know about *that* restriction."

Jason and Rutherford exchanged a look. No words were needed to express their joint conclusion: these people had had about all they could handle for now.

"The answer will become clear in due course," said Rutherford smoothly. "In the meantime, I suggest you all get some rest. We have a busy day ahead of us tomorrow, including the implantation of your temporal retrieval devices."

Their faces reflected their distaste, which performed the distraction function Rutherford had intended.

CHAPTER THREE

THE FOLLOWING DAY, they underwent the biological cleansing process of which Rutherford had spoken—painless, but involving a certain degree of discomfort and indignity. In accordance with his usual policy, Rutherford also hastened them through something he had no desire to let them stew about.

"The temporal retrieval device, or TRD, is very tiny." He held up a metallic object no larger than a small pea. "It can be implanted anywhere; we generally prefer to use the inside of the upper left arm. It is a very simple in-out surgery."

Landry rubbed his itchy face (Rutherford had ordered all three of the men to start growing beards), scowled, and asked the question they always asked. "Do we *have* to have it implanted?"

"The Articles of Agreement you signed state that you consent to it."

"Yes, yes, I know. But is it *really* necessary?" Landry's uneasiness was reflected in Chantal Frey's face and, to a lesser extent, in Mondrago's. They had all grown up in post-Transhumanist society, and to them anything that blurred the line between man and machine was both illegal and flesh-crawlingly obscene.

"The Authority," Jason explained, "is responsible for getting you back to your proper time. Yes, we could build the TRD into some in-period object that you could carry. But then you might lose it, by inadvertence or theft. And with no TRD to restore your temporal energy potential, you'd be marooned in the fifth century B.C. permanently." He saw that he'd gotten through to them. "You *can't* lose something that's inside your flesh."

As was often the case, Chantal's voice was so quiet and hesitant as to be almost ignorable. "But . . . didn't you say that the third member of your expedition remained in the Bronze Age. How could that be, if—?"

"That was due to unforeseen circumstances, Dr. Frey." Jason's features and tone were carefully neutral. "The Teloi detected Dr. Sadaka-Ramirez's TRD and had it cut out of her."

Chantal's color didn't look particularly good.

"That sort of thing doesn't normally happen," Rutherford put in quickly. "In point of fact, that was the only time it has *ever* happened. At any rate, you now understand the importance of this procedure. And please be assured that the implant is a totally passive one, not involving any kind of direct neural interfacing." Their expressions combined relief with revulsion at the very concept. "The TRD activates at a predetermined moment, timed by atomic decay, at which moment you will find yourselves back on the displacer stage."

"And until that moment," said Jason, forestalling another question that always got asked, "there is no way to return to the present. You're going to be in the past for a fixed duration, come hell or high water. This accounts for the stringent health and fitness qualifications you had to meet, and the low-tech survival course you had to pass . . . and also for the non-liability clause the Authority has written into the Articles of Agreement."

"But," Landry persisted somewhat peevishly, "why can't you take along a . . . er, switch, or whatever, so you can activate the TRDs and bring us back if we find ourselves in difficulties?"

"Retrievals must be according to a rigid, entirely predictable schedule. That way, the Authority can assure that at the time you are due to return the displacer stage is clear of all other objects—objects with which you might otherwise find yourself sharing a volume of space." Jason smiled at his listeners' expressions. "Admittedly, the likelihood of this happening is small. But its consequences don't bear thinking about."

"One problem, Commander," said Mondrago. "We *don't* have inner atomic clocks. Isn't it going to be kind of startling when, to our eyes, the universe suddenly disappears without warning and is replaced by what we can see from the displacer stage?" From their expressions, it was clear that Landry and Chantal found the prospect unsettling to say the least.

Jason's eyes met Rutherford's. This could no longer be put off.

"It won't be without warning," said Jason. "I'll give you advance notice—not only to preserve your mental equilibrium, but also to make sure we vanish in private, so as not to alarm the locals."

"But how can *you* predict when the moment is going to be?" Mondrago persisted, in the tones of a man who was more than half sure he already knew the answer, at least in its broad essentials.

"My ability to do so relates to what I said before about recordings of the aliens we encountered in the Bronze Age Aegean. The fact of the matter is that I have an actual, neurally interfaced computer implant. Among other things—and this is almost the least of its functions—it provides me with a countdown to the time all our TRDs activate. It also has a recorder feature, spliced directly onto my optic and auditory nerves: whenever I activate that feature by mental command, it records everything I see or hear on media that can be accessed after I return to the present."

He studied their faces. Mondrago was taking it with equanimity—he had doubtless heard Service rumors about this sort of thing. The other two bore the excruciatingly embarrassed look of people who were too polite to reveal the prejudice they felt.

One of the human race's keys to survival is that human beings almost never carry any idea to its ultimate logical conclusion. There are, of course, exceptions: the Nazis and the Khmer Rouge come to mind. So it had been with the Transhuman movement, which, in the two or three generations it had ruled Earth before being swept away in fire and blood, had sought to exploit to the fullest the possibilities inherent in late-twenty-first-century cybertech and genetic engineering, splintering humanity into specialized castes serving an elite of super-men. The human psyche had never recovered from that abuse. The result had been the Human Integrity Act, which by now enjoyed the kind of quasi-sacred status the people of the old United States of America had accorded their Constitution. Any tampering with the human genome was forbidden. So was anything that blended human brains and nervous systems with computers. So was any application of nanotechnology that made nonlife difficult to distinguish from life. All of this had been seared into the human soul by the Transhumanists and their experiments upon themselves; legislation was almost superfluous.

"It has other useful—in fact, indispensable—features," Jason continued before the abhorrence could crystallize. "It gives me access to a great deal of information. For one thing, it can project directly onto my optic nerve a map of our surrounding area. We'll never be lost. And the recorder function is especially necessary in an era like the one we're going to, when paper and other such conveniences don't exist. Remember, what you bring back to the present, like what you take into the past, is limited to what you can carry—which, like the clothes you're wearing, is effectively part of the same 'object' as your body, as far as temporal energy potential is concerned." He saw that he had scored a point with the academics.

"So," Rutherford said briskly, "you can see why the Authority was able to make a case for the kind of limited exemption from the Human Integrity Act enjoyed by certain law enforcement agencies. And now, let us proceed to have the TRDs implanted—a very brief, practically painless procedure." He ushered Landry and Chantal out of the room. Jason was about to follow when Mondrago caught his eye.

"Question, Commander," he asked when the others were well out of earshot. "This computer implant of yours: as a fellow Temporal Service member, do I also get one?"

"No," Jason stated flatly. "That limited exemption Rutherford mentioned is *very* limited, and subject to constant scrutiny. We have to demonstrate a genuine need. As a practical matter, this means only the mission leader has one. You'll get one at such time as your seniority and experience qualify you for the mission leader function."

Mondrago looked thoughtful. "If you should buy it, sir, then as next senior Service member I'll be acting mission leader, and if so—"

"—You'll just have to get by without it. Sorry. We couldn't justify extending the exemption to cover potential acting mission leaders."

"Understood, sir." Mondrago's expression was unreadable.

"However," Jason continued, "as you've pointed out, you're a Service member, unlike Drs. Landry and Frey. So there's something you need to know and they don't. I'll take this opportunity to reveal it to you. Their TRDs—and yours—incorporate a passive, micro-miniaturized tracking device. Remember what I said about the map I can summon up? Well, the current locations of the three of you are going to appear on that map as little red dots."

"I can see how that might come in handy." Mondrago showed no sign of resentment.

"Extremely handy. Especially when a member of the expedition is lost or a prisoner." *And most especially when the TRD in question has been chopped out of its owner and we're trying to recover it.* Jason's hand strayed toward his pocket, but he was getting better about halting it. "Drs. Landry and Frey are having enough trouble accepting the necessity for any kind of implant. The fact that it has an additional function would only upset them unnecessarily. So you won't reveal it to them except with my permission. Clear?"

"Clear, sir."

"Good. Now let's get to the lab."

There followed the standard three-week orientation period . . . only in this case it lasted a little more than three weeks. The reason became apparent when Rutherford discussed the matter of language.

"The obvious pointlessness of sending people into the past unable to communicate in the target milieu," he declaimed, "enabled us to obtain yet another variance of the Human Integrity Act—a minor one. In the interest of practicality, the Ionic dialect of Classical Greek—the speech of Athens—will be imposed on the speech centers of your brains by direct neural induction. The process is harmless and non-invasive, although it can be disorienting, which is why our standard procedures call for rest and, if necessary, antidepressant drugs afterwards."

Landry was clearly unconcerned. In his excitement, he reflexively fumbled for the pipe that was no longer there. "Yes! Of course, this process won't enable us to speak the language like natives. But that works out perfectly, since we're supposedly from Macedon. Fifth century B.C. Greek was divided into four distinct dialects: Ionic,

Doric to the south, Arcado-Cypriote (a survival of the old Mycenaean idiom) and North-West Greek. The last one—of which we'll supposedly be native speakers—was the most divergent. In fact, Athenian snobs affected to be unable to understand it at all."

Rutherford's intellectual forebears, Jason thought with a mental snigger.

"Our very thoughts," that worthy acknowledged with a gracious nod to Landry. "In this case, however, we will also be providing you with a *second* language, which you will find more difficult to assimilate: that of the Teloi."

Chantal—who clearly hadn't shared Landry's Classical Greek enthusiasms—now showed definite signs of interest at the prospect of learning a nonhuman tongue. "But how is this possible?"

"I was, for a time, a prisoner of the Teloi, Dr. Frey," Jason explained. He didn't elaborate. "In order to expedite interrogation, they rammed their language into my brain by a brute-force version of what you are going to be undergoing, with no chemical cushioning. The language's utterly alien structure didn't help either. Nevertheless, I came through the experience with about the level of comprehension that would be expected of a reasonably bright secondary-school graduate in a foreign language. By a reversal of the process, this was downloaded from me, and can now be provided to you—with great gentleness, of course. If we do encounter any surviving Teloi, you ought to be able to haltingly communicate with them . . . if the opportunity to do so should arise, and if you should want to."

Chantal, in her excitement, ignored the cautionary tone of Jason's last few words. With her and Landry both properly motivated, the team proceeded to the labs.

The rest of their linguistic preparation was relatively free of emotional hurdles, involving as it did conventional learning techniques supplemented by the kind of neuro-electronic "sleep teaching" technology that was an accepted part of their social background. They acquired a basic ability to read the Classical version of the Greek alphabet—unnecessary for Landry, who would be available to see them past any difficulties—for literacy was widespread among Greeks of their assumed social status. It was an accomplishment that Athenians would find impressive in natives of an ill-regarded place like Macedon, and would help offset the social stigma of such an origin.

Also, Rutherford drilled them in the Ionic Greek speech that had been impressed on their brains, assuring himself that they could actually converse in the language. This was more difficult for Chantal and Mondrago than for Landry, who already knew it as a written language, and Jason, for whom it fell somewhere between his own ancestral Demotic Greek and the harsh ancestor of Mycenaean Greek he had acquired for his last expedition.

For the Teloi tongue, Jason was of course the only one who could perform this training function. He took them through exercises, playing the role of a Teloi.

"Is something bothering you?" Landry asked him solicitously during one of these sessions. "A few times I've noticed—"

"No," replied Jason, more curtly than he had intended, for in fact he *did* find this more disturbing than play-acting should have been, awakening memories that he'd thought he had suppressed, and other memories he'd forgotten—or never known in the first place—that he had. His annoyance with himself for feeling this way, and for taking it out on Landry, helped clear his mind of his distaste. "All right," he said briskly, "you next, Chantal."

She stepped forward eagerly, showing no signs of having shared Landry's observations. It was during this part of the training that she seemed to truly come alive, and this, too, disturbed Jason, for reasons he could not put his finger on.

CHAPTER FOUR

ORIENTATION OFTEN INVOLVED an actual jaunt to the target area, for purposes of familiarization. In this case, Rutherford deemed it unnecessary and possibly counterproductive, given almost twenty-nine hundred years' worth of changes. And in Landry's case—and, to a lesser extent, in Jason's—modern Greece was old hat anyway. Instead, he took them on virtual tours, enhanced by modern scholarship's best guesses as to what the landscape in question had looked like. Jason knew from experience that those guesses were sometimes surprisingly good . . . and sometimes not. He dared hope that the former was the case for the city of Athens, which had been the subject of centuries of dedicated and painstaking archaeological work.

They were also drilled in the historical background of the period—or at least Jason, Chantal, and Mondrago were. Given his academic credentials, Landry was an integral part of the instructional staff, and quickly came to dominate it. For this, Jason eventually came to be grateful. Landry, a product of the same sort of social background as Rutherford, could be something of an irritating know-it-all at times. But he was a true teacher, not to be confused with an educational bureaucrat who held that title. In his introduction, he managed to clarify the labyrinthine complexities of fifth century B.C. geopolitics.

"To put it in the simplest possible terms—"

("Please do," Mondrago was heard to mutter.)

"—the Greek, and specifically Ionian, colonies on the Asiatic shore of the Aegean were loosely dominated by the kingdom of Lydia in the mid-sixth century B.C." Landry manipulated a remote, and a cursor ran over the area in question—the western fringe of what would much later become Turkey—on the map-display that covered the rear wall of the briefing room. "Then the Persians, under their first Great King Cyrus, conquered Lydia, including the Ionians. In order to keep the Ionian city-states under control, the Persians established tyrannies in them."

"They must have loved that," Modrago grimaced.

"Actually, that word doesn't have the blood-stained connotations it later acquired in English. A Classical Greek 'tyrant' was simply a man who ruled a city from outside the normal constitutional framework, with the support of one of the popular factions. The closest later-day parallel would be a North American big-city 'boss' of the late nineteenth and early twentieth centuries, although the position of Greek tyrant had more formal recognition than that."

"So he was well advised to take good care of his constituency," Jason opined.

"Precisely. But the tame tyrants of Ionia tended to lose sight of that because their other constituency—the one they *had* to keep happy—was the Great King of Persia."

"Why?" asked Chantal. "If their own people were behind them, couldn't they defy him?"

Landry gave her a look of rather supercilious annoyance, as though he considered the question naïve. Instead of answering it directly, he held up the remote and expanded the map to the east and south. And expanded it. And expanded it, until the peninsula of Greece and the entire Aegean basin had shrunk to kind of an afterthought at the upper left corner.

"The Persian Empire," he explained with almost patronizing care, "was the world's sole superpower. It had conquered the entire Near East and Egypt, as well as parts of Central Asia and the Indus Valley over here to the right of the map, in western India. It is believed to have had a population of at least sixteen million people, while Greece and the Aegean islands had, at most, two and a half million. Furthermore, it was not the result of gradual expansion over a span of centuries. Cyrus didn't begin his career of conquest until around 550 B.C. This unprecedented empire had burst on the world in a mere sixty years."

Mondrago studied the map intently. "How could the Persians possibly hold an empire that size together, at that technological level? I mean, infantry marching on foot. . . ."

"Yes. The Greeks were incredulous when they learned that the Persian capital of Susa was three months' march eastward from the Aegean shore. They would have been even more incredulous if they had known that the empire extended *another* three months' march beyond that."

"Then how—?"

"The Persians were the first empire-builders in history to recognize that communication was the key to control. They used a combination of fire beacons, mounted couriers using a system of highways with posting stations, and other techniques, including aural relay in mountainous regions."

"'Aural relay'?" queried Mondrago.

"Yes. They had men trained in breath control who could literally *shout* to each other across valleys and ravines where the acoustics were good, with lots of echoes, thus transmitting messages almost instantaneously across the right kind of terrain. By using all these various means the Great King was able to get information from the frontiers and send orders back in mere days, which seemed supernatural to the Greeks."

"I'm beginning to understand why the Ionian tyrants had to kowtow to him," Mondrago said seriously. "The *capo di tutti capi.*"

"Yes. But by so kowtowing they were swimming against the tide of the Greeks' inveterate xenophobia, and thereby running the risk of alienating their own people. So their rule was always teetering on a knife-edge, and they were ready to jump either way: gain still greater favor with their master; or, failing that, go into rebellion out of sheer desperation.

"In 500 B.C. Histaeus, the tyrant of Miletus, the largest and richest of the Ionian cities, tried the first option. He himself was living at the Persian court in a kind of gilded hostage situation—they gave him the title 'Royal Table-Companion'—but through his nephew Aristagoras, who was standing in for him at Miletus, he offered to expedite a conquest of the Aegean island of Naxos, where he had contacts among the disgruntled aristocracy. As it turned out, Aristagoras made a total botch of the expedition. Rather than sit with folded hands and await the usual fate of Persian puppets who failed, Aristagoras reversed himself: he declared himself a convert to democracy of the kind Athens had had for the past eight years. He also called on the other Ionian cities to establish democracies and join Miletus in rebellion."

"The expression 'big brass ones' comes to mind," commented Jason.

"Indeed. The rebellion spread like wildfire through Ionia and beyond, and Aristagoras persuaded the Athenians to come to the aid of the new democracies. In 498 B.C. they sent an expeditionary force which marched inland and burned Sardis, the seat of Artaphernes, the local Persian satrap, or governor." Landry caused the cursor to flash on Sardis.

"Mission accomplished," Mondrago remarked drily.

"Not quite. The town was burned but the citadel held out and the Greeks were forced to retreat to the coast. On the way, they were cut to pieces by the Persian cavalry."

Mondrago looked perplexed. "I've studied the ancient Greek style of warfare, and I've always gotten the impression that the Persians had no answer to the hoplite, or heavy infantryman. That seems to be the pattern all the way up to Alexander the Great's conquest of the Persian Empire."

"One gets that impression because, as you've pointed out, the Greeks won in the end," Landry explained with a chuckle. "It's always the ultimate winner's successes that are remembered. It comes as a shocking surprise to most people that George Washington was soundly trounced whenever he came up against professional British troops in the kind of open-field set-piece battle they were organized and trained to fight. However, your point is well taken as applied to the phalanx of hoplites. When it could be brought to bear under the right conditions—head-to-head combat on a narrow front—it was indeed unstoppable by anything except another phalanx. But it was a rigid, inflexible formation, and the hoplites who comprised it, loaded down with fifty to seventy pounds of armor and weapons, were incapable of rapid maneuvering."

Landry manipulated his controls again. An image appeared on the screen, superimposed on the map. It showed a man who seemed to have stepped out of a Grecian vase-painting. He wore greaves on his lower legs, a cuirass with curving metal shoulder-plates, and a face-enclosing helmet with an impressive-looking but (to Jason's eye) impractical-seeming horsehair crest. He carried a large round shield and a spear a couple of feet longer than he was. At his side hung a leaf-shaped sword. The image represented modern scholarship's best reconstruction, which had turned out to be very much like those vase paintings after all.

"When hoplites armed and equipped like this couldn't form up, as in the retreat from Sardis, the Persian cavalry could ride circles around them and shoot them to pieces with arrows. In 479 B.C., that Persian cavalry nearly won the Battle of Plataea, before the Spartan phalanx could be effectively brought to bear. But the Persian style of warfare was, at bottom, a raiding style. The Greeks finally won by forcing decisive battles. Alexander became 'the Great' because he could catch his enemies between a phalanx and the heavy shock cavalry his father Phillip had invented—the most effective heavy shock cavalry the world would see before the advent of the stirrup. But the point is, we're going to be seeing the first of those decisive hoplite battles." Landry's eyes glowed with anticipation, then he shook himself and returned to his subject.

"At any rate, after the debacle of the retreat from Sardis, Athens withdrew into isolationism, leaving its Ionian allies to be brutally subjugated, a process that was completed by 494 B.C. with the destruction of Miletus. After which the Great King Darius decided it was time to punish those Greeks across the Aegean who had aided the rebels. In 491 B.C. his emissaries toured Greece demanding 'earth and water'—the tokens of submission. Athens and Sparta violated the diplomatic niceties by killing the emissaries, in the case of the Spartans by throwing them down a well, at whose bottom they were told they could find what they sought." Mondrago smothered a guffaw. Landry shot him a primly disapproving look before resuming.

"This was very bold, you see; the Persians had already established a satrapy in Thrace, to the north of the Aegean, and had an army there. But their accompanying fleet was wrecked by a storm, which made invasion from the north impractical. Instead, a new fleet was prepared—six hundred ships, including some specialized for transporting cavalry horses. It carried an army we believe numbered as many as 35,000 infantry and 1,000 cavalry—the Greeks later claimed it was hundreds of thousands, but they always believed in making a good story even better. It also carried Hippias, the last tyrant of Athens, who had been working for the Persians since being deposed in 510 B.C. He was now over eighty years old, but still hoped to be restored to power. Instead of working its way north, the fleet island-hopped directly across the Aegean and took the city of Eretria on the island of Euboea, an Ionian ally, with the help of fifth columnists. They then burned it and enslaved the population . . . which was also meant to be the fate of Athens."

"Which brings us to your mission," said Rutherford, who had entered the room unnoticed. "You omitted one thing, Bryan: in 492 B.C King Alexander I of Macedon, who was reliable only as a weathervane, made his kingdom a Persian client-state. This is convenient for us, for your cover story is that you are Macedonians who opposed submission to Persia and are in exile as a consequence. This should assure you of a friendly reception in Athens—particularly from the man we intend for you to contact. But for now, I believe it is too late in the day to begin your detailed briefing on the Marathon campaign itself—which, at any rate, should be left to the end, so as to be as fresh as possible in your minds. Also, we have other matters to take up tomorrow."

CHAPTER FIVE

THEIR ORIENTATION INVOLVED a great many mundane things, such as their wardrobe.

The fabrics had to be authentic, of course—mostly wool, but also flax and the coarse animal-hair cloth called *sakkos*. But the Authority's specialists had a lot of practice at producing such things. The basic male garment—there was no such thing as underwear—was the tunic known as the *chiton*, fastened at both shoulders and tied at the waist with a girdle. Over this was worn the *himation*, a large rectangular woolen cloak draped around the left shoulder and back around under the right arm and across the front. Anything even remotely resembling trousers was regarded as hilariously effeminate, which was one reason why the Athenians had underestimated the Persians before their disastrous expedition in support of the Ionian rebels. By 490 B.C., of course, the trouser-wearers from the East were no longer quite so funny. The *chlamys*, or cold-weather cloak, shouldn't come into the picture in the time of year they were planning to spend in ancient Greece. As travelers from afar, they would be able to justify wearing sturdy boots rather than the more typical light sandals, and also the broad-brimmed felt hat, or *petasos*.

Chantal would wear an ankle-length linen tunic, held up by pins at the shoulders and at other points to form loose sleeves. Over this she would be expected to drape the *himation*, preferably wrapped around her head—or, alternatively, a head-scarf. Classical Athens was not all that unlike fundamentalist Islam where the status of women was concerned. At least she should be able to get away with light sandals rather than bare feet. Her hair was long enough to be pulled back with ribbons into the orthodox ponytail or bun.

The men would naturally not be lugging around the hoplite panoply. As Landry explained, even hoplites only burdened themselves with that load of armor and weapons a few minutes before taking their places in the phalanx for battle. And at any rate, Jason didn't expect to be doing that sort of fighting; still less did Mondrago, given his assumed social class, and least of all did Landry. There were no such things as professional soldiers in fifth century B.C. Greece, aside from the Spartans, who were considered freakish for the degree to which they specialized in war. Athenian hoplites were simply the male members of the property-owning classes of citizens, who could afford (and were expected) to equip themselves with the panoply. They were liable for military service from eighteen to sixty, and given Greece's chronic internecine wars they were likely to spend the majority of their summers that way. In between, training was minimal. In phalanx warfare, what counted was the steadfastness that held the shield-wall unbroken even in the shattering clash of spears. Those men weren't flashy martial artists, but theirs had been the collective courage in whose shelter Western civilization had survived infancy.

However, the team's supposed homeland of Macedon was a backwater which had retained the simple monarchy of the Bronze Age while the other Greek states had been evolving into civic societies. In fact, Macedon probably came closer in some ways to what Jason remembered from the seventeenth century B.C. Jason would pose as a minor nobleman, Mondrago as a disaffected former member of the "King's Companions," a Macedonian holdover of the Bronze Age war-band. As such it would be normal for them to carry swords. Rutherford let them choose their blades off the rack.

One day Jason was in the station's gym, putting himself through some exercises with the double-edged, slightly leaf-shaped cut-and-thrust sword he had chosen—the most typical Greek pattern of the period—when Mondrago walked in from the adjacent courtyard, wiping his brow. The Corsican was holding a very simple sling: a small leather pouch with two strings attached, one of which was looped over a finger and the other gripped by the thumb. The user then swung the sling around the head and sent the stone or lead bullet on its way, propelled by centrifugal force. Jason had never used one, although he knew it was the favorite missile weapon of the Classical Greeks, who had never made any secret of their disdain for archery.

"Can you really get any accuracy with that?" Jason asked.

"You'd be amazed, sir," Mondrago said, with a jauntiness bordering on insouciance. "It takes a lot of practice, but I've been getting some. I asked the shop to make me some in-period lead bullets. They swear these are very authentic." He took one from his pouch. It was oval, an inch long, and bore on its side the Greek words for "Take that!"

"I'll take their word for it," Jason laughed. "By the way, did you ever pick out your sword?"

"Yes, sir." Mondrago went to the sword rack and took down a weapon quite different from Jason's: a single-edged Spanish sword, or *falcata*, forward-curved for maximum efficiency at chopping, although it had an acute point for thrusting—a vicious-looking weapon somewhat resembling the *kukri,* or Gurkha knife, but longer and with a finger-guard. Like Jason's more conventional weapon it was iron—strictly speaking, extremely low-carbon steel—and made to authentic specifications, although very well made within those limits.

"I know it's a slightly eccentric choice where we're going," said Mondrago, as though anticipating an objection. "But it's pretty common there. I've seen it in Greek vase paintings. And I kind of like it." He gave Jason an appraising look and lifted one expressive eyebrow. "Would you like to see a demonstration, sir?"

"Sure." They went to another rack and took down the small round wooden shields carried by Classical Greek light troops, not the heavy, awkward things carried by hoplites in phalanxes. Then they went through a couple of passes. Mondrago was good, Jason had to admit, and the *falcata* was like an extension of his sinewy arm. Jason found himself on the defensive, barely able to interpose the shield between himself and Mondrago's chopping strokes, until he got into the rhythm of the thing and began to use his superior size and weight to push aggressively, forcing his way in to closer quarters.

Mondrago backed off and indicated the shield. "Even these light versions kind of slow you up. Want to try it without them, sir?"

"Fine. Let's get suited up." Without allowing an opportunity for any reckless suggestions, Jason turned and walked toward the locker room, leaving Mondrago no option but to follow.

They put on impact armor, flexible but with microscopic passive sensors that detected incoming blows and caused the electrically active nanotech fabric to go to steel-like rigidity at the instant of contact. The stuff was standard equipment for riot police and certain others . . . and regulation safety equipment for weapons practice. Then they returned to the exercise floor and went at it in earnest.

Mondrago now altered his technique, using the *falcata* almost like a long knife, holding it low and emphasizing the point. Again, Jason had to adjust, parrying a dizzying series of thrusts. Then, abruptly, Mondrago shifted again, chopping down. As Jason raised his sword to parry, Mondrago brought his right foot around in a sweeping *savate*-like move, knocking Jason's feet out from under him. He brought the *falcata* up and then down in another chop.

But Jason brought his sword around and up. At the moment the *falcata* hit the instantly rigid fabric at Jason's left shoulder in a blow that otherwise might well have severed his arm, Jason thrust upward into Mondrago's crotch. There was no impact armor there. Jason stopped the thrust with his sword-point less than an inch short.

For a moment their eyes met. Then, with a crooked smile, Mondrago extended a hand and helped Jason to his feet.

"Very good, sir," he said. "But then, I've heard stories about some of the stuff you did in the Bronze Age, on your last expedition."

"Probably exaggerated. You're good, too. Very good. But I imagine a ranged weapon like that sling would be more useful than a sword if we should happen get into any trouble with the Teloi."

"Yes . . . the Teloi." Mondrago's eyes took on a look Jason thought he could interpret . . . and that he wasn't sure he liked, in light of what he had learned of the Corsican's background.

"In that connection," he began, "I've naturally studied your record. . . ."

Mondrago went expressionless. "Yes, sir?"

"Oh . . . never mind." Jason decided not to pursue the matter, at least for now.

And maybe not at all, he thought. *There's no point in making an issue of something that I'm hoping will never become an issue.*

In addition to clothing and weapons, something else produced with careful attention to period detail was the money they would be carrying. It was a great convenience that money existed in this target milieu, unlike the Bronze Age, where Jason and his companions had had to carry a load of high-value trade goods, well-concealed (but stolen anyway, to Jason's still unabated annoyance). The coinage of the period was chaotic, with each city-state issuing its own, but all were widely accepted. They carried Athenian silver *oboloi,* six of which made a *drachma,* which would buy a tavern meal with wine, and four of which made a *stater.* Also, because it would be natural for people coming from Macedon, which had been under Persian influence for a couple of years, they carried Persian gold *darics* worth about twenty-five *drachmai,* showing the Great King drawing a bow.

"The street name for these coins was 'archers,' for obvious reasons," Landry told them. He chuckled. "In the next century, when the Persians finally learned that the way to neutralize the Greeks was to subsidize them to fight each other, one Great King quipped, 'It would seem that my best soldiers are my archers.'"

In addition to gear, they needed names. Jason could use his own given name. So could Mondrago; "Alexander" wasn't uncommon enough to make his being a namesake of his former king remarkable. There was nothing in Greek even close to the other two's names, so Rutherford let them choose from a list. Landry would go by Lydos, Chantal by Cleothera. In the relatively elementary society of Macedon, people generally had no second names, identifying themselves as "son/daughter of so-and-so" if necessary. Chantal would be a cousin of Jason's, under his protection and that of his follower Alexander. Landry would be a part-Thracian family retainer, son of freed slaves, educated in Athens years earlier before returning to Macedon, who had been "Cleothera's" tutor and was still in her service.

Rutherford lectured them on the timing of their expedition.

"Traditionally, it was believed that the Battle of Marathon took place on September 12. But for this to make sense the Persian fleet would have had to spend an inordinate amount of time getting across the Aegean. Furthermore, it is based on the Spartan calendar, which may have been a month ahead of the Athenian. And finally, it rests on unrealistic assumptions about logistics—specifically, the ability of the Persians to keep an army of such size fed. So the weight of scholarly opinion has shifted steadily in favor of a date in August. This is one of the questions you will be able to settle.

"You will arrive in Attica on July 15, 490 B.C. This will give you time to establish yourselves in a position to observe events, and also to discover the answers to the various unsettled questions concerning the preliminaries to the battle. But this expedition does not involve the evaluation of long-term effects, so an extended stay will be unnecessary. You will only remain for sixty-five days, after which your TRDs will activate on September 18, almost a week after the battle's latest possible date, although no one really takes the September 12 dating seriously anymore."

Landry's disappointment at the brevity of their stay was palpable.

"The experience of temporal displacement," Rutherford continued, "is a profoundly unnatural one which can cause disorientation. We have learned that this effect is intensified—sometimes dangerously so—if it takes place in darkness. Therefore, despite our preference for minimizing the chances of local people witnessing the, ah, materialization, you will arrive not in the dead of night but just after daybreak. Commander Thanou, with his extensive experience, will recover first and will be able to assist the rest of you until the effect wears off.

"You will arrive on the road—the Sacred Way, it was called—from Athens to Eleusis, a little to the east of the latter. There should be no one about at dawn there."

"Eleusis!" Landry's eyes took on a dreamy look. "The central shrine of the Eleusinian Mysteries! The ancient Greeks believed that Hades, the God of the Dead, abducted Persephone, daughter of Demeter, the harvest-goddess, and the resulting compromise was how they explained the seasons. A cave at Eleusis was believed to be the actual site where Hades emerged from the underworld and returned Persephone to her mother." He seemed to do a quick mental calculation, and his dreaminess turned to excitement. "Kyle, couldn't we stay for just a *little* longer? The ceremonies—about which we have very few hard facts, as the initiates were forbidden to speak of what they had experienced—took place just slightly after your return date, with the procession from Athens the thirteen miles to Eleusis, where—"

"—Where the initiates went through a series of purification rites for which they had been carefully and secretly prepared," Rutherford reminded him gently. "What, exactly, would you plan to do?" Landry looked crestfallen. "No, Bryan. With only one displacer stage in existence, our schedules are, of necessity, inflexible, as Commander Thanou has long since explained. And we have to draw the line somewhere. There would always be just one more enigma you'd want to unravel.

"You will proceed directly to Athens, where you should arrive in the afternoon. Commander Thanou, using the resources provided by his computer implant, will have no difficulty guiding you. He can neurally access a map showing all the main thoroughfares. I doubt very much if a complete map of ancient Athens *ever* existed, and if it had, it would have resembled a plate of spaghetti; most of the city was a maze of narrow pathways, lanes, and alleys. But you are going to be seeking hospitality from an individual whose area of residence is known. He is a prominent public figure, so once you are in that area, minimal inquiries should suffice to locate his house. And your politics should assure you a welcome there, as he is a leading advocate of resistance to Persian aggression." Rutherford looked annoyed. "Or rather, he *was*. Tenses are such a problem when discussing time travel!"

The rest of their orientation passed rapidly, and toward its end Rutherford allowed them a day of relaxation. On the last evening before displacement, Jason found himself at the bar of the station's lounge. As he ordered the last Scotch and soda he would have for two and a half months, he heard a familiar quiet voice behind him.

"Commander Thanou? May I join you for a moment?"

"Of course, Dr. Frey. But please call me 'Jason.' And may I call you 'Chantal'?"

"Certainly . . . Jason. We're going to be working together closely for some time."

They found a table and he ordered Chablis for her. She took a couple of sips as though to fortify herself.

"I've been hoping to speak to you privately," she began, "but the opportunity never seems to have arisen. You see . . . I can't help being fascinated by that neurally interfaced implant inside your head."

"Fascinated? Most people are repelled by the concept."

"I know. I'd be less than honest if I didn't say *I* was, just a little, at first. But at the same time there's something exciting about it—the way it almost takes you beyond the ordinary human experience. I mean . . . what's it *like?*"

"There's really nothing transcendent about it. It's very utilitarian—just an extremely convenient way of accessing information in various forms and recording sensory impressions. That's as far as exemptions from the Human Integrity Act ever go, even in cases like ours where there's clearly a legitimate need." Jason laughed grimly. "Anything more is altogether too reminiscent of the Transhuman movement for most people's taste."

"Yes, I know. And of course they did many terrible things. And yet . . . I sometimes wonder if we're right to automatically reject all their goals. Surely there must have been some power in their ideals, at least at first, before the movement took power and grew corrupt. Perhaps some of the things they sought could be made to benefit the human race without resorting to their extreme methods."

Jason gave her an appraising look and ran over in his mind what he knew of her people's history.

They had been among those who had left Earth on slower-than-light colony ships in the early days of the Transhuman movement's rise to power, fleeing what they could see coming. The bulk of colonizers had gone to the nearer stars. The settlers of Arcadia, however, wishing to exile themselves even *more* irrevocably, had dared the thirty-five-light-year voyage to Zeta Draconis, most of that time spent in suspended animation. They had awakened to find that the second planet of that binary system's Sol-like primary component was a hospitable world, fully deserving of the name they had bestowed on it. And there they had remained in the utter isolation they had sought.

Meanwhile the near-Earth colonists had returned to Earth on the wings of the negative-mass drive they had invented, blowing in like a fresh wind that had begun the toppling of the Transhumanist regime. Only *afterwards* had the main body of the human race reestablished contact with Arcadia.

Thus, Jason reflected, this woman came of a society that had opted out of history and avoided the entire titanic, blood-drenched drama. Now, of course, in this day of faster-than-light travel, the Arcadians had reentered the mainstream of human society and subscribed to its dominant ethos. But perhaps they—and she—could not be expected to feel exactly the same thing the rest of humanity felt at the sound of the word "Transhuman."

"You won't find many people who'll agree with you," he said mildly.

"I know," she acknowledged. "And I'm not even sure *I* agree with it, if you know what I mean. It *certainly* isn't something I feel strongly about. I just can't help wondering." She fell silent, and remained so for a few moments before speaking up again.

"Com . . . Jason, I hope you won't mind if I ask you another question."

"Go right ahead. As you pointed out, we're going to be working together. We shouldn't have any secrets."

She took another sip and laughed nervously. "One thing I almost wish you *had* kept a secret: what happened to Dr. Sadaka-Ramirez's TRD." She shivered.

"Please don't let that prey on your mind. Rutherford was telling the truth when he said it doesn't generally happen, and that in fact it had *never* happened before. People of past eras have no way to detect implanted TRDs. It was her misfortune that the Teloi did." Jason halted his hand almost before it began to stray.

"And now we're going in search of the Teloi. . . ."

"The surviving Teloi, if any," he corrected. "If we do encounter them, they'll be in a far less powerful position than they were in the Bronze Age. Furthermore, this time their existence won't take us by surprise."

"I keep telling myself that. But there's something I'm puzzled about. Why couldn't she have been rescued?"

"Rescued?"

"Yes. It seems as though it would be possible—at great expense, admittedly—to send a second expedition back to the time just after your departure, carrying a new TRD for her, timed the same as those of the expedition members."

"Temporal energy potential doesn't work that way. You're linked to the time from which you come. Such a TRD would have returned to the time from which we brought it—but *she* wouldn't have, because she didn't come from that time." Jason took a long pull on his Scotch and soda. "And besides, you misunderstand. She didn't remain because she had to. We succeeded in retrieving her TRD. The self-sacrifice of Dr. Nagel, our third member, made that possible. She could have held it in her hand and returned. But she chose to stay."

"Why?" Chantal's question was barely audible.

"Very simple: she fell in love." Jason laughed shortly. "You know the old cliché about the hero getting the girl. Well, in this case the Hero did. Remember what I was telling you about the origin of demigods? She got herself a prime specimen: Perseus. Yes," he added as Chantal's eyes grew round, "*that* Perseus. One of the female skeletons Schliemann found in the shaft graves at Mycenae must have been her."

"I suppose he never knew what she had given up for him," Chantal whispered.

"You know, I never thought of it from that angle. But then, I'm not a woman."

"So," Chantal said after a thoughtful silence, "when you came back, I suppose her TRD appeared on the displacer stage with you . . . as did Dr. Nagel's corpse."

"Neither. Dr. Nagel's remains, TRD and all, were taken inside the Teloi pocket universe just before its access portal was atomized. And as for Dr. Sadaka-Ramirez's TRD. . . . Remember I mentioned that I spent time as a prisoner in the pocket universe? We all did—and she spent more time there than Dr. Nagel and I. And the Teloi kept the time-rate there slower than in the outside universe—it helped them seem immortal to their human worshipers. And the atomic timers of the TRDs. . . ." Jason saw that she had grasped it. He grimaced. "I was the first time traveler in the history of the Temporal Regulatory Authority to return behind schedule. I don't mind telling you I was nervous about appearing on the displacer stage at an unforeseeable moment! Fortunately, Rutherford had gone to great lengths to keep the stage clear."

Chantal wore a look of intense concentration. "If, as you say, Dr. Sadaka-Ramirez was in the pocket universe longer than you—"

"Precisely. At some completely unpredictable time, her TRD will be found on the floor of the displacer stage."

Chantal looked at him very thoughtfully. "I've noticed that whenever this subject comes up you have a habit of reaching for something in your pocket."

"You are extremely observant. Just before my displacement back to the present she burned her last bridges by giving me her TRD." Jason brought out the little plastic case and opened it, revealing the tiny sphere. "Still there, I see."

"But sometime you'll open the case and it won't be. It will be on the displacer stage. And you'll have a kind of closure."

"You're as perceptive as you are observant—uncomfortably perceptive, in fact. Not that I'm complaining. It will be a highly useful quality where we're going." He regarded her with new eyes. "This isn't the most tactful thing to say, Chantal, but I think I may have underestimated you."

"People sometimes do."

"I've had my doubts about your ability to hold up under the conditions we're going to be experiencing," he told her bluntly. "I've also had doubts about your usefulness. But to some extent, that last has been wishful thinking on my part."

"I don't understand."

"Then let me put it this way. I hope your specialized field of knowledge will turn out to be irrelevant to our mission. In other words, I hope we'll find that by 490 B.C. every last Teloi on Earth is dead and only remembered in myth. You'd probably consider them fascinating. I consider them abominations."

"You're very forthright. Actually, the same sort of doubts about what I can contribute have been worrying me. If you get your wish about the Teloi, I'll try to make myself as useful as possible, and not be a burden."

"I can't ask for more than that. And every member of an expedition is always needed. You can never foresee everything that's going to come up, and you never know what talents and abilities are going to come in handy."

"Thank you for the reassurance."

"Not at all. Let's have another round. By the way, have you ever tried any authentic Greek wine in the present day?"

"No, I haven't."

"Well, you'd better drink as much of that Chablis as you can while you've got the chance."

The day came, and they entered the vast dome that held the thirty-foot-diameter displacer stage, surrounded by concentric circles of control consoles and instrument panels. Rutherford gave each of them the handshake he always bestowed before withdrawing to the glassed-in mezzanine that held the control center. As he turned to go and the others climbed onto the stage, Jason spoke. "Uh, Kyle, I'd like you to keep something for me."

"I rather thought you might." Rutherford took the plastic case that would have been very hard to explain in the fifth century B.C.

Jason took his place on the stage and waited.

CHAPTER SIX

NO ONE HAD EVER SUCCEEDED in putting the sensation of temporal displacement into words. Words are artifacts of human language, and this was something outside the realm of natural human experience.

There was nothing spectacular about it—except, of course, from the standpoint of the people in the dome, to whose eyes the four of them instantaneously vanished with a very faint *pop* as the air rushed in to fill the volume they had occupied. As far as they themselves were concerned, there were no such striking visual effects. There was only a dreamlike wavering of reality, as though the dome and the universe itself were receding from their ken in some indescribable fashion. And, as though awakening from that dream, they were left with no clear recollection of having departed from the dome and no sensation of time having passed. Instead, crowding out the dream-memories, as the waking world will, was the dirt road they stood on, with the rising sun just clearing a ridge of hills and spreading its bronze illumination across the body of water that lay close to their right and the island of Salamis that could be glimpsed across that gulf. There was no one else in sight.

As predicted, Jason recovered from the disorientation first. Mondrago wasn't too far behind him. The other two both pronounced themselves ready to travel not too long thereafter.

"All right," said Jason, "let's cover as much ground as possible as early as possible. It's going to get hot later, at this time of year." As they hitched up the sacks holding their belongings and set their faces eastward toward the sun, Landry cast a wistful look over his shoulder at the barely visible hump of the acropolis of Eleusis to the west.

"Maybe we can find time for a side trip later, Bryan," Jason consoled him.

They proceeded along the Sacred Way with the aid of their four-and-a-half-foot walking sticks, skirting the Bay of Eleusis, as the sun rose higher into the Attic sky whose extraordinary brilliance and clarity had been remarked on by thousands of years of visitors, even during the Hydrocarbon Age when Greece had been afflicted by smog. Looking about him, Jason could see that the deforestation of Greece was well advanced since he had seen it in the seventeenth century B.C. Presently the road curved leftward, turning inland and leading over the scrub-covered ridge of Mount Aigaleos, which they ascended in the growing heat. They reached the crest, turned a corner, and to the southeast Attica lay spread out before them, bathed in the morning sun. In the distance—a little over five miles as the crow flew, with the sun almost directly behind it—was the city itself. Like every Greek *polis*, it clustered around the craggy prominence of its acropolis, or high fortified city . . . except that this one would forever be known simply as *the* Acropolis. It wasn't crowned by the Parthenon yet, but Jason knew what he was looking at, and what it meant.

He let Landry pause and stare for a few moments.

As those moments slid by, the sun rose just a trifle higher, and its rays moved to strike a certain cleft in the rocks. For a split second, Jason got a glimpse of—

At first his mind refused to accept it.

Mondrago must have been looking in same direction. He ripped out a non-verbal roar, grasped his walking stick in a martial-arts grip, and sprinted for the cleft.

Chantal's eyes had been following Landry's in the direction of Athens. Neither of them had seen it. Now they whirled around, wide-eyed.

"Stay here!" Jason commanded, and ran after Mondrago, who was already out of sight.

He scrambled up to the cleft and looked left and right. Mondrago was just vanishing from sight behind a boulder. Jason followed and caught up with him in a tiny glade where he stood, gripping his walking stick like the lethal weapon which, in his hands, it was. He was looking around intently and, it seemed, a little wildly.

"Gone?" Jason asked, approaching with a certain caution.

"Gone," Mondrago exhaled. He relaxed, and something guttered out in his eyes.

"Did you see what I saw?"

"Depends on what you saw, sir."

"I *think* I saw a short humanoid with wooly, goat-like legs and, possibly, horns."

"On the basis of a very brief glimpse, I confirm that. Doesn't seem likely that we'd both have the same hallucination, does it?"

"It's even less likely that we'd actually see something corresponding to the mythological descriptions of the god Pan."

"I don't know, sir. You saw some actual Greek gods on your last trip into the past—or at least some actual aliens masquerading as gods."

Jason shook his head. "Even if any of the Teloi are still around eleven and a half centuries after I encountered them, what we saw was definitely not one of them. It also bore no resemblance to any nonhuman race known to us in our era. And speaking of nonhuman races . . . I couldn't help noticing your reaction to this particular nonhuman."

Mondrago's face took on the carefully neutral look of one being questioned by an officer. "I was startled, sir."

"No doubt. But what I saw went a little beyond startlement." Jason sighed to himself. This could no longer be put off. He should, he now realized, have brought it up that day in the exercise room. But his hopes had led him to avoid the issue. He paused and chose his words with care. "As I mentioned to you once before, I studied your record during our orientation period. Among other things, I learned that you served with Shahanian's Irregulars in the Newhome Pacification."

"I did, sir," Mondrago said stiffly. His expression grew even more noncommittal.

As far back as the end of the twentieth century, the end of the

Cold War had led to a proliferation of PMCs, or "private military companies" like Executive Outcomes and L-3 MPRI, offering customized military expertise to anyone who could pay. This had proven to be a harbinger of the future. The need of fledgling extrasolar colonies for emergency military aid had soon outstripped the response capabilities of the chronically underfunded armed services, leading to a revival of the "free companies" of Earth's history, although in a strictly regulated form. The need arose in large part from the recurring failure of human colonists to recognize until too late that a new planetary home was already occupied by a sentient race, simply because that race lacked all the obvious indicia of civilization. Civilization, it had turned out, was a statistical freak. Tool-using intelligence, however, was not. Neither was the capacity to feel resentment at the environmental disruption that even the most minimal terraforming unavoidably caused.

Newhome, DM-37 10500 III, had been a case in point. The autochthones had been physically formidable to a degree that was exceptional for tool-users: steel-muscled hexapods whose three pairs of limbs could all be used as legs, propelling their quarter-ton mass faster than a cheetah. The forward pair could also be used as arms, the middle pair as relatively clumsy ones. The saberlike claws, the whiplike tail, and the tusklike fangs were, on some basic level, more frightening than the proficiency that the beings had acquired with captured and copied firearms. The colony had survived, thanks to imported professional soldiers who had inculcated the natives with a certain respect for the human race. But it had been too close for comfort, and an accommodation had been worked out under which human developments were restricted to geographically and ecologically distinct enclaves. By all accounts, the natives were now avid customers for the products of human civilization, and would soon be as peaceable and corrupted as one could wish.

During the fighting, though. . . .

"I've read some pretty harrowing accounts of that fighting," said Jason. "Some of them were almost unbelievably so."

"You can believe them, sir."

"You say that like a man who knows whereof he speaks. And I seem to recall a couple of comments in your record. . . ."

Mondrago's features remained immobile, and his eyes stared

fixedly ahead. But they burned. "They used a captured M-47 AAM launcher to shoot down one of our transport skimmers. Some of the men survived and were taken, including a couple of friends of mine. We did a search-and-rescue sweep and found them . . . or what was left of them. I won't try to describe what had been done to them. Another time, we were a little too late responding to a distress call from a terraforming station. These weren't soldiers like my friends. There were women and children—although you could barely tell. We made those filthy alien vermin pay the next time we hit one of their villages."

A quaver had crept into Mondrago's tightly controlled voice by the time it reached the word *alien*.

"Yes," Jason nodded. "All this was touched on in those comments I mentioned. There were other comments in later stages of your career, whenever your duties brought you into contact with nonhumans. Never enough to actually get you in trouble, but. . . ." Jason met Mondrago's eyes squarely. "There's always been a possibility that we'd encounter aliens on this expedition. On the basis of what's just happened, I'd say that possibility has to be upgraded to a strong probability. Are you going to be able to handle that in a disciplined manner?"

The fire had gone out in Mondrago's eyes, and the stiffness had melted from his expression. He spoke with his usual insouciance, something short of insolence. "I was under the impression that protecting this party from aliens was what I was here for, sir."

"Wrong! You're here to protect the party from whatever I tell you to protect it from. And I have no intention of provoking any unnecessary conflicts with anybody, human or otherwise. That's not our purpose." Jason spoke quietly, but Mondrago unconsciously came to something resembling a position of attention. "Compared to some of the outfits you've served in, I'm sure the Temporal Service seems like a mildly well-supervised excursion agency. But you've read the Articles, including the provisions concerning the authority of a mission leader."

"I have, sir."

"Good, because it's not just boilerplate. Let me explain a little history to you. On Earth, about five and a half centuries before our time, a sailing ship or a military unit overseas was effectively out of communication with its home base. The commander therefore had to be granted a very high degree of authority to act on his own initiative—and to enforce discipline. Then electronic communications came in, and brought with them—"

"Micromanagement."

"No argument. But now the pendulum has swung back. With no such thing as faster-than-light 'radio,' messages have to be sent on ships, and a captain in the Deep Space Fleet is about as much on his own as a wet-navy skipper before they had the telegraph, and his legal status reflects that. With us, it's even more extreme. The 'message-drop' system gives us a not-very-satisfactory way to send information to our own time, but there's absolutely no way we can get information—or instructions—*back*. The Temporal Service may look like a loose-jointed quasimilitary organization, with no formal rank structure and everybody on a first-name basis, but in the crunch, a mission leader has legal enforcement powers that Captain Bligh would have envied. And I *will* have my orders obeyed, even if they cause you trouble because of the way you feel about aliens. Is that clear?"

"Yes, sir."

"I thought it would be. You're military, and you understand the necessity for this. The civilian members of extratemporal expeditions can't be expected to, and we prefer not to rub their noses in it unless it's absolutely necessary, which it usually isn't." Deciding that he had struck the right balance, Jason turned away. "Now let's get back to Drs. Landry and Frey. They're probably getting worried."

The two academics did in fact look jittery, but they still waited by the roadway. *Thank God*, Jason breathed inwardly. *They're the kind that can follow orders.* He'd had altogether too much experience with the other kind.

"What happened?" asked Landry, not unreasonably.

Jason never kept secrets from expedition members unless he had to. He forthrightly described what he and Mondrago both believed they had seen and had tried unsuccessfully to catch. His listeners' excitement—Landry's at the possible grain of truth in a Greek myth, Chantal's at a possible unsuspected nonhuman race—was palpable. He firmly squelched it.

"For now we're going to have to file this away under the heading of 'unexplained mysteries, to be deferred until later.' And we won't mention this incident to any of the locals. Clear? Now let's get going."

They descended into the rocky lowlands of Attica and walked on along the dusty road, past clumps of marjoram and thyme, and asphodel-covered meadows. They began to encounter people, but no one took any particular notice of them, save for an occasional glance occasioned by the oddity of a woman traveling abroad. But Chantal had wrapped her *himation* modestly around her head and face, so no one looked scandalized.

In this era long before automobiles, there could be little "sprawl." Besides which, there was something to be said for living within the protection of the walls. So the city was sharply defined. Landry had mentioned that historical demographers estimated its population at this time at a little over seven thousand, and that of the entire *polis* or city-state of Attica as maybe a hundred and fifty thousand counting slaves and resident foreigners.

"Athens was almost the only 'city-state' that really was one," he explained as they approached the walls. "Most of them were almost completely rural, with a little *asty*, or town, of not more than two or three thousand at the center of the *agros*, or countryside. So 'city-state' is a completely misleading translation of *polis*."

"Then why did the term become so well established?" inquired Chantal.

"Because we historians have always fixated on Athens, which was atypical to the point of being *sui generis*. It became—or 'will become,' I suppose I should say—even more atypical after the Persian Wars in the Periclean era, as the capital of an empire of 'allied' states, with a previously unheard-of population of over thirty thousand for the city itself and maybe as many as half a million for the entire *polis*."

They entered Athens through the Dipylon Gate, whose fortifications lacked the moat and forward defenses that would be added later, after this era's thoroughly unimpressive wall had been destroyed by the Persians in 480 B.C. and afterwards rebuilt. The man they were seeking was destined to be the driving force behind that rebuilding, and much else besides.

They passed through the labyrinthine alleys of the malodorous potters' quarter known as the Ceramicus, although in truth it was as noted for its cheap whores as for its ceramics. A number of the former were in evidence, or at least the women they saw had to be assumed to be such, for Athens's sixth-century B.C. lawgiver Solon (one of the most consummate misogynists ever to draw breath, according to Landry) had laid it down that any woman seen in public alone was presumed to be a prostitute. Only the direction-finding feature of Jason's computer implant enabled them to find their way through that maze, for they knew in general that their destination was south—and, unfortunately, downwind—of the Ceramicus, away from the potteries and whorehouses but near the Hangman's Gate outside of which was the dumping ground for the bodies of executed criminals and suicides. And the streets (by courtesy so called) still teemed with dogs, goats, pigs, and their fleas.

In addition to all the actual stenches, Jason detected a psychic one—that of fear. He had been in cities living under the threat of invasion before.

As they traversed the winding, unpaved, filth-encrusted alleyways, Jason frequently glanced at his followers. He knew from experience the difficulty twenty-fourth-century people had in adjusting to the urban aromas of antiquity, and those aromas were a particularly ripe combination in this part of Athens. Mondrago looked stoical, and the other two seemed to be holding up reasonably well.

"What made him decide to live in *this* area?" asked Chantal. Her tone implied that there *must* be more desirable neighborhoods.

"Politics," Landry chuckled. "He's of aristocratic birth, though not from a politically prominent family. But his pitch is to the poorer elements, so he moved here from the family estates so he could be closer to his constituency. It was also a good location for an attorney—yes, he was the first man in history to parley a legal practice into a political career. And finally, it's within walking distance of the Agora, where all the political and legal business is conducted. As far as we know, he's still living here now even though three years ago he was elected Eponymous Archon—the head of state for a year."

"A year? Then what's he doing now?" Chantal wondered.

"It is believed that at the time of Marathon he was *strategos*, or general, of his *phyle*, or tribe, called the Leontis. You must understand, this is an elective office. Every year each of the ten tribes into which the Athenian citizenry is divided elects a *strategos*, who can be reelected an unlimited number of times. The official commander-in-chief is the *polemarch*, or War Archon, who is elected by the whole citizen body."

"More lack of military professionalism," Mondrago commented with a sniff.

Political prominence naturally made him easy to find. Jason's first inquiry—which incidentally confirmed that they could make themselves understood in the Ionic dialect—yielded directions to a house larger than any of those nearby. It looked like it had been extended as its owner's political prominence had waxed. Still, it had the same basic look as all the others: built of plaster-covered mud brick, with rooms organized around three sides of a small courtyard, the fourth side facing the street with the main door in its wall. All the larger windows faced inward to overlook the courtyard; only narrow slits faced the street. From within came the sound of flute and cithara music.

Jason was wondering if it would be good form to knock on the door when a sound of voices came from around a corner of the street. A small group appeared, clustered around a man in his mid-thirties to whom they were talking animatedly. Never mind sandals and chitons; Jason knew political networking when he saw it.

But he only had eyes for the man at the center of the group. It wasn't every day that he gazed on someone to whom Western civilization at least arguably owed its survival.

Besides the conventionally idealized sculptures of the man they sought, Jason had seen a later Roman bust which was believed to have been a copy of one done from life. Now he realized that belief was correct, as he stared at the solid, powerful, thick-chested build, the blunt features, the massive jaw covered by a beard as dense and black and close-cropped as the head hair. The overpowering impression was one of unsubtle strength. That impression, Jason knew, was completely false, at least as far as the lack of subtlety was concerned.

The hangers-on departed, and Jason took the opportunity to approach. "Rejoice," he said, giving the conventional general-purpose greeting. He immediately found himself on the receiving end of a politician's smile, over which eyes of a very intense brown-black studied him. He launched into the stock story of their lives. "So," he concluded, "we departed Macedon because we could not live with our king's willingness to grovel before trousered barbarians. We were told that, as enemies of the Great King of Persia, we could hope for hospitality from the *strategos* who lives in this house."

The smile widened into something a little more genuine. "Well, Fortune has smiled on you, for you have found him. I am Themistocles."

CHAPTER SEVEN

THE COURTYARD WAS COBBLESTONED, as was typical of the better class of houses. As they entered it through the door in the street-side wall, they saw the duo that was the source of the music they had heard.

"It's not always easy getting Eupatrids to come to an address like this," said Themistocles in the tone of one anticipating an oft-asked question. The word he used was best translated as "the well-bred"— the monumentally snobbish Athenian aristocracy's term for itself. "So I like to invite the most popular musicians to use my house for rehearsal." He sounded ebulliently pleased with himself for his own cleverness. Jason had a feeling that he not infrequently sounded that way.

Themistocles led the way through the courtyard, with its surrounding portico which supported a balcony of the second-story women's quarters, to a doorway leading to the kind of reception room Jason's orientation had led him to expect. It was a small room—almost all Classical Greek rooms were—with an elaborate black and white pebble mosaic floor. The walls were painted in a singularly handsome pattern, with a baseboard in white-lined black and the main wall above in dark red. Themistocles motioned to servants to bring in the chairs and stools which, in sparsely furnished

Athenian homes, were constantly moved from room to room as needed. Like everything else the Classical Greeks made, their furniture was beautiful.

The slaves also brought wine. It was the resinated wine that unkind non-Greeks all through history compared, unfavorably, to turpentine. In this case it tasted like turpentine-flavored water, for as custom dictated the wine was diluted. It was easy to understand why alcoholism had not been a widespread social problem in ancient Greece.

"You are most kind, *strategos*," said Jason, "to extend your hospitality to refugees." The word he used actually implied even more, for a Greek without a *polis* was in a very real sense a non-person, without an identity. *And not registered voters in Athens*, he left unsaid.

Themistocles gave an indulgent hand-wave. "Who am I to quibble about background? My mother Abrotonon was a Thracian." He bestowed a smile on Lydos/Landry.

"Ah," said Landry. "So your mother was not . . . that is, we had heard stories that a Carian—" He shut up under a surreptitious glare from Jason. *He's already told us all we need to know, Bryan*, his glare said.

It was the answer to yet another question. They had hoped that this version of Themistocles's parentage would prove to be the correct one, as it would give their host a certain sense of kinship with them. A second theory had held that his mother had been a Carian woman from Halicarnassus named Euterpe. Either way, there was no doubt that his aristocratic descent on his father's side had not saved him from being a youthful outsider in the maniacally exclusive society of Athens.

"In the old days," Themistocles continued, confirming Jason's unspoken assumption, "that was enough to deny me citizenship. We lived in Cynosarges, the immigrant district outside the city walls, when I was a boy. But then, eighteen years ago, came the reforms of Cleisthenes. The Pisistratid tyranny was overthrown, and the law changed."

"As I understand it, *strategos*," Landry ventured cautiously, with a nervous side-glance at Jason, "the need to fill out the numbers of the tribes into which Cleisthenes divided the Athenian people also helped extend the citizenship."

"No doubt about it," Themistocles nodded. "That was one of Cleisthenes's masterstrokes. Faction-fighting among the Eupatrid dynasties had brought Athens to the edge of ruin and opened the way for the tyranny of Pisistratus and his sons. His solution was to simply sweep away all the old family and clan identities by dividing Attica into ten tribes, made up of demes scattered all over. He even made people take their second names from those demes." He chuckled. "One of the demes was named after the Boutads, one of the grandest of all the aristocratic families. Instead of sharing it with every goatherd in the deme they gave themselves a new name: the *Authentic* Boutads!"

They all laughed. Actually, Jason had already heard the story from Landry, who'd said it reminded him of an incident in the history of his native North America, where vaporing beyond description had erupted in Boston around the turn of the twentieth century when a certain unpronounceable Eastern European immigrant had taken it into his head to shorten his name to "Cabot." It was good to have another anecdote verified. So far, this was proving to be one of those expeditions whose findings tended to confirm orthodox expectations.

Except, of course, for a certain sighting on the Sacred Way near the crest of Mount Aigaleos. . . .

"But," Themistocles continued, sobering, "it worked. For the first time, everyone—regardless of birth or wealth—could speak and vote in the Assembly. Athens became the first true *demokratia*."

Jason and Landry exchanged a look, for it hadn't been certain that this word—meaning a state in which power, or *kratos*, was invested in the people, or *demos*—had actually been in use this early.

"You have no idea what it was like," Themistocles continued. "Under the tyrants, we Athenians had never amounted to very much. Suddenly we behaved like heroes. Enemies from Sparta and Thebes and Chalcis descended on us like vultures, thinking we'd be easy prey—and we defeated them all!"

Actually, internal dissention—probably incited by Cleisthenes' bribery—stopped the Spartans, Jason mentally corrected, recalling his orientation. But for a fact, the Athenians had seemed transformed overnight by their democratic revolution. Themistocles's next words helped him understand why.

"So a whole new world of opportunities had been opened up for me and others like me—there seemed no limits any more. When I reached the required age of thirty, my ancestry through my father made me eligible to run for Archon." Jason nodded, recalling that even though every citizen could vote only the upper classes could run for high office. "I could never have dreamed of such a thing before!"

Which, of course, gave you a very intense and personal commitment to the new order, thought Jason.

A servant entered and signaled to Themistocles, who excused himself. They were left to themselves for a few minutes, and Jason motioned them to silence, bestowing a special cautionary look on Landry. Presently their host returned, looking a little preoccupied.

"That was Euboulos, a shipbuilder," Themistocles explained. "I needed to talk with him. He's been offering to support me in the Assembly, in exchange for my influence in sending certain contracts his way in the future."

"When you were running for Archon," Landry prompted, "did you not argue for a new harbor, and expansion of the fleet?" Jason kept his features immobile, for this would be well known enough to make the question legitimate.

"Expansion of the fleet?" Themistocles snorted. "We have practically none to expand! Seventy triremes! And if we did, where would we base it—that miserable open bay at Phalerum? It's absurd! We can't even protect our shipping from the flea-bitten pirates who infest the island of Aegina, only fifteen miles south of Salamis and squatting across our trade routes! And that's the least of the threats we face. That very year, the Persians wiped out the Ionian fleet at Lade, after which they sacked Miletus and ended the rebellion."

"Wasn't the Ionians' defeat at Lade the result of the desertion of the ships from Samos, who wanted to doom their traditional commercial rivals in Miletus?"

"You're very well informed, Lydos." Jason held his breath, but Themistocles continued, for this was obviously a pet subject. "Yes, that's the curse the gods seem to have laid on us Greeks: we can never unite. Show us a common enemy, and all that most Greeks can see is an opportunity to betray some other Greek to him, for private gain or to avenge some age-old slight." He gave the exasperated sigh of a brilliant man forced to work with short-sighted fools while pretending to respect them. "Well, anyway, as Archon I was able to get work started on a new seaport for Athens at Piraeus, just to the east of Phalerum. That's the place!"

"Isn't Piraeus two miles farther from Athens than Phalerum is?" asked Jason, mentally calling up the glowing map that seemed to float a few inches in front of his eyes.

"A small price to pay! That easily defensible rocky headland offers *three* natural harbors. It allows space for our merchant fleet to grow, as it's been growing along with all the rest of our economy now that people know they can work for their own betterment without fear of having all they own taken from them by a tyrant. It will also provide a base for the war-fleet we need . . . if I can ever persuade the Assembly that we *do* need it, and if we can ever find the money to pay for it. That's the prospect I keep holding out to Euboulos and others like him."

Themistocles paused, brooding for a moment. Looking at him, Jason reviewed in his mind the things he knew but could not reveal: that in seven years a rich lode of silver would be discovered at Laurium, near the southern tip of Attica; and that under Themistocles's urging the Assembly would excel itself, spending the windfall on the fleet of triremes that, three years later in 480 B.C., would (with the help of Themistocles's genius for adroit disinformation) win at Salamis the victory on which the future of this planet and a great many others rested.

All at once, the full realization of just who it was whose watered wine he was drinking truly hit Jason.

Landry interrupted their host's thoughts. "We have heard that there were other issues as well . . . such as the impending trial of Miltiades the Younger."

"Ah, yes," said Themistocles, animated once more. "As you probably know, being from the North, the elder Miltiades was a member of a Eupatrid family called the Philaids who was forced out of Athens sixty years ago because he opposed the tyranny of Pisistratus. He founded a colony in the Thracian Chersonese." (*The Gallipoli Peninsula*, Jason translated automatically.) "He died childless, and his step-nephew Miltiades the Younger ruled the colony as a tyrant. He joined the Ionian revolt and fought heroically, capturing the islands of Lemnos and Imbros in the name of Athens.

When the revolt collapsed, he fled to Athens. And what did the
Assembly do when the most renowned Persian-fighter of them all
landed at Phalerum and offered his services? Put him in prison for
the crime of tyranny in the Chersonese!" Themistocles gave another
sigh of utter weariness and frustration. "Fortunately, his trial was
scheduled after that year's election. As Archon, I was able to exert
some small influence on the proceedings."

I'll just bet you were! It was, thought Jason, yet another reason
why that election had been one of the most crucial ever held in all
history. Aloud: "Yes, we'd heard that he was triumphantly acquitted,
and has now been elected one of the ten *strategoi.*"

"True. We need him now, in light of the current situation.
Speaking of which. . . ." With an air of getting down to business,
Themistocles proceeded to ask them a rapid-fire series of very
shrewd questions about the state of affairs in Macedon, now a
Persian satellite. Drawing on their orientation, they were able to give
very specific answers. As heirs to centuries of painstaking historical
research, they knew far more about Macedon, Thrace and adjacent
areas in the early fifth century B.C. than contemporary Athenians did.
Themistocles was clearly impressed.

"Yes," he finally said, leaning back. "You've been very informative.
That obligates me to help you in any way I can—which is my
inclination anyway, since you obviously hold the same views I do on
appeasement of the Persians. The first need is to get you established
as *metoikoi.*"

Resident non-citizens, Jason translated: accepted in polite society
and not without certain civil rights, but unable to vote, own land, or
marry citizens—and at the same time liable for military service. For
Classical Greeks, *polis* identification was everything. As *metoikoi*
they would at least have a recognized status in Athens.

"You'll also need a place to stay," Themistocles continued. "I
know people who have accommodations to let. I assume. . . ." His
voice trailed off. As an aristocrat—at least on his father's side—he
naturally could not bring up so crass a subject as ability to pay.

"Of course, *strategos*," said Jason, earning a smile of approval
from Themistocles for his ability—surprising in a hick from the
north—to grasp what had been left unspoken. "We are indebted to
you for your help in arranging all this."

"And," Mondrago spoke up, "we doubt whatever information we have been able to provide will be useful enough to repay your kindness, now that the main Persian threat is no longer from the north."

"No, it isn't." Themistocles's brooding look was back, but now it held a new undertone of discouragement. They didn't break into his black study with matters of common knowledge.

The natural approach for the Great King Darius to take in chastising the Athenians for their support of the Ionian rebels had been a southward advance from his satrapy of Thrace through his new client-state of Macedon. But such a strategy required the support of a fleet working its way around the northern end of the Aegean—a fleet that had been wrecked in a storm off Mount Athos. Then Mardonius, the swashbuckling Persian general in command of the northern front, had buckled one swash too many and gotten himself seriously wounded in an attack on some mountain tribe of goat-stealers.

So the Great King had adopted a new strategy—an unsettlingly original one.

"When the newly assembled Persian fleet of six hundred ships departed from Cilicia earlier this year," said Themistocles, speaking more to himself than to them, "nobody was too alarmed at first. Surely, everyone thought, it must be headed north, to follow the coast around the Aegean. That was the way it had always been done. But then, once past the ruins of Miletus and through the strait between Mount Mycale and the island of Samos, it turned *westward*, straight out across the open sea from island to island! First they obliterated Naxos and enslaved the population. Then they stopped at Delos, the sacred birthplace of Apollo and Artemis, and their commanders Artaphernes and Datis—he's the real commander; Artaphernes is just a blue-blooded Persian figurehead that they had to have because Datis is a Mede—put on a hypocritical display of respect for Apollo. This, after the Persians had burned Apollo's oracle at Didyma and plundered his bronze statue! Maybe some Greeks will actually be stupid enough to be taken in by it."

Carrot and stick, thought Jason.

"Do you know what that smooth-tongued snake Datis had the nerve to tell them on Delos?" Jason could have sworn Themistocles' indignant tone held just a touch of professional envy. "He actually claimed with a straight face that the Ionian rebels hadn't been worshiping the *true* Apollo at Didyma, but rather a kind of imposter: one of the *daiva*, the Persian demons or false gods or whatever. What a gigantic load of goat shit!"

Themistocles, Jason reflected, was even more right than he knew. As Landry had explained during their orientation, Datis' propaganda line was nonsense in terms of Zoroastrian dualistic theology. Just as Ahura Mazda, the supreme god of truth and light, had his counterpart in Ahriman, god of lies and darkness, so his six emanations, the *amesha spenta* or "beneficent immortals," had dark shadows in the form of the *daiva*. A Zoroastrian priest would have gagged on the idea of Apollo—one of the *daiva* himself, according to them—having such a shadow. But the Greeks of Delos hadn't been up to speed on such subtleties, and with the Persian army occupying their island they hadn't been disposed to dispute the point.

"I understand the Persians have Hippias with them," said Landry.

Themistocles gave him a sharp look. "You really are *very* well informed, Lydos."

Jason shot Landry a warning glance, for once again he was displaying an implausible level of knowledge. "We heard people in the streets saying so," he explained quickly.

"Well, it's true. The last tyrant of Athens, chased out twenty years ago, has been a faithful toady of the Great King ever since. And now the doddering old bastard has convinced himself that if he betrays Athens to them the Persians will restore him as tyrant. Ha! He's a fool as well as a traitor. They'll just use him as a source of information."

"And," Jason suggested, "maybe for any contacts he still has within the city." The term *fifth column* would of course mean nothing to Themistocles.

"Yes." Themistocles grew very grim. "And even if there aren't really any of his fellow traitors within the walls, the suspicion that there *may* be some aristocratic faction ready to open the gates from the inside poisons our air." He shook his head. "Ah, well, it's just one more reason why we're lucky to have Miltiades. I only hope that he was right in talking the Assembly into trying and executing the Persian ambassadors that came last year demanding earth and water." He was clearly worried that Athens, at Miltiades' urging, had forfeited the moral high ground.

"If possible," Landry said diffidently, "we'd like to meet him, having heard so much about him."

"Hmm. Yes, I think that could be arranged. I'll see what I can do. But for now, you're welcome to stay here tonight."

As they got up, murmuring their thanks, Jason spoke up, hoping his interest sounded only casual. "Oh, by the way, we've heard certain odd rumors on our journey. Have there been any incidents of . . . well, of people claiming to have seen manifestations of the gods?"

Themistocles gave him a look which he could not interpret. It was never easy to know just how literally the people of pre-scientific societies really took their gods. One of the few things of which the Classical Greeks were intolerant was atheism . . . strictly speaking, *asebia*, or failure to worship the gods. It was the crime for which Socrates would be sentenced to drink hemlock eight decades from now. But what was the real gravamen of the offense: impiety, or a dereliction of civic duty? Jason knew he had to tread very warily.

"No, not that I've heard of," said Themistocles after a pause. "Why do you ask?"

"Oh, only curious," said Jason hastily. They made their exit as soon as was gracefully possible.

CHAPTER EIGHT

THIS WAS NOT THEIR ACROPOLIS.

The serene perfection of the Parthenon, the inspired eccentricity of the Erechtheum, and all the rest lay half a century and more in the future, when Pericles would loot the treasury of the League of Delos—Athens's subordinate "allies"—to build them, replacing the temples the Persians had burned in 480 B.C. Now, ten years before that, even those earlier temples were for the most part nonexistent.

Seven centuries earlier, the five-hundred-foot-high crag had been the citadel of a semi-barbaric Bronze Age king like those of Jason's recent acquaintance. That age-old megaron had long since vanished, for starting three generations ago, the Eupatrid clans had cluttered the summit with private building projects, competing with each other in the efflorescence of gaudily painted statuary, culminating with the large, flamboyant "Bluebeard Temple" reared by the supremely rarefied Eupatrid family of the Alcmaeonids for its own glorification and the overshadowing of its rivals, the Boutads (who hadn't become "authentic" yet). But even such monuments to aristocratic self-importance had not robbed these precincts of their sacredness, for here was the olive tree, believed to be immortal, that Athena herself had granted to the city, besting Poseidon in the matter of gifts and winning the Athenians' special worship. (Jason wondered if some

Teloi power-struggle lay behind the legend). And the old, shabby temple of Athena Polias held an archaic olive-wood statue of the goddess believed to be a self-portrait, fallen from the sky.

Jason and his companions shouldn't have been seeing any of this, as the crest of the Acropolis was supposedly barred to all but native-born Athenians. But it was becoming more and more apparent that a lot of exclusionary legislation was honored more in the breach than in the observance, in this state without a nit-picking bureaucracy. And besides, they were friends of Themistocles. So Landry had gotten his wish and they now walked among all the schlock that would eventually be swept away by Persian fire or Athenian urban renewal or both. Jason dutifully recorded it all through his implant simply by looking at it, knowing how interested Rutherford would be.

As far as he was concerned, the most edifying thing about the Acropolis at this stage of its history was the view from it. To the west was Mount Aigaleos, scene of the unexplained sighting that still rankled in Jason's mind. To the south was the bay of Phalerum, Athens's port whose inadequacy was such an insistent bee in Themistocles's entirely metaphorical bonnet. To the northeast was the marble-quarry-scarred Mount Pentelikon, beyond which lay the beach and horse-breeding plains of Marathon. Two roads led there, one to the north and one to the south of the mountain—roads which were going to acquire a vital strategic significance in the next few weeks.

Closer than any of these things—almost directly below to the southeast, in fact, within the city itself—was what looked like an unfinished construction site. Which, in fact, was precisely what it was: the longest-unfinished construction site in history.

When Pisistratus had taken power as tyrant in 560 B.C., all the competitive building on the Acropolis had come to an end; *grands projets* were only to be for the glorification of the tyranny. And his sons and successors, Hippias and Hipparchus, had had a perfect opportunity, given that the Athenians had been so remiss as to neglect to raise a temple to Zeus, the king of the gods. In a precinct traditionally sacred to Zeus, they had begun work on a temple of truly Pharaonic grandiosity. It had been uncompleted in 510 B.C. when the tyranny had been overthrown and Hippias sent into exile. Afterwards, the new democracy had neither finished it nor torn it down. Instead, they had simply left it standing, half-finished, as a mute testament to the tyrants' megalomaniacal folly. And so it would stand until the second century A.D., when the Roman Emperor Hadrian would deign to complete it.

Jason, who had known Zeus personally, tried to imagine just how that second, generation Teloi would have taken all this.

He touched Landry's shoulder. "Let's go, Bryan. It's time to meet Miltiades down in the Agora." The historian reluctantly complied.

The four of them turned away, toward the gates, past the immense bronze four-horse chariot placed by the democracy in this one-time aristocratic showcase as a monument to its victories over those who had tried to strangle it in its cradle. They proceeded on down the great ramp and through the crumbling old wall that still marked the outline of the Bronze Age lower town. There they turned right and followed the Panathenaic Way, past the temple enclosure of the Eleusinium on their right, from which the procession to Eleusis for the Mysteries would depart in October. After the next intersection, on the left, was the fountain-house where the women of Athens came in the morning to collect water—one of the tyrants' more useful projects. Then, beyond that, the Agora opened out to their left.

It had been called the Square of Pisistratus, after the tyrant who had cleared it. Like the fountain-house, and unlike the temple of Zeus, this was something the democracy could use. In fact, it had needed such a gathering-place for its public business. So the detritus of the tyranny had been cleared away and replaced by public buildings like the Bouleuterion where the *boule* that prepared the agenda for the popular assembly met, and the circular Tholos where its members ate at public expense. Emphasizing the political change was the bronze statue of two men, heroically nude, with drawn swords— Aristogiton and Harmodius, "the tyrannicides," who had killed Hippias's brother and co-tyrant Hipparchus, and died for it.

As they passed that statue, in the center of the Agora, Landry provided an amused elucidation. "They were homosexual lovers. Hipparchus took a shine to Harmodius and tried to use his political power to have his way with him. Eventually he pushed the two of them just a little too far. They decided their only way out was to murder him."

"And for this they put up a statue of you in this city?" Mondrago wondered.

"Well, the new democracy needed all the heroes it could get," Landry explained. Jason, who had visited the late twentieth and early twenty-first centuries, recalled the word *spin*.

They continued on, through the noisy merchants' stalls. The shady plane trees that featured in so many artists' impressions of the Agora still lay in the future, waiting to be planted after the Persians' retreat in 480 B.C. Jason would have welcomed them, on this sunny late-July afternoon. He paused for an instant under a merchant's striped awning and looked at the crowd. There was a subtle difference from what one would expect in such a marketplace—an unmistakable undercurrent of tension. This was, unmistakably, a city under threat.

One head stood above the general run. The man's exceptional height was the first thing that attracted Jason's attention. What held his eyes was that, unlike most of the people who made up the Agora's sweaty, dusty, entirely ordinary bustle, this man looked the way Classical Greeks were supposed to look, complete with the straight, high-bridged nose and regular features. The longer Jason looked, though, there was something about him that wasn't specifically Greek at all, but was ethnically unidentifiable. Unlike most mature men in this setting, he had no beard, and in fact looked like he had very little facial hair to grow.

Jason took all this in as the man passed them in the opposite direction, headed toward the Panathenaic Way. He thought the man's eyes—large, golden-brown—met his own for a fraction of a second, but he couldn't be sure. Then he felt a tug on the shoulder of his *chiton*.

"Jason," said Chantal, in as close to a whisper as she could come and still make herself heard. "That tall man who just passed us—I saw something under his *himation*. I just got a quick glimpse . . . but it was something that didn't belong in this time."

"Huh?" Jason stared at her. "What was it?"

"I don't know. I probably wouldn't have been able to identify it even if I'd seen it for longer than a fraction of a second. But it was some kind of . . . device. And it had an unmistakable high-technology look."

"Chantal, this is impossible! We're the only time travellers in the here and now—and even if we weren't, nobody is ever allowed to bring advanced equipment. And while that man may look a little out of the ordinary, there's no possibility that he's a Teloi. You must have imagined something."

Chantal took on a look of quiet stubbornness. "You once told me that I'm very observant. You might as well take advantage of that quality." A trace of bitterness entered her voice. "It's the only thing about me that's been any use so far."

Jason chewed his lower lip and looked behind them. The man's wavy dark-gold head could still be seen above the generality. He reached a decision and turned to Mondrago.

"Alexandre, follow that man. Don't reveal yourself, and don't take any action. Just find out where he's going, then come back and report. We'll be over there near the Tholos."

"Right." Mondrago set out, blending into the throng. The rest of them continued toward the Kolonus Agoraeus, the low hill bordering the Agora on the west, with a small temple of Hephaestus at its top and the civic buildings grouped at its foot. To their left was the Heliaia, or law court: simply a walled enclosure where the enormous juries of Athens—typically five hundred and one members—could gather. Just to the left of the Tholos, a street struck off to the south-west, passing another walled quadrangle: the Strategion, headquarters of the Athenian army.

Landry was staring raptly at a small building—a workshop of some kind, it seemed—tucked into an angle of a low wall across the street from the Tholos, near a stone that marked the boundary of the Agora. "What is it?" Jason asked him.

Landry seemed to come out of a trance. "Oh . . . sorry. But that building there . . . I don't know who's occupying it now, but a couple of generations from now it will be the house and shop of Simon the shoemaker." Seeing that this meant nothing to Jason, he elaborated. "It's the place Socrates will use for discussions with his pupils—like Plato and Xenophon."

"Oh," was all Jason said. Inwardly, he was experiencing an increasingly frequent tingle: a sense of just exactly where he was, and what it meant . . . and what would have been lost had the men of Athens not stood firm at Marathon.

Up the street from the Strategion came a group of men, as Jason had been told to expect around this time of day: the *strategoi*, the annually elected generals of the ten tribes, who advised the War-Archon. Jason recognized the latter from descriptions he'd heard. Callimachus was older than most of the *strategoi*, a dignified, strongly built gentleman, bald and with a neat gray beard, wearing a worried expression that looked to be chronic. Themistocles walked behind him.

At Callimachus' side, and talking to him with quiet intensity, was one of the few *strategoi* of his own age. This was a man of middle size, lean and wiry, obviously very well preserved for his age, which Jason knew to be about sixty. He still had all his hair, and it was still mostly a very dark auburn, darker than the still visible reddish shade of his graying beard.

The group began to break up, with Callimachus shuffling off as though stooped under the burden of his responsibilities. Jason wondered if he remembered how to smile. Themistocles led the man who had been expostulating to Callimachus to meet them.

"These are the nobles from Macedon I mentioned, Miltiades." He performed introductions, then excused himself. Jason explained that "Alexander" was currently indisposed.

"I would be, too, if I shared the name of that lickspittle king!" Miltiades gave a patently bogus glare, then laughed. He showed no sign of being scandalized at the presence of a woman in the group, which Jason had hoped would be the case given his background in the wild and wooly frontier of Thrace, where he had married Hegesipyle, the daughter of the Thracian King Olorus. He asked them a series of rapid-fire questions concerning the current state of affairs in those parts, which they were able to answer as they had answered Themistocles.

"We hope we have been of assistance to you, *strategos*," Jason said afterwards. "And we are grateful to you for taking the time to talk to us. We know how much you have had to concern you, ever since . . . well, the news from Naxos and Delos."

"Yes," said Miltiades grimly. He swept his hand in a gesture that took in the Agora crowd. "Can't you feel the suspense as we wait to hear where Datis and his fleet will strike next? And just think: the whole thing could have been avoided if only the Ionians had listened to me twenty-three years ago!"

"You mean," Landry queried, "the matter of the Great King's bridge of boats across the Danube?"

"Yes! Darius, puffed up from his conquests in India, had led his great cumbersome army into Scythia. Of course he couldn't catch the Scythian horsemen, who harried him so mercilessly he was lucky to escape." (*Ancestors of the Cossacks*, thought Jason, remembering what he knew of Darius's invasion of the Ukraine in 513 B.C.) "He'd ordered his subject Greek tyrants—including me—to build that bridge, and await his return before the horrible winter of that land set in. I proposed to the others that we destroy the bridge and leave him stranded north of the river, to either freeze or be feathered with Scythian arrows. We would have been free! But that crawling toad Histaeus, tyrant of Miletus, persuaded the others that my plan was too bold, too risky. So the bridge remained, and the tyrants welcomed back their master."

"Including you," Landry ventured.

"Of course. Do you take me for a fool? Yes, I groveled with the best of them. But later I joined the rebellion Histaeus instigated through his nephew Aristagoras." Miltiades's scowl lightened as though at a pleasant recollection. "The only good outcome was what happened to Histaeus after the rebellion had been crushed. He had the effrontery to demand that the Persian satrap send him to Susa to appeal to his old friend the Great King! The satrap complied—by sending his head there, pickled and packed in salt."

"There was one other good outcome," Landry demurred. "You yourself escaped."

"Yes—twice. First from the Persians, and then from the Athenian Assembly after arriving here! This, even though after capturing the islands of Lemnos and Imbros from the Persians I gave them to Athens! I have Themistocles to thank for my acquittal. I'll never forget that, even though he and I don't agree on everything."

"Like the fact that you persuaded the Assembly to execute the Persian emissaries who came demanding submission last year," Chantal suggested diffidently. "He mentioned that he had reservations about that." Even Miltiades looked slightly taken aback at a woman speaking up unbidden, but after a slight pause he continued.

"A lot of people discovered that they have reservations, after the fact. They said the person of an ambassador is sacred, and that we'd brought down the disfavor of the gods on ourselves." Miltiades's scowl was back at full intensity. "They just don't understand. In a city like this, so traditionally riven by the feuds of aristocratic cliques, so uncertain of its new democracy that hasn't had time to acquire habitual loyalties. . . ." Miltiades seemed to have difficulty putting it into words. In this land with so few rivers worthy of the name, there was no metaphor of burning bridges. "We needed to make our rejection irrevocable, by taking a dramatic step that left us with no alternative but to resist. Besides which, as a practical matter, it aligned us unbreakably with Sparta, which had killed the emissaries without even the formality of a trial."

Jason was silent, remembering the twentieth-century debate over the pros and cons of the Allies' "unconditional surrender" policy in World War II—a debate which hadn't entirely died down among historians even in the twenty-fourth century. Miltiades had argued the Athenians into something like a mirror image of that: unconditional defiance.

"Can Sparta truly be relied on?" asked Landry, probing again for an historical insight.

"If Cleomenes were still alive, I'd be sure of it," said Miltiades, referring to one of the Spartan kings, of whom there were always two. "Yes, I know, he was an enemy of the democracy in its earlier days—tried to force us to take Hippias back as tyrant! But . . . well. . . ." Fifth-century B.C. Ionic Greek also didn't have anything about politics making strange bedfellows. "Lately, he was as staunch an enemy of Persia as any. And four years ago he did us all a favor by crushing Argos, which was threatening to stab us all in the back by joining the Persians at the Battle of Sepeia." Miltiades chuckled. "He attacked them by surprise on the third night of a seven-day truce. When someone asked him about it, he said he'd sworn to the truce for seven days but hadn't said anything about nights! And then when the Argive survivors retreated into the sacred grove of Argos, he ordered his helots to pile brush around the grove and burn it."

"How horrible!" exclaimed Chantal.

"Exactly. Burning a sacred grove was just one more affront to the gods, added to the Spartans' throwing the Persian emissaries down a well. And of course the gods wouldn't be fooled by that trick of having the helots light the fire; they knew who gave the order."

Clearly, Miltiades was more concerned with the trees than with the Argives. "But that was Cleomenes for you. An unscrupulous conniver, to be sure, but *our* unscrupulous conniver. However, he finally outsmarted himself. He bribed the Oracle of Delphi to pronounce his co-king Demaratus illegitimate, so he could bring in that pliable little rat-fucker Leotychides in Demaratus' place. When the story came out, Cleomenes was killed—pay no attention to that goat shit about suicide. Too bad. But his successor, who'd married his daughter Gorgo, may have promise. Young fellow named Leonidas."

Leonidas, thought Jason, and the familiar tingle took him once again. *Leonidas, who ten years from now will lead three hundred Spartans to Thermopylae, where they will leave their bones under a tomb inscribed with "Stranger, go tell the Spartans that we keep the ground they bade us hold," and sear into the very soul of Western civilization a standard against which every subsequent generation of Western men must measure themselves.*

"And now you must excuse me," said Miltiades. "I have people to talk to, people to persuade of what we must do when—not if—the Persians come. And the debate has already begun in the Assembly." Landry restrained himself with an effort as they said their farewells. He would, Jason suspected, have sold his soul for the opportunity to observe the Assembly, but they all knew it was out of the question for resident foreigners like themselves.

As Miltiades receded into the Agora crowd, Mondrago reappeared. "I followed that man as ordered, sir," he reported crisply. "He went back in the direction of the Acropolis, and through the gate in that old wall at the base—but not up the ramp to the summit. Instead, he turned left when nobody was looking and skirted the side of the hill—pretty rough footing, I can tell you. He scrambled partway up the side, past some really old-looking shrines or whatever."

"The sides of the hill," Landry interjected, "especially the northern side, were riddled with tiny shrines, some of them of Bronze Age vintage, in Classical times. In fact, come to think of it, there was a shrine to Pan in a grotto there. Although," he continued, sounding puzzled, "it's always been believed that that shrine was established *after* the Battle of Marathon."

"Well," Mondrago resumed, clearly uninterested, "he vanished into one of those shrines. I expected him to reappear soon—it seemed barely large enough for him to take a leak in! But he never came back out. I thought I ought to get back here and report."

"You did right." Jason turned to Landry and Chantal. "You two get back to our rented house. Alexandre and I are going to look into this."

CHAPTER NINE

IT WAS LATE AFTERNOON when Jason and Modrago passed through the gate at the base of the Acropolis ramp, and there was almost no one about. So they turned unnoticed to the left and began to scramble along the steep, craggy northern side of the Acropolis.

Looming above them to the right were the walls that surrounded the summit. Below to the left spread the sea of small, tile-roofed buildings and winding alleys that was Athens. They had eyes for neither, for it was all they could do to keep their footing on the crumbling ancient pathways that clung to the almost cliff-like face.

Here and there, they passed the mouths of shallow caves holding the worn-down remnants of shrines carved into the hill in ages past, often holding barely recognizable statues which must surely predate written history.

Jason knew full well that humans were quite capable of imagining gods for themselves without the help of the Teloi—the entire religious history of humanity outside the Indo-European zone bore witness to that. So he didn't know how many of these Bronze Age sculptures represented the alien "gods" and how many reflected images that had arisen from the subsoil of the human population's own psyche. All he knew was that these shrines, sacred to the forgotten deities of a forgotten people, belonged to a different world from the bustling city below or the self-conscious monuments above. Child of a raw new world, he had always found Old Earth's accumulated layers of ancientness oppressive—almost sinister. Now he had passed into a realm of ancientness beyond ancientness, and the tininess of his own lifespan shook him.

"This is the one," he heard Mondrago say.

It was much like the others, little more than a rough indentation in the hillside. Inside and to the left was one of the crude sculptures, in a roughly hewn-out niche with an opening to the sky. It got no direct sunlight, here on the north side of the Acropolis, but there was enough illumination to make out the statue's outlines. With a little imagination, it was possible to see a goat-legged man.

"He's gone," said Mondrago.

"Gone from *where*?" Jason demanded irritably, waving his hand at the little cavern, which hardly deserved the name; it was barely deep enough for a man to stand up inside. "Are you sure this is the right shrine?"

"Of course I'm sure!"

"But he could barely have squeezed in here, much less remained for a long time."

"I tell you, this is where I left him!" Mondrago angrily slammed the rocky rear wall of the cavern with his fist for emphasis.

With a very faint humming sound, a segment of the rough stone surface, seemingly indistinguishable from the rest, slowly swung inward as though on hinges.

For a moment the two men simply stared at each other, speechless in the face of the impossibly out-of-place.

"I must have hit exactly the right spot," Mondrago finally said, in an uncharacteristically small voice.

Jason shook his head slowly. No one in the twenty-fourth century had any inkling of anything like this under the Acropolis. "This has to be the work of the Teloi."

"Why? Chantal said she saw high-tech equipment on a *human*."

"I know what Chantal said. But she had to be mistaken. The Authority doesn't allow it. *Ever*."

Mondrago's brown face screwed itself into a look of intense concentration. "Look, ours is the only expedition that's ever been sent to this era, right? So if there *are* other time travelers around here, they must have come from *our* future."

Jason shook his head. "The Authority has a fixed policy against sending multiple expeditions to the same time and place, where they could run into each other. God knows what paradoxes *that* could lead to!"

"But you told us—"

"—That there are no paradoxes. Right. But I also told you that we don't go out of our way to *invite* paradoxes, because the harder we push, the harder reality is apt to push back—maybe so hard as to be lethal."

"Yes, I know, that's another fixed policy. But think about it: maybe sometime in our future, the Authority's policies will change. Maybe the Authority itself will change . . . or even cease to exist."

Jason was silent. This had of course been considered, for it was obviously not impossible that it could happen in the unforeseeable scope of the twenty-fourth century's future. But while no one had ever denied the possibility, no one ever seemed to think about it very much either. Its implications didn't bear thinking about; the mind reeled from the potential consequences of unregulated *laissez-faire* time travel. And as more and more expeditions had returned from the past and reported no indication of other time travellers from further in the future, the thought had receded to the back of people's minds. Everyone had settled into the comfortable assumption that, for whatever reason, the restrictions imposed by the Temporal Regulatory Authority and the Temporal Precautionary Act under which it operated must be forever immutable.

"Anyway," said Mondrago, interrupting his thoughts, "why are we standing here speculating? Let's investigate this."

Jason eyed the opening dubiously. "We're unarmed."

"No, we're not." Mondrago lifted his *himation*, which he was wearing hanging from his left shoulder and draped around despite the late-July heat, and the *chiton* under it. He had contrived a heavy cloth sheath with leather strings, by which his short Spanish *falcata* was strapped tightly to his left thigh.

Jason frowned. Going armed was not customary in Athens, and the sword would have taken some explaining if anyone had spotted it. But this was no time to raise the issue. He peered through the doorway, which admitted enough light to reveal a flight of shallow steps carved in the stone, leading downward into the gloom.

"We'll see how far we can get before the light gives out," said Jason. As they passed through the doorway, he looked for whatever machinery had opened it, but it was concealed beyond his ability to find it in the dimness.

They descended the steps, and as their eyes accustomed themselves, they saw they were in what appeared to be a small, natural cave from whose opposite side a tunnel had been dug. At the tunnel's far end was a faint glow.

"My God," whispered Mondrago. "How far under the Acropolis does this extend?"

"Shhh!" Jason motioned him to silence. Straining their ears, they detected a murmur of voices from the tunnel.

Without waiting for orders, Mondrago drew his sword.

They advanced into the tunnel, in which Mondrago could just barely stand up straight and Jason had to stoop slightly. The sides were too smooth and even to be entirely the work of nature. But it was crude excavation, and Jason began to think that humans of the Bronze Age or earlier were responsible for the basic work, to which the Teloi had later added high-tech touches like the door.

The glow grew brighter as they approached, and they could smell the aroma of burning oil lamps. The sound resolved itself into voices joined in a kind of low chant—a dark, weird, unmelodious drone that was somehow repellent. Jason was wondering if it was bringing to the surface of his consciousness certain memories from the Bronze Age that he had no desire to recall.

Nearing the tunnel's end, they flattened themselves against opposite walls in shadow and cautiously peered through the opening. In the light of the lamps they saw a large, roughly circular cavern, clearly of natural origin but shaped by human tools as the tunnel had been shaped. Its floor had been flattened and smoothed, and it was crowded with figures in nondescript local clothes, who were producing the chanting. Those people—they were humans—were arrayed in a half-circle, focused on an idol on a rough dais toward the rear of the cavern and somewhat to the left. It was a crude idol similar to the one in the outside shrine, but in better condition as consequence of being sheltered, and therefore more readily recognizable, even in the dim flickering lamplight, as representing the Pan of mythology.

But Jason's attention was riveted on the tall man standing behind the idol—the man they had seen in the Agora. He stood with arms folded, not joining in the chanting but surveying the chanters. His eyes looked down on them with a cold remoteness reflected in the set of his thin lips. It was an expression too far removed from the merely human to be arrogant. He did not sneer, any more than a man sneers at dogs.

He's definitely no Teloi, thought Jason, *but he could scarcely seem any less human if he was one.*

Abruptly, the man unfolded his arms and spread them wide. The chant instantly ceased, leaving a palpably expectant hush.

Then the man spoke. His voice was a rich, deep baritone. But there was more to it than that. Below the level of audibility there was something that compelled one to listen to it, to the exclusion of every other sound, and to believe what it said in defiance of all critical faculties. Jason wondered if certain otherwise inexplicable historical figures as disparate as Joan of Arc and Adolph Hitler had possessed the same quality.

"Rejoice!" he said. "The time is at hand—the time you have been promised. And this time was chosen for a reason. Your god knew that this would be the time when your city would stand in its greatest danger. Even now, the barbarians close in on Athens! Everyone knows it! Nothing your leaders can do will save you from death, your sons from being gelded, your daughters from being raped, and all your children from being enslaved and scattered like dust among the rabble of slaves all across the vastness of Persia. And after another generation, no one will remember that the Athenians ever existed!"

A low moan of utter desolation filled the cavern.

"But your god will save Athens!" The extraordinary voice rose like a clarion. "Your devotion is enough to cause him to withhold his righteous anger against this city for its failure to worship him. He will cause the barbarians to go mad with fear, as he has the power to do, and they will flee, howling, to their ships!"

A rapturous sound arose from the worshipers.

"Afterwards, Athens will erect a proper shrine out there on the north slope where our poor shrine now is, and offer sacrifice to him every year. But," he continued, and his voice dropped, "no one must ever know of the secret doorway to this, the god's *true* shrine. For you and your successors will continue as you always have to be the custodians of his innermost mysteries. And every few generations, at the prophesied times, the god's promise to you will be kept, as it has been before."

The air of the cavern was now thick with breathless anticipation.

"Such a time is now come, as was foretold to your ancestors. I and my companions are only the heralds. Now there comes among you . . . *the Great God Pan!*"

Without warning, some well-concealed lighting fixture in the wall behind the idol—and hence at about ten o'clock, from Jason's perspective—activated, and a harsh glare flooded the cavern. The worshipers' eyes, which had been focused on the idol, were dazzled. But Jason's, viewing it from an angle, were not. So he was able to discern, in the glare, the idol sinking into the floor with a practically inaudible hum, leaving a hatchway through which a living being emerged—a being at which Jason's mind reeled. But he didn't doubt his sanity, for it was inarguably the figure he had briefly glimpsed on the slopes of Mount Aigaleos.

The artificial light—supernatural to the worshippers in the cavern—faded to a relatively dim glow. In that glow stood revealed an outrage against nature, with the legs of a goat and the upper body of a brown-skinned, hirsute, muscular man—very definitely a man, for it was grotesquely male, almost ridiculously so. The head was that of a man—broad, snub-nosed, full-lipped, with thick, curly hair and beard of a dark reddish brown. From amid that hair grew a pair of horns.

An ecstatic, almost orgasmic moan gusted from the worshipers.

The tall man from the Agora turned toward the apparition with the air of a magician who had produced a rabbit from a hat. The motion caused him to face the tunnel opening.

It belatedly occurred to Jason that the opening where he and Mondrago had crouched in shadows was no longer shadowed.

The classically handsome face of the speaker contorted into a mask of rage. "Intruders!" he bellowed. "Seize them!"

"Run!" Jason yelled to Mondrago as the worshipers began to

emerge from shock. They ran back along the tunnel, as fast as its cramped confines permitted.

That slight head start enabled them to reach the steps ahead of their frantic pursuers—who then caught up as they struggled up the steps. Jason felt his legs grappled from behind and below. He wrenched one leg free and kicked backwards, feeling facial bone and cartilage crunch under his hard-driven heel. Momentarily free, he ascended the rest of the way to the area just inside the tantalizingly open doorway, where there was more room. Mondrago was already there. Jason saw him spring backwards after delivering a slicing sideways lunge with his Spanish sword that ripped through a pursuer's throat and sent him silently to the floor, his head flopping loosely on a neck that had been severed to the spinal column. Jason recognized the Afghan fighting technique, but he had only a split second to admire Mondrago's mastery of it before a crush of bodies from behind bore him to the floor and a shattering impact to his head caused the universe to explode into a shower of stars and then go dark.

CHAPTER TEN

JASON AWOKE to a nauseatingly painful headache. He didn't want to open his eyes, but to fail to do so was out of the question. He parted his eyelids very cautiously.

The light sent fresh pain stabbing through his head, but it was not quite as bad as he had feared—he could sense that it was dim interior lighting. Lying on his back as he was, all he could make out was a completely nondescript ceiling. He slowly turned his head to the left.

He found himself looking into a pair of brown eyes, somehow like the eyes of an animal, but not quite, for they held something that no animal would ever know. Those eyes looked out at him from under bushy brows of the same dark russet color as the curly hair and beard that framed a face whose expression he could not interpret. The head lowered to look more closely at him, a motion which caused the horns to dip.

Unconsciousness mercifully took him again.

When he awoke again his head was clear. Another difference was that he was sitting up, in a chair to which he was tied. One of the first things he noticed in the light of the oil lamps as his eyes darted around the small, windowless room was that Mondrago was similarly seated and bound to his right, although he was only just stirring from unconsciousness. He also saw a man in local garb walking out the door, holding a hypospray injector by which he and Mondrago had presumably been awakened.

But mostly he noticed that now he was looking into a human face. Human . . . but inhumanly perfect.

It was the man they had seen in the Agora and in the inexplicable cavern under the Acropolis. Now he sat at his ease in a chair of local manufacture. His wavy hair was an unmistakable shade: a unique kind of blond-black, like an alloy of gold and iron. His eyes were large and luminous, the color of amber. His lips were full without being thick. There was no indentation between his brow and the bridge of his ruler-straight nose.

"Well," he said in his strangely compelling voice, "what are we to do with you?" He spoke in twenty-fourth century Standard International English.

Jason made himself blink with incomprehension before swallowing to moisten his dry throat and speaking in indignant Greek. "What is this barbarian babble? Who are you? And how dare you hold us prisoner? I am a nobleman of Macedon, and this is my retainer. And we are friends of the *strategos* Themistocles! Release us at once or it will go hard on you."

The perfect lips quirked in a momentary smile. "It's no use. Our instruments detected the energy surge your arrival produced. It was just by chance that we happened to be in the vicinity at the time, between Athens and Eleusis." The man gave an irritated headshake. "And it was an *unfortunate* chance that you happened to spot Pan. It's all your fault, you know. We would have preferred to simply avoid you and let you return to your own time, blissfully ignorant. We still wish we could have. If only you hadn't meddled—!"

Jason had almost stopped listening after the word *instruments*, for he suddenly recalled what Chantal thought she had seen, and what he had definitely seen in the shrine on the Acropolis north slope. "Who the hell *are* you?" he blurted, all thoughts of dissimulation forgotten. "You're brought advanced technology back in time! That is flatly contrary to the regulations of the Temporal Regulatory Authority, besides being a felony under the Revised Temporal Precautionary Act of 2364."

This time the full lips formed a smirk. "We don't concern ourselves with either."

Jason stared at him. "You must be from our future."

"Evidently not, since we didn't know you were going to be here in this time-period. If we had known, it would have made things awkward for us, as this expedition is essential to us but, like you, we make it a point to avoid creating possibilities for different time travelers to encounter each other. That's one rule of the Authority which we follow—an uncharacteristically sensible one. We would have had to go to great lengths to avoid attracting your attention."

"But if you're not from our future, how can you be here? The Authority certainly didn't send you."

Another smirk. "We have our own arrangements."

"You keep saying 'we.' Will you kindly answer my question and tell me who you are? What's your *name*, for God's sake?"

For an instant the man seemed to weigh the pros and cons of revealing the information. Then he smiled as though pleasurably anticipating the effect his answer would have.

"I am Franco, Category Five, Seventy-Sixth Degree."

Jason stared. "But that's a—"

"Yes. I am a genetically upgraded agent of the Transhuman Dispensation."

"What are you trying to put over on us?" demanded Mondrago, now fully awake. "The Transhuman movement was wiped out a generation before Weintraub discovered temporal energy potential."

"So you Pugs think." From history lessons, Jason recognized the Transhumanist acronym for *products of uncontrolled genetics*—their term for the human race in its natural form. "You truly believe you successfully stood in the way of evolutionary destiny. You merely delayed it. Our inner circles withdrew into concealment, in various hidden places all around Earth and the Solar System, where we have secretly continued our great work."

"Too bad," remarked Jason. "We really did think the universe had been cleansed of the Transhuman abomination."

Franco leaned forward, and his amber eyes glowed as though fervor burned like a flame behind them. "It is you who are the abomination: a form of life that has outlived its time but refuses out of mere parochialism and nostalgia to step aside and get out of the way of its successors. Humanity is clinging to its primordial state—a race of randomly evolved apes—when for centuries it has had the technology to transform itself into a consciously, rationally self-created race of gods—"

"—And monsters." Jacob shook his head irritably. "Why am I wasting my breath talking to you? I have no idea who you really are, but you're obviously a liar in addition to being a raving lunatic. The fact that you're here and now proves that. The Authority has never sent any diehard Transhumanist fanatics into the past, and it never will."

Franco took on an infuriatingly complacent look. "Who said anything about the Authority?"

"Talk sense! The Authority operates the only temporal displacer in existence."

"So it pleases the Authority to think. Shortly after Weintraub's initial experiments, we stole his data—it was pathetically easy, and we were *very* interested in its potentialities. Our research ran parallel to, but in advance of, Fujiwara's. She and Weintraub were brilliant, for Pugs, but they followed several false trails. The result was a 'brute force' approach to temporal displacement, requiring a titanic installation and a lavish expenditure of energy. We soon spotted the flaws in their mathematics. O*ur* displacer is relatively compact and energy-efficient, and therefore concealable."

"Are you saying," said Jason, thunderstruck, "that there are *two* displacers on Earth in our era?" He wanted to believe it was a lie, because it removed the foundations of his accustomed structure of assumptions. But, try as he might, he could see no other way to account for the presence of unauthorized time travelers with proscribed equipment.

"Only since the Authority's came into operation," said Franco, amused. "Ours was the first. We'll probably build more, as the one we have is getting somewhat overworked. As I mentioned, we have been intensely interested in time travel ever since Weintraub demonstrated that it was a theoretical possibility."

"Why? I've never heard that the Transhumanists had any interest in historical research."

"We don't." Once again Franco leaned forward avidly. "We look to the future, not the past. We don't want to study history. We want to change it."

For a heartbeat or two, Jason stared openmouthed. Then he burst out laughing.

"Now I *know* you're a lunatic!" he finally gasped. "History *can't* be changed! But please don't let me stop you. I hope you try—I really do. In fact, I hope you try very, very hard!"

"I never said we thought we could change *observed* history. But have you ever considered how much of the human past is unobserved and unrecorded? There are vast empty stretches of territory and time in which we are constantly changing the past, filling up those stretches with what will, in the end, turn out to have been humanity's secret history—a history inevitably leading to our eventual triumph at a date which . . . I don't believe I'll reveal to you. We call it, simply, *The Day*."

"And how, precisely, are you doing that?" Jason inquired, unable to keep a reluctant and horrified fascination out of his voice. In one corner of his mind, he wondered why Franco was telling him all this. Probably the Transhumanist simply felt a need for someone besides his own underlings to brag to. Jason had known enough blowhards, in his own time and others, to be able to recognize the type.

Of course, there was another, more unsettling explanation: Franco thought his revelations could do no possible harm because he had no intention of letting his listeners live.

"We have various techniques. For example, we plant genetic flaws in the unmodified human population by infecting populations with gengineered retroviruses, which by The Day will have rendered those populations vulnerable to a biochemical warfare using tailored proteins or polysaccharides. Another approach is to plant retroactive plagues, spreading mutagens whose genetic time-clocks result in the poisoning of certain vital food supplies on The Day. And there are even more subtle 'time bombs' that we plant, some of a purely psychological nature."

"But," said Jason with an incredulous headshake, "things like that would be extremely long-term, and require repeated visits to various eras in succession." Inwardly, he fought to hold at bay an obscene vision of Earth as a rotten apple, seemingly sound on the outside but a writhing mass of worms inside the skin, waiting to break through it.

"To repeat, our temporal displacement technology is less expensive than yours by orders of magnitude. We are therefore less constrained in how far into the past we can go, and how often. This is particularly helpful in my own work: the establishment of cults and secret societies, which we nurture over the centuries by repeated visits from the same, seemingly ageless agent at prophesied times. At those times the agent foretells the next visit, dazzles the faithful with technological 'magic,' and gives them enough foreknowledge of the future to confirm the succeeding generations in their faith. As the ages pass and the scientific worldview takes hold, we will begin to reveal the truth to them. By then their loyalty will be practically hereditary, and we will offer them suitable rewards in the new order."

"A promise which naturally won't be kept," Mondrago stated rather than asked.

"Naturally. Promises to Pugs mean nothing. By the time The Day arrives, Earth will be riddled with such cadres, not knowing of each other's existence. Like all our other projects, it will not contradict recorded history. But recorded history will turn out to have been a mere ornamental façade, behind which *real* history has been building all along toward a Transhumanist future."

"And," Jason said slowly, "I imagine it helps to no end when you have some kind of pre-existing cult to build on." He wanted to keep Franco talking as long as possible, revealing as much information as possible.

"You're surprisingly perceptive. Yes, my first appearance in this region was in the late Bronze Age—the thirteenth century B.C. Pan, you see, is a very ancient god. And, since we are not limited by the irrational restrictions you labor under, my genetic code was resequenced by nanotechnological means, altering my appearance to godlike standards, as you've doubtless noticed."

"Actually I hadn't."

Franco's eyes narrowed a few microns and chilled a few degrees, but otherwise he showed no reaction to Jason's jab.

"At the same time," Jason went on, "it must limit you that you can't send any of your radically specialized—and unhuman-looking—gengineered castes back in time. Nor can you send those of your servitors with blatantly obvious bionics. They couldn't exactly blend, could they?"

"It is a handicap," Franco acknowledged. "But this was one of those cases in which we were able to make use of recorded history, rather than merely avoiding it. We knew, of course, of the later belief that Pan had intervened at Marathon. It was the perfect opportunity to reinforce our cult's fervor."

"And, of course, you've been able to show them their god Pan in the flesh. Another of your gene-twisted obscenities, of course—although I didn't realize that even you were able to produce anything so grotesquely divergent from the human norm."

"We're not, at least not without great difficulty. We had help. You see, in the course of my earlier visits to Greece, we acquired allies." Before Franco could elaborate, a door opened and a handsome but relatively nondescript man came in and whispered to him. He nodded, said "Bring him in," and turned back to Jason with a dazzling smile. "By a most fortunate coincidence, the leader of those allies is here now." He stood up and, to Jason's amazement, went to his knees.

"Greetings, Lord," he said, oozing a reverence that would not have deceived a child. But it seemed to satisfy the figure who entered, bending low to get through the door and unable to stand up straight without brushing his gold-shot silvery hair against the ceiling. His huge, disturbingly alien eyes stared at Jason, empty of recognition.

"Hi," said Jason in the Teloi tongue, eliciting a satisfyingly startled reaction from Franco. "It's been a long time. Well, actually it hasn't been all that long for me. But for you it's been almost eleven hundred and forty years."

Zeus looked puzzled.

CHAPTER ELEVEN

"YOU SEEM SOMEHOW FAMILIAR," said the Teloi, with a frown, stroking the beard he shared with some but not all males of his race. His deep voice held the indefinably disturbing quality Jason remembered.

"Let me refresh your memory," said Jason. "Do you recall your 'son' Perseus? It was at the time Santorini—or Kalliste, as it was called then—exploded. Surely you must remember that." While waiting for a reply, he glanced around and saw that Mondrago was staring, wide-eyed, in spite of having seen video imagery of the Teloi.

"Oh, yes," Zeus finally nodded, a little vaguely. "Perseus was one of the superior strain that we created for the purpose of leading the ordinary human masses into a proper state of submission to their creators. They were a great disappointment to us, from Gilgamesh on. But Perseus was better than most. He kept his word and established my worship at Mycenae after I had imprisoned the Old Gods forever."

Wait a minute! thought Jason, speechless. *What's this?* You *imprisoned them?*

"And now I remember you," Zeus continued. "You were one of the time travelers who appeared around that time. You were of some assistance to me." He turned to Franco. "He must be spared, for I pay my debts to mortals."

91

He's gone senile, Jason realized. *He really believes it. He thinks he really is a god. And he's forgotten how the senior Teloi got permanently trapped in their pocket universe. The myths and legends that his human worshipers have woven around what happened have become more real for him than the truth.*

And why should I be surprised? For almost eleven and a half centuries he and his faction of younger-generation Teloi—the ones who didn't *get trapped—have been stranded on low-technology Earth without their extradimensional hidey-hole and with none of their advanced technology except what they happened to have with them when Santorini blew up and their tame human empire based on Crete was wrecked by the tsunami and other side effects. All that time, they've been running a bluff with the aid of whatever flashy displays of techno-magic they could manage.*

All things considered, I suppose it's surprising he's retained any vestige of sanity at all.

Franco broke into his thoughts. "So you already know about the Teloi?"

Jason saw no point in evasion or denials. "We encountered them on an expedition to observe the Santorini explosion."

"Ah, yes . . . that expedition had departed from the twenty-fourth century shortly before we did. So you must be Jason Thanou. I hadn't realized we had such a distinguished guest. By the time we encountered the Teloi, four centuries after you did, they had forgotten about you."

"But now I remember," Zeus broke in. "Yes, you were useful to me. And now new time travelers have arrived." He indicated Franco, who inclined his head graciously. "And they too recognize true divinity—not to be confused with a silly legend like 'Pan'! We helped them produce a living image of that legend, with which to gull the local human cattle, who deserve no better. In exchange, they will help restore my worship to this disrespectful city!"

"What?" Jason managed.

Zeus's voice had been steadily rising. Now he was almost raving. "Yes! Athens has sought the patronage of my daughter Athena, while neglecting me!" Familial affection, Jason recalled, was not a trait of the vastly long-lived Teloi, who produced children but rarely. In fact, the being Oannes who had told Jason the story of the Teloi on Earth had been of the opinion that their second generation, including Zeus, were infertile. Jason wondered if, in his increasing dementia, Zeus had come to believe the local mythology's version of his relationship to Athena. "At least the tyrant Hippias, son of Pisistratus, began building a suitable temple to me. But then the Athenians drove him out and failed to complete it. Instead they have left it standing unfinished, as though wishing to flaunt their impiety!

"But now, thanks to Franco—a member of an improved human stock called the *Transhumans* who have returned to the worship of us, the true gods, as he assures me—matters will be set right. The Persians are coming, and bringing Hippias back with them. Franco will enable them to win the coming battle, conquer Athens, and restore Hippias as tyrant. And then Hippias will put the Athenians to work completing his great temple, thus atoning for their ingratitude to me!"

Behind Zeus and out of the Teloi's range of vision, Jason saw Franco smile.

"What has this Transhumanist pimp been telling you about time travel?" Mondrago suddenly burst out. "He's lying. It doesn't work that way. History is fixed—and it says that the Athenians are going to kick the Persian army's ass up between the ears and then pull it out through the nose!"

"And even if Franco could prevent that," Jason added, "he wouldn't, because it's precisely what he's promised his cult of Pan-worshipers is going to happen, thanks to their 'god.'"

"Lies!" Zeus was truly raving now. He loomed up, standing as straight as he could, shaking with the extremity of his passion. His right hand grasped Jason's throat with choking force, half-lifting him from the chair. "All lies! Franco warned me to expect this. He told me you would be jealous of him as a more highly evolved form of life."

"Can't you see?" croaked Jason desperately. "He's just using you—making a fool of you!"

"No! He is my true worshiper. It is all clear to me now. But," Zeus continued, with the abrupt tone-change of the insane, "you served me well, long ago. Franco, this man and his follower must be spared." He released Jason, who sagged back down in his bonds, gasping for breath.

"Yes, Lord," said Franco smoothly. Zeus gave a vague nod, and departed. As he stooped to get through the door, there was, in spite of everything, a quality about him that could only be called pathetic.

"You heard him," Jason wheezed to Franco through his bruised throat. "About not killing us, that is."

"He'll get over it." Franco's smile was charming. He shook his head with what Jason would have sworn was sincere regret. "We really would have preferred to just let you complete your studies and go home, ignorant of us. As it is. . . ."

"If you cut our TRDs out—TRDs that nobody in this era is supposed to be able to detect—and we don't reappear in our time on schedule, a lot of questions are going to be asked. The Authority isn't stupid, you know." Jason wasn't absolutely certain of the last part, but saw no useful purpose to be served by sharing his skepticism with Franco.

"Oh, we won't do that. We'll simply kill you in some acceptably 'in-period' way, and your corpses will appear on the Authority's displacer stage. Very sad. But we all know that human history is a violent place."

Without moving his head, Jason turned his eyes as far to the right as he dared and met Mondrago's. The latter nodded imperceptibly. He understood. Chantal and Landry, about whom the Transhumanists might be ignorant, must not be mentioned.

Franco seemed to read his mind, or at least read the byplay correctly. "And as for the other two members of your party, we will deal with them in due course. Oh, yes, we know about them. Since capturing you, we have brought certain intelligence sources to bear, and we've learned about Themistocles' Macedonian guests, and where they are lodging now." His eyes took on the unfocused look of one sending a command via direct neural induction through an implant communicator of a sort prohibited even to someone in Jason's position, involving as it did a proscribed melding of mind and computer.

Taking advantage of Franco's distraction, Jason mentally activated his map-display, with its red dots representing the party's TRDs. Chantal and Landry were still at the house. He forced himself not to let his relief show.

Presently, four of Franco's underlings entered the room. "Take them back to separate cells," he ordered.

The goons cut Jason's and Mondrago's bonds with unemotional efficiency and hoisted them to their feet. It took some hoisting, for they were horribly stiff, and Jason realized for the first time how hungry he was—they must have been unconscious for at least the better part of a day. As they were being led out of the room, a sudden impulse made Jason twist out of the grip of one of his two handlers and turn to face Franco. He had no time to try and understand his own motivations—what was the point of arguing with a Transhumanist?—but he looked into those large, perfectly shaped amber eyes and waved his one free hand at the door through which Zeus had passed.

"That thing that just left this room is the inevitable end product of the Transhuman movement's vision of humanity's future! Is that really what you want?"

Franco's face showed no resentment or anger, or anything at all except the certitude of the true ideologue. "Oh, no. You're wrong. Don't confuse us with the Teloi. We won't repeat their mistakes. Remember what you said earlier about gods and monsters? The Teloi sought to turn themselves into gods. They neglected the monsters. We won't."

The goons tightened their grip and marched the two prisoners through the door, into a corridor even more dimly lit than the room they had departed. As they proceeded, a short figure appeared from a side corridor to the right.

It took a heartbeat for it to register on Jason's mind, as his eyes met the brown ones of Pan. From Mondrago's direction, he heard a non-verbal growl.

Without consciously formulating a plan, he used a basic release technique: he went limp, ceasing to resist the two men holding him. By an instinctive reaction, they relaxed their grip.

With a Judo-like wrenching motion he freed himself and forced his still-stiff muscles to propel him forward. He grasped the startled Pan from behind, locking one arm around the hirsute throat. With his other hand, he grasped one of the horns. He took the creature halfway to the floor and pressed his right leg behind the creature's knees to prevent a backward kick of its cloven hooves.

"If you cry out," he snapped at the guards, "I'll break his neck. And then where will your 'god' be?"

He was betting that the guards didn't have implant communicators like Franco's. He recognized their sort from history disks. They were nondescript-looking, low-grade Transhumanists, doubtless with high but very specialized intelligence and little initiative. His intuition seemed to be paying off, for they stood seemingly paralyzed with indecision.

"I'll also break his neck," he continued, pressing his advantage, "if you don't release my companion."

They released Mondrago, who hurried to join Jason behind Pan.

"Don't hurt me."

It took a second for Jason to realize the voice was Pan's. It had an odd timbre to it, and was unexpectedly high-pitched, and it was difficult to sort out the emotions behind it. But he found himself thinking it was an undeniable—if odd—*human* voice. And it was pleading.

"I won't hurt you if you do as you're told," Jason said. "Show us to the nearest exit from this building."

With Jason still holding him in the same potentially neck-snapping grip, Pan moved in a cautious sidewise gait back along the corridor from which he had emerged. The four guards followed closely but cautiously, making no moves that might precipitate the death of the god the cult-worshipers expected. The corridor was a very short one, terminating in a door.

And here Jason faced a dilemma. They couldn't take Pan with them out into the city, where he would have been conspicuous to say the least.

"Kill it now!" hissed Mondrago, seeming to read his mind. "We don't need it as a hostage anymore—they won't be able to pursue us once we're outside in public. Kill it just before we bolt out the door. And that will be the end of their little scheme for a cult of the 'Great God Pan'."

"No," Jason heard himself saying. "We're not murderers."

If telepathy had been a reality, Mondrago's searing contempt could have been no more obvious. "'Murderers'? This thing isn't human. It isn't even a decent animal. It's just a filthy, obscene mutant! Have you gone soft in the head?"

"We don't kill any sentient being without a reason! Remember that. And get ready to move . . . *now.*" With a sudden movement,

Jason thrust Pan back into the narrow corridor. The four guards rushed, but got in each other's way in the confined space even before stumbling over Pan. Jason and Mondrago hit the door with their shoulders. It burst open, and they were out, into one of the crooked streets of Athens.

While running, Jason summoned up his map-display and saw that the red dots of his and Mondrago's TRDs were in the area south of the Agora, on the terraced lower slopes of the Areopagus hill—the vicinity of their rented house, where the dots of Chantal's and Landry's TRDs still glowed reassuringly.

Good! Jason thought as they sprinted through the winding, uneven alleyways. *Even in this maze, it won't take us long to find it. We'll get Chantal and Landry out of it before Franco can "deal with them in due course" . . . and find a new address.*

There were no such things as apartment blocks in fifth-century B.C. Athens. But there were blocks of houses—as many as six houses. Their quarters were in such a block. All the houses had the inward-looking design of Athenian residences, organized around miniscule courtyards and having upstairs rooms. A narrow street-front door in the mud-brick wall gave access to the courtyard.

It was ajar.

Off to the left, out of the corner of his eye, Jason barely glimpsed a figure hurrying around a corner of the block, seeming to push another figure ahead. He was about to investigate when he heard shouting from within, in Landry's voice. Without waiting for Mondrago, he plunged through the open door.

The shouting was coming from one of the small rooms opening off the courtyard. Jason rushed in, to see one of the goon-class Transhumanists grasping Landry by on arm and holding a dagger in his other hand.

Without thinking, Jason sprang forward, reaching out to seize the wrist of the dagger arm.

With the strength of desperation, Landry broke the Transhumanist's grip and rushed frantically forward. He succeeded only in tripping himself and Jason. The Transhumanist grasped him from behind, under the chin, and brought his dagger-edge across the historian's throat. With a gurgling shriek, Landry fell across Jason. Mondrago, desperately trying to get into the room, stumbled over the fallen body. The Transhumanist, with the quickness of his unnatural kind, shoved him aside and plunged out the door.

Mondrago got to his feet and gave chase. By the time Jason could get out from under the body atop him, it was too late. That which had been Bryan Landry, Ph.D., lay in a pool of blood and excreta, his slit throat like a ghastly, grinning second mouth—an 'in-period' death.

Of Chantal Frey there was no sign. Jason checked his map-display again. It was unchanged, still showing both Landry's and Chantal's TRDs right here.

Mondrago returned. "The bastard got away," he gasped. "Where's Chantal?"

"She ought to be here." Jason began to look around frantically.

"Look," Mondrago said expressionlessly, pointing at the floor in a corner of the room. The small smear of blood was barely noticeable. So was the tiny metallic sphere that had been cut out of Chantal's arm.

Jason clamped calmness down on himself. "They can't have gotten too far with her. Let's go!"

As they reemerged onto the street, they heard a roar of voices from the direction of the Agora, like a disturbed sea with an undertow of terror. People were running along the street, wild-eyed.

Jason grabbed one such passerby. "What has happened?" he demanded. "What's going on?"

"You haven't heard? The news has just arrived. The Persians have sacked Eretria! Burned it to the ground and enslaved the people!"

Eretria, thought Jason, frantically summoning up information from his implant. *The one Greek city, other than Athens, that aided the Ionian rebels and therefore was marked for destruction by the Great King. Located on the island of Euboea, just across a narrow strait from Attica—within sight of Attica at its narrowest point, in fact.*

"The Eretrians resisted," the man went on. No Greek could resist recounting a story. "For five days they defended their walls. But then they were betrayed. Two members of an aristocratic faction sold out, opened the gates, and let the Persians in."

Uh-huh! thought Jason, remembering what Themistocles had said. *That's all the Athenians need to hear at this point.*

"And they'll be here next!" The man must have suddenly

remembered just how close Eretria was, for he grew wild-eyed and fled.

Jason consulted his implant for the calendar. It was still late July.

Well, I suppose we've settled the question of whether the Battle of Marathon took place in August or September. Kyle Rutherford will be interested.

It didn't seem terribly important at the moment.

CHAPTER TWELVE

THERE WAS NO SIGN OF CHANTAL. And no one was in a position to help find her, under the circumstances in which Athens now found itself.

"It's a shame about Lydos," Themistocles said distractedly as they hurried across the Agora. "I was glad to have the body taken care of, and of course I'll do what I can to find the murderer later. And I wish I could help organize a search for Cleothera. But now there's no time. The Assembly is about to bring the question of our strategy against the Persians to a final vote."

Jason saw that the Agora crowd was moving steadily southwestward, in the direction of the Pnyx hill where the *Ekklesia*, or Assembly of all citizens, had met since the establishment of the democracy. They were being herded in that direction by the exotically costumed "Scythian" police force of Athens. Some of these men were really Scythians; most were merely dressed up to resemble those famously fearsome barbarians from north of the Black Sea. But all were public slaves, and Jason had a feeling they relished any opportunity to ram it to the free citizens. This was such an opportunity, as they advanced through the Agora toward the Pnyx in a line, holding a long rope daubed with red powder. Any citizen found outside the meeting area with red marks on his clothing was fined. Athenian democracy was not just participatory; it was compulsory.

"Miltiades mentioned that the debate had been going on even before the news from Eretria," Jason remarked.

"Yes, and now we no longer have the luxury of time. A little time, true: the north coast of Attica, just across the strait from Eretria, is too rugged for a landing. They have to sail back down the strait. But we can't afford to let the debate drag on any further. The Assembly has got to act now and approve Miltiades's proposal."

"What proposal is that?" asked Jason, who already knew.

"The Eretrians made a big mistake: they took shelter within their walls and let the Persians land and deploy unopposed. A lot of fools in the Assembly want us to repeat that mistake. Miltiades—and he's got Callimachus and most of the *strategoi* behind him—argues that we should march out and meet them. And," Themistocles added grimly, "it's not as though there was much question about where they're going to land."

"Where is that?"

"Marathon. After they leave the strait and turn south, it's just around the headland. It's a wide, sheltered bay with room to draw up even a fleet the size of theirs. And beyond the beach is a flat plain that's always been horse-breeding country—perfect terrain for their cavalry. And not one but two roads lead from there to Athens, one north and one south of Mount Pentelikon." Themistocles looked grim. "They'll know all this—that traitorous dotard Hippias will have told them. Oh, yes, they'll be landing there any day now."

A man passed them. Jason recalled having seen him among the *strategoi*. He was about forty, tall for this milieu—taller than Jason, in fact—and distinguished-looking, with smooth deep-brown hair and a neatly sculpted beard of the same color, with a reddish undertone. His expression was one of studied seriousness, and he moved with a kind of self-conscious dignity, as though very aware of having an image to uphold. He and Themistocles locked eyes. *If looks could kill*, Jason thought, *there'd be two corpses in the Agora*. But they exchanged a glacially polite nod, and the tall man moved on in his grave way, nose in the air.

"Aristides," Themistocles told them with a scowl. "*Strategos* of the Antiochis tribe, as I am of the Leontis. He knows as well as I do that Miltiades is right. But, knowing him, he may argue against Miltiades just because I'm for him."

"So the two of you are political opponents?" Once again, Jason knew the answer full well but hoped to draw Themistocles out. He succeeded beyond his expectations. Clearly, Aristides was a subject on which Themistocles would expound to anyone who would listen.

"That pompous hypocrite! He poses as a model of old-fashioned, countrified virtue, preening himself on never accepting bribes while implying that I do!" Jason noted that, for all his indignation, Themistocles didn't actually deny it. "Ha! He doesn't *need* bribes— he's got a large estate outside Phalerum, and a whole network of rich relatives. But that doesn't stop him from letting his sycophants go around calling him 'Aristides the Just.' In fact, he cultivates the title." Themistocles looked like he wanted to gag. "Ah, well. Here we must part. Come see me afterwards and I'll tell you what happened."

Jason would have given a lot to have heard the debate on the Pnyx—arguably one of the most crucial in history—and he knew Landry would have given even more, a thought which caused him to feel a twinge like an emotional nerve pain. But it was, of course, as impossible as ever. One of the defining features of the Athenian version of democracy was its single-minded exclusivity. Only voting citizens were allowed in the Assembly. As *metoikoi*, or resident foreigners, he and Mondrago were no more likely to be admitted than women and slaves. They said their farewells and turned away, looking around them as they went for any sign of Chantal—or of any of the Transhumanists they had seen. As usual, there was none. As they walked through the now practically deserted Agora, Jason chuckled, despite his bleak mood.

"What's so funny?" asked Mondrago.

"Aristides the Just. I was remembering a story Bryan told me." As he spoke Landry's name, Jason found himself unable for a moment to continue. He would, he knew, be a long time coming to terms with the fact that a member of an expedition he led was now dead—at least one, for God knew what had happened to Chantal. And Landry had died, not in an act of heroic self-sacrifice like Sidney Nagel's, but butchered by murderous enemies in Jason's very presence. And Jason hadn't saved him. Knowing he couldn't let himself dwell on his oppressive sense of failure, he resumed briskly.

"You see, the Athenian constitution provides for something called 'ostracism.' That doesn't mean what it will later come to mean in English. It means that they hold a kind of election where everybody can write someone's name on a potsherd, called an *ostrakon,* and if your name appears on over six thousand potsherds you're exiled for ten years."

Mondrago whistled. "Pretty harsh."

"It's not quite as bad as it sounds. The exile's property isn't confiscated. It's just a way of temporarily removing individuals who are felt to be getting too big for the britches they haven't got, for the health of the democracy. Sometimes it's the only way of breaking irreconcilable deadlocks. Anyway, at the present time, it's never been used. The first ostracism won't happen until 487 B.C. And then, in 482 B.C., Aristides will be ostracized. It will be a kind of referendum on Themistocles's naval policy, of which Aristides is a die-hard opponent. As a result, Athens will have the fleet it needs to defeat the Persians at Salamis in 480 B.C. when the *big* invasion comes. That's what I meant about breaking deadlocks."

"But what's the funny story?"

"During the election, an illiterate voter walks up to Aristides, not knowing who he is, and asks him to write the name 'Aristides' on a potsherd for him. Aristides asks him why—has Aristides ever done him any injury? Does he know of any wrongdoing Aristides has done? 'No,' the man replies, 'it's just that I'm so sick and tired of hearing him called Aristides the Just all the time!'"

Mondrago guffawed. "I'm with him!"

"It gets better. Aristides, without another word, goes ahead and complies with the man's request."

"Maybe at that point he decides there are worse things than exile from Athens and its politics."

Jason smiled wryly. "And then, in 470 B.C., Themistocles will be ostracized."

"*What?* Themistocles? After saving this city's bacon at Salamis?"

"Precisely the problem. By then the Athenians will have gotten just so sick and tired of him being so insufferably right all the time. Anyway, he'll go to Susa and end his life as a valued advisor of the Great King of Persia. Many people in our era are shocked to learn that. They find it crushingly disillusioning and disappointing—a colossal let-down."

"Not me. This self-opinionated, back-biting town doesn't deserve him." Mondrago shook his head and looked around at Athens. "I'm beginning to think I'd be willing to write my own name on one of those potsherds."

Jason said nothing, for now that he had told the story, his dreary inward refrain—*I've lost a team member*—was back in full force. The fact that they were, for the second time, unable to witness the Athenian Assembly in session made it worse, for he knew how unendurably frustrated Landry would have been.

It got even worse as they walked along, parallel to the South Stoa. It wasn't the long open-fronted building, with offices for governmental market inspectors, which would one day give its name to the Stoics, philosophers who would declaim in its colonnaded shade. That wouldn't be built until the late fifth century B.C. But Landry had been delighted to discover that an earlier version—just a long portico, really, fulfilling some of the same functions but never suspected by the archaeologists—existed in 490 B.C. He had insisted that Jason look at it and thereby record it. The recollection caused Jason another jag of emotional pain. He found himself compulsively glancing backward over his right shoulder, in the direction of the Pnyx.

I'm frustrated too, he suddenly realized. *Not as much as Bryan would be, of course. But still . . . considering the importance of what's going on there today. . . .*

Abruptly, he halted, and a sudden wild resolve drove the depression from his mind.

"Alexandre," he stated firmly, "we're going to that Assembly!"

Mondrago stared at him, goggle-eyed. "Uh . . . we haven't exactly been invited."

"Who said anything about invitations?" asked Jason with a grim smile.

"Sir, are you trying to get us in trouble—and jeopardize the mission?" Mondrago pointed back in the direction they had come, where the police had by now rounded up the last of the stragglers. "Those guys in the odd costumes don't strike me as having much of a sense of humor."

"We're not going that way, back through the Agora." Jason consulted his map-display of Athens. It confirmed his hunch. "There's a roundabout alternate route, where nobody ought to be just now. We'll work our way around to the side of the Pnyx."

"Won't somebody there notice us?"

"I have a feeling that everyone will be so focused on the debate that two extra men will be able to slip in unobserved. We'll have to keep our mouths shut, of course, and not draw attention to ourselves. And we probably won't be able to stay too long. But the outcome of this Assembly session is a matter of recorded history, so nothing we do should cause any harm."

"So you're always telling me, sir: no paradoxes. But you've also told me that there's no predicting what will happen to prevent paradoxes, and that whatever it is might be hazardous to your health." Mondrago's tone was respectful but determined, and Jason had to respect him for sticking to his guns. "If this debate is as important to observed history as you say, then reality, or fate, or . . . God, or whatever, might be even less particular about it than usual this time."

"I can't deny the hazards. And of course we won't be able to appreciate what we see and hear to anything like the extent Bryan could have. But my implant will record it all. It will be priceless data for historians, when we return. It's what Bryan would have wanted. We owe it to him." All at once, Jason could no longer meet the other's eyes. "Or rather, *I* owe it to him."

Mondrago's face wore an expression Jason had never seen, or expected to see, on it. "*You* didn't kill him, sir. Those Transhumanist vermin did. Now it's up us to get home with the information we've got on them, so that maybe they can be made to pay!"

Every word of which, Jason admitted to himself, was demonstrably true. Only. . . .

"I may not have killed him, but I didn't prevent it either—any more than I prevented Chantal's abduction. It may not make sense to feel that way, but I'm stuck with it. And I need to do this. If you don't want to come, I won't order you to. You can go back to the house and wait for me."

"Hell, somebody's got to keep you out of trouble," said Mondrago gruffly. "I've been doing it for officers for years."

"You'll pay for that," said Jason with a grin. "Let's go!"

They hurried on to the eastern end of the South Stoa. There, between the Stoa and the fountain-house, stairs ascended to a street that ran parallel to the Stoa, behind it and at a higher level. Here they turned right and followed the raised street a short distance, with the upper parts of the Stoa's rear elevation to their right. To their left were the low, white-plastered walls that enclosed the rear yards of the houses clustering on the lower slopes of the Areopagus hill. At the first break in those walls, they turned left onto an upward-sloping alley.

So far, it was the same route they would have taken to return to their quarters, now haunted by the ghost of Bryan Landry. But instead of taking the next turn, Jason led the way straight ahead, further up the slope. The houses began to thin out. As Jason had foretold, hardly anyone was about.

Beyond the houses, they worked their way to the right, scrambling around the middle Areopagus slopes toward the hill's northern side. Down to their right, they looked over the sea of tiled roofs to the southwest of the Agora. Ahead rose the Pnyx, their destination, from which a sound of distant voices could be heard.

Reaching the valley between the two hills, they came among more houses. Here, too, the steep, narrow streets were practically deserted. There was, Jason reflected, something to be said for Athenian society's domestic seclusion of women, at least from the standpoint of one trying to get around unnoticed. Starting up the Pnyx, they passed between houses cut so deeply into the hillside that their rear rooms were semi-basements. Then they were on the undeveloped slopes, and began scrambling to the left and upward. The sounds of the thousands of men gathered ahead grew louder.

CHAPTER THIRTEEN

IN THE COURSE OF THEIR ORIENTATION, Jason had learned that the *Ekklesia,* or Assembly of all Athenian citizens, had originally been held in the Agora. After the overthrow of the tyrants the new democratic regime had decided to move it to the Pnyx, and a great workforce had been employed carving a fitting meeting place out of that hill's rocky slopes, a project that had only been completed fifteen years previously.

He also knew that in 403 B.C. the Athenians would erect a truly impressive artificial platform on the Pnyx, earthen but supported by a massive stone retaining wall set against the northwestern slope, with concentric semicircles of seats sloping downward in a theater-like way to a speaker's dais backed up against the higher slope that rose on the southeast side. Jason had seen a holographic image of that platform, based on the archaeologists' deductions, and he was very glad that it still lay eighty-seven years in the future. The only way to its top would be two steep and rather narrow stairways on the northwest side, rising from the twin termini of the road leading up from the Agora, along which the citizens were driven. With such limited access, there would have been no way a pair of *metoikoi* interlopers could have gotten past the vigilance of the police. That very consideration, Jason suspected, would at least unconsciously go into the design—an architectural expression of Athenian exclusivity.

But in 490 B.C. no such platform and no such stairways existed. The meeting-place was a shallow depression sunk into the slope. Thus it was possible to approach unnoticed, climbing the slope to the rim of the "bowl." That rim was lined with the backs of standing figures, for the rough-hewn seating only accommodated five thousand and the Assembly's quorum was six thousand. But everyone's attention was riveted on the speaker's platform below. No one noticed the two figures ascending the slope from behind and insinuating their way into the overflow crowd. Jason and Mondrago worked their way forward as inconspicuously as possible and reached the rim, just above the highest seats. They looked out over the packed amphitheater-like womb of democracy.

I'm getting all this for the historians, Bryan, thought Jason, activating his implant's recorder function. He held no belief that Landry could hear him or would ever know. But he himself knew. That was enough.

He ran over in his mind what he knew of the Assembly. Each of the ten tribes presided for one-tenth of the year—the *prytany,* or "presidency." Normally, meetings were on the average every nine days, to consider legislation proposed by the *boule,* or "Council," of fifty members from each tribe, selected by lot for a one-year term. But emergency sessions, of which this was emphatically one, could be called. Any citizen—not just those of the upper classes, as had previously been the case—could speak, but in practice only trained speakers did so. Voting was by a simple show of hands.

Looking toward the speaker's platform, stage to the amphitheater, Jason saw that the elite got the best seats. There were gathered the nine *archontes,* or administrative officers, and the ten *astynomoi,* or magistrates, all chosen by lot. In the same favored area were the ten elected tribal *strategoi.* He could pick out Themistocles' jet-black head and Miltiades' graying-auburn one.

There was, Jason thought, more than a quorum here today— hardly surprising under the circumstances. And the orientation of the meeting-place was such that the participants got an unrivaled view. For Jason, on the upper rim, the panorama was especially breathtaking. To the right rose the acropolis in all its awesomeness.

Below spread the city, and beyond that the plain of Attica. In the distance Mount Pentelikon could be glimpsed, and the two roads to Marathon.

I can see why they moved the meeting-place here, Jason thought. Unlike the people of other Greek city-states, who invented fanciful foundation legends of heroic migrations and divine descent, the Athenians believed themselves to be autochthonous, sprung from the soil of the corner of Greece they inhabited, as much a part of the landscape as the vineyards and the olive trees and the very rocks. Up here, looking out over that landscape, it was hard for them to forget that.

The day's debate had begun while he and Mondrago had followed their indirect route, and was obviously well under way. And Themistocles had indicated that, after days of discussion, both sides were down to summations of their arguments. That seemed to be the case at present. A speaker was holding forth even now, untypically portly for this society, and evidently a Eupatrid, judging from his obviously imported himation, dyed Phoenician purple and lined with gold figurings. "We all know the Persians will have us hopelessly outnumbered. I have it on good authority that their army numbers *two hundred thousand men!*"

There was a collective gasp.

"I heard *six* hundred thousand!" somebody yelled from the seats. A shudder ran through the throng, accompanied by moans.

"Shit!" Mondrago muttered in Jason's ear. "How many men do these people think each of Datis's six hundred ships can carry, over and above its own crew?"

"Not to mention supplies," Jason whispered back, nodding. "What would all those men be eating? Each other?" He motioned Mondrago to silence, so as not to interfere with the audio pickup.

"And," the speaker continued, "They are bringing their cavalry!" A hush settled over the crowd. The memory of the retreat from Sardis was all too fresh among these people, many of whom had lost relatives to the arrows and javelins of the Persian horsemen. "And no Greek army has ever defeated them in open battle! We have no choice. We cannot submit and expect mercy—not after. . . ." He left the thought unspoken and glared in the direction of the *strategoi,* and specifically at Miltiades, who had advocated the trial and execution of the Persian envoys. "No. We must remain inside our walls and place our trust in the gods!"

"Like the Eretrians did?" came a coarse jeer. A commotion erupted. Jason recalled being told that the Assembly was a tough audience.

The presiding officer, chosen from the current *prytany*, called for order and sought for the next speaker to recognize. Miltiades stood up. A respectful silence gradually descended, for everyone knew his background.

"The last speaker," he began, "has addressed you with an eloquence I cannot hope to emulate, for I am only a rough, simple soldier who has spent his years fighting the Persians while *he* has perfected his oratorical skills." A titter arose from the audience, with outright laughs rising like whitecaps above it. The Eupatrid turned as purple as his himation. "Nor do I need to, for he has set forth, far more persuasively than I could have, the arguments for marching forth and confronting the Persians in the field!"

A flabbergasted hubbub arose. Miltiades raised his hands to silence it.

"Yes, the Persians are coming in overwhelming force, and are bringing their cavalry. And after the last few days' debates, we are all agreed that they will probably land at Marathon." Miltiades pointed theatrically toward the distant outline of Mount Pentelikon. "From there, two roads lead around that mountain to this city. If the Persians seize even one of those roads, their horsemen will have the freedom of the plain all the way across Attica!" He let the breathless silence last a couple of seconds. "*But,* if we can get there in time and deploy across those roadways, we can pen them up in their beach-head where the cavalry will have no room for maneuver."

Miltiades paused, and someone else got the attention of the presiding officer, clearly seeking leave to answer him. While that byplay was in progress, the Assembly seemed to lose focus as discussions began everywhere. Jason could sense a trend, which doubtless had been building up gradually over the last few days' debates, in Miltiades' favor. Nearby, among the standing-room crowd, one man's voice rose above the rest as he addressed those around him. "Miltiades is right! Let's all of us speak out in support of him when someone stands to argue with him."

"Right!" agreed someone else. "All of us. . . ." He looked around, and his eyes narrowed as they rested on Jason and Mondrago.

Uh-oh, Jason thought. *I knew this was bound to happen sooner or later. These men naturally clump together in tribal groups, and they all know each other—Aristotle considered that a basic precondition of democratic government. Any outsiders are bound to stand out. They've been fixated on the speakers so far. But now—*

"Who—?" the man began.

Time to fight fire with fire, Jason decided. "Who's that?" he shouted, pointing off to the side. Heads swiveled in that direction, and a commotion spread—a commotion that, Jason saw, was disrupting the new speaker's opening remarks. But that was all he stayed to see. He grasped Mondrago's arm, and while everyone's attention was distracted, they slipped back and scrambled back down the slope, working their way back the way they had come.

When they were back on the slopes of the Areopagus and could afford to relax their haste a little, Mondrago finally spoke. "Remember that speaker you threw off his stride, there at the end?"

"Yes."

"Well . . . what if he *hadn't* been thrown off his stride? He might have been more effective, and talked the Assembly out of approving Miltiades' strategy."

Jason gave him a sharp look. It was the sort of unexpected thing Mondrago occasionally came out with. And it was one of the questions that gave the Authority headaches.

"I suppose," he finally said, "that if what I did influenced the outcome, it *always* influenced the outcome, if you know what I mean. In other words, it was always part of history. That's just what we have to assume."

Mondrago said nothing more, and neither did Jason, because he was still brooding over their enforced early exit from the Pnyx. *God, but I wish I could have stayed to the end!* he thought in his frustration. He consoled himself with the thought that Themistocles had promised them a recap that evening.

Themistocles looked drained but triumphant. He took a swig of wine with less water in it than usual. "We won! I have to admit, that canting prig Aristides came around in the end, even though some of his usual allies advanced strong arguments that we should squat inside the walls and settle in for a siege. The same arguments we've been hearing for days. But Miltiades was brilliant. He stood the whole argument on its head and turned the fear of the Persian cavalry to his own advantage."

"And, as Miltiades has more experience fighting the Persians than anyone else, his opinion naturally commanded respect," Jason nodded.

"Naturally. But nobody ever mentioned aloud what was really at the back of everyone's mind. It was too touchy a subject to raise in the Assembly." Themistocles smiled rather grimly. "The Eretrians didn't contest the Persians' landing, but withdrew inside their walls to resist. And all it took was two traitors to open the gates from inside. And now Eretria is a smoldering heap of rubble." He took a pull on his almost-neat wine. "In this city, with all its irreconcilable factions and aristocratic family feuds brought to a boil under the pressure of a siege, what are the chances that *no one* would accept Persian gold or take revenge for some old slight or seek to curry favor with the new rulers? Ha! I doubt if we'd last the five days that Eretria did before somebody betrayed us."

"Still, Miltiades's strategy seems to carry risks of its own," Jason prompted.

"Oh, yes. That nonsense about hundreds of thousands is just old women's rubbish, of course, but the fact remains that the Persian army is going to number several times the nine or ten thousand we can put in the field." (*Thirty-five thousand or so, by modern estimates, Bryan told us,* Jason thought. *Rutherford wants us to confirm that. All at once, like so many of Rutherford's priorities, it doesn't seem quite so important any more.*) "So if we're to have any hope of victory we're going to have to commit every man we have—which means that Athens itself will be left defenseless." Themistocles tossed off the last of the wine. "Ah, well, it's irrevocable now. By solemn resolution of the Athenian people, we will march as soon as the beacon-fire atop Mount Pentelikon is seen, confirming that the Persians have landed."

"Not before that?" inquired Mondrago with a frown. "If you could get there earlier, and secure the beach—"

"No. That was something even Miltiades had to concede. We can't be *absolutely* certain the Persians will land at Marathon, even though everything points to it. No, we have to wait until it's confirmed. Then we'll march, with every available man. Speaking of which," Themistocles continued without a break, "about your own military obligation. . . ."

"Yes, *Strategos*?" Jason had been waiting for this. One of the peculiarities of the Athenian system was that *metoikoi*, while denied practically all political rights, were liable for military service. "We naturally expect to serve the city that has so generously taken us in, as *ekdromoi*." The term referred to light-armed infantry, not very numerous and with a marginal role. The hoplites who made up the phalanx were members of the three uppermost property-owning classes, who could afford a panoply of armor and weapons costing seventy-five to a hundred drachmas, which was what a skilled worker could expect to make in three months. Jason was fairly confident that his and Mondrago's broad-spectrum expertise with low-tech weapons should enable them to function as hoplites, but that wasn't what they were here for. As skirmishers, around the fringes of the battle, they should be able to observe with minimal risk. More importantly, now, they would be in a position to watch for Transhumanist intervention.

"Ordinarily, that would be true," Themistocles nodded. "And in fact it *is* true in your case, Alexander. Coming from Macedon, you ought to be familiar with *that* kind of fighting." The remark held a note of unconscious condescension. The Thracians whom "Alexander" would naturally have fought were noted for hit-and-run skirmishing by light infantry called *peltastes*. It was looked down on by the southern Greeks, for whom *real* warfare meant the head-on clash of phalanxes composed of the Right Kind of People—which, Landry had speculated, was why the role of light troops at Marathon had always been ignored by historians. "But you, Jason, as a Macedonian nobleman . . . well, it would hardly be fitting for you not to take your place in the phalanx."

Jason groaned inwardly. He hadn't thought of this. He should have, for it went to the heart of the paradox of Classical Athens. Politically, it had the most radically democratic constitution in human history, a record it continued to hold in the twenty-fourth century. Socially, it was class-conscious to a degree that might have seemed just a bit much in Victorian England.

"Ah . . . *Strategos*, I have no armor, and no weapons other than my sword, and am in no position to supply myself with them." There was, Jason knew, no such thing as "government issue."

"Don't worry about a thing," Themistocles said expansively. "Remember, over the last twenty years, we Athenians have captured a lot of equipment in our victories over the Thebans and Chalcians. Most of it has been put on the market—a good thing, as it's reduced the prices and enabled more of our men to afford it. But there's a reserve of equipment, to be supplied at public expense to the sons of men who've met an honorable death in battle." Jason knew of the custom. He had wondered how the distribution was organized. Themistocles proceeded to enlighten him. "As *strategos* of the Leontis tribe, I have control of a portion of that reserve, for our people." He winked broadly. "I've always felt I have a certain latitude in exercising my discretion with regard to that portion."

No doubt, thought Jason drily. Aloud: "But, *Strategos*, I belong to no Athenian tribe." This, he knew, was an important point. The phalanx was organized by tribes, for the Greeks understood some-thing that had eluded various bureaucrats throughout history. Men do not face the pain, death, and simple horror of combat for nationalistic abstractions, and they assuredly do not do it because some politician has made a speech. They do it for the other men in their unit. Never—not even in a Roman legion or in a regiment of the old British army—had this been more true than in a phalanx, where every man depended on the others, for if one man's cowardice broke the shield-line, all were dead. In the Roman legion or the British regiment, such solidarity was instilled by discipline, training, and unit traditions. In a phalanx it was inherent; the men to either side of you were men of your tribe, known to you from childhood and linked to you by kinship ties. To break ranks in their sight was unthinkable.

"Don't worry, Jason," Themistocles assured him, growing serious. "You'll stand with the Leontis tribe. I know it's a little irregular." (*Not that you've ever let that stop you,* Jason thought.) "But I'll tell those men that you have reason to hate these Persians who made slaves of your people and a puppet of your king. They'll know you can be relied on."

I hope they're right, Jason thought bleakly.

CHAPTER FOURTEEN

JASON LIFTED the little white-ground ceramic vase called a *lekythos*. It held the ashes of Bryan Landry.

Themistocles had arranged the cremation—an acceptable though non-compulsory rite. They had placed the traditional coins over the eyes—a tip for Charon, the ferryman who would convey the spirit across the River Styx into Hades. Due to their ambivalent status in Athens, and the general social disruption, they had been able to short-circuit the customary preliminaries of anointing the body with oils and wrapping it in waxed cloths. Nor, for the same reasons, were they under any pressure to have the *lekythos* interred in the Ceramicus beyond the wall. Jason intended to have it with him when their TRDs activated. Naturally Landry's own TRD—indestructible by mere fire—now lay, invisibly small, in the ashes at the bottom of the cremation oven and would appear on the displacer stage.

So would Chantal Frey's TRD. Jason had left it with Themistocles for safekeeping, concealed in melted wax at the bottom of one of the small *pyxides,* or cosmetics-holding covered jars, that were among her possessions. Jason was grimly determined that it would arrive in the twenty-fourth century clutched in her living hand.

The second expedition in a row when I've gotten somebody killed, he thought, knowing how unreasonable the self-reproach was but unable to dismiss it. *It's getting to be a habit.*

It wasn't the only thing preying on Jason's mind. Whether or not any of them got back alive, the Authority *had* to be made aware that a Transhumanist underground was operating an unlawful temporal displacer. His plan had been to hire a local bronzesmith to hammer a message—unreadable by anyone of this milieu—onto a thin sheet of bronze, which he would deposit in this expedition's message drop, located on the slopes of Mount Pentelikon. But he'd had no opportunity. Besides, in Athens's current miasma of fear and paranoia, what was obviously writing in an unknown language and alphabet would surely draw suspicion onto the head of a foreigner like himself.

"It's time," he heard Mondrago say. He nodded. The great beacon-fire atop Mount Pentelikon had been sighted, confirming that the Persians were landing at Marathon.

They stepped out into the early morning coolness that unfortunately wouldn't last, and moved toward the Agora with all the other mustering men. Athens' unique economy, with over half of its wheat supplies imported and stored in granaries, had made it possible to concentrate the army at a central location rather than having to call men in from farms all over Attica. This, in turn, made the strategy of a rapid response to the Persian landing possible. Slaves carried the armor and weapons; the miserably uncomfortable fifty-to-seventy-pound hoplite panoply was intended to be donned no sooner before battle than was absolutely necessary, especially in the August heat. Of course, *ekdromoi* like Mondrago marched in their own lighter equipage of small round shields, leather shirts, slings, and two javelins, with light helmets hanging from the waist for travel.

As they descended the steps between the South Stoa and the fountain house and entered the Agora, Jason searched for the Leontis muster, hoping to spot Themistocles among the throngs. As he stood looking around, an older man approached him.

"You're Jason, the man from Macedon, aren't you? Rejoice! I'm Callicles, of the Leontis tribe. The *strategos* Themistocles—he's done a good turn or two for my family—asked me to look you up and sort of give you any help you may need, since you're new here."

Which, Jason thought, was damned nice of Themistocles. In the not-exactly-open society of the Athenian tribes, having a buddy in the ranks would help an outsider like himself to no end. He studied

Callicles with interest. He already knew that hoplites were liable for active duty up to sixty, with no concessions of any kind to their age, and Callicles was fifty if he was a day—a much riper age than it was in Jason's world. But he looked like a tough old bird.

"Thanks," Jason said. "I know I'll be grateful to have you around, not being a member of the Leontis tribe at all."

"Don't worry about it," Callicles reassured him. "Themistocles told us about you. He explained that you're a well-born soldier in your own country." *Not a tradesman like most* metoikoi *in Athens*, was left unsaid. "Some of the men's sense of humor may be a little rough around the edges, I grant you. But nobody will really give you a hard time. Come on. We're over here." As he turned and led Jason toward his fellows of the Leontis, he spoke to Mondrago over his shoulder, as an afterthought. "The *ekdromoi* are over there," he said shortly.

Jason saw Mondrago make a gesture in the direction of Callicles' back—a gesture he suspected was a very old one in Corsica.

They joined the Leontis ranks, and Callicles greeted various fellow veterans of numerous campaigns in defense of the Athenian democracy. As he did, Jason noticed a knot of older men off to the side, surrounding a much younger man wearing only a loincloth and a headband. They seemed to be giving him last-minute instructions. A gooseflesh-raising thought occurred to Jason: *Could that possibly be . . . ?* Moved by a sudden impulse, he turned to Callicles. "Who is that young man over there?"

"Pheidippides. You wouldn't know about him, not being from Athens. He's the best runner we've got. We're sending him to Sparta to ask for their help." Callicles spat expressively and rubbed his grizzled beard. "Small chance, if you ask me. But even the Spartans ought to be smart enough to see that they're next, after throwing those Persian emissaries down a well."

Jason stared, and brought up information from his implant. Pheidippides was in his late teens or early twenties, tall and long-legged, with barely an ounce of body fat overlaying muscles that were long and flowing rather than massive and knotted. He looked like what he was: one of the greatest long-distance runners the human species would ever produce. For he would run the one hundred and forty miles of rough, winding, hilly roads to Sparta in two days—something a few athletes would duplicate starting in the late twentieth century, wearing high-tech running shoes and served by numerous watering stations. Then he would turn around and return to Athens in the same incredible time. And then he would fight in the Battle of Marathon. And then—if legend was to be believed—he would carry the news of victory the twenty-six miles to Athens in full armor, with an urgency that caused him to fall dead after gasping, "Rejoice! We conquer!" The last part had given rise to the Marathon race of the modern Olympic games (whose runners were not required to wear armor), but modern historians had been inclined to pooh-pooh it, asserting that Pheidippides's run to Sparta had become confused in popular imagination with the Athenian hoplites' rapid march back to Athens from Marathon after the battle. Rutherford wanted them to settle the question.

But there was another story that was somewhat more relevant to their present situation. On his return run from Sparta to Athens, on the heights just this side of Tegea, Pheidippides would afterwards swear that the god Pan had appeared, greeted him by name, and asked why the Athenians did not worship him, promising to aid them in the coming battle if they would do so henceforth. Historians had naturally written this off as an exhaustion-induced hallucination. It was, Jason reflected, an assumption they might just have to rethink.

He was, however, puzzled about one thing: how was Franco going to get his pet "god" to the Tegea heights, roughly two thirds of the way to Sparta, for the occasion? Even assuming that they had already departed, travel by daylight would be out of the question, as Pan was not exactly inconspicuous.

But then there was no time to dwell on the matter further, for Themistocles was bawling orders and the roughly nine hundred strong muster of the Leontis tribe was shaking itself into marching order. Jason consulted his implant's calendar function. It was August 5.

The optic display read August 7 as Jason leaned on the camp's earthen defensive barrier, still drenched with sweat under the early afternoon August sun even though he was now out of his armor, and gazed out over the plain of Marathon.

He had always regarded himself—accurately—as being in excellent physical condition. It had been fortunate that he was, for the hoplites had marched from Athens to Marathon at a pace he was surprised that Callicles and the rest of the older men could sustain. Hoplites, he was learning, were very, very tough—especially the hoplites of Athens, who had been at war more or less continuously in defense of their fledgling democracy for almost twenty years. These men might not be professional soldiers—unlike the Spartans, they had day jobs, normally in agriculture, the only really respectable occupation for men of their class—but all of them except the very youngest were seasoned veterans.

They had arrived in time, while the Persians were still organizing themselves on their beachhead, amid the inevitable chaos of all amphibious landings. They had deployed across the two roads to Athens in a strong defensive position, facing northeast from rising ground with the higher wooded slopes of Mount Agriliki behind them and a temple of Heracles with its sacred grove shielding their right flank. Callimachus and Miltiades—who seemed to function as unofficial chief of staff *cum* operations officer, not that either term existed in this era—had set them to work establishing a fortified camp. From there they could look out across a scene that Jason was sure caused these men, brought up on Homer, to imagine what the defenders of Troy must have witnessed.

The beach curved away to the northeast, where the bay was sheltered by a rocky promontory called the "Dog's Tail." For miles, that beach was black with six hundred ships hauled up on the sand. About half of these were triremes—fighting galleys that could have overwhelmed Athens's seventy-trireme fleet had the Athenians been suicidal enough to commit it. The rest were transports of various kinds, including fifty specialized ones that carried twenty horses each. The almost fifty thousand rowers and other sailors stayed on or near the ships. Just inland from the base of the promontory was a marsh. Between it and the Athenian position stretched a flat, barren plain, hemmed in by hills and divided into northern and southern halves by the Chardra, a stream mislabeled a river. To the southwest of the marsh, just inland from the narrow sandy beach, was the vast Persian camp, three miles from where Jason stood, pullulating with thousands and thousands of outlandishly clad invaders. Jason's practiced eye confirmed the modern estimate of their numbers, which meant the Athenians were outnumbered about three to one, even counting their light troops (which almost nobody ever did) and the addition of almost a thousand hoplites who had arrived, to vociferous cheers, from the small city-state of Plataea—its entire levy. It wasn't a large reinforcement, but it was the only help the Athenians were to get, and Landry had mentioned that Athenian gratitude to the Plataeans would endure for generations.

Then a stalemate had commenced. Something like a ritual had been established. The Greeks would form up their line in the morning, with light troops like Mondrago carrying forward *abittis* cut from the trees on the slopes to shield the phalanx's flanks. The Persians would also form up, and their dread cavalry would ride forth in their colorful trousered costumes, perform show-off caracoles, and shout taunts—the language was incomprehensible, but the tone was unmistakable—at the Greeks, who had no archers to respond. It was, of course, intended to draw the Greeks out, off the high ground and onto the plain. The Greeks would not rise to the bait; and the Persians, armed for raiding and not for shock tactics, would not venture to charge uphill against the shield line. And thus another day's morning ceremonies would conclude.

Jason became aware of Mondrago at his side. The Corsican was bathed in sweat even though he hadn't been encased in hoplite armor. "This is ox shit," he said with feeling.

"You look tired," said Jason solicitously.

"Tired? You'd be tired too. All you hoplites have to do is go through this morning charade, then sit on your asses the rest of the day while we *ekdromoi* go out on patrol!"

My God! thought Jason. *Is Athenian class consciousness getting to him?*

"But," Mondrago continued, calming down a little, "I'm sure Callimachus and Miltiades are happy as clams at high tide."

"How so?" asked Jason, who thought precisely the same thing but was curious to see if Mondrago had come to the same conclusion by the same path.

Mondrago waved an arm in the direction of the Persians. "They can't sit here forever. The food supplies for that horde must be getting used up fast, and they've been trying to gather some locally.

Remember what I said about going out on patrol? At least I've been getting some practice with my sling. We've been going out into the hills to keep them from foraging—us and the horsemen."

"Horsemen?"

"Yes. Athens does have a tiny cavalry force, you know. It's largely ceremonial. Nobody around here even claims it would be close to being a match for the Persian cavalry even if the numbers were equal."

"I know." Jason recalled the Panathenaic frieze, and the flowing artistry of its procession of splendidly mounted young men—magnificent, but somehow not seeming very combat-ready. And that frieze had been from the Parthenon, as completed in 437 B.C. He somehow suspected that the current generation of Athenian cavalry, more than half a century earlier, would be even less impressive in battle.

"Still," Mondrago grudgingly admitted, "they've got heart. And they're good enough to help us cut up forging parties. I can guarantee you the Persians are still consuming the supplies they brought with them."

"Logistics," Jason nodded. "It's the most important part of war, and the part that historians and novelists are most likely to forget."

"Something they're even more likely to forget about than food is what comes out the other end," said Mondrago with a nasty grin. "Can you imagine what that camp must be like, with that many men crammed into it? Ours is bad enough!"

Jason gave a grimace of agreement. With the exception of the as-yet-unborn Roman legions, camp sanitation had not been the strong suit of ancient armies. He, with his experience of past eras, and Mondrago with his military background, could endure it—barely.

"Right," Jason said. "No large army in this era can sit encamped in one place for long. It's only a matter of time—and not much of it—before disease, the real killer in ancient warfare, is going to hit, starting with intestinal ailments."

"And then they'll have tens of thousands of men with diarrhea packed in there." Even Mondrago, hardly the most fastidious of men, shuddered at the thought. "No doubt about it: time is on our side. Hence this miserable standoff we're in. Why should Callimachus seek battle when he can just watch the Persian army rot?"

"Besides," Jason reminded him, "Callimachus expects the Spartans to come. Why rush things when you're waiting to be reinforced by an army of full-time professional killers?" He was about to say something else, when, at the outermost left-hand corner of his field of vision, a tiny blue light began blinking for attention.

At first it didn't even register on Jason. His implant had a number of standard features which had often come in handy in the Hesperian Colonial Rangers but which were irrelevant in past eras of history. He therefore never used them on extratemporal expeditions, and it was easy to forget they were there. So it took him a heartbeat or two to remember this one, from his time with the Hesperian Colonial Rangers, when it had been useful to have a sensor that detected the space-distorting effects of grav-repulsion technology. In retrospect, he could have used it in the Bronze Age; but, as he recalled, the Teloi "chariots" had always been upon him before such use had occurred to him.

Now, however, that blinking light told him that an aircar or some such vehicle was being used in the near vicinity.

Mondrago seemed to notice his distracted look. "What—?"

"Quiet!" Jason concentrated furiously, attaining the mental focus necessary for direct neural activation of the sensor's directional feature. He had barely done so before the blue light winked out.

"Something to do with your implant, right?" said Mondrago after a moment of silence.

Jason took a deep breath. "Yes. Somebody around here is operating a grav vehicle."

This got Mondrago's undivided attention. "The Teloi?"

"Presumably. But whoever it is, they just switched it off—" he turned to the left and pointed to the hill to the northwest "—up there, on Mount Kotroni."

Mondrago's gaze followed his pointing finger. It wasn't really a mountain, at seven hundred and eighty feet. Like the rest of the hills defining the plain of Marathon, it was forested in this era. "We've got to check this out."

"No, *I've* got to check it out. My implant will enable me to zero in on it if it's reactivated. I'm going up there." He instinctively reached for his waist and confirmed that he still had his leaf-shaped sword.

Mondrago looked around. "I have a feeling these guys don't exactly approve of people going AWOL. Least of all now."

"So you have to stay here and cover for me. If anybody wonders where I am, make up some excuse."

"Like what?"

Jason started to try to think of one . . . and then came to the realization that he trusted Mondrago fully to handle it on his own. And, in fact, the further realization that he was glad to have the Corsican at his back in general.

"You'll think of something." Without waiting for a reply to this gem of brilliance, Jason turned away and headed for the camp's eastern perimeter. At least everyone seemed too relieved to be out of armor to notice him.

CHAPTER FIFTEEN

IN THE EARLY AFTERNOON AUGUST HEAT, Jason was grateful for the shade of the foliage as he scrambled up the slopes of Mount Kotroni.

As he neared the crest, a level clearing opened out before him. At that moment, the tiny blue light began flashing again.

He looked around and saw nothing where the sensor assured him he should. But experience-honed instinct caused him to take cover behind a boulder and take a fighting grip on his short sword. No sooner had he done so when he heard a faint, whining hum. And he saw dust swirling upward from the clearing, as though from the ground-pressure effect of grav repulsion.

Above the ground, now that he knew what to look for, he recognized the shimmering effect of a refraction field, which achieved invisibility by disrupting the frequencies of light and causing them to "bend" or "slip" around the field and whatever was within it. It was cutting-edge technology in Jason's world.

And I never saw the Teloi using it, he thought, puzzled.

Then the dust settled, and the field evidently was switched off, for an aircar appeared out of nowhere, settling to the ground—and Jason's puzzlement turned to shock.

It was a small model, little more than a flying platform with a transparent bubble and two seats, for the pilot and one passenger.

This one held only the pilot—a human, who proceeded to raise the canopy and emerge. And it was not one of the overdecorated, somehow Art Deco-reminiscent Teloi designs Jason remembered. He recognized it as a Roszmenko-Krishnamurti model, a few years old as his own consciousness measured time.

Until this instant, he had been able to tell himself that Franco's claims of radically superior time-travel technology were mere braggadocio, or perhaps an attempt at disinformation. Now he knew he could no longer take shelter in that comfortable assumption. The Transhumanists had temporally displaced this aircar—along with all their personnel and God knew what else—almost twenty-nine centuries. The Authority couldn't have done that without an appropriation request that would have precipitated an all-out political crisis. The Transhumanists had done it using a displacer so compact, and drawing so little power, that it could be concealed somewhere on Earth's surface.

Rutherford has *to be told about this!* He cursed himself for not having somehow managed to leave word at the message-drop on Mount Pentelikon.

The pilot stepped to the ground and, with his back to Jason, fumbled for a hand communicator. Jason suddenly realized that, after the man reported in, his own window of opportunity to take any action would vanish. Without pausing for further thought, he bunched his legs and launched himself over the boulder.

It was fairly artless. Jason hit the totally surprised Transhumanist from behind, smashed him over prone. His sword-holding right arm went around the man's neck, while his left hand grasped his left wrist and pulled that arm up behind his back.

But this Transhumanist was one of the genetic upgrades designed for, among other things, strength. His free right arm went up behind Jason's neck while his legs sent both of them surging upwards until he had Jason practically piggy-back. Then, with a further surge, he threw Jason over his right shoulder.

Jason's trained reflexes took over for him. He kept his grip on his sword, and hit the ground in a roll which brought him back up to his feet even as he whirled to face his enemy. The Transhumanist was already rushing him, hands outstretched in what Jason recognized as one of the positions of combat karate.

Jason's options suddenly became very simple. He had hoped to take the man alive, but he had no desire to have blade-stiffened hands smash through his rib cage and pull out his lungs. With a twisting motion, he evaded those hands while driving his sword into the Transhumanist's midriff. Then he dropped to his knees, wrenched the sword point-upward inside the guts in which it was lodged, and rammed it straight up. Blood gushed from the Transhumanist's mouth as he fell to his knees and toppled forward, pulling the sword out of Jason's hand by his sheer weight.

Jason retrieved his sword, wiped off the blade, and used the pommel to smash the communicator the Transhumanist had never had a chance to use. Then he examined the aircar. It was, as he had thought, a standard model aside from the decidedly non-standard invisibility field. He activated its nav computer and brought up its last departure point on the tiny map display.

It was a point in the heights just east of Tegea, just over ninety miles to the southeast as the crow or the aircar flies.

Just about where Pheidippides swore that Pan appeared to him, came the thought, bringing with it a flash of understanding.

Jason summoned up his implant's clock display. He really needed to be getting back to camp. But at the aircar's best speed he could cover the distance in less than half an hour. And this had to be looked into.

He had neither time nor tools to bury the Transhumanist's body, but he didn't want to leave it to be found. With difficulty, he hauled it into the passenger seat and tied a heavy stone to it. Then he set the computer to retrace its last course, lowered the canopy, activated the invisibility field, and took to the air.

Jason's route took him over Mount Pentelikon and just north of Athens, but he was in no mood to appreciate the view, and at any rate the outside world appeared in blurry shades of gray when viewed from inside the field. He flew on into the dim-appearing afternoon sun. Soon he was over the island of Salamis, and the waters where ten years from now the navy that was now only a gleam in Themistocles' eye would scatter the fleets of Xerxes. Then the waters of the Saronic Gulf were beneath him. He stopped, hovered only twenty feet above the waves, and made certain there were no boats nearby whose crews might have noticed a body appear out of nowhere in midair and fall into the sea. He raised the canopy and pushed his deceased passenger out.

Resuming his flight, Jason went feet-dry over the Argolid. He did not permit himself to glance to the right, toward Mycenae and the bones that lay buried there. Instead, he spent the few remaining minutes of flight wondering just what the aircar had been doing landing on Mount Kotroni. No answer came to him, and none would now be forthcoming from the former pilot.

Approaching the end of the route, Jason resumed manual control of the aircar. Zooming the map display to its largest scale, he narrowed the landing site down to a flat area on a ridge overlooking the road from Sparta. He set the aircar down as gently as possible, to minimize the telltale dust-swirl. After satisfying himself that there was no one about, he deactivated the invisibility field and stepped out and walked to the edge of the ridge.

Looking cautiously down, he could see the winding road. On a lower level of the ridge, two humans were observing the road from concealment. Above them, but slightly lower than Jason, Pan crouched behind a boulder.

To Jason's right was a smooth, gentle slope which allowed easy access to Pan's position. He slipped very quietly down the slope, taking advantage of the fact that he was facing the sun and therefore casting his shadow behind him. He worked his way close behind the obviously preoccupied Pan and, with an adder-sudden movement, his left arm went around the being's neck, forcing the chin up. With his right arm, he pressed the edge of his sword against the exposed throat. It wasn't much of an edge—these swords were primarily for thrusting—but it would do.

"Quiet!" he hissed. The two Transhumanists below, their attention riveted on the road, hadn't noticed. "Don't make a sound."

Pan remained rigid but did not struggle. "What are you going to do with me?" he whispered.

Which, Jason realized, was a very good question. He hadn't formulated a plan, and when he thought about it he wondered why he hadn't simply killed Pan outright. Arguably, it would be the rational course—at least Mondrago would have so argued.

"What are you here for?" he whispered back, temporizing.

"I'm waiting for the Athenian runner who is returning from Sparta. He should be passing here soon. I am to accost him and ask him why the Athenians fail to honor me, and promise to aid them nevertheless in the coming battle by causing the Persians to flee in terror. And at the height of the battle, I am to appear to the Athenians, so they will believe they owe me their victory."

"And are you going to do it."

"I must!" The whisper held a quavering squeak. "I have been ordered to."

"Do you always follow orders?"

"I have no choice!" For an instant Pan's voice rose almost to a full squeak. Jason pressed his sword-edge harder against the hairy throat, and Pan subsided into a dull whisper. "You don't know what it's like!"

"You mean they torture you?"

"They don't need to. My entire existence is torture! Only they have the power to deaden it."

"I don't understand."

"How could you? Franco and his people came to this country fifteen years ago and persuaded the Teloi to help them create me, knowing this was the year they would need me to be available. They used . . . medicines to make me mature faster," Pan explained, coming as close as fifth-century B.C. Greek could to the concept of artificial growth accelerants. "They needed the help of the Teloi to do all this."

Jason nodded unconsciously. Of all the perversities forbidden by the Human Integrity Act, species modification—genetic tinkering which introduced genes not native to the original human genome— was the ultimate obscenity. The Transhumanists, of course, had had no compunctions about it. But even they had never developed it to the level that must have been required to create a thing like Pan. Evidently, though, they and the Teloi together had been equal to the task.

"But," Pan continued, still struggling with the limits of the language, "the parts of me that are not human could not be made to really *fit*. And my forced growth made it worse. Almost everything I do, especially walking, is unendurable . . . or would be without the medicines they constantly give me."

Again, Jason understood. It was one of the reasons species

modification was regarded as such a unique abomination. The human organism was a totality. It was not designed to support, say, a digitigrade walking posture. Pan was a living mass of incompatibilities—a biological *wrongness*. And applying growth accelerants to such a ramshackle skeleton must have made it even worse, especially considering that the Transhumans and their Teloi allies probably hadn't bothered with any of the usual precautions.

Yes, Pan would never be free of pain, or at least discomfort, for a second of his waking life—and how would he ever sleep?—without chemical analgesia. He surely would have long since escaped into madness had it not been for the drugs that only his creators could supply . . . or withhold.

Now Jason understood how they controlled him. And from what he had heard in Pan's whisper, he dimly sensed how much the twisted being must hate them.

Killing Pan now would be the merciful thing to do as well as the expedient one.

Only, thought Jason as his grip tightened on the sword-hilt, *he might be a valuable source of information on the Transhumanists.*

"Listen," he said, improvising, "you can get away from them. You can get help from the Temporal Regulatory Authority." Of necessity, he said the last three words in English.

"How?" whispered Pan in a tone of dull scorn.

"Well. . . ." This was no time for a lecture on the physics of time travel, even had it been possible in the language. "After I return to my own time, I'll come back to this time with soldiers to kill those two men down there—it can be a few minutes after this point in time, in fact—and I'll bring with me the medicines you need." Once Rutherford knew what was at stake, Jason was sure he could get an appropriation for such an expedition, and a waiver of the rules to allow him to bring back a substantial supply of advanced medications.

"Can you take me to your time?"

"No." Jason found he could not lie. "You are of this era. There can be no travel forward in time."

"But *you* travel forward in time!"

"No." How to explain temporal energy potential? "I only return to the time from which I came, and where I belong. You belong here, and must remain here. But we can free you from your dependence on Franco and the Teloi."

Afterwards, Jason was always certain that Pan wavered for a heartbeat before stiffening convulsively. "No! I can't trust you! They created the agony that is my life, and only they can grant surcease from it. I must do as I am told."

At that moment, before Jason could reply, one of the Transhumanists below—from whom Jason had never entirely taken his eyes—rose to his feet and gestured at the road from Sparta. In the distance was a tiny, running figure.

The sight of that figure—Pheidippides, returning with the news that the Spartans would be delayed—distracted Jason for a fraction of a second, causing him to lower his sword. That was enough. With the strength of desperation, Pan broke free of him and scrambled recklessly downhill despite Jason's efforts to catch him by his caprine legs. Jason could only watch, cursing under his breath, as he joined the Transhumanists.

He really ought, Jason knew, to return to his aircar while the Transhumanists' attention was riveted on the road and get back to Marathon. But curiosity held him. He compromised with caution by ducking behind the boulder and watching as Pheidippides reached a point almost directly below. He saw one of the Transhumanists manipulate a remote control unit. A concealed device by the side of the road erupted into a flash of light and a thunderclap of sound. With a cry, the runner staggered and fell to his knees. While his eyes were still dazzled, one of the Transhumanists shoved Pan forward and up into plain sight. When Pheidippides could see again, the "god" stood on the ridge looking down at him.

"Pheidippides of Athens," said Pan in more-in-sorrow-than-in-anger tones, "why have the Athenians failed to worship me?"

Pheidippides groveled in the dust of the road. "We do, Great God, we do," he stammered frantically.

"No. My sacred grotto on the slope of the Acropolis is neglected, save by a few. The smoke of sacrifice does not rise from my altar there."

"We will neglect you no longer, Great God. I swear it! After I tell what I have seen, we will make amends. We will offer sacrifice."

"It is well. Continue on your journey, and assure the Athenians of my affection for their city. Tell them also that I know the peril in which Athens now stands, and that I mean to come to its aid very soon, because I trust that your promise to me will be kept."

Pheidippides looked timidly up. "Aid us how, Great God?" he dared ask.

"You know, Pheidippides, the power I possess to arouse unreasoning fear in men," Pan replied obliquely. "Now go, and complete your errand, and bear my words to the Athenians!"

The hidden Transhumanist touched his remote again, and the bogus thunder and lightning sent Pheidippides flat on his face with a wail. Pan scurried back to join his two handlers. After a few moments, Pheidippides cautiously looked up and rose to his feet. Still blinking, he cast nervous glances all around. Then a slow smile awoke on the young face—a smile of serenely confident hope, the kind of smile rarely seen among Athenians these days. The smile broadened into a grin as he resumed his run.

The Transhumanists crouched, preparing to leave as soon as the runner was out of sight, and Jason dared delay no longer. He retraced his steps, flung himself into the aircar, reactivated the invisibility field, and set his course back to the clearing on Mount Kotroni, over-looking the Greek camp on the plain of Marathon.

Once in the air, he had leisure to reflect wryly. *Of course I didn't kill Pan. History says Pheidippides claimed to have met him on the road.*

Only . . . if I had killed him, then maybe Pheidippides would have hallucinated him anyway, as historians think he did.

He shook his head and flew on, with the westering sun behind him.

CHAPTER SIXTEEN

MOUNT AGRILIKI ROSE two thousand feet to the southwest of the plain of Marathon, with the Athenian camp backed up against its lower slopes. Jason found a clear ledge about halfway to the summit and shielded from the view of those below. He doubted if the Transhumanists had a means of locating it when it was powered down. Of course they might have installed some kind of beacon that had enabled them to track its flight, but concealing the aircar was worth a try. He might well want to use it again, and what Rutherford didn't know wouldn't cause him to have a stroke.

He scrambled down the forested slope in the late-afternoon shadows. He slipped into the camp without difficulty, as nobody was being particularly careful about guarding its mountain-protected rear when the Persians were bottled up on the plain.

Mondrago, who had not been required to account for Jason's absence, greeted him with relief. They found a relatively private spot toward the rear of the camp and Jason recounted his story.

"It would be nice to think you stranded them there on that ridge in the Peloponnese," Mondrago remarked when Jason was finished. "I can't believe the Transhumanists could have displaced more than one aircar almost twenty-nine hundred years into the past."

Jason shook his head dourly. "They must be able to call in Teloi aircars, even if those are restricted to flying at night because they lack invisibility fields. In fact, they must be using them already. The aircar I took can only carry two, and I saw four: the pilot I killed, two more on the Tegea heights, and Pan."

"And that nauseating little mutant is still alive!" said Mondrago venomously. The look he gave Jason was accusing.

"I'm still hoping to turn him. I've told you how much he resents his own existence."

"He should. And I'll bet it's not just the things you told me about." Mondrago grinned nastily. "That gigantic dong of his must have been designed for nothing but show. It probably hurts him to piss."

"I hadn't thought of that," Jason admitted with a grimace.

"So what's the plan?"

"I'm just going to have to improvise. Remember, they'll be bringing him here before the battle—come to think of it, that must have been what their aircar was doing on Mount Kotroni, scouting out a suitable landing spot. Maybe that will be my chance."

"You say they're going to have him appear here so he can take credit for spreading panic among the Persians. That sounds like they're planning to create the panic themselves. I can think of ways that might be possible."

"So can I," nodded Jason. Such effects could be achieved in ways involving focused ultrasonic waves affecting the human nervous system, sent along a laser guide-beam. And the Teloi might have other techniques.

"Well, then, sir," Mondrago continued, his tone changing to one of formal seriousness, "has it occurred to you that maybe this is why the Greeks end up winning the battle?"

"You mean, that the Transhumanist intervention has *always* been part of history? That *it's* the reason Western civilization survives?" Jason knew his voice probably reflected his unwillingness to believe it.

"Can you rule out the possibility? And if it's true, and if our theories about time travel are correct, you won't be able to undo it. Something will prevent you—maybe something lethal. And if those theories *aren't* correct. . . ." Mondrago left the thought dangling.

Jason drew a deep breath. "Remember when we were at the

Athenian Assembly? This is sort of the opposite side of the coin from that. Once again, I don't deny that there are risks involved. But if the opportunity presents itself, I plan to try again to offer Pan our help in exchange for his cooperation."

Mondrago looked disgusted.

Pheidippedes half-ran and half-staggered into the camp the following night. He had paused only briefly at Athens to impart the news he now brought to the army. In the immemorial way of armies everywhere, Rumor Central promptly conveyed that news to everyone.

"Carneia!" old Callicles snorted, with his patented eloquent spit. "The Spartans are celebrating Carneia, their holy festival—quite a big festival, I've heard—and they can't march until the moon is full!"

Mondrago shared his feelings. "Greatest warriors in history!" he muttered to Jason in an English aside. "More like the greatest party animals!"

"Mark my words," Callicles continued, "if that bastard Cleomenes was still running things in Sparta, he wouldn't let any stupid 'period of peace' stop him. But now he's dead, and the Spartans are shitting in their chitons with fear that they may have offended the gods by throwing those Persian emissaries down that well, not to mention burning that sacred grove at Argos. So they're being very careful to observe their religious holidays—and never mind that we Athenians get butt-fucked by the Persians while they're doing it!"

A pair of men passed within earshot, heading toward the tents of the Aiantis tribe. One of them paused. In the light of the campfires, Jason saw he appeared to be in his mid-thirties, beginning to go prematurely bald. "But," he called out to Callicles, "if they set out at the full moon and march as fast as Pheippides says they promise to, shouldn't they be here in a week? Surely we can hold the Persians at bay that long."

Jason expected a scornful reply accompanied by another expressive spit. But Callicles's "Maybe you're right" was no worse than grudging. He sounded as though he knew the man, at least by reputation.

"Come on!" the man's companion called. "We're already late."

"Coming, Cynegeirus." The man waved to them and hurried on.

"Who was that?" asked Jason.

"Fellow named Aeschylus, from Eleusis," said Callicles. "Writes plays."

Jason stared at the retreating back of the man who was to become Greece's greatest dramatist—but whose epitaph would say nothing about that, only that he had fought at Marathon. And the familiar tingle took him.

"You've heard of this guy?" Mondrago asked him.

Jason nodded. "In our era he's going to be known as the Father of Tragedy."

"He seemed pretty cheerful to me."

"He may not be quite as much so after what is going to happen to the man with him—his brother Cynegeirus." Jason shook himself, recalling what Landry had told him. In the final phase of the battle, on the beach, Aeschylus would watch as Cynegeirus had a hand chopped off as he tried to grab the stem of an escaping Persian ship, a wound from which he would subsequently die. "I've got to go. The generals must be meeting now to decide where we go from here, and I want to get that meeting on my recorder—there have always been a lot of unanswered questions about it."

"They're going to just let anybody listen in?" Mondrago sounded scandalized by such sloppy security.

"Maybe not. But I'll never know if I don't try." And Jason slipped away through the camp.

Security almost lived down to Mondrago's expectations—indeed, it was a barely understood concept in this place and time. In the heat of the August night, Callimachus and the ten *strategoi* were meeting under an open tent. Herodotus had claimed that command of the army had been rotated among those ten tribal generals, one on each day, and that as the day of battle had approached the others had handed command over to Miltiades on their allotted days. Mondrago had scoffed at that, declaring roundly that no army could or would have tried to function under such a nonsensical system. He had turned out to be right. Their initial impression—that Callimachus the war archon was in actual as well as honorary command, assisted by Miltiades as *primus inter pares* among the *strategoi*—had proven to be correct. Mondrago, whose sole intellectual interest was military history, had mentioned the names "Hindenburg" and "Ludendorff."

Jason had a great deal of experience at making himself inconspicuous. He now brought all the subtle techniques he had learned to bear as he moved among the campfires and approached the open tent. He saw Pheidippides walking groggily away from that tent, where he must have finished rendering his formal report and would now doubtless collapse into a very long sleep that no one would begrudge him. Jason continued on in his unobtrusive way toward that tent and its murmur of voices, working his way inward until he could see the figures within, illuminated by flickering torchlight, and his implant's recorder function could pick up the voices.

"You heard Pheidippides," said someone Jason didn't recognize. "All we have to do is hold out until the Spartans arrive: seven days if they keep their promise, and he's convinced they will."

"And there's no reason why we can't keep this stalemate going that long," said someone else. "All we have to do is stay here, in this fortified camp on ground of our choosing."

A murmur of agreement arose from what seemed to be a clear majority of the generals. The murmur rose to a pious pitch when one voice added, "And remember, according to Pheidippides we have Pan's promise of assistance!"

Miltiades rose to his feet, the torchlight glinting from the remnants of red in his beard. The self-convincing murmur gradually subsided. All the *strategoi* were veterans of wars against the enemies of Athenian democracy—*Greek* enemies. But Miltiades knew the Persian way of war from inside and outside, and they all appreciated that fact.

"We can't just sit here behind our earthworks and wait for the Spartans," he said as soon as he had absolute silence. "The Persians have spies and well-paid traitors everywhere. Anything we know, we must assume *they* know. So don't you suppose they're taking account of Spartan schedules themselves?"

The silence took on an inaudible but perceptible quality of uneasiness. "Military intelligence" was still a barely understood concept among the Greeks, and there was something sinister, almost uncanny about it. But the Persians were the first people in history to recognize that information was the key to control. And Miltiades knew the Persians.

"Furthermore," Miltiades continued, "Datis is running out of time. Even on half rations, his food stores can't last more than a few days. I know we've seen some coming and going of ships, bringing in supplies from islands under Persian control. But with harvest season coming on, even those supplies must be running low. Before the Spartans arrive, and before his army starves, Datis is going to have to try a new strategy."

"What strategy?" someone demanded. "What can he do? He can't attack us here in this position."

"What he can do," explained Miltiades patiently, "is embark his army and sail around Cape Sunium and land at Phalerum, with nothing between them and Athens, leaving us still sitting here, looking stupid."

A shocked silence fell. None of these men, Jason was certain, were under any illusions as to the likelihood that the undefended city wouldn't contain a single fifth columnist to open the gates as the gates of Eretria had been opened.

"When they begin to embark," Miltiades resumed into the silence, "We will have no choice. We will have to advance onto the plain and attack."

If possible, the silence deepened into still profounder levels of shock as the *strategoi* contemplated the prospect of doing exactly what Datis had been hoping they would do.

"But," said Miltiades before anyone could protest, "that will be our opportunity. Think how difficult an operation that embarkation will be for them—especially because they'll want to break camp at night, to conceal it from us. And the hardest part will be getting the cavalry aboard. Whenever they've loaded horses aboard ships before, they were able to use the docks in Ionia and at Eretria; they didn't have to get them up gangplanks on a beach in shallow water. They'll have to do that first, before daybreak. If we can strike them at exactly the right time, they'll be without their cavalry, and off balance. We've never had such a chance! And we'll never have it again!"

"But," protested Thrasylaos, *strategos* of the Aiantis tribe to which Callimachus himself belonged, "we'll need to know in advance when they're preparing to depart."

Even at a distance, Jason could see Miltiades' teeth flash in a grin. "The Persians aren't the only ones with spies. They have a lot of Ionian conscripts over there, and among them are some old associates of mine from the rebellion. I still have contacts among them. They and I have arrangements for meeting and exchanging information, over there in the Grove of Heracles." Miltiades raised a hand to hush the hubbub. "That's all you need to know at present."

"But," Thrasylaos persisted, although his voice was that of a man who was wavering, "if we advance out onto the plain, they'll be able to outflank us, with their superior numbers." An uneasy murmur of agreement arose, for a phalanx was always terrifyingly vulnerable to flank attacks. "And they'll have their archers," he added, in a tone that held a mixture of conventional disdain—the Greeks had always looked on archery as the unmanly expedient of such dubious heroes as Prince Paris of Troy—and healthy apprehension.

Callimachus rose to his feet. His bald scalp gleamed in the torchlight, but he looked younger than he had when Jason had first seen him in the Agora, for he no longer had the stooped, careworn look. He now exuded calm confidence.

"We will prevent them from outflanking us," he explained, "by lengthening our line. To accomplish this, our center—the Leontis and Antiochis tribes—will form up four men deep." He gave Themistocles and Aristides, the generals of the two tribes in question, a meaningful look. "The right and left wings will be eight deep as usual."

Themistocles and Aristides looked at each other, their mutual detestation for once in abeyance as they considered the implications of this order.

"*Polemarch*," said Themistocles respectfully, "we have observed over the past several days that the Persian center is always the strongest part of their formation." There was no fear in his voice. He was merely inviting his commander's attention to certain facts, with scrupulous correctness.

Aristides amazed everyone present by nodding in agreement. "It's where the Medes and the Persians themselves are concentrated, and the Saka from the east—the best troops they've got."

Miltiades answered him. "Yes. That's the standard Persian formation, with their weaker troops—levies from all over the empire—on the wings. And that's precisely why we're making our wings stronger."

Callimachus quieted the hubbub that arose. "You'll all understand why soon, for I mean to explain my plan to you so you can tell your men what to expect. And as for Thrasylaos' other point, about their archers. . . ." For the first time, Jason saw Callimachus smile. "Well, we'll just have to give them the least possible time to shoot their arrows!"

Out of the corner of his eye, Jason noticed men beginning to take notice of him. Reluctantly, he moved on, carefully projecting the casual air of a man who had paused for no particular reason. Given the reputation of the Persians for espionage, he couldn't risk any suspicious behavior.

And besides, he had a very good idea what Callimachus was about to say.

CHAPTER SEVENTEEN

ANOTHER DAY OF DEADLOCK WENT BY, and then another, and another.

The ritualistic morning confrontations continued, and Jason saw what Callimachus and Miltiades meant about the Persian formation. The Medes and Persians and their eastern ethnic relatives, the Saka, were massed in the center, with archers behind the protecting lines of infantry carrying wicker shields and armed with short spears and the short swords known as *akenakes*. Here as well were the lightly clad horse archers, and cavalry armed with spears and—alone among the Persian army—wearing bronze helmets. It was a typical Persian array, except that, having had to cross the sea, it contained a lower percentage of horsemen than was normal. And, just as typically, it was flanked by polyglot masses of troops from all over the empire, visibly less smart about getting into formation each morning and staying there in the baking August sun.

"Rabble," sniffed Mondrago with reference to the latter troops, late in the afternoon.

"Don't be too sure," Jason cautioned. "Remember, this army has spent six years crushing the Ionian rebels and conquering Thrace. They're veterans, and all that experience fighting and training together has probably given them about as high a degree of operational integration as is possible for such a multiethnic force. And they have a tradition of victory—they've never been defeated." He looked around to make sure no one was observing them. "Anyway, I need to get going."

Jason inconspicuously gathered up the fruits of his surreptitious labor over the past two nights. Mondrago looked at the small satchel dubiously.

"Do you really think these things are going to last over twenty-eight hundred years?"

"Why not? Archaeologists dig them up all the time." Jason took out one of the ceramic potsherds he had been collecting and inscribing with his report. Only a small amount of the English lettering would fit on each one, but he had numbered them; Rutherford should have no trouble puzzling them out when they appeared at the message drop.

"So now I'm going to have to cover for you again," Mondrago grumbled.

"Well," said Jason reasonably, "I have to be the one to go. Would you be able to find the message drop on Mount Pentelikon?"

"I know, I know. You're the one with the map spliced into his optic nerve." This clearly didn't sweeten it for Mondrago.

"I'm still going to need daylight, though. So I'd better get going now."

Jason slipped out of back of the camp and made his way up Mount Agriliki to the ledge where he had left the Transhumanists' aircar. It was still there, to his relief; the Transhumanists evidently had no way of locating it. He took it aloft and made his invisible way to Mount Pentelikon, rising over thirty-five hundred feet a few miles to the southwest.

Before their departure from the twenty-fourth century, he had taken a virtual tour of the mountain, and his implant had been programmed to project a tiny white dot on his neurally activated map display where an overhanging rocky ledge sheltered the spot that had been chosen as a message drop.

At this moment, in the linear present of the year 2380, it was empty. In a few minutes, Jason's potsherds would be there, to be discovered in the course of the next of the inspections of the site. But no one would be there at the precise instant of the linear present when

Jason put them there. Something would prevent it. He suppressed the eerie feeling that always took him at moments like these.

He cruised about in search of a place where the aircar could rest concealed from any goatherds who might be about, finally settling for a kind of small glen. Save for being more extensively forested, all was as it would be in his era. He hefted his satchel and set off on a narrow path leading around the mountainside toward his destination. Turning a corner, he saw the flat top of the ledge under whose far end was the message drop, a few feet below.

But he had eyes for none of that, for he was not alone. Ahead of him stood Franco, Category Five, Seventy-Sixth Degree, and one of his strong-arm men . . . and Chantal Frey.

For a heartbeat the tableau held, as they all stood in shocked surprise. Then the low-ranking Transhumanist sprang into action, as he was genetically predisposed to, whipping out a short sword and lunging toward Jason.

Jason dropped his satchel and let his trained reflexes react for him as he took advantage of the tendency of a lunge to put the swordsman slightly off balance. Twisting aside to his left and gripping the wrist of his assailant's sword-arm, he pulled the man forward while bringing his right knee up, hard, into his midriff. The wind whooshed out of him as Jason pulled him forward, continuing the lunge, and his grip on the sword-hilt weakened enough for Jason to twist it out of his hand as he fell.

Jason whirled toward Franco, who was too far away for a thrust. He knew he had only a few seconds before the swordsman recovered. His sword wasn't designed for throwing, but it would have to do. He drew it back. . . .

With an almost invisibly quick motion, Franco grabbed Chantal in his left arm, swung her in front of him as a shield and, with his right hand, put a dagger to her throat.

"Drop the sword or she dies," he said emotionlessly, in his strangely compelling voice. Chantal's eyes were huge in her frozen face.

A measurable segment of time passed before Jason let the sword slip from his fingers and hit the flat rock ledge with a clang. The guard retrieved it, and Franco released Chantal. She took a step toward Jason.

"I'm sorry, Jason." She seemed barely able to form words, and her features seemed about to dissolve in a maelstrom of conflicting emotions.

"It wasn't your fault," he said dully. But then he looked into those enormous eyes, and began to understand what he was seeing in them.

No, he thought as a horrible doubt began to dawn.

Then she stepped back and stood beside Franco, half-leaning against his side as he put an arm around her shoulders.

"No," said Jason, aloud this time but almost inaudibly.

"Yes," said Franco with a smile. "This works out very well. When she returns to her own time she'll be able to explain how you and the others met your unfortunate end."

"Returns to her own time? Haven't you made that impossible?" Jason jerked his chin in the direction of Chantal's left arm, which still had a bandage around it. She seemed to seek refuge deeper in the crook of Franco's arm. "Why did you do that, by the way? Just sheer, random sadism?"

"Oh, we had to, in order to keep you from being able to track her whereabouts. Oh, yes, we know about your brain implant, and the passive tracking devices incorporated in the other team members' TRDs." Franco pursed his lips and made a mocking *tsk-tsk* sound. "Whatever happened to your precious 'Human Integrity Act'?"

"You never told me about that, Jason," Chantal said with a kind of weak resentment in her voice. She snuggled even closer to Franco. "*He* did!"

"Chantal," said Jason, still struggling with his bewilderment, "don't you understand? He's made it impossible for you to return to your own time. You'll have to spend the rest of your life in this era!"

"Oh, no," Franco denied, shaking his head, before Chantal could speak. "Now that we have you, and while that thug of yours is otherwise occupied at Marathon, we'll find her TRD."

"You're lying, as usual. Why would you want to do that?"

"You'll learn in a moment. But, to resume, it must be at your house in Athens or, more likely, the house of your friend Themistocles." Jason tried to keep his features immobile and not confirm Franco's supposition. From the latter's expression, he saw that he had failed. "We'll retrieve it—sonic stunners will take care of his servants, and we have sensors that can detect it. We also have some field dermal regeneration equipment among our first-aid supplies. It will be a simple matter to re-implant it in her arm and restore the tissue."

"That will never get past a careful examination."

"But why should there be such an examination? There will be no reason for anyone to suspect her. At the same time, there will be a tendency to want to spare the single survivor of the expedition any further distress."

"So there will. It's called ordinary human decency."

"Yes—an obsolete concept that continues to serve a useful purpose simply because we have always been able to exploit it. She'll be welcomed back with open arms after she arrives accompanied by her companions' corpses, and receive a great deal of sympathy for the harrowing experience she has been through. She will therefore be in an excellent position to be a useful agent of ours."

Jason shook his head as though to clear it of a fog of unreality. "Chantal . . . *why*?"

"Jason . . . I'm sorry. I know what you're thinking. But he's made me understand—made me see things clearly for the first time. Remember our conversation in the lounge the night before our departure? I'd always wondered, but now, thanks to him, I *know*. Our society is trying to stand in the way of destiny—the destiny that the Transhumanists represent. It's . . . it's as though we're like the Persians at Marathon, unconsciously fighting to prevent a better world from being born. The human race can transcend itself, become something *better*."

"Chantal, I can't believe I'm hearing this claptrap! Surely you can't believe it—not after he murdered Bryan and did *that* to you!" Jason pointed at her left arm.

A convulsive shudder went through her. "He's explained to me that they never intended to kill Bryan. They were just going to take him as a hostage, like me. You *forced* them to kill him, by interfering. And as for me . . . he had to do that. He didn't know yet that he could trust me. He had no choice. But he truly regretted it—he's told me so." She looked up into Franco's face.

Jason saw the look she gave Franco, and Franco's smile. And all at once he understood.

A plain, shy, insecure girl, he thought. *Attracted to the study of aliens because she's always found them easier to cope with than her fellow humans—especially the male ones. And suddenly, at a time of special vulnerability, she's exposed to a man whose genes were tailored to maximize his charisma. He must have really turned on the charm, and the flattery. . . .*

"Chantal," he burst out desperately, "can't you see he's just using you? He's lying to you. He's not capable of love. And even if he was . . . to him you're nothing but a Pug!"

Jason's consciousness exploded into a spasm of sickening pain as the guard punched him from behind, hard, in the right kidney. He fell to his knees, gasping. When he finally looked up he saw Franco examining the contents of the satchel he had dropped.

"Very ingenious," said Franco, holding up one of the laboriously inscribed potsherds. He dropped it on the ground, and poured all the others out to join it. Then, with his foot, he crushed them into fragments.

"Chantal told us your message drop was up here on this mountain," he explained. "But of course she didn't know the exact location. We have patrolled the area periodically in the hope of encountering you. But it was just good fortune that we happened to be up here today on . . . other matters."

"You still don't know the message drop's exact location," Jason reminded him.

"No. But it would be useful to us—we could leave whatever messages we want, to be found by your superiors. That—and also the location of the aircar you stole—is information we will now obtain from you."

"You can try."

"And succeed. I don't have access to any high-tech means of torture, but I won't need them. To tell you the truth, I've always considered them overelaborate. Come, Chantal," Franco said offhandedly, turning on his heel and striding off without waiting for her. "And," he called out over his shoulder to the guard, "bring him."

Chantal, her face still working as though she was on the verge of an emotional collapse and her body moving as though it could barely remain upright, turned slowly and followed Franco like a sleepwalker. Jason, responding to a prod by the guard's sword, fell in behind her.

They were walking along the ledge when Chantal abruptly swayed, lost her balance, and began to crumple to the flat rock, near its edge.

The guard automatically reached out past Jason to catch and steady her. But his position was awkward, and she continued to fall, pulling him down.

Jason had only a split second to react, and he was not in a good position to do it. The best he could manage was a kick that caught the guard in his ribs and sent him sprawling over the ledge to the ground a few feet below. He bellowed in rage, but kept his grip on his sword and sprang back to his feet almost immediately. From up ahead, Franco was roaring with rage and running back toward them. All Jason could do was spin around and, without even a backward glance at Chantal, sprinted for his aircar.

He was around the bend in the path and in the aircar before his pursuers could see it. He activated the invisibility field just before the guard, with Franco behind him, came around the cliffside. In the murky grayness of the outside world, they looked around in bewilderment. Jason smiled grimly as he took off, blowing a satisfying amount of dust into their faces.

Once in the air, he released a long-pent-up breath, sank back into the seat cushion, and tried to sort out his swirling thoughts.

She looked like she was fighting off a nervous breakdown, he told himself. *It was just a lucky break that she collapsed when she did.*

Or . . . was that a deliberate stunt on her part, to let me escape?

I may never know.

Back in the camp that night, in the light of the full moon that had enabled him to scramble down the now-familiar slope of Mount Agriliki from his concealed aircar, Jason related the story to Mondrago, who muttered something about the Stockholm Syndrome. "And now," he concluded, "I've got to get back to Athens, go to Themistocles' house, and retrieve that jar containing Chantal's TRD."

"Back to Athens? Now? Are you crazy?" Mondrago shook his head. "It's just lucky you got back here no later than you did."

"What are you talking about?"

"Haven't you noticed all the commotion around here?" Jason hadn't, in his emotional uproar. "Well," Mondrago continued, "it seems that after sunset some unusual noises were heard from the direction of the Persian camp. Then, just before you got here, there were some comings and goings in and out of the Grove of Heracles over there to our right."

"Miltiades' Ionian spies!"

"Good guess. Anyway, there hasn't been any official announcement but the word has spread: the Persians are beginning their embarkation, starting with the cavalry. And we're going out there to attack them at dawn."

Jason hadn't looked at his calendar display in a while—he'd had other things on his mind. Now he did. It was August 11.

The Battle of Marathon would take place on August 12, as Rutherford had assumed on the basis of an increasing consensus among historians starting in the early twenty-first century. Kyle would doubtless be interested. Jason, at the moment, didn't give a damn.

CHAPTER EIGHTEEN

NO ONE GOT MUCH SLEEP THAT NIGHT, under the light of the full moon that meant the Spartans were starting to march. The slaves were kept busy burnishing the shields and armor, the generals went over the plan repeatedly as they moved among their tribes with whatever pre-battle encouragement they could give . . . and everyone could hear the distant tramping of tens of thousands of feet as the Persians moved forward onto the plain, and the more distant sounds of the embarking cavalry.

The Greeks were not great breakfast eaters—a crust of bread dipped in honey or wine, at most—but before the afternoon battles that were customary in their interminable internecine wars they were wont to take a midmorning "combat brunch" including enough wine to dull fear. Not this time. This army mustered before dawn, sorting itself out into the tribal groupings. There was surprisingly little confusion, given that the light was limited now that the full moon had passed.

"At least we won't have to fight in the heat," old Callicles philosophized grumpily.

Jason, standing beside the elderly hoplite with the rest of the Leontis tribe, saw Aeschylus and his brother Cynegeirus, hurrying to the right flank to join the Aiantis. The playwright waved to

Callicles—he must, Jason thought, have a good memory for faces. Then, with the help of slaves and each other, they began the task of donning the panoply that was never put on any earlier than necessary before battle, such was its miserable discomfort.

The greaves were the least bad: rather elegant bronze sheaths that protected the legs from kneecap to ankle, so thin as to be flexible and so well shaped that they needed no straps—they were simply "snapped on," with the edges nearly meeting behind the calves. But despite their felt inner linings they were apt to chafe with the movement of the legs and lose their snug fit. They were put on first, while the hoplite could still stoop over.

Next, over his chiton, came that which prevented him from stooping: a bronze corselet of front and back segments, laced at the sides and connected over the shoulders by curved plates. Jason had been given a choice from Themeistocles' stock and had found one that seemed to fit him reasonably well—an absolute necessity. But the weight and inflexibility of the thing, and its efficiency as a heat-collector in the August sun, made him understand why later generations of hoplites in the Peloponnesian Wars would abandon it in favor of a cuirass made from layers of linen. Feeling his chiton already begin to grow sweat-soaked even before sunrise, he decided he didn't need to worry about the Persians; heat prostration would get him first. The skirt of leather strips hanging from the lower edge was the only protection the groin had.

Even more uncomfortable was the bronze "Corinthian" helmet, covering the neck and with cheek pieces and nose guard, practically encasing the entire head and face. It had no interior webbing or other suspension, only a soft leather lining; its five-pound weight rested on the neck and head. Jason now understood why hoplites grew their hair as long and thick as possible, despite the problem of lice, and he wondered what it must be like for older, balding men. With no real cushion between helmet and cranium, blows to the head—such as those dealt by the axes favored by the Persians' Saka troops—were often fatal. And, of course, the heat and stuffiness inside such a bronze pot were stifling. Given all this, it was easy to understand why Classical Greek art usually showed the helmet propped back on the head; it was worn this way until the last possible moment before battle, at which time it was finally lowered over the face. At this point, the hoplite became semi-deaf (there were no ear-holes) and able to see only directly ahead. But, Jason reflected, in a phalanx that was really the only direction you needed to see. And it occurred to him that this was one more bit of cement for a phalanx's unique degree of unit cohesion. A hoplite need not worry about his blind zones as long as the formation held; but alone, he was locked into a world of terrifying isolation.

At least, Jason consoled himself, his helmet was not one of those with a horsehair crest, intended to make the wearer look taller and more fearsome but adding to the helmet's weight and awkwardness. He had made sure to draw one of the plain, crestless versions, whose smooth curved surface would have a better chance of deflecting a Saka axe.

Then the slave handed Jason his most important piece of defensive equipment: the shield, or *hoplon*, that gave the hoplite his name. It was circular, three feet in diameter, made of hardwood covered with a thin sheet of bronze that didn't add much to its protective strength but which, when highly polished as it was now, could dazzle the enemy. Its handgrip (*antilabe*) and arm grip (*porpax*) distributed its weight along the entire left forearm, making it usable. But there was no getting around the fact that the thing weighed sixteen pounds, and was damned awkward. Fortunately, its radical concavity made it possible to rest most of its weight on the left shoulder. Of course, carried that way, the *hoplon* couldn't possibly protect the right side of the man carrying it. For that, he was utterly dependent on the man to his right in the formation keeping *his* sixteen-pound shield up. Again, solidarity was survival.

Finally, Jason was handed his primary offensive weapon, far more important than the short leaf-shaped sword at his side: a seven-and-a-half-foot thrusting spear, carried shouldered while the phalanx was advancing, then held underhand for the final change, but afterwards generally gripped overhand for stabbing. It was made of ash with an iron spearhead and, at the other end, a bronze butt spike. The latter was useful because the spear, only an inch thick, often shattered against hardwood shields and bronze armor in the thunderous clash of two phalanxes; a man deprived of his spearhead could reverse what was left of the spear and stab with the spike. Also, the ranks behind, still carrying their spears upright, could jab downward into any enemy wounded lying at their feet as the phalanx advanced.

Speaking of feet, there was one thing Jason could not understand, and never would. The human foot, as he knew from painful experience on his last extratemporal expedition, was a vulnerable thing composed of numerous small and easily-broken bones. Hoplites went into brutal, stamping, stomping battles with nothing on their feet but sandals. Why men already wearing and carrying fifty to seventy pounds of bronze, wood, iron, and leather didn't go one step further and avail themselves of the fairly sturdy boots their society was quite capable of producing was a mystery he was never to solve. He had, with careful casualness, put the question to Callicles, and had gotten a blank look for his pains. Evidently, it was just the way things were done—which, as Jason already knew, was more often than not the answer to questions about the seemingly irrational practices of preindustrial societies.

Finally the outfitting was done. Jason looked at Callicles and knew that what he saw mirrored how he himself looked. *Dressed to kill,* he thought.

Themistocles moved among the Leontis, telling dirty jokes, calling men by name and asking how their children were, recalling various men's former heroisms, and generally being Themistocles. The fact that he was here told Jason that the customary sacrifices had been offered to the gods by the generals, and that the omens had proven favorable. Now the order was given, and in the first glimmerings of dawn the hoplites moved through gaps in the defensive earthworks and took up their positions in accordance with the plan on which everyone had been repeatedly briefed over the past few days. There was little talk, and most of that was in whispers, as older men offered advice and encouragement to newbies.

Themistoicles positioned himself in the front line, of course, as Aristides was doing in the Antiochis front rank to their immediate right. There, they and the other tribes' *strategoi* would fight as ordinary hoplites, which was precisely what they would revert to being after their tenures in office expired. Very few Classical Greek generals who held repeated commands died in bed; when phalanxes clashed, the commander of the defeated side was almost invariably killed, as were not a few victorious commanders. The idea of a general standing safely on a hill in the rear and issuing commands was utterly foreign to these men. The concept of "leading from the front" went without saying, and it was one more layer of psychic cement for the phalanx. Jason knew that Callimachus was taking up a similar position on the right flank, the traditional place for the war archon, among his own Aiantis tribe. The Plataeans were on the left. Only Miltiades, in his capacity of "chief of staff," was somewhere around the center, overseeing the big picture.

According to Herodotus, Jason told himself, *a hundred and ninety-two Athenians and eleven Plataeans get killed today, out of a total of ten thousand. Pretty good odds against being one of those two hundred and three.*

The sun cleared the hills of Euboea, visible in the distance across the water to the east, and for the first time the panorama on the plain was visible, with the dense masses of the enemy, and, beyond that, their camp, which must be mostly broken down by now. Along the curving beach, it could be seen that the Persians had gotten most of their ships into the water during the night, but the activity swirling around them suggested that the loading of the horses—obviously in progress, since very few cavalry were visible in the Persian formation—was still incomplete.

Jason stared at the Persian line, just under a mile away. Then he looked left and right at their own formation. *Let's see,* ran his automatic thought processes, *ten thousand hoplites, of whom two thousand in the center are arrayed four ranks deep and the rest eight ranks deep. . . . That makes a front line of fifteen hundred. Assuming each man has a total of three feet of space, that's a front forty-five hundred feet long, plus a little more to allow for spaces between the tribes. It looks like the Persian front is very little longer than that, and, our right is sheltered by the Grove of Heracles. But their formation is a hell of a lot deeper, with maybe thirty thousand men packed into it.*

He became aware that all the muttering and whispering in the ranks had ceased. Everyone was staring fixedly at the outlandishly costumed horde a mile across the plain, and especially at the center, directly ahead of them—the core, or *spada,* of the enemy array, ethnic Iranians all, and veteran soldiers. This was the army that had, in a mere two generations, conquered all the known world to the east, and beyond into the fabulous reaches of India. The army that had crushed the Lydians, the Babylonians, the Elamites, the Egyptians, and all the rest of the seemingly eternal ancient civilizations and ground their rubble into a new universal empire. The army that no Greeks had ever defeated in pitched battle.

It was, Jason thought, understandable that he could feel a kind of collective shudder run through the tight formation. He also caught a whiff of an unmistakable aroma. From his expression, Callicles also recognized it.

"Always some who do it about now," he chuckled. "I've never done *that*, but I've occasionally been known to let the water run down my legs." The old hoplite's voice held no embarrassment, and no condemnation of the men who were voiding themselves. Fear was nothing to be ashamed of. The only shame was in failing to hold the all-important line. A hoplite could feel as much natural fear as he wanted, as long as he overcame it enough to keep formation.

Themistocles took a few steps forward and turned to face his men. He didn't shout, or even seem to speak loudly, but his voice carried. He pointed with his spear at the Persian multitude.

"Men of Leontis! These barbarians stand on Attic soil, where they do not belong—the soil from which *you* are sprung." A murmur of agreement ran through the ranks, for as Jason knew, this was no mere figure of speech to these men, with their literal belief that they were the autochthonous race of this land, unconquered for all time. "They are here to carry out their Great King's command: after killing you they are to castrate your sons and scatter your daughters in slavery all across his vast mongrel empire, as they have scattered so many conquered peoples. Thus your bloodlines are to be extirpated and Athens itself forgotten."

A paralyzing silence held the phalanx. But Themistocles knew what he was doing. He allowed the silence to hold for only a couple of heartbeats before resuming.

"Yes, this is the most terrible fear that any Greek can imagine. But by being here, you have chosen to come face to face with that fear, and defy it, and thereby conquer it. You have chosen to prevent the obliteration of your families and your *polis*. You can make these choices because you are free men, not slaves. That freedom to choose gives you a power that the Persians will never know, for there are no free men among them, only slaves and slavemasters. It is a power that is new in the world—a power that you are going to unleash here, today, on this plain. And after you do, the world will never be the same again."

Themistocles fell abruptly silent and resumed his place in the line. There was no cheering or boisterousness, just a grim, steady determination which settled over the formation like a cloak.

Orders were passed. The Corinthian helmets were lowered into position, and the hoplites ceased to be individuals and became faceless automata. *Rutherford will bitch about the limited input my recorder implant has to work with*, Jason thought, looking through his tiny eye-slits. *To hell with him*. With a shuffling of feet and a clanging together of shield rims, the phalanx locked itself into rigidity.

In unison, ten thousand voices began to sing the holy paean.

Greek music—all ancient music, really—had rhythm and melodies, but no harmonies. That was true even of the instrumental music, and still more so of the singing. This was more of a chant. It sounded eerie inside Jason's helmet. He followed along as best he could, not that anyone could make out any individual voice.

Trumpets sounded, reverberating inside the bronze helmets. In accordance with the plan they all knew, the phalanx advanced, at a walk at first. Then, after just a few steps, double time. The air began to fill with dust as all those thousands of feet pounded the dry ground of summer, and the bronze-against-bronze clatter of jostling armor rose to a clanging roar.

Jason, peering through his helmet's eye-holes, became aware of something. Unable to see more than a small range of vision, barely able to hear at all, he was dependent on the *feel* of the shoulder-to-shoulder phalanx around him: the pressure and the pushing and the shoving. It became clear why every man drew courage from all the others, and why all were caught up in an irresistible compulsion to advance, ever forward.

He was also beginning to understand why men in their forties, fifties, and occasionally even sixties were to be found in the phalanx alongside those in their twenties. They weren't expected to hold up under the kind of endless campaigning endured in the trenches of World War I or the jungles of Southeast Asia or the high desert of Iota Persei II. Hoplite warfare wasn't like that. The whole point was to avoid ruinous protracted war between city-states by deciding matters in one brutal afternoon. The toil and the fighting and the bloodshed were concentrated and distilled into a single decisive clash of appalling violence but short duration. Callicles and his ilk could handle that. It also explained why men were able and willing to endure the awkwardness and discomfort of the hoplite panoply: they didn't have to do so for long.

They were getting closer, and up ahead Jason saw that the Persians were starting, rather belatedly, to firm up their formation. At first they must have been unable to believe what they were seeing: the Greeks, with no archers, were actually coming out onto the plain and attacking three times their number. And then the rapid Greek advance had left them with less time than they had thought they had. But there was no panic. These were veterans. Now the spear-bearing infantry were forming up in front and grounding their wicker shields to form a palisade, while thousands and thousands of archers massed behind them, ready to release a sky-darkening sleet of arrows that would decimate the crazy Greeks, after which the infantry (and the few horsemen in the formation) would advance and slaughter the disorganized remnant. Such were the standard Persian tactics, and no army in the known world had ever stood before them.

Then the trumpets gave another signal. At what Jason estimated was a distance of six hundred yards from the Persian front, the double-time became a fast trot.

Herodotus had said the Athenian hoplites had run the entire distance of almost a mile, a unique event. Historians had hooted at that, flatly denying that men so equipped could have done it and been fit to fight afterwards. But, in the surge of adrenaline now singing through their veins, Jason didn't doubt that for the rest of their lives these men would remember what they were doing as a run. And those skeptical historians had overlooked one thing: hoplites trained, in the task-specific way of all successful exercise programs, to run in armor. In fact, one Olympic event was a foot-race whose contestants wore armor and carried shields. No, these men couldn't sprint a mile. But they could cover ground at a pace that few athletes of any other era, however well-conditioned, could have matched carrying the particular burden they carried. Jason only hoped he'd be able to keep up.

At the same time they began to trot, they began to scream their war-cry: a terrifying *alleeee!* calculated to fray the nerves of any who heard it. The ululation rose even above the clattering of shields. Jason recalled what a colleague who had observed the American Civil War had once told him about the "Rebel yell." Between that and the cacophony of moving armor, the noise reverberating inside Jason's bronze helmet was deafening.

The air was filling with the dust kicked up by ten thousand pairs of trotting feet, the August sun was getting hotter, and breath was coming in painful gasps. No one cared. They were all half-crazed now, and their trot covered the ground much faster than Persian tactical calculations allowed for. Blinking the sweat out of his eyes, Jason thought he could see frantic movement in the Persian formation up ahead.

Then, at a distance of two hundred yards, the war-cry rose to a collective nerve-shattering scream . . . and the trot became a run.

It was more than a run. It became, in the insanity of the moment, almost a race, as the phalanx thundered down on the now visibly rattled Persians.

Now the Persian archers let fly, and thousands upon thousands of arrows arched overhead with a *whoosh* like a rushing of wind and plunged downward. But most of them missed entirely, for the speed of the running attack had thrown the archers' timing off. And of those that hit, most were ineffective. Jason heard and felt them clattering off his shield and helmet. The advance did not slow, and the formation did not waver. If anything, it picked up speed. Exhaustion didn't matter anymore; adrenaline was irrelevant. These ten thousand screaming madmen were carried forward on a tide of sheer impatience to start killing these barbarians who had come to destroy their world and everything that gave their lives meaning.

Now, with a collective crash, the spears of the first two ranks were brought down into an overhand position and leveled.

The Persian archers scrambled to reload. But there was no longer any time for that.

Even through his helmet, Jason could hear new screams. They came from up ahead, and they were screams of panic, for the Persians now knew that these bronze killing machines in human form were not going to stop. Jason could see that horrified realization in the faces of the infantry just ahead. They were instinctively flinching backward, their shield-palisade dissolving.

Now, then, let's see, thought Jason in the calm, detached corner of his mind that was still running calculations even in these final seconds. *Ten thousand men, weighing an average of maybe a hundred and fifty pounds and carrying an average of maybe sixty pounds of weapons and armor. That comes to. . . .*

Over a thousand tons of bronze and hardwood and bone and muscle, bristling with iron spearpoints and moving at the velocity of a sprint, smashed into the Persian army.

CHAPTER NINETEEN

JASON HAD WITNESSED the Fourth Crusade's sack of Constantinople. He had seen the ghastly bloodbaths of the Thirty Years' War. He was no stranger to the brutal madness of battle waged with weapons driven by human muscle at face-to-face range amid the stench of sweat and blood and shit. But none of that had really prepared him for the crashing impact of a running phalanx.

In all the other low-tech clashes he had experienced, there had always been a last second instinctive flinching, an avoidance of an actual full-tilt collision. But hoplites were trained to smash straight in, rocking the opposing phalanx back and hopefully opening up tears in its shield-line, after which the battle would cease to be a battle and become a slaughter. The result of such a collision was one for which Jason doubted his generalized expertise in low-technology combat would have prepared him: a thunderclap of din and violence as the two phalanxes came together, the pressure of the rear ranks forcing the front rank ever forward into a nightmarish thunderclap of shields bashed against shields, of thousands of splintering spears.

But not this time. The front rank of the Persian army was simply pulverized as the thrusting spears went through wicker shields and quilted cloth and occasional armor of loosely hanging metal scales to punch into bodies. The phalanx ground on, trampling the shield palisade and seeking out the even less well-protected archers.

Jason drove his spear into the midriff of a Persian, looking into the man's terrified eyes and smelling his shit as the spearhead ripped through flesh, muscle, and guts before coming up against the spine. Yanking the spear out of the squalling Persian, he came to a realization that was simultaneously dawning on the Greeks all up and down the line: *their spears weren't breaking.* This time they weren't up against another phalanx. There were no hardwood shields and bronze breastplates for the spears to break against. A rectangular Persian wicker shield, made by threading sticks through a wet framework of leather, might as well not have been there when a hoplite thrust his iron-headed ash spear through it. So the spear could be used again . . . and again . . . and again.

The front ranks pushed on. Now the unbroken spears were being used overhand, for stabbing. Jason felt his sandaled feet almost slip in blood and entrails, and heard a scream as he stepped on a wounded Persian. He reversed the spear and slammed the butt-spike down into the terrified face, through the eye-socket into the brain, and jerked it out jellied and bloodied. He couldn't let himself think about it. But the next time he stepped on a screaming man he moved on, and heard the scream abruptly cease behind him. One of the men in the rear ranks must have brought his spear's butt-spike down.

In the midst of the crushing press of armored men, forging ahead through a welter of gore and a din of endless screams, Jason could see nothing of what was happening elsewhere on the field. He could only advance, thrusting again and again, through the abattoir that was the battlefield of Marathon. But he knew that the Greek flanks, eight ranks deep and facing second-rate troops, were advancing more rapidly than they were here in the center, where a formation only four deep faced a massive concentration of Persians and Saka. Soon the enemy flanks would give way entirely and flee in howling panic, seeking the safety of their ships. The Greek flanks would follow . . . but only for a hundred yards or so.

This, Jason knew, would be the crucial moment. And it would disprove what a small but persistent school of revisionists had been claiming ever since around the turn of the twenty-first century: that the Athenians had fought Marathon as a disorganized mob. None of those revisionist historians, Mondrago had remarked archly, had ever commanded infantry in combat. If they had, they might have spared themselves the embarrassment of making such a silly assertion, for they would have known that no disorganized mob could possibly do what the Greek flanks were about to do. First of all, they would halt their pursuit of a routed enemy on a trumpet-signal, leaving the light troops, or *thetes*, to harry the Persians along. And then they would pivot their formations ninety degrees, facing inward toward the center from left and right.

Even as Jason was thinking about it, he realized that their own advance in the center had halted, as the massive Persian numbers began to tell. He even had a split second to wonder at the courage of the Persian and Saka elite troops they faced here, for they were pushing back against the terrifying, spear-jabbing front line of the phalanx, forcing it back by the sheer weight of their mass of human flesh. The tide began to turn against the Athenian center.

Time lost its meaning. The sun was rising in the sky, and in the midst of heat and exhaustion and thirst the men of the Leontis and Antiochis tribes fought on, giving ground stubbornly, their thin line bending back but not breaking. From behind, their tribes' *thetes*, including Mondrago, kept up a supporting rain of javelins and sling-stones. They could do so over the heads of the hoplites because the withdrawal was now slightly uphill.

Jason's spear had finally broken, and the stump of it had been knocked out of his hand before he could reverse it and use the butt-spike. He frantically drew his short sword as the crush of enemy troops, sensing victory, pressed the Greek center further back. Now the Athenians were backing up into the wooded terrain in front of and to the right of their camp. That terrain had been their friend over the past days, screening their right flank from the Persian cavalry; now it turned traitor, causing the phalanx to begin to lose its cohesion. Now it was individual fighting, more a brawl than a battle, and the awkward *hoplon*, intended as an interlocking component of the phalanx rather than an individual defense, was almost more hindrance than help.

Jason saw a huge Saka—instantly recognizable as such by the distinctive pointed hat they wore—break free of the press and turn toward him, swinging his battle-axe in a powerful downward cut.

Jason managed to raise his heavy shield in time to block it, but the hard-driven axe, striking off-center, knocked the *hoplon* aside. With a roar, the Saka recovered and brought his axe around for a second blow before Jason could get the sixteen-pound shield back in line. Jason raised his sword to parry the cut, deflecting the axe's arc, but it struck his helmet a glancing blow that caused stars to explode in his eyes. He instinctively whipped the sword around and drove it into the Saka's midriff, a vicious twisting thrust that brought a rope of entrails out with it when he withdrew the blade.

As the Saka sank, groaning, to the ground, Jason looked around him, cursing the helmet's limited field of vision. To his left, he saw Callicles, using the butt-spiked stump of his broken spear to fend off an *akenake*-wielding Persian. But exhaustion was finally beginning to tell, and the old hoplite was slowing. With a visible effort, he raised his shield to counter what turned out to be a feint. The Persian rushed in under it and brought his short sword upward, driving into Callicles' groin. Callicles shrieked. The Persian heaved the *akenake* out and stabbed again.

Jason lunged, swinging his *hoplon* around like a weapon. Its edge caught the Persian on the back of the neck, smashing his face into Callicles' shield, crushing his nose and breaking his teeth. Before the Persian could recover from the stunning impact and pain, Jason raised his sword and chopped down where neck met shoulder. Blood sprayed. The Persian and Callicles collapsed together, their blood mingling. It was all the same color.

At that moment, Jason became aware of a sea-change in the battle. He must, he thought, not have heard the second trumpet call. For now the Persian center, so exultant mere minutes ago, was dissolving in consternation. A deafening cacophony of shouts and clashing weapons and armor to left and right told Jason why. The victorious Greek flanks, having wheeled inward in a way impossible for any but veteran troops well-briefed on a prearranged plan, were crunching into the Persian center, which was now boxed in on three sides. The Leontis and Antiochis men of the Greek center were now advancing again as the screaming Persians and Saka fled for their lives in the only direction left open to them, having had their fill of the horror, the sheer awfulness, of hoplite warfare. But as always in warfare at this technological level, running for one's life was precisely the wrong thing to do, for fleeing men could not protect themselves. The Athenians of the center went in pursuit, cutting them down in the ever-shrinking killing ground as the flanks pressed in from the sides. Jason was left behind.

He sank to his knees, feeling in his left temple the pressure from a dent the Saka's axe stroke had made in his helmet. He laid down his sword and shield, pulled the helmet off, threw it away, and took great gulping breaths now that he was free of its stifling confines. He also looked around, relishing the full field of vision. The slope was littered with the dead and dying, a wrack left behind as the roaring tide of battle receded. Otherwise, he was alone.

Now's my chance to get away, go up this hill to the aircar, get back to Athens and retrieve Chantal's TRD from Themistocles' house—assuming that Franco and his merry men haven't already beaten us to it, he told himself. *First, I have to find Alexandre.* He forced his brain, still numb from what he had just experienced, to start forming the mental command that would bring up a map of the locality complete with TRD locations. . . .

At that moment, he saw out of the corner of his eye that he wasn't alone after all. A hoplite, still fully armed and equipped, was coming toward him at a trot, his face hidden by one of the crested Corinthian helmets.

Who is that? he wondered, looking at the inhuman facelessness of the Corinthian helmet. *And what's he in such a hurry for?*

"Rejoice!" he called out, one fifth-century B.C. Greek to another.

Instead of replying, the hoplite brought his spear up overhand and stabbed with it. For some infinitesimal fraction of a second, Jason clearly saw the spearpoint coming toward his unprotected face.

Jason's paralysis broke. He scooped up his shield and, with no time to get his arm through the *porpax* arm-grip, he awkwardly grabbed the shield by the hand-grip and the left edge and shoved it up and out as he surged to his feet.

The iron point, driven by all the strength of his onrushing assailant, punched through the shield's thin bronze covering and the hardwood beneath, protruding from the inner surface inches from Jason's arm. Jason twisted the shield sharply to the side, and the spear-shaft broke. Before the attacker could reverse it and use the butt-spike, Jason shoved the shield forward against him, pushing with his entire weight, bowling the man over. Taking advantage of the momentary respite, he scrambled backwards and retrieved the sword he had laid on the ground. At the same time, he frantically tried, using his left arm alone, to grip his shield properly. Clumsy and burdensome as the sixteen-pound *hoplon* was, it was all he had.

But the man had gotten to his feet with remarkable speed for one wearing hoplite armor, and was carrying his shield very easily—he must, Jason thought, be very strong, to be able to use the *hoplon* for personal defense. He swung the remainder of his spear-shaft almost like a mace and struck the rim of Jason's shield just as Jason was still trying to correct his grip, sending it flying. The spear-shaft also went flying, and the attacker whipped out his sword and rushed in. Jason knew himself for a dead man, for he stood no chance in a sword fight, shieldless and helmetless.

Only . . . at least I can see, *without that damned helmet!*

It was the only card he had to play. He lunged forward, evading the sword-slash and moving into the attacker's right-hand blind zone.

Even with these short blades, it was too close for swordplay. But taking advantage of his instant of invisibility, Jason got his right arm under the attacker's from behind and, holding both their sword-arms locked into temporary uselessness, used his free left hand to grab the man's helmet by its crest and wrench it off.

At appreciably the same instant, the attacker brought his clumsy shield sharply back, smashing its rim into Jason's left rib cage. The breastplate prevented it from breaking any ribs, but the impact caused Jason to lose his grip and the man flung him away. He landed supine, and a sandaled foot came painfully down on his right wrist, pinning his sword-arm to the ground.

Jason had time to look up into his assailant's face. It was one of the unpleasantly similar faces of Franco's gene-enhanced underlings. Jason recognized him as Landry's killer. The man raised his sword. . . .

There was an odd and unpleasant sound, which seemed compounded of those usually characterized as *whack* and *crunch*. The Transhumanist's face went abruptly expressionless, and blood began to seep from a small round hole in the exact center of his forehead. His raised sword fell to the ground, and he followed it there with a clang of armor as his legs crumpled.

Jason looked behind him. Mondrago held the sling that had sent its little lead pellet into the Transhumanist's brain.

"You really *do* know how to use that thing," Jason remarked, inadequately.

"You helped by getting his helmet off," Mondrago grinned, helping Jason to his feet. He glanced at the body. "So I suppose his job was to provide us with an 'in-period death.'"

For a moment they stood and looked to the northeast over the plain of Marathon, where the battle was roaring along toward the Persian ships. Jason knew what was happening up there. Datis, the Persian commander, had managed to get enough of a new line formed to hold the Greek light troops. But when the re-formed phalanx—moving slowly this time, for there were limits to the endurance even of hoplites—arrived, a final, desperate battle would rage. The Persians would hold the narrow beach long enough for all but seven of their ships to get away. But many of them would be driven into the great marsh behind their camp, and the sixty-four hundred Persian dead that would be counted after the battle didn't even count the ones drowned there.

Still, the surviving Persians, including the dread cavalry that had embarked before the battle, would be at sea, and the way around Cape Sunium, to Phalerum and undefended Athens, lay open to them. And at the same moment that horrifying realization dawned on the Greeks, they would see a signal, like the sun reflected from a polished shield, flash atop Mount Pentelikon—surely the work of the traitors whom everyone feared lurked amid Athens' labyrinthine political factions.

So the weary victors would send a runner to assure the city that the victory had been won. And then they would set out for Athens, leaving the Antiochis tribe to guard the captured loot of the Persian camp. (Apparently only Aristides "the Just" was trusted with that particular assignment, and Jason had to admit that he himself wouldn't necessarily have trusted Themistocles with it.) These men who had just fought a battle would march, in full armor, the twenty-six miles back to Athens, starting at ten in the morning and arriving at Phalerum by late afternoon, barely in time. And the Persian fleet would sail away.

And as a result of all the sickening butchery on this plain Western civilization would live, to one day give humankind—for the first time—an economic system that allowed for at least the possibility of prosperity, a legal system that allowed for at least the possibility of justice, and a governmental system that allowed for at least the possibility of individual liberty . . . including the liberty of free scientific inquiry that would lead to the stars.

Rutherford wanted us to find out if there's any truth to the tradition that the runner is none other than Pheidippides, and that he drops dead after delivering his message, Jason recalled, *or if historians have been right to ridicule it . . . just as they've ridiculed the idea of the hoplites running to the attack. He also wanted us to find out the truth about the "shield signal" from Mount Pentelikon, because the mystery of that was never solved.*

Too bad, Kyle. We don't exactly have time for any of that at the moment.

"Come on," he told Mondrago as he discarded his breastplate and greaves and tried to discard his exhaustion with them. "Let's go. The aircar is concealed about halfway up here on Mount Agriliki. We'll take it to Athens and—maybe—make it to Themistocles' house and get that jar containing Chantal's TRD before Franco does."

They ascended the wooded slope behind the Greek camp, the sounds of shouts and screams and clashing weapons diminishing as the battle moved on. Jason concentrated on retracing his steps to the clearing. As a result, he almost missed the flicker of motion among the shadow-dappled underbrush.

"What?" Mondrago exclaimed, and bounded toward the barely-glimpsed movement. A figure broke cover and skittered frantically away.

It was Pan.

CHAPTER TWENTY

MONDRAGO SCRAMBLED UPHILL and plunged forward, catching the fleeing Pan around the legs. A backward kick of cloven hooves caused him to lose his grip and yelp with pain.

But the split second that kick took enabled Jason to catch up. Avoiding the goatish legs, he landed atop Pan's thrashing back, wrapping his left arm around the throat and gripping one of the horns with his right hand. The hybrid being was immobilized, and the force of his struggles confirmed an impression Jason had gotten when grappling with Pan before: that his muscularity was deceptive, or perhaps the word was "decorative." He didn't seem very strong, and there was an odd but unmistakable feeling of artificial fragility about him.

Mondrago got to his feet and drew the dagger that was part of standard *thetes* equipment. "I'll kill the miserable little—!"

"As you were! I want information, not a corpse." Mondrago subsided, and Jason addressed Pan, with a jerk on the horn for emphasis but a slight relaxation of the throat-hold. "Talk! What are you doing here? And how did you get up here anyway?"

"I came in a Teloi aircar," rasped Pan in his squeaky voice, through a still-constricted throat. "The Transhumanists have to use them, since you stole the only one they brought with them."

"Doesn't that limit their mobility, having to use aircars with no invisibility fields?"

"Yes. Franco's fury is terrible. But they have no choice. I came with one of his men, who was sent to kill the two of you. We were dropped off here on Mount Agriliki because of its location; the killer could slip down unnoticed behind the Greek center as it was being forced back. He ordered me to wait here."

And of course you had to obey, thought Jason. The Transhumanists had no need to worry that their "god" would run away and cut himself off from the drugs that made his existence endurable.

"Afterwards," Pan continued, "I am to be picked up and taken to Mount Kotroni." He pointed northward, to the left of the plain. "Franco has a machine set up there, which he is very shortly going to use to induce uncontrollable fear in the Persians when they form their second line, protecting the departing ships."

Jason called up his map-display; it made sense.

"That will have to be very soon," he said, listening to the distant battle-sounds.

"Yes. They'll be here for me any minute now. I am to show myself on the slope, so the Greeks can see me. The Persians' panic—" (Pan did not smile) "—will be attributed to me."

Well, well, thought Jason, *so that was what their aircar was doing on Mount Kotroni when I took it. They were scouting out a good location.*

"Afterwards," Pan went on, "we are to return to Athens in the Teloi aircar. Even traveling cautiously to avoid being observed, we will arrive there in not many minutes—long before any runner that can be sent from here. I will appear to my worshippers in the cave under the Acropolis and tell them of the victory before anyone else in Athens knows. The Teloi will signal from Mount Pentelikon the instant the battle is over."

"Aha!" Mondrago burst out. "So that's the famous 'shield signal' that everybody has always wondered about."

"Right," Jason nodded. "The Greeks will think it's traitors signaling to the Persian fleet, even though the meaning and purpose of such a signal will be hard to understand, and afterwards no treason will ever be proved. But now we know what it's really for: to let Franco & Co.

know exactly when they can proceed with the ceremony. It'll make it even more of a belief-strengthening miracle for the true believers when their god appears to them and tells them about the battle just as it's ending. A very precisely choreographed operation all around."

"And one which we're now in a position to abort!" said Mondrago wolfishly. "You've gotten your information out of him. Now let me kill him."

Pan stiffened with fear.

"No!" said Jason, without really knowing why.

"Why not? Franco will have egg on his face when the 'god' doesn't show up as promised."

Which, Jason was forced to admit to himself, made sense. Only. . . .

All at once, it came to him. He wondered why he hadn't thought of it before. But of course he *had* thought of it before, when he had last spoken to Pan on the Tegea heights above the road from Sparta.

"Listen, Pan," he said hurriedly. "We've got to go. I just need to know one thing: do you know how to pilot the Teloi aircars that the Transhumanists are using?"

"Why, yes." Pan seemed puzzled, as did Mondrago. "They taught me how, in case I should ever need to do it when alone." He didn't need to add that he could always be relied on to go to the destination he was ordered. In light of that utter reliability, it made perfect sense that the Transhumanists would have availed themselves of the flexibility of training him to pilot himself. But Jason had had to be sure.

"Good. Now, if I let you live, I know you've got to stay and do as Franco tells you . . . and I know why. But I'm going to do it anyway."

Mondrago began to splutter, inarticulate with outrage. Jason shushed him.

"I'm going to leave you here. But I'm going to stop the Transhumanists from using you as they intend to, over there on Mount Kotroni. And afterwards I'm going to take you to Athens."

"How will you accomplish all this?" Pan asked in a tone of dead incredulity, too hopeless even to sneer.

"Good question," muttered Mondrago.

"Never mind that for now. Just remember what I told you before about getting help for you, and freeing you from your dependence on the Transhumanists and the Teloi? Well, I swear to you that I'll do exactly that, in exchange for your cooperation."

"Cooperation in what?" The high-pitched voice was no longer entirely lifeless, for a flicker of eagerness had awakened in it.

"I'll want you to appear to the cult members and tell them that you're no god, and that the Transhumanists are some kind of evil supernatural beings—I'll leave the details to you—who've duped them. Do you agree to my terms?"

"If you do indeed take me to Athens, and protect me from Franco and the others, I'll do as you ask."

"Good." At that moment, the tiny blue light began to flash that told Jason a grav repulsion vehicle was approaching. In this era, when such vehicles weren't supposed to exist, it could mean only one thing. "The Teloi aircar is coming for you. We have to go. Remember what I said." He got to his feet and motioned the still visibly thunderstruck Mondrago to follow him. Mondrago looked at Pan, and then at his dagger, with obvious longing, but he obeyed.

The two men hastily ascended the short remaining distance, flung themselves into the Transhumanist aircar, and engaged the invisibility field. As they went aloft they saw, in the ghostly grayish world viewed through the field, an open-topped Teloi aircar flying low for concealment.

"Well," said Mondrago with a gust of released breath, "here they come to take Pan over to Mount Kotroni so he can put on his little performance—and there's not a damned thing we can do about it about it now. What, exactly, was the purpose of all those lies you told him?"

"I wasn't lying," said Jason distractedly as he set a course for Athens. "I meant every word."

"*What?* But how—?"

Jason turned to meet Mondrago's eyes, and all the distraction was gone. When he spoke, the bullwhip crack of command was in his voice. "At the present time, you have no need to know that. For now, you will simply follow orders. And any more borderline insubordination on your part will go into my report. *Is that clear?*"

Mondrago came to as close to a position of attention as the aircar's cramped passenger seat permitted. "Yes, sir!" he said with a new snap.

"Good." Jason allowed his expression to soften into a smile. "Oh, and by the way, thanks for saving my life. That also will be in my report."

With no need to conceal the movements of a vehicle that was, in the present milieu, supernatural, they were at Athens in minutes and were able to pick a landing spot with care.

While he was doing it, Jason spared a moment to consult his map display. The red dot that marked Chantal's TRD was still at Themistocles' house. He ordered his weary body not to go weak with relief. Now, no matter what happened to him and Mondrago, he would be able to scupper Franco's plan to use Chantal as a mole.

There was a small clear area just within the city wall near the "Hangman's Gate." Jason settled the aircar gently down and made sure no one was in sight. Leaving Mondrago to keep the power on, Jason got out with the invisibility field still activated. To an observer, he would have seemed to step into existence from nowhere. Fortunately, there were no observers. He hastened through the narrow alleys, encountering no one, for all the women and old men and children who currently occupied Athens were either keeping to their homes or milling uneasily about the Agora, waiting for news.

Reaching Themistocles' house, Jason pounded on the door. The slave who opened it gasped at the sight of him—either from recognition or from sheer horror at the apparition, encrusted with dust and gore. This was no time for subtlety. While the slave was still goggling, Jason jabbed him in the solar plexus just hard enough to double him over, then wrapped an arm around his throat in a choke-hold that induced prompt unconsciousness. Then he rushed into the house, sending maidservants fleeing screaming as he went to the storeroom where he had left "Cleothera's" possessions. The jar was still where he had left it. He opened it to confirm the presence of the TRD, then ran from the house and retraced his steps to the open area and the carefully-memorized location of the aircar.

"Got it!" he told Mondrago as he took the aircar aloft. "We beat Franco to it."

"He probably thought he had plenty of time and no need to hurry," Mondrago opined. "Now he's going to be shitting rivets."

"Maybe." Jason frowned. "We've got to get out of Attica—and

not just because the Transhumanists are going to be hunting for us. Themistocles is going to think we're deserters—and if the house slaves recognized me, he's going to think I'm a thief as well. I hate that."

"So do I. I like Themistocles. I'm glad he survives the battle."

"Not everyone does. Callimachus, for example, dies in the final battle on the beach, by the Persian ships, transfixed by so many spears he's propped up and can't fall to the ground."

"Shit." Mondrago shook his head at the thought of the gallant old war archon, to whom history would never accord as much credit for the victory as he deserved. "At least Miltiades lives, right?"

"Right—but he probably would have been better off getting killed." Seeing Mondrago's puzzled stare, Jason explained. "Later this year, the Athenians will give him command of their fleet, and he'll take it around the Aegean on an expedition against islands that collaborated with the Persians. At Paros, though, he'll be defeated and badly wounded in the leg. On his return to Athens, his political rivals, the Alcmaeonid family, will smell blood. They'll put him on trial and hit him with a fine of fifty talents—an impossibly large sum—as an alternative to execution. But by then he'll have gotten gangrene in his wound, and will die shortly after the trial."

"Shit!" Mondrago repeated, but in a very different tone. "So these people are going to do *that* to the man who, along with Callimachus, masterminded the victory of Marathon for them. And you told me how they're going to ostracize Themistocles after he does the same thing for them at Salamis when the Persians come back ten years from now. And I seem to recall something about making Socrates drink hemlock." He looked down at the receding maze of Athens. "Tell me again about how these are supposed to be the *good* guys!"

Jason was silent for a moment. When he spoke, it was to himself as much as to Mondrago. "Infants are awkward and messy—even the ones who end up growing into worthwhile adults. Democracy in Athens in this era is awkward and messy. But it had to survive this day. Otherwise, the world we come from could never have been." He fell silent again, then spoke briskly. "Anyway we're going to have to lay low for a month and six days, and as I said, we've made Attica too hot to hold us now, even if there weren't Transhumanists running around in it looking for us. We'll need to go somewhere else."

Mondrago held his peace about the promises Jason had made to Pan concerning the events of this very day, here in Attica. "Where?" was all he said.

Jason smiled. "Well, I remember a place I hid out once before."

He set a course for the island of Crete.

The shepherds and goatherds around Mount Ida now spoke the Doric dialect of Greek instead of a Hittite-Luwian language, and Jason noticed the occasional iron tool among them. Otherwise, they were exactly as he remembered their ancestors in 1628 B.C.

He had brought the aircar over Crete and across the Tallaion Mountains (as the Kouloukounas range was called in this era) and along the Mylopatomas Valley to the upland plain of Nidha, with the snow-capped mass of Ida looming up eight thousand feet above sea level. At least this time he hadn't had to struggle, lamed by a broken foot, over all that dramatic terrain. A slow circle of Mount Ida had revealed the well-remembered cave, under a looming shelf of rock, where he and Deirdre Sadaka-Ramirez had sheltered.

He had cut off the invisibility field as he had brought the aircar in for a landing on the nearest piece of level ground he could find, allowing any locals who happened to be around a glimpse of it. Rutherford, he knew, would have had heart failure. But among a profoundly illiterate population like this, any tales would die out after a couple of centuries at most, and never be believed by anyone in the greater world outside this totally ignored backwater of an island. And a little supernatural cachet wouldn't hurt.

And so it had proved. They had taken up residence in the cave, believed by some to have been the nursery of the infant Zeus. It, too, was much as he remembered, although this time it didn't lie under a sky polluted with the ashes of Santorini in the aftermath of the most cataclysmic volcanic explosion in history. After a while the locals had timidly sought them out. A series of hints, haltingly delivered through the barrier of dialect differences, had persuaded them to supply the uncanny pair of strangers with cheese and wine (by courtesy so called) and certain other items, while keeping their presence a secret lest the displeasure of certain baleful deities be called down on the whole region. Jason and Mondrago had certain skills—first aid, for example—that enabled them to repay the favors and in the process acquire even more prestige. And they were both experts in wilderness survival, who quickly improvised bows with which to hunt the wild goats. They passed late August and early September with no great difficulty.

As September 18 approached, Jason programmed a fairly complex navigational command into the autopilot of the Transhumanists' aircar. He sent it looping, pilotless, in a circle that brought it around to the opposite side of Mount Ida . . . and then, with all the acceleration it could pile on, directly into the mountain-side. After his return, any investigators the Authority might find it worthwhile to send to that mountainside might find a few bits of wreckage that hadn't been there before.

Through it all, Mondrago remained stoically silent on the subject Jason had ruled off limits.

Finally the time came when they stood (it seemed undignified to arrive on the displacer stage sitting on one's butt) awaiting retrieval. Jason held the little jar stolen from Themistocles' house tightly in his hand. The digital countdown projected onto Jason's optic nerve wound down. It was nearing zero when Mondrago finally blurted, "Sir, I just don't get it!"

"What don't you get?"

"You know what I mean. If there's one thing I've learned about you, it's that you're a man of your word. And you told me that you meant what you said to Pan. But all the things you said you were going to prevent—the performances on Mount Kotroni and under the Acropolis—happened over a month ago, back in Attica. So you didn't keep your promise."

"Didn't I?" Jason grinned. "Aren't you forgetting something?"

"What, sir?"

"We're time travellers!"

Mondrago's bug-eyed stare of realization was the last thing Jason saw before the indescribable unreality of temporal transition took them.

CHAPTER TWENTY-ONE

AS ALWAYS, the glare of electric lighting in the great dome was blinding after instantaneous transition from a relatively dim setting—and practically all settings in past ages were relatively dim. It made the disorientation of temporal displacement even worse, affecting even an old hand like Jason. Between the blindness and the dizziness, it was a moment before he became aware of the hubbub among the people behind the ranks of control panels. They had been expecting four people to appear on the stage, not two.

Blinking the stroboscopic stars out of his eyes, Jason saw Mondrago shamefacedly getting to his feet. "Don't worry," he assured him. "Everybody loses his balance the first time." Looking around the floor of the stage, he spotted Landry's TRD, covered with the ashes of the crematory furnace. Then he saw Kyle Rutherford advancing toward the stage, his face a question mark.

"Dr. Landry was killed," said Jason, pointing at the tiny, ashy sphere on the floor. He offered no further explanation. Rutherford restrained himself from demanding one.

"And Dr. Frey . . . ?"

"She remained in the target milieu. Her TRD is in here." Jason held out the ceramic vase.

Rutherford stared wide-eyed. Jason had a pretty good idea what he was thinking, after his own last extratemporal expedition. He recalled the words of a probably mythical twentieth century figure with the unlikely name of Yogi Berra: "*Déjà vu* all over again."

"Yes, it was cut out of her," he said, answering Rutherford's unspoken question.

Rutherford went pale. "The Teloi?"

"No . . . or at least not principally. There are a lot of things you need to know—things that can't be made public. Can we go somewhere for an informal preliminary debriefing?"

"Yes . . . yes, of course." Rutherford started to lead them away, then paused. "But from your choice of words, do I gather that Dr. Frey was alive when you last saw her?"

"Yes. I left her in the fifth century B.C. still alive. And. . . ." Jason paused, and his face took on a look that caused Rutherford to flinch backwards. "And *this* time I'm going to get her back!"

Reducing Rutherford to a state of inarticulate shock had long been an ambition of Jason's. Now he had achieved it . . . and the circumstances made it impossible for him to enjoy it.

They sat in Rutherford's private office. It was more austerely furnished than the one in Athens that he preferred whenever he didn't need to be in Australia, but like that one it held a display case containing items brought back from the past. And here, also, the prize exhibit was a sword—in this case, a seemingly undistinguished medieval hand-and-a-half sword. A teenaged French peasant girl who believed the saints had told her to liberate her people and crown her Dauphin had found it buried behind the altar of the church of Saint Catherine of Fierbois in 1429 and carried it to the relief of Orleans. More to the point, the office contained the necessary equipment for playing the sights and sounds recorded on the tiny disc Jason had removed from his implant through an equally tiny slot in his skull, concealed by a flap of artificial skin. They had corroborated a story Rutherford clearly didn't want to believe.

Now Jason and Mondrago—uncharacteristically subdued, unaccustomed as he was to such surroundings—waited while Rutherford shook his head, slowly and repeatedly as though in a semi-daze. Jason wasn't sure which revelation had hit the old boy hardest: that a surviving Transhumanist underground still existed, or that they were operating an illicit temporal displacer on a higher technological level than the Authority's, or that they were taking high technology equipment into the past, or the objectives for which they were using their displacer. Now he sat amid the rubble of his well-ordered world.

"One thing in our favor," Jason concluded, trying to end on a positive note. "The Transhumanists are limited to sending their varieties that look more or less like normal humans—that's the only sort we saw—back in time. Their more extreme species variations would be pretty conspicuous in past eras, not to mention the cyborg warriors with grossly obvious bionic parts."

"But," said Mondrago, spoiling the effect Jason had intended, "there's no reason they can't have all of those on Earth in the present day, in the various concealed strongholds Franco bragged about." They all shuddered inwardly, as members of their culture always did at the thought of the grotesque and unnatural abominations the Transhuman movement had spawned, all of which were believed to have been extirpated a century before.

Rutherford gave his head a final shake, this time a decisive one. "This is terrible! It must be stopped! The potential consequences of what you have discovered are simply incalculable."

"Agreed," Jason nodded. "But the Authority can't handle it alone."

"I know." Rutherford's voice was desolate. The prospect of having to compromise the Authority's sacrosanct status as an independent agency was one more blow. "We shall have to involve the government's law enforcement agencies. Earth must be combed from pole to pole. This illegal displacer must be found!"

"Easier said than done," Jason cautioned. "Remember, they didn't steal the Authority's technology; they developed it themselves from Weintraub's original work, in a superior form. It won't be like searching for an installation the size of this one. *Their* displacer is compact enough to be hidden, and so energy-efficient that they could send a fairly numerous party equipped with an aircar twenty-nine hundred years back using a concealable power source."

This time a low moan escaped Rutherford. "And in the meantime," he said in a dead voice, "we have no idea where to look for their various schemes of temporal subversion. You said the Transhumanists you encountered were from a time slightly earlier than the present—"

"Yes, Franco let that slip."

"—but we don't know how long they have been pursuing their nefarious program, nor how much further into our future they will be continuing to send expeditions back, nor where and when those expeditions will go. Our field of investigation is impossibly large. And we don't know where to begin!"

"Not altogether true. We know exactly what one of their schemes is: the Pan cult. And we know exactly how to scupper it." Before Rutherford could speak, Jason leaned forward and spoke with grim, tightly controlled urgency. "I propose that you send me and Alexandre and a couple of other combat-trained Service men back to the moment after I left Pan, the point of arrival to be Mount Kotroni, where they were about to take him."

"But . . . but . . . you and Mondrago were already there," stammered Rutherford, scandalized. "So you and your own earlier selves will be present simultaneously!" What Jason was proposing violated one of the most basic policies of the Authority.

"Once there," Jason continued, ignoring the interruption, "we'll stop them from using high-tech means to induce panic in the Persians while staging an appearance by Pan. Then, as per my agreement with Pan, we'll take him to Athens where he'll tell the cultists that they've been played for suckers. Of course," he added as an afterthought, "we'll need certain rather special equipment and supplies." He launched into a list. As he proceeded, Rutherford experienced more and more difficulty breathing, and by the time he was done the older man seemed on the verge of a stroke.

Rutherford gradually regained the power of speech. "But the expense! The illegality! The. . . ." He pulled himself together. "You realize, of course, that while I have a great deal of discretion as regards the Temporal Service's ordinary operations, I could not possibly take it upon myself to authorize anything like this. The entire governing council of the Authority will have to consider your proposal."

"Bring 'em on."

If Mondrago had seemed uncomfortable in Rutherford's private sanctum, he was positively fidgeting in the understatedly ornate conference room that held a quorum—indeed, almost the entirety—

of the council, sitting around a long table with him and Jason at one end and Rutherford at the other.

The councilors had been summoned from around the planet to Australia—a summons sent under conditions of maximum security, for it had included the essential elements of Jason's findings. Since their arrival they had seen and heard the supporting evidence, and no one was inclined to doubt those findings. Not that there had ever been any serious doubt, given Jason's well-known reputation for competence, despite his equally well-known reputation as a wise-ass.

His proposal, however, was something else.

Helene de Tredville, a small woman of almost ninety standard years with white hair pulled tightly back into a severe bun, stared down the table at him. "So, Commander Thanou, do I understand that you want us to let you take modern weapons back to the fifth century B.C.?"

"Modern weapons and *medical supplies*?" Alistair Kung's voice—unexpectedly high-pitched, coming from such an overweight body—rose to a squeak on the last two words.

"Yes to both. Actually, I'd also considered asking you to send back an aircar with an invisibility field." Jason knew it was wicked to relish the signs of incipient cardiac arrest around the table. He relished it anyway. "Fortunately, Pan knows how to pilot the Teloi aircars, so we can use one of those, even though the lack of invisibility technology will be inconvenient. But as for modern weapons . . . the Transhumanists surely have them, and we can hardly be expected to go up against them with in-period swords and spears."

"But the medical supplies," Kung began, only to be silenced by Jason's expression. All the flippancy slid away, revealing what lay beneath it.

"I promised Pan that if he did as I ask I would free him from his dependency on his Transhumanist and Teloi masters. I keep my promises. Since we've been back, I've had a chance to confer with medical specialists and ascertain precisely what he needs. We can take back a supply that will, quite frankly, last him as long as a twisted organism like him is likely to live. I intend to leave him the Teloi aircar and advise him to go somewhere out-of-the-way—maybe the part of Crete where Alexandre and I hid." A ghost of Jason's trademark raffish smile reawoke. "He can start a 'cult' of his own there to assure his safety. In a historyless place like fifth-century B.C. Crete, it won't cause any problems."

"But," dithered Alcide Martiletto with a flutter of slender wrists, "it's all so *improper!* We'd have to violate our own rules and protocols in just *so* many ways!"

"Desperate times call for desperate measures," Jason philosophized drily. Then, doing his best to make it seem an afterthought, he added, "There's one additional benefit. We can rescue Dr. Chantal Frey."

"What?" Jadoukh Kubischev leaned forward. Unlike the frankly corpulent Kung, he could be described with minimal charity as "well-fleshed." And in his case, the flesh was held up by a substantial bone structure. "Whatever are you talking about, Commander? You know perfectly well that this is impossible. The TRD restores the temporal energy potential of a person or other object, causing it to return to the time from whence it came. Dr. Frey's TRD was separated from her and came back with you. Even if you were to take an extra TRD with you and give it to her to hold, it would be inseparably linked to the linear present of the time from which it made transition—as is she. It would return to its own linear present, but she would not. This is axiomatic." He shook his head with a force that set his wattles jiggling. "No. That is the end of it. She is permanently stranded in Classical Greece."

"And besides," Martiletto honked, "by your own account, the bitch turned traitor!"

"No!" Jason took a deep breath and forced himself to keep his tone deferential. "I was there, and I ask you to believe me when I say she was . . . conflicted, and that I can win her back." He turned to Kubischev. "And as for how . . . well, you all know the rule of thumb for bringing objects back with you when retrieved. The restored temporal energy potential, in a manner still imperfectly understood, seems to encompass not just your clothing but any objects you can conveniently carry, and therefore such objects require no separate TRDs of their own. Dr. Frey is a slightly built woman, and I'm a reasonably strong man. Yes," he continued hurriedly, before the murmur around the table could coalesce into flabbergasted rejection, "I know, it's never been tried with a human before. But I know of no theoretical objection to it."

From the far end of the table, Rutherford studied him shrewdly.

"So *that* was what you meant about 'getting her back.' This, despite the fact that the Transhumanists were planning to send her back as an infiltrator—a scheme which was prevented only by your recovery of her TRD before they could re-implant it, and which must have had at least her passive acquiescence. Jason, are you certain that, after your last extratemporal expedition, this isn't a matter of . . . working out guilt over what happened to Deirdre Sadaka-Ramirez?"

Once again, Jason recalled the Yogi Berra quote. He decided the humor wouldn't be appreciated here. He kept silent, fearing that anything he could say might damage his credibility even more than Rutherford had.

"However," Rutherford continued, addressing the meeting at large, "that is really immaterial. Whatever deep-seated feelings and motivations may lie behind Commander Thanou's proposal, the fact remains that he is *right*. This is the only point we presently know of where the Transhumanists' plans can be attacked—their only current point of vulnerability. We must exploit it. For one thing, we may be able to acquire valuable intelligence about the Transhumanist underground in the course of the operation."

"Maybe from Dr. Frey, if she can in fact be turned and brought back for debriefing," Mondrago ventured.

"Yes," Jason nodded. "Franco must have spilled *something* to her in the course of their . . . relationship." He trusted himself to say nothing more. He was coping with the unaccustomed—not to say unimaginable—sensation of feeling gratitude to Rutherford.

"An excellent point," nodded Rutherford.

"But the expense!" wailed Martiletto. "We just sent one expedition of four persons back nearly three millennia. Now you want us to send another!"

"The Authority has fairly substantial contingency reserve funds," said Jason, refraining from commenting on the council's notorious stinginess in spending them. "If this isn't an extraordinary emergency, I don't know what is."

"It would require extensive preparation," said Kubischev, wavering.

"Of course," agreed Jason. "But that doesn't matter. What counts is not the time we depart from, but the time we arrive in the target milieu."

"Quite true," said Rutherford with another nod, this time a brisk subject-closing one. "If there is no further discussion, I call for a vote."

CHAPTER TWENTY-TWO

THE TEMPORAL REGULATORY AUTHORITY solemnly maintained that its enforcement arm was not even quasi-military in nature. And, for a fact, the Temporal Service had never been noted for military punctilio. Nevertheless, the two new members of the team rose to their feet into something resembling the position of attention when Mondrago called out "Attention on deck!" and Jason entered the briefing room. They knew his reputation in the Service, and that he held the permanent rank of Commander in the Hesperian Colonial Rangers, not exactly an ill-regarded outfit.

"As you were," he said, studying the two as they resumed their seats. Like every officer who has ever led troops into battle, he would have liked to have had more of them. But he hadn't dared to press his luck by demanding that more than four people be displaced such a vast—and correspondingly expensive—temporal "distance." And he had to admit that, on short notice, it had been hard enough to find even two combat-trained people, not otherwise occupied, who possessed the particular qualifications required, including the ability to blend in fifth-century B.C. Greece. He didn't really expect them to have to do any blending, but Rutherford had been adamant.

It was that very difficulty in finding suitable people that had led Jason to accept a woman, despite his misgivings in light of the social milieu into which they would be displaced. And he couldn't quarrel with Pauline Da Cunha's combat record—in fact, on further reflection he'd decided he was lucky to have her after all. She was wiry, deceptively small, and dark enough to require a cover story as a Hellenized native of Caria in Asia Minor.

Adam Logan was of average size (hence on the large side, where they were going) and unobtrusively muscular, with nondescript features and medium-brown hair and eyes. He was sufficiently unremarkable-looking to pass in a wide range of Caucasian-inhabited historical settings, which made him valuable to the Service. His quiet competence made him even more valuable.

"By now," Jason began, "you've gone through all the preliminary procedures, including your microbiological 'cleansing' and the acquisition of the appropriate dialect of ancient Greek through direct neural induction." Jason didn't really expect them to be doing any hobnobbing with the locals on this expedition; it was just something else Rutherford had insisted on. "You have also received extensive orientation on the target milieu in general terms. This is in the nature of your actual mission briefing.

"You both volunteered on the strength of the highly classified information that was offered to you, including the involvement of the Teloi aliens. So you know that this mission is not our usual escort duty—nursemaiding teams of researchers. In fact, it's unique in the history of the Service. This time we're going up against illegal time travelers—a surviving cadre of Transhumanists, in fact."

"That last part helped induce us to volunteer, sir," said Da Cunha. Logan's expression confirmed it.

"I know. I'm sure there would have been no lack of volunteers if we had put out a general call for them. We didn't, partly due to security considerations but mostly because we could only use people with certain qualifications. We're almost certainly going to be facing modern weapons, so we've obtained special permission to use such weapons ourselves. And you two are experts with those as well as with the various low-technology weapons we in the Service normally take with us into the past."

"What kind of firepower are we going to be dealing with, sir?" asked Da Cunha, who clearly did the talking for this duo. "We've heard that you had some run-ins with these, uh, Teloi when you were in the Bronze Age."

"The Teloi use rather low-powered neural paralyzers, designed to resemble heads—'Heads of the Hydra' they're called—when dealing with the primitive local humans. For serious work, they have weapon-grade lasers; the only ones I saw were pistol-sized, so I can't say whether or not they have anything heavier. As for the Transhumanists, I simply don't know. I never encountered any of their stuff—I got the impression that they preferred to use the local stuff whenever possible, thus minimizing the chances of having some awkward explaining to do. But since they have no scruples about taking modern equipment, up to and including an aircar, back in time, we dare not assume that they didn't take modern arms as well."

Da Cunha spoke up again. "What about us, sir? We *do* have scruples. Surely we've had to give some thought to avoiding the possibility of our weapons being observed."

That's an understatement, thought Jason, recalling Rutherford's jitters. "You are correct. A bit of forced-draft engineering was required. I had a hand in the design myself." He reached out an arm, and Mondrago handed him what appeared to be a four-foot walking stick of the sort typically used by the ancient Greeks, perhaps a trifle stouter than most such sticks.

"You will note a row of small knobs along the shaft, about a foot from one end, appearing to be natural bumps on the wood. If you depress the forward one. . . ." He did so, and the far end of the "stick" flipped open and folded out into a set of focusing lenses about three inches in diameter.

"The basic mechanism is that of the standard Takashima laser carbine, but miniaturized and redesigned to fit into this shape. Like the standard Takashima, it functions in two modes: 'kill' and 'stun.' In the former mode, it is a weapon-grade laser; in the latter, the laser is powered down to a guide beam to ionize the air, along which an electrical charge is carried. These functions are activated by pressing the second and third knobs respectively. The fourth knob back is the actual trigger. The fifth knob activates a harmless visible-light setting, which may be useful as we're going to be spending part of our time underground. Finally, the energy cells that provide power are fed in through this slot, opened by pressing the sixth knob. We are under orders to retrieve all ejected cells and bring them back with us." Jason ignored his listeners' expressions on hearing this, hardly the kind of order a combat infantryman wants to hear.

"As you know," he continued, "even the standard Takashima is not a battlefield weapon; you wouldn't want to take it up against opposition in powered combat armor. That is doubly true of this little improvisation, given the amount of power we've had to sacrifice on the altar of inconspicuousness. But it ought to be adequate for our needs, as any action we see should be at very short ranges."

Da Cunha looked thoughtful. "The stunner setting ought to work particularly well on this mission. For one thing, Greece has a dry climate; as we all know, the electrical charge does stupid things in rain or even high humidity. And as we also know, metal armor conducts the charge and actually attracts it."

"Agreed, with the caveat that our targets almost certainly won't be wearing armor. However," Jason continued, and his expression turned more chilling than he knew, "in the absence of orders to the contrary, your weapons should be permanently set on 'kill.' Remember, it's impossible for us to bring back prisoners for interrogation, however much I'd like to. There are two exceptions to this, which I'll get to in a few minutes."

Jason turned toward the rear wall of the room and touched a remote-control unit. Part of the wall flickered and became a screen displaying a map of the Marathon plain. He indicated Mount Kotroni, to the northwest of the plain. "We will materialize here, a few minutes after the point in time—precisely ascertainable thanks to my recorder implant—when Alexandre and I left Pan on Mount Agriliki." His listeners' looks of distaste at the mention of Pan were unmistakable, though quickly smoothed over. Their orientation had included imagery of the artificially engendered hybrid being. "At that time, the Transhumanists were on their way in a Teloi aircar to take him to Mount Kotroni, overlooking the current phase of the Battle of Marathon." He touched more controls, and color-coded battle lines appeared. "The Persians will have hastily formed a new line, adjacent to their camp, to shield the embarkation of their ships. As the Greeks—advancing slowly at this point—approach this line, the Transhumanists' plan to induce panic in the Persians by means of a sonic projector—a technique which, as we know, is useless against modern countermeasures, but which ought to serve this purpose—

while having Pan appear on the slopes about here." He zoomed in on Kotroni and used a cursor to indicate its eastern slopes. "Our point of appearance will be here, so we can arrive unobserved by them. The element of surprise should be total." The cursor moved a third of the way around the peak, westward, to a level area on the opposite slope.

"We will proceed around behind them and kill all Transhumanists present. I want to emphasize that Pan must not be killed or even stunned, for he is essential to the next phase of the operation. He knows how to pilot the Teloi aircar—I ascertained that before making an agreement with him. In exchange for the pharmaceutical supplies we are bringing, he will take us to Athens in the aircar, which must be a model capable of carrying several passengers, given the use the Transhumanists were making of it. There we will make our way to the cavern under the Acropolis, where more Transhumanists— probably including their leader—and the members of the cult of which you learned in your orientation will be awaiting Pan. Here we will have to play it by ear: the Transhumanists must be neutralized with as few manifestations of out-of-period technology as possible. And Pan will tell the cultists that he's not really a god and that the Transhumanists are evil supernatural beings who have been deceiving them."

"That might not be easy, sir," said Logan slowly. "The ancient Greeks didn't have 'devils' or 'demons', and none of their gods were either purely good or purely evil. They were just a kind of super-powerful immortal humans."

"Very astute," said Jason with a sharp look. Evidently there was more to Logan than met the eye, or the ear. Rutherford had raised the same objection. "That's why I told Pan to use his imagination. But while awaiting retrieval on Crete I had time to think about it some more. In particular, I thought about a line of theological propaganda that the Persian commander Datis used on the Greek island of Delos on his way to Athens. There's no point in going into the details at this time, as it would sound like mumbo-jumbo to you. As a matter of fact, it *is* mumbo-jumbo. But since my return, after consultation with Rutherford and various experts on the period, I think it may work. It doesn't really fit into the conventional Greek version of metaphysics, but maybe Pan's word will carry weight anyway. As always, flexibility and adaptability are going to have to be our watchwords.

"At any rate, afterwards we will use the small gravitically focused explosive charge we're taking with us to seal the tunnel without doing any damage to the buildings above. The cavern will be gone, but the historically attested grotto sacred to Pan on the north slope of the Acropolis will remain. The Athenians will continue to offer annual sacrifices to Pan there, as history says they did, but the Transhumanists' twisted cult will be aborted.

"Now, there's one other matter—the second of the two 'exceptions' I mentioned in connection with weapon settings. At some point in this operation, it is highly probable that we will encounter Dr. Chantal Frey, a member of my prior expedition to this milieu. As you know from your orientation, she had her TRD surgically removed and may have defected to the Transhumanists." Jason said this in a very even tone of voice, and he noted his listeners' carefully neutral expressions at his choice of words. "She must not, under any circumstances, be killed. It is permissible, if the situation seems to warrant it, to stun her. I intend to bring her back with us, willingly or otherwise, by actual physical carriage just as we have always brought various items back. It is a method that has never been tried before with a human or any other living organism. In fact, the idea of doing so has never occurred to anyone before, doubtless because we're so accustomed to thinking exclusively in terms of our standard procedures. But I am advised that it is within the bounds of theoretical possibility.

"Now, as to your TRDs. You're probably wondering why they haven't been implanted yet. The reason is that they've only just become available. They are a new model, hastily developed and rushed into production for this mission. They are somewhat larger than the standard models, but the implantation will still be a minor operation. Unlike all TRDs up until now, these are not set to activate at a pre-set moment. Instead, they are designed to activate on command. The command is transmitted through my brain implant. I will decide when we are to be retrieved."

Da Cunha and Logan stared, for this was beyond unprecedented. "But how will anyone here know when to expect us?" Da Cunha asked.

"They won't." Jason permitted himself a wintery smile. "This, as we all know, would normally be out of the question due to 'traffic control' considerations on the displacer stage. Which, of course, is why TRDs like these have never been developed before; no one could imagine a use for them. But that issue won't arise this time, because the stage will be kept clear until we return. Which, in turn, won't be much of a problem because this is going to be the briefest extratemporal expedition in the entire history of the Authority. A couple of hours, if that, ought to be long enough for us to accomplish this mission, if it can be accomplished at all. And every additional minute we spend in the fifth century B.C. is just one additional chance for some kind of screw-up.

"Finally, Alexandre here is my second in command. This is due to his familiarity with the target milieu, despite his junior status in the Service. If either of you has a problem with this, now's the time to get it off your chest." Total silence answered him. "Very well. If there are no further questions, you are dismissed. We'll have further briefings, and opportunities to practice with these rather unique versions of the Takashima, at a later time."

As they filed out of the room, Mondrago lingered. "Sir, may I have a word?"

"Sure. What's on your mind?"

"Well, sir, about the 'all you can conveniently carry' rule on which you're basing your plan to bring Dr. Frey back to our time in the linear present. . . ." Mondrago trailed to a halt, looking uncharacteristically abashed.

"Yes?" Jason prompted. "What's the matter? You don't think it will work?"

"I'm sure I'm not qualified to say, sir," replied Mondrago, armoring himself in military formality. "If the experts say it will, I believe them. It just occurs to me that at the same time you're doing it . . . well, Pan is a fairly small being, and if it works at all I ought to be able to do the same with him."

Jason stared. "Are you saying you've decided you want to rescue Pan?"

"No, sir!" said Mondrago, a little too emphatically. "I'm just thinking that he might be a useful intelligence source, if we could bring him back for debriefing."

"I see." Jason carefully kept his face expressionless. "You know, you may have a point. I hadn't thought my idea out to its logical conclusion. I was thinking exclusively in terms of using it for Dr. Frey, because this is her proper time. But on reflection, that shouldn't matter; we're always bringing inanimate objects with us from their own periods in the past this way, and they stay here. Otherwise Rutherford wouldn't be able to keep that sword and the other souvenirs in his display case! And the experts keep telling me that whether the object is living or nonliving shouldn't matter. I'll tell you what: if the opportunity presents itself, without jeopardizing the success of the mission, I'll let you make the attempt. Good enough?"

"Yes, sir."

The time came, and the four of them filed onto the displacer stage with their "walking sticks." They also carried in-period daggers. Logan and Mondrago also carried the kind of satchels that ancient Greeks normally carried when going on lengthy walking journeys. The former contained the explosive charge; the latter the medical supplies for Pan, just in case Mondrago's idea didn't work. All of them carried, in the usual sort of waist-tied wallets, a supply of the energy cells for which they were strictly accountable.

Rutherford met them at the edge of the stage for the traditional handshake. On this occasion it seemed overlaid with a new grimness. In the past there had sometimes been a possibility that Rutherford was sending time travelers into battle; this time it was a certainty. As mission leader, Jason was the last to shake hands. But at the last moment he paused.

"Ah, Kyle . . . what with one thing and another, I haven't gotten around to asking you. But . . .?"

Rutherford's eyes met his. "Yes. It's still there."

Jason nodded. No more needed to be said. He mounted the stage.

CHAPTER TWENTY-THREE

THEY WERE ALL EXPERIENCED, so the disorientation didn't hit them too hard when the dome surrounding the displacer stage faded into oblivion as though it had never been and they stood on a ledge in Mount Kotroni's shadow.

Still, there was a moment when they would have been helpless had there been any hostiles present—assuming, of course, that those hostiles hadn't been stunned into immobility by their appearance out of thin air. It was why Jason had chosen the side of the hill opposite the side from which the Transhumanists would be overlooking the plain of Marathon, their attention riveted on the battle below and to the east.

That fixation couldn't be counted on, though, and the all-important element of surprise had to be preserved. Using the Service's standard hand signals, Jason motioned the others to follow him to the right. They silently worked their way around the hill's southern slopes, emerging into the morning sun. Jason spared an instant for a glance to the south, where the taller Mount Agrliki loomed beyond the Greek camp, defining the southeast end of the plain. Mere minutes ago, he thought with a sudden chill, his own three-months-younger self had left those slopes and was now flying his invisible aircar toward Athens. He couldn't let himself dwell on it, lest the sense of strangeness immobilize him.

They rounded the hill and the plain lay spread out before them. To the southeast the ground was choked with corpses, the detritus of the initial clash, where the inward-pivoting Greek flanks had crushed the Persian center a lesser trail of carnage extended northeast of that, following the path of the re-formed, grimly advancing phalanx that was now nearing the improvised Persian line defending the ships, almost directly to the east. Beyond that, the narrow beach was a scene out of hell, with the ships putting out to sea and the shallows choked with frantic men trying to find a ship, any ship, that would take them. On the Persian right, the Greek light troops were hunting scattered Persian stragglers into the great marsh.

The noise from the plain, compounded of the screams of the wounded, the panicked cries of the Persian fugitives, the shouted command, and the tramp of the phalanx's twenty thousand feet, was horrifying. But Jason knew it was about to rise to a truly hellish crescendo, for this was a lull in the battle, before the final clash.

Jason tried to imagine the exhaustion of the dust- and gore-encrusted hoplites of the phalanx, moving toward what by some accounts was to be the fiercest fighting of the day, where Callimachus and many others would fall. He knew that their exhaustion would allow the Persians to hold out long enough for all but seven of their ships to escape. He also knew—although it almost defied belief—that these same men would turn around later that same morning and march twenty-six miles *in armor* to Phalerum, where the Persian fleet would find them drawn up on the shore. Jason had to wonder how much of a fight they would really have been able to put up at that point, had it come to that. But after what the Persians had just experienced, they would have no appetite to put it to the test. They would sail away.

Then Jason turned the final corner of the goat-trail they were following. There, on a ledge beyond a boulder, were three Transhumanists—none of whom was Franco—and Pan. He motioned his followers to a halt and crept forward to peer over the boulder.

The Transhumanists, who had a good view of the Persian line that Datis had somehow managed to improvise, were aiming a subsonic projector of the kind he had imagined they would use. It was a small model, with barely enough range. But all that would be required of it would be to induce emotional turmoil in just a few men, here and there in a hastily organized formation of men already badly shaken. That would be enough to dissolve that formation. Off to the side was the Teloi aircar, an open-topped model large enough to carry four passengers besides the pilot, not quite as overdecorated as the "chariots" Jason remembered.

Only three of them, Jason thought. No doubt there had originally been a fourth, but that one—the murderer of Bryan Landry and would-be murderer of Mondrago and himself—now lay near the Greek camp with Mondrago's sling-pellet in his brain. *And they're preoccupied. This ought to be easy.* He signaled the others to slide forward and join him behind the boulder. They noiselessly took up their positions and he prepared to give the signal.

At that instant, at the far end of the ledge beyond the Transhumanist group, an inhumanly tall figure appeared.

One of the Transhumanists cried out. They all whirled to face the new apparition. Pan cowered. Jason, his tactical calculations thrown off, motioned Mondrago and the others to lay quietly as he tried to evaluate the situation's new dynamics. Da Cunha and Logan stared over the top of the boulder wide-eyed, for this was their first sight of Teloi in the flesh.

Zeus stalked forward. Three other Teloi followed him: a male who somewhat resembled him, another male who seemed more powerfully built than the Teloi norm, and a female who, like Zeus, exhibited the Teloi indicia of aging. Jason didn't recognize any of the three, but certain hard-to-define qualities about them made him wonder if he was looking at Poseidon, Ares and Hera.

One thing was certain: none of them looked happy, Zeus least of all. And all wore, on the belts of their tunics, laser pistols of the kind that had killed Sidney Nagel on the island of Kalliste shortly before it had exploded, leaving the remnants that would one day be known as the Santorini group.

The Transhumanist who seemed to be the leader—he looked to be one of the varieties gengineered for intelligence and initiative, at the expense of some of the physical attributes—bowed and addressed Zeus in the tone of patently bogus servility Jason had heard Franco use. "Why, greetings, Lord. This is most unexpected." He looked around in vain for an aircar. "How did you—?"

"The sky-chariot that brought us has departed," said Zeus, his voice thick with an emotion that made it even more disturbing than Teloi voices normally were. "Aphrodite took it away, for we will not be needing it. We mean to reclaim this one, which we unwisely let you use before we learned of your impious betrayal of us, your gods."

"Whatever do you mean, Lord?" The Transhumanist's reverential tone was getting a little frayed around the edges. As a member of one of the upper Transhumanist castes, he was struggling to suppress a heritage of arrogance. "As our leader Franco has repeatedly told you, we wish only to serve you."

"You lie, as Franco has lied to us from the beginning. He promised to enable the Persians to restore Hippias to power in Athens so he could complete his great work: the raising of a temple almost worthy of me. But now I see your true aim. You mean to give the victory to the Athenians!"

"A minor change in plans, Lord—a mere tactical adjustment." The Transhumanist's struggle to maintain his pose of obsequiousness was now comically obvious—or at least it would have been comical under any other circumstances. "Rest assured that our long-term goal is unchanged: leading Athens back into its proper reverence for you."

"More lies! It is all clear to me now! Your only concern is to establish a cult of this grotesque artificial being Pan which we enabled you to create but which is now under your control. And you intend to commit the ultimate blasphemy by establishing him as a god, for your own selfish purposes!"

Pan looked like he wanted to burrow into the stony soil of the hillside.

Zeus was raving now, his features working convulsively. "You are no better than all other humans—the original stock, and the Heroes we created in an effort to guide the others back to their proper role. You 'Transhumanists' claim to be a superior strain, but you are like all the rest: treacherous and disloyal and, above all, ungrateful to us, your creators and your gods! We should never have summoned your species up from apedom!"

A strong shudder convulsed the Transhumanist and his façade of worshipfulness seemed to fall from him and shatter, revealing what lay beneath. Not just his face but his entire body was one great sneer of loathing and contempt.

"Our gods? You senile, decayed, demented fool! You are inferior even to the lesser breeds of humans. You have long since outlived your time—and you have now outlived your usefulness to us, your supplanters—the new gods!" And with motion of almost insect-like quickness, possible only to genetically upgraded reflexes, the Transhumanist reached inside his chiton, pulled out an extremely compact laser pistol, and shot Zeus in the upper chest.

In the late twentieth century, after the invention of the laser but when weapon-grade applications of it had been only a theoretical possibility, people had had peculiar ideas about them. The vision of a blinding but silent beam of light was wrong in every particular; it was invisible in vacuum, and in atmosphere there was only a sparkling trail of ionized air, accompanied by a sharp but not very loud crack as air rushed in to fill the tube of vacuum that had been drilled through it. And a continuous laser beam swinging back and forth and reducing its target to sizzling salami slices was out of the question; even aside from the impossible energy demands, any attempt to do it in atmosphere would have come to grief on the hard facts of thermal bloom. Instead, a pulse of directed energy burned a hole in the victim, with a burst of superheated pinkish steam—the human or Teloi body is, after all, seventy percent water—whose knockback effect now sent Zeus' body toppling over backwards.

The other two Teloi drew their weapons, as did the two subordinate Transhumanists. There was an intense instant of crisscrossing, crackling beams. One of the Transhumanists went down, as did all the Teloi.

It all happened so quickly that the last Teloi was sinking to the ground before Jason could react.

"Get them!" he snapped, rising to his feet from behind the boulder and activating his "walking stick." He speared the Transhumanist leader with a series of rapid-fire laser pulses more powerful than those of the pistols. Mondrago and the others opened up at appreciably the same instant, and the Transhumanists died, practically incinerated by multiple laser burns.

Jason turned away toward Pan. But as he did he heard a low, croaking "Jason." Zeus was still barely alive.

Moved by some impulse, Jason walked over to the Teloi with whom he had once conspired the "imprisonment of the Titans," and looked down into the nonhuman face. It was contorted with pain, but the strange pale-blue-and-azure eyes held an odd clarity, as though the clouds of insanity had dissipated.

"Jason," Zeus repeated, though this time it was more a whisper than a croak. "Yes, I do remember you. It was so long ago, when Kalliste exploded and our older generation were trapped forever." He stated it matter-of-factly—nothing about imprisoning the Titans in Tartarus. All his delusions were gone, burned away by the fires of agony. "You made that possible."

"I and my two companions," Jason nodded. "Both of them died to do it. One was Oannes."

"Yes, I remember him too—one of the Nagommo." The Teloi's voice held none of the hate that would once have suffused it at the name of his race's mortal enemies. Even that was gone now. "And I remember Perseus, who afterwards established my worship at Mycenae as king of the gods. King of the gods!" The huge eyes closed, and Jason thought Zeus had spoken his last. But then they fluttered open, and were empty not just of lunacy but of everything, holding the ultimate horror of absolute nullity as he looked back over thousands of barren, pointless years with the pitiless clarity of impending death. His desolate whisper was barely audible.

"Lies. All lies. No, not even lies. Just . . . nothing." The Teloi's last breath whistled out in an oddly humanlike way.

Jason turned away and looked around him. In the usual way of laser firefights, it had been very quiet, without spectacular visual effects. None of the battling thousands on the plain below—none of whom were looking up the hill in any case—had noticed. Besides, even as the Transhumanists were dying, the Athenian war-cry of *Alleeee!* had arisen again, and the grinding crash as the phalanx had rammed into the Persian holding force.

Jason couldn't pause to admire the view. He rushed over to where Pan crouched in a fetal position. Grabbing a shoulder, he rolled the being over. Large brown eyes went even wider.

"It's you!" squeaked Pan. "How—?"

"It's a long story, and we haven't got time. What I need to know is this: does the agreement we made a few minutes ago over there on Mount Agriliki still hold?"

"Yes. But now you're suddenly dressed differently, and you seem somehow changed. And who are these others?"

"Never mind. You said you knew how to pilot this Teloi aircar. I need for you to take us to Athens, as fast as it can possibly be managed while maximizing concealment."

"Yes . . . yes, that was always the plan. And there is a prearranged landing site—the precinct that's always been sacred to Zeus, and where his unfinished temple is located. Nobody ever goes there now."

"Good." The irony was not lost on Jason, as he glanced at the detritus of the erstwhile king of the gods. "Do you also know how to program the aircar's autopilot?"

"Yes, I do."

"Then let's go." Jason turned to his subordinates. "Put that sonic projector into the aircar's baggage compartment—it should fit, and we ought not to leave it here. Move!"

They piled into the aircar. Jason had intended to be the last one in, but Mondrago, standing on the rim of the ledge, called to him. "Sir, look down here."

Jason joined him. He had forgotten the roar of battle from the plain below. But now he followed Mondrago's pointing finger to the east. The makeshift Persian line had given way, and the battle was dissolving into a chaotic melee on the narrow beach as the Greeks pursued the fleeing Persians through the sands and the shallows as they sought rescue, desperately scrambling aboard the ships that Datis' last stand had enabled to disembark before it had collapsed in—

"Panic," Mondrago stated. "The Persians panicked after all, even though the Transhumanists never got a chance to use that sonic projector! Ah . . . what's funny, sir?"

Jason brought his chuckling under control. "Of course the Persians panicked! I mean, after the hell they had been through in the first stage of the battle, the one we were involved in . . . and remember, this Persian battle-line was a pick-up force of stragglers Datis somehow put together to cover the embarkation. And now they saw that blood-spattered phalanx coming at them again. What could be more natural than panic? So you see . . . *it happened anyway!*"

Mondrago nodded his understanding. "And because of the 'prophecy' that Pan gave Pheidippedes on the road from Sparta a few days ago, the Athenians will attribute it to Pan and sacrifice to him in that grotto every year, just like history says."

"Exactly. As usual, reality protects itself. Come on, let's go."

They departed, leaving the bodies of the would-be gods to the carrion birds.

CHAPTER TWENTY-FOUR

THEY FLEW SOUTHWESTWARD, relying on the aircar's low altitude and high speed to avoid being observed—or, at least, to assure that anyone who *did* observe it would not be believed. As they curved around the lower northern slopes of Mount Pentelikon, Jason reflected that somewhere up there on the summit was at least one Transhumanist, ready to flash the "shield signal" that would so perplex contemporary Athenians and later historians. He would subsequently return to his own time and place, for they had no leisure to attempt a search for him. Then the mountain was behind them and they sped across the plain of Attica.

As they went, Jason spoke to Pan in haste, because they had little time. "Do you know anything about the beliefs of the Persians? The teachings of their prophet Zoroaster?"

"Some," said Pan, clearly puzzled by the question. "Franco and others have spoken of it."

"Good, because when you address the cultists, this is what I want you to say." Jason set it out in a few swift sentences, which was all he had time for. Pan frowned but claimed to understand. Jason could only accept that.

Pan brought them carefully around to approach Athens from the southwest, where no one's attention was fixed. There, tucked into an angle of this century's unimpressive city walls, was the dust-blown, weed-choked precinct sacred to Zeus. Here stood the forest of unfinished columns that had been intended to uphold the immense temple the tyrant Hippias had begun to erect, ostensibly to the glory of Zeus but in reality to his own and that of the Pisistratid dynasty of political bosses. It was what Napoleon might have built as a monument to his own ego if he had been a Classical Greek. Now it stood in its permanently unfinished state, left by the Athenian democracy as an object lesson in the futility of dictatorial megalomania.

Pan landed the aircar in the roofless space that was to have been the temple's vast central aisle. As they got out, alert to the possibility of stray bystanders—even more unlikely than ever, on this day—Jason spoke to Pan. "Now, I want you to set a course into the autopilot which will, when signaled to do so, send this aircar out over water— I don't care where, as long as it's a remote stretch of coast—and then into a crash dive. I don't really expect to use it," he added, seeing Pan's expression. "It's just in case of contingencies."

Pan obeyed, as he was conditioned to do, then handed Jason a remote-control unit, small and austerely functional by Teloi standards. "You need only press this stud to activate the command."

"Good." Jason put the unit in the pouch at his waist. "All right, everybody, let's go!"

It was only about a third of a mile to their destination-point on the Acropolis' north slope, as the crow flew. Of course, crows didn't have to negotiate the twisting narrow streets of Athens. But Jason's map display helped keep them from deviating from the most nearly direct route. And those streets were practically deserted, with the old men and women and children thronging the Agora on the far side of the Acropolis, waiting for news of the battle. The baggage compartment had held a hooded cloak in which the Transhumanists had customarily wrapped Pan when it was necessary to move him about where he might be observed. Swathed in it and hunched over, he might be mistaken for an elderly woman, as long as the cloak fell to the ground and concealed his hooves.

As they hastened through the streets, Jason briefly wondered if that slightly younger Jason Thanou was even now on the far side of Athens retrieving Chantal's TRD from Themistocles' house, or if he had already departed for Crete.

Moving along the narrow roadway that ran along the north side of the Acropolis, with the steep hillside immediately to their left, they reached a point directly below the grotto of Pan. The decaying Bronze Age wall did not extend here, for it only enclosed the area around the Acropolis' western end. The hillside here was regarded as unscalable. Jason understood why as they scrambled up it, not wishing to waste time and risk notice by proceeding around to the gate in the wall and backtracking along the pathway Jason and Mondrago had followed before.

There was no one outside the grotto. Pan had explained that the cultists would not arrive until later, although they were probably already on their way, following the pathway from the gate, which was another reason Jason hadn't wanted to take that route. The question was whether Franco was already inside. It was at this point that they were going to have to begin playing it by ear.

"Do you remember where you hit the rear wall?" Jason asked Mondrago.

"About here, I think." Still, Mondrago had to pound several times before finding the right spot. The door-sized segment they remembered swung open. He and Jason led the way in, down the crude, shallow steps and across the small cave and into the tunnel. They activated their laser weapons' "flashlight" feature as the light from the doorway dimmed. There was no light from up ahead, and no sound. Jason dared to breathe a sigh of relief.

They entered the large cavern holding the eerily archaic cult statue. But the idol was not on its dais. Rather, it was sunk into the floor, leaving the hatchway Jason remembered Pan emerging from in a glare of artificial light.

"Franco will be here any moment," said Pan nervously as he busied himself lighting oil lamps.

"With how many others?" demanded Mondrago.

"No more than one. Aside from the one on Mount Pentelikon, that's all he has left." Jason nodded; he'd always thought there had to be a limit to how many people the Transhumanists, however advanced their time-travel technology, could displace, especially when they were also displacing the mass of an aircar. "He'll be expecting the four others from Marathon to be waiting here with me. Oh . . . and he'll also probably bring the woman defector. He's represented her to the cultists as a priestess."

Jason made no comment. He looked down into the chamber into which the idol had sunk. "It looks like there ought to be room for all of us to squeeze in down there. Pan, you wait up here where Franco expects you."

The four of them descended a short ladder and crowded together. It was at least as tight a fit as Jason had thought . . . and though the cavern was cool, they had all been sweating profusely in the outside August heat.

"It's just as well," whispered Mondrago, as though reading Jason's thoughts, "that none of us have been eating the local diet. All those beans—!"

"Shhh!" Jason shushed him, for there was a faint sound of approaching footsteps above.

They hadn't long to wait before Franco's unmistakable voice spoke, curtly and without preamble. "Where are my men?"

"Dead, Lord," squeaked Pan. "Zeus and three other Teloi arrived atop Mount Kotroni and accused you of betraying them. A fight broke out and everyone, on both sides, was killed. Afterwards, I took the aircar and came here according to the plan, as I knew you would wish."

"You lie, you nauseating piece of filth! *All* of them, on *both* sides killed? Do you take me for a fool?" There was a meaty smack, followed by a high-pitched whimpering.

"Don't, Franco!" came a female voice—Chantal Frey's voice. "After all, he came back as ordered."

"He had no choice." Franco's voice held a dismissiveness that transcended contempt.

"They're coming!" said a male voice unknown to Jason.

Franco's voice muttered a non-verbal curse. "All right, we have no time. We'll get to the bottom of this later. You: get down there and be prepared to play your role." Franco didn't look down into the compartment below the dais, for he had no reason to. Pan scurried down the ladder and crammed himself in with Jason and the others. His body odor was oddly acrid, but none of them were particularly squeamish. Above, Franco must have activated a control, for the cult statue rose up to its position on the dais and the hatch closed. Darkness settled over them.

Sounds from above were now muffled, but Jason could discern

shuffling feet as the cultists filed into the cavern. It didn't sound to him like as large a group as he had seen here before, but that made sense on this day; this would be mostly women and older men, with only those younger men who had managed to evade military service. Then he heard the droning, somehow sinister chant he had heard before. Soon the chanting began to be responsive, alternating with various ritual signals. Jason paid no attention to the sounds of the ceremony, which had probably been crafted to conform to the type of ritual that members of the various mystery religions would expect. Then it stopped abruptly, replaced by the stirring sound of Franco's voice.

"Rejoice! Civilization is saved! While other Athenians huddle in the Agora, quaking with fear, Pan now grants you, his elect, the news they await. Know, then, that at this very moment, the battle is already won. The barbarians, driven mad with fear by Pan, have fled shrieking to their ships. The only ones left on Attic soil now lie dead on the plain of Marathon or drowned in the marshes."

The rapturous collective sigh was audible.

Franco's voice dropped an octave. "But those barbarians who escaped still believe they can defy the will of the gods and vent their rage on Athens. They have now set their course for Cape Sunium, and Phalerum beyond it, where they mean to land and descend on this defenseless city."

There was a faint hissing sound of indrawn breath.

"But fear nothing!" Franco's remarkable voice again became a clarion. "Pan has granted to his priestess Cleothera a vision of the future. Hear the prophecy!"

There was a pause, either intentionally or unintentionally dramatic, before Chantal spoke. Jason thought he could discern a quavering hesitancy in her voice. To the cultists, the effect must have been one not of ambivalence but of eeriness. And her singsong tone of recitation by rote must have been exactly what they expected of an oracle through whom a god spoke to mortals.

"Rejoice," she intoned. "At this moment, the men of Athens have recognized the danger, and are girding themselves to march back. And they will arrive at Phalerum in time! The Persians, seeing the men who had just bested them drawn up on the shore, will wet their barbarian trousers in fear and sail away."

Another, even more relieved sigh arose.

"And now," Franco resumed, "your god has once again shown the favor in which he holds you. You have already received oracles that will enable your families to enrich themselves when the events they foretell—the second Persian invasion ten years from now, the wars between Athens and Sparta, and all the rest—come to pass. Thus you will be able to profit at the expense of this city that has never accorded Pan proper worship! And he will always hold you and your descendants in this same favor, as long as you unquestioningly obey his commands, as told to you by us, his messengers, while keeping your vow of secrecy."

There was a chorus of frantically affirmative noises.

"Finally, even though his previous appearance was spoiled by impious intruders, you will now receive the ultimate reward of your devotion . . . for now *the Great God Pan appears to you!*"

All at once, the hatch above Jason's head was outlined in light that shone through the cracks as the harsh electrical light he had seen before flooded the cavern. He heard the gasps of the cultists as they were temporarily blinded by the unnatural glare. Then the hatch, with the idol atop it, sank down, leaving the opening. Pan ascended the short ladder and the light above faded, allowing the cultists to see the apparition in the dimness.

Jason, crouched in the darkness below, heard the weird half-moan and half-sigh that arose above. It was a sound that no group of people in Jason's world could have produced, for it held the kind of skepticism-free terrified ecstasy that the human race had lost the capacity to feel when it had emerged from the shadows of superstition. Gradually it droned down into silence, leaving a breathless hush.

The silence seemed to last a long time.

Jason felt Mondrago's body, pressed up against his in the confines of the chamber, go rigid with tension.

Pan's not going to go through with it, thought Jason, with a sickening sense of defeat. *He can't. The habit of obedience is too strong, and now it's reasserting itself. He's going to do exactly as Franco told him to do. I was an idiot to think otherwise.*

All at once, the silence was shattered by a high-pitched sound. It took Jason a second to recognize the sound for what it was, for he had never heard it or even imagined it could be.

It was the sound of Pan laughing.

"You *fools!* Are you really such idiots that you still think I'm your god Pan? Now the time has come when I can enjoy telling you how you've been deceived."

Jason tried to imagine Franco's state of shock. It must, he thought, be as complete as that of the worshippers, though for different reasons. And there was nothing Franco could do. He could hardly shoot or otherwise silence the "god." He could only stand, paralyzed, and listen as his creation's jeering voice went on, tearing down his edifice of intrigue with every syllable.

"Know, then, simpletons, that I am come from the East, for I am of the *daiva*, the anti-gods who impersonate and thwart the gods just as black smoke rises along with the sacred fire. Even as the Ionians of Didyma worshipped one of my fellows thinking him to be their god Apollo, so you have worshiped me! Oh fools, fools, fools!"

As Zoroastrian theology it was, of course, perfect gibberish. But these people didn't know that. They had some vague knowledge of the religion's concepts and terminology, for their fellow Greeks in Ionia had long been in contact with the Persians. And they had heard of what Datis had told the Apollo-worshipers of Delos about the oracle at Didyma. So this all held a ring of horrible verisimilitude for them, and continued to do so as Pan raved on.

"You think what I have done at Marathon today was to save Athens, this stinking pig-wallow you call a city? Ha! I did it to punish the Persians for their failure to worship the one *true* God: Ahriman, lord of the darkness which must inevitably engulf the universe when the last light finally gutters out, no matter how many futile fires the priests of Ahura Mazda ignite. But the Persians have chosen to worship Ahura Mazda, following their stupid prophet Zoroaster, and now they have paid for their folly. *And so shall you, fools!* For my servants are here to destroy you!"

It took a fraction of a second for Jason to realize what Pan meant. Then he barked "Move!" at the others and forced his stiffened legs to propel him up the ladder, to stand beside Pan.

The light in the cavern was dim enough that his eyes required no real adaptation. He saw the cultists, still immobilized with shock, and, off to the side, Franco with Chantal beside him, staring wildly. Another figure, which he recognized as one of the middle-level

Transhumanists, lunged at him, drawing a dagger as he moved. Jason brought up his "walking stick" and speared the man with a laser beam.

Behind him, Mondrago and the others were scrambling up the ladder and, as they emerged into the cavern, firing laser bolts into the mass of cultists. In this dimness, the trails of ionization were almost bright enough to resemble lightning. And the vicious crack was loud in this confined space.

The cultists went mad with terror. They pelted toward the tunnel mouth, trampling and crushing each other in their hysterical haste to be gone from what had become a chamber of inexplicable horror.

The rapid-fire laser bolts stabbed again and again into that writhing, screaming mass of bodies, and the stench of burned flesh filled the cavern.

But Jason had eyes for none of that. He swung his weapon toward Franco.

With that unnatural quickness of his, Franco whipped out from under his tunic a small laser pistol of the same model his fellows had used earlier on Mount Kotroni. But he did not point it at Jason. Instead, he grasped Chantal by the upper arm, twisted it up in an obviously painful grip, and swung her in front of him, placing the pistol's focusing lens against her head.

Chantal gave a cry of pain and something worse than pain. "Franco . . . darling. . . ."

"Shut up, you pathetic Pug cunt!" Franco snarled, and yanked her arm further up, eliciting a fresh cry. "You're useless for my purposes without your TRD—except as a shield."

Jason forced himself to remain calm and do nothing reckless like trying for a head shot, for even if it succeeded it might well cause Franco's trigger finger to spasm in death. He looked around. The last of the surviving cultists had by now fled down the tunnel, and Mondrago, Da Cunha, and Logan were also covering Franco and his captive with their weapons. Pan groveled beside Jason's feet.

Franco looked them over for a moment, then smiled at Jason. "So . . . you've come back, while an earlier version of you is simultaneously here. The fuddy-duddies who run the Authority will never recover!"

Jason was in no mood to appreciate Franco's perspicacity, which would doubtless also enable him to recognize the falsity of any offer to let him live. "Let her go," he said evenly, "and you can have a quick, clean death. Your choice."

Franco gave another infuriating smile. "I believe I'll choose no death whatever. I'm taking her with me. If anyone tries to stop me, she dies. If I see anyone following me, she dies."

Jason put on a devil-may-care expression. "What makes you think a threat to the life of a defector is going to deter us?"

"It shouldn't. But if I know Pugs, it will." The false levity abruptly slid away, and Franco's face, for all its designer Classical handsomeness, grew very ugly. "No more childish bluffing! I'm going now, to the precinct of Zeus, where that repulsive little genetic monstrosity must have brought the Teloi aircar." He gave Pan a look of loathing. "I wish I were in a position to kill it now, for its betrayal. But no; that would be kinder than letting it live."

Beside his legs, Jason felt Pan stiffen, and a kind of convulsion go through the misshapen body. All at once a high-pitched scream of pent-up hate split the air of the cavern and Pan's goatish legs propelled him forward like a projectile.

Startled, Franco pulled Chantal with him as he tried to avoid that sudden attack. He almost succeeded. Pan careened against his and his prisoner's legs, knocking them both off balance. He tried to grapple Franco's legs. Instinctively, Franco brought his laser pistol down hard. The butt struck Pan's right temple, under the horn, with a sickening crunching sound. Pan went limp.

Mondrago was the first to recover. With an inarticulate shout, he fired at the now partially exposed Transhumanist. But Franco was still staggering, and the aim was off. The laser beam brushed against his left arm, and also Chantal's, which Franco had never quite let go. Her scream immobilized them all just long enough for Franco to bring his laser pistol back up against her head.

"Now, where were we?" said Franco, although his face was too contorted with pain to manage a mocking smile. "Remember, nobody is to follow us, or she dies. After I reach the aircar, I'll let her go. After all, I think I've had the full use of her! You're welcome to her now, Thanou—not that I'd give her much of a recommendation." He gave Chantal's laser-burned left arm a particularly vicious jerk and pulled her along with him as he backed into the tunnel. The sound of their footsteps and Chantal's whimpering gradually receded.

Jason dropped to his knees beside Pan. As expected, the artificial being whose fragility Jason had thought he had sensed was dead.

"I'm sorry, sir," said Mondrago miserably. "I didn't mean to hurt her. I thought I could—"

"Forget it." Jason held up a hand for silence, and waited until he was sure Franco had had time to exit the tunnel. "All right. The three of you set up the explosive charge in the tunnel, as per the plan. And . . . leave Pan's body in here. After you've set the timer, come to the precinct of Zeus. I'm going there now."

"What?" Mondrago goggled. "But, sir—"

"Don't worry. Of course I'm not going to let Franco see me—at least not until he reaches the aircar. There . . . well, I think I have a way of dealing with him."

"Let me come too!"

"No. There's less chance of him spotting just one of us. Now just follow orders for once, damn it!" And Jason plunged into the tunnel.

Franco had closed the outer door, but like Houdini's safes it was easy to open from the *inside*. Jason scrambled down the steep, rocky slope of the Acropolis and slipped through the twisting alley-like streets. Once he caught a glimpse of Franco and Chantal far ahead, and instantly flattened himself against a wall before resuming his stealthy pursuit.

He emerged from the labyrinth of alleys and buildings into the open area where the unfinished temple stood, just in time to see Franco drag Chantal between two of the topless columns. He followed, circling around and passing through the colonnades at another point. Franco had mounted the open-topped aircar and was pulling Chantal up onto it.

"But you said you'd let me go!" she protested, struggling to resist.

"Don't be even stupider than you have to be. I lied, of course. No, I think I'll take you with me. I can amuse myself with you in various ways before my TRD activates. By then, you'll be begging me to kill you. But I probably won't. No, I believe I'll just leave you permanently stranded . . . an unattached woman with no family, in this society . . . maimed and disfigured, as you'll be by then after what I'll have done to you . . . yes." With a final heave of his good arm, Franco hauled her up onto the aircar.

Jason stepped out from behind his concealing column. "Hi!" he called out with a jaunty wave. In his hand was a small black object: the remote control unit Pan had given him.

Franco and Chantal, standing on the aircar's edge, both stared.

Jason pressed the stud.

The autopilot awoke, and under its control the aircar lurched aloft.

Chantal lost her balance and fell a few feet. The impact, landing on her burned left arm, brought a gasping shriek of pain.

But Jason's attention was fixed on the swiftly rising aircar. Franco was windmilling his arms, frantically trying to regain his balance. But he toppled over the side. He managed to catch the rim and hold on as the aircar rose still higher and began to swing into a southward course.

Jason took careful aim with his disguised laser carbine and burned Franco in his good right shoulder. With a cry of pain, the Transhumanist lost his grip and fell. He hit the stump of an unfinished column face-first with bone-cracking force, then fell the rest of the way to the ground and lay still. The aircar continued on its way, and would plunge into the sea, vanishing from an era in which it did not belong.

Jason walked over to Franco. The Transhumanist's ribcage was crushed, and when he tried to speak only a feeble, gurgling hiss of agony emerged from between his splintered teeth, along with a froth of blood.

Jason drew his dagger, but then stopped. *Why bother?* He sheathed the dagger, turned away and went to examine Chantal. Her breathing was shallow, and aside from her laser burn, she had broken her right leg. But she would live. Franco's noise had ceased by the time she regained consciousness.

"Lie still," he told her. "You're safe. Franco's dead."

"Jason," she whispered weakly, "I've been a fool. I wish I could make amends, but I know I can't, ever. I deserve to stay in this century and die."

"You're not going to. We're going to take you back."

"*What?* But how—?"

"Never mind. Just lie still," Jason repeated. He heard footsteps behind him. It was his team.

"All done, sir," Mondrago reported. "The charge is set. In fact, it ought to be—"

From the direction of the Acropolis, Jason thought he heard an extremely faint *crump*, but he knew it was probably his imagination. The explosive device they had used generated a momentary sound-deadening field at the instant of its detonation, rendering it effectively inaudible to Athens' preoccupied citizens. If he'd heard anything, it must have been the rumble as the subterranean tunnel collapsed.

"We left Pan in there as ordered, sir," Da Cunha added.

"Good. It's a fitting tomb for him." Jason smiled. "No one will ever know who's lying under the Acropolis."

"When the Athenians offer their annual sacrifices to Pan at the grotto," mused Logan in the thoughtfully deliberate way he always seemed to speak, on the rare occasions when he did it at all, "they'll never dream that the real thing is entombed inside it."

"Interesting point." Jason handed his "walking stick" to Mondrago and, with great care, put one arm under Chantal's knees and the other behind her back, and lifted her up. She gasped with pain but clung to his neck. He focused his mind, preparatory to giving a neural command. "All right. Is everybody ready? Let's go home."

CHAPTER TWENTY-FIVE

THE GREAT DOMED DISPLACER CHAMBER was almost exactly as they had left it a couple of hours earlier. Rutherford had to all appearances never moved. After his initial startlement at their appearance, he brusquely motioned forward the waiting medical team. Jason handed Chantal over to them.

"How is she?" he asked as soon as they had laid her on a stretcher and brought their medical sensors to bear.

"She's in a great deal of pain," a doctor replied as he gave her a hypospray injection against that same pain. "And she's in mild shock. But none of her injuries are life-threatening. She's going to be fine." He gestured, and his orderlies lifted the stretcher.

Chantal turned her head to meet Jason's eyes, and spoke weakly. "Jason . . . thank you. I'm—"

"Hush. Don't try to talk."

"No, let me finish. I already knew I was wrong. But you've shown me just how very wrong I was, because what you've done has reminded me of what it is to be truly *human*. So now I know why—whatever humanity's imperfections—we must always *remain* human. That is too precious a thing to be gambled away against the chance of something 'superior'." The effort of speaking seemed to exhaust her. The doctor gave a more peremptory gesture, and she was borne away. Only when she was out of sight did Jason turn to face Rutherford.

"Mission accomplished," he reported wearily, "in all particulars. I'll tell you the details later, in private. But the Transhumanist operation has been scotched, and their leader was killed. And I don't think Dr. Frey's loyalties are going to be in any question after this."

"And the, uh, 'cleanup' aspects of the plan?" asked Rutherford anxiously.

"All done. The tunnel under the Acropolis behind the grotto was sealed, and no anachronistic hardware was left lying around."

"Good." Rutherford's relief was palpable.

"Also, the being 'Pan' was killed by his own Transhumanist master."

"Just as well," said Rutherford offhandedly.

Jason glared at him. So, he noticed to his surprise, did Mondrago. "I suppose it could be regarded that way, from the standpoint of 'cleanup.' But . . . well, he kept his bargain with me, and he died trying to aid us. I think he's entitled to just a little respect."

"I meant no offense." Rutherford seemed genuinely contrite, and Jason's annoyance ebbed.

"None taken. And before we head for your office, there's one other thing you'll want to know, because it relates directly to one of the questions the original expedition sought to answer. As we learned then, the Olympian 'gods' were still alive and active in the flesh—at least the Teloi flesh—up to 490 B.C. But after that, for the most part, they became just what they've always been assumed to have been: myths."

Rutherford's eyes kept going to the sword that was his private office's prize exhibit. Jason wasn't sure why.

Finally Rutherford swung around to face Jason and Mondrago. "So not all of the Teloi were wiped out in this final confrontation with the Transhumanists?"

"No. Zeus, before he died, mentioned Aphrodite—or whatever names she was known by in the other Indo-European cultures—as being the pilot of the aircar that had dropped them off. So she and various others must have lived on afterwards; I can't account for Athena or Artemis or Apollo, for example. And they could have continued to play the god game with the help of the self-repairing Teloi techno-magic devices. But remember, they were all members of the youngest Earth-born generation, which Oannes assured me suffered from a drastic reduction in life expectancy. They must have died off, and even before they did, the literal belief in their pantheon began to dissipate, leaving a void that was filled by various Eastern mystery religions and, finally, by Christianity." Jason chuckled. "Knowing the Teloi, I have a feeling that the loss of human belief in them helped hasten their end."

"Quite likely." Rutherford turned brisk. "But, more to the point, about the Transhumanists. . . ."

"Yes. That's the real problem. At least one of them survived, as we knew from the first was going to happen, since we didn't have time to hunt down whoever sent the signal from Mount Pentelikon. So one or more of them were retrieved on schedule, as were the corpses of Franco and the others. The survivor or survivors didn't know the details of Franco's death, but they *did* know in general about our discovery of their presence. And they knew that Alexandre and I may have gotten back with that knowledge, even though we were earmarked for assassination down there on the battlefield.

"Incidentally, I've been using the past tense deliberately, because as you know, their expedition came from, and therefore returned to, a time somewhat prior to ours. So their linear present lies in our past—"

"I know," interjected Rutherford bleakly, for he understood the implications.

"—and therefore by now they know that their scheme for a Pan cult was foiled, although they don't know how. And they must regard it as at least a possibility that, as of a point slightly in their own future, we know about their underground and its extratemporal activities, so they'll be on their guard. One good thing: when we went back we killed all the ones who actually saw us, so just exactly what happened on Mount Kotroni and at the grotto in Athens must be a mystery to them."

"One other good thing," Mondrago spoke up. "They know that we got Dr. Frey's TRD back, so they'll assume she was left to die in the fifth century B.C."

"That's right," Jason agreed. "I suggest that we keep her presence here strictly under wraps, even to the extent of providing her with a new identity. I'm certain she'll cooperate. And a debriefing by intelligence specialists ought to be productive."

"Surely Franco didn't give her a great deal of detailed and specific data about the Transhumanist underground," said Rutherford dubiously.

"No, of course not, but he could hardly have avoided dropping some information in the course of her . . . association with him. He was an incorrigible braggart. She may turn out to be an ace in the hole for us." Jason paused. "I don't know what the final judicial determination of her case will be, or if it will even come to that. But if she ends up being sentenced to incarceration, I recommend that the time we keep her here be credited against her term."

"I will pass along your recommendation, with my endorsement. Coming from a man whose death she almost caused, it should carry some weight. And you may quite possibly be right about her usefulness to us. But it goes without saying that she can provide no information on what the Transhumanists have been doing since Franco's expedition. And as to what they may do in the future, the expeditions they may send back before we find this compact and energy-efficient temporal displacer of theirs, as we *must* find it . . . !" Rutherford shook his head slowly and looked at least his age.

"And," said Mondrago, "we don't know how riddled Earth is with these long-term secret organizations of theirs—we only aborted one of them, remember. We also don't know when 'The Day' is scheduled to be, when all their long-term schemes are scheduled to come to fruition. Basically," he concluded with a kind of pessimistic relish, "we don't know much of anything at all."

"One thing we do know," said Jason grimly, and his eyes held Rutherford's. "We know that the Temporal Service is going to have to change. The days of us being a sort of glorified tour guides are over. Oh, of course we'll continue to send historical research expeditions back. But those expeditions are going to have to have more guards— very watchful guards. And above and beyond that, the Service is going to have to have a new unit whose full-time job is hunting down the Transhumanists across time the way we just did—a specialized combat section."

Rutherford winced. "Perhaps we could call it the 'Special Operations Section.'"

"Sounds good. Call it whatever you want. But for that section, at least, the old loose-jointed style isn't going to work anymore. It's going to have to be a military, or at least paramilitary, outfit—and outfits like that have the kind of organization they do, including a formalized rank structure, for a reason."

"And I think I know just the man to head it," Rutherford told him, with a very brief smile. Then his expression grew desolate again, as he contemplated the coming era of time wars. It was the look of an old man seeing his life's assumptions and verities slipping irretrievably away into the past and vanishing, leaving him face to face with a harsh, unfamiliar, and unfriendly future in which he did not belong.

But then his eyes strayed to the fifteenth-century sword in his display case, the sword that had been borne by she who had come to symbolize the capacity of human beings to fight bravely and die gallantly for something they knew in their souls was worth dying— and killing—for. He seemed to draw strength from it. He turned back to Jason and spoke matter-of-factly.

"You will, of course, need to commence recruiting without delay."

"Right. Da Cunha and Logan are, of course, obvious candidates. And we'll need as wide a range of ethnic types as possible."

"Sir," Modrago blurted. "I want to be the first to sign up for this Special Ops Section of yours."

"Satisfactory, Jason?" asked Rutherford with a lift of one eyebrow.

Jason pretended to consider. "Well, he's an insubordinate wise-ass—"

"I can see how there might be a certain affinity, however reluctantly acknowledged," Rutherford interjected drily.

"—but he's an insubordinate wise-ass who is very handy to have around in a fight." Jason turned to Mondrago. "I just might be able to use you. But I need to be sure you've got the right kind of motivation."

"Well, sir, let me put it this way. Of course I've always hated Transhumanists, but mostly just because *everybody* hates them, if you know what I mean. Now I understand why I *ought* to hate them." Mondrago seemed to seek for words to explain further, but then shook his head and spoke briefly. "It's just something that has to be done."

"Like what those men we fought beside at Marathon did," Jason nodded. "Yes, I think you may possibly do." He turned to Rutherford. "Will that be all for now?"

"Yes." Then, as Jason and Mondrago got to their feet, Rutherford seemed to remember something. "Oh, yes, Jason, I almost forgot. A most remarkable coincidence occurred." He took out the little plastic case Jason had left in his care. It was empty. Then he held out his other hand. It held a tiny TRD.

"Do you recall our last exchange just before your departure? Afterwards, still thinking about it, I looked in the case and found it was empty. A subsequent search revealed this on the displacer stage. Would you like to keep it?"

"No. I don't think I need it anymore." Jason smiled. "Come on, Alexandre. We've got work to do."

HISTORICAL NOTE

That Marathon was one of the most crucial battles of world history has been recognized by such diverse authorities as Sir Edward Creasy and the U.S. House of Representatives, in a resolution on its 2500th anniversary. I fail to see how any other view is possible.

The events of Xerxes' invasion of Greece ten years afterwards—the immensity of the Persian host, even when discounted for exaggeration; the heroic last stand of the three hundred Spartans (and their seven hundred forgotten Thespian allies) at Thermopylae; the stunning naval victory at Salamis; the titanic clash of massive armies at Plataea—have an epic quality which causes them to get most of the attention. But none of these things would ever have happened had the Athenians lost at Marathon, or submitted without fighting. No subsequent Persian invasion would have been necessary. It would have all been over in 490 B.C.—or perhaps the following year, if Sparta had not yielded and another campaigning season had been required to complete its obliteration.

A few historians—including Arnold Toynbee, in one of his less brilliant passages—have attempted to minimize the criticality of the Persian Wars. And in the 2006 collection *Unmaking the West*, Barry Strauss presented a counterfactual scenario suggesting that even if the Persians had conquered Greece and gone on to conquer the rest of the Mediterranean basin, it is not impossible that Western civilization—or at least *a* Western civilization, sharing many of the characteristics and values we associate with that term—still *could*, maybe, just possibly, have arisen. As an intellectual exercise, the essay is as original, ingenious and thought-provoking as one would expect from Professor Strauss . . . and it doesn't convince for an instant. Not even he can succeed in defending the indefensible.

No. When those ten thousand hoplites broke into a run and charged three times their number of a hitherto invincible enemy, our future went with them. We cannot calculate the debt we owe them.

The scholarly literature relevant to Marathon is intimidating in its voluminousness. For the interested reader with finite time, I recommend three books on which I have leaned heavily and to which I take this opportunity to acknowledge my debt.

The first is *The Western Way of War*, by Victor Davis Hanson, a brilliant study of Classical Greek warfare and its long-term historical repercussions, which latter theme is further developed in the author's subsequent *Carnage and Culture*. Hanson has been on the receiving end of a great deal of hysterical invective and politically correct name-calling. He must be doing something right.

The second is *Persian Fire,* by Tom Holland, a compulsively readable overview of the Persian Wars which achieves an almost unique degree of evenhandedness without ever seeming to lean over backwards to be evenhanded. Rather, the author simply accepts each side on its own terms while skewering both with his trademark sardonic wit. He is particularly good on the little-known and less-understood subject of what can only be called the ideology of the Persian Empire.

Third and most recent is *The First Clash*, by Jim Lacey, which focuses on the Marathon campaign and benefits from the fact that its author, aside from his academic credentials, is an experienced infantry officer and defense analyst. And unlike all too many historians, he does his math. On narrowly military questions I have tended to defer to his judgment, or at least to give it respectful weight when balancing it against Holland's. I have not always done so in less specialized areas such as the much-disputed chronology and sequence of events.

For example, I agree with Holland and an ever-increasing number of other historians that the battle took place in August. Lacey, in his Prologue, does perfunctory obeisance to the traditional date of September 12, but he doesn't mention it again—which is understandable, inasmuch as his own reconstruction of the campaign (and, in particular, of the logistical constraints under which the Persians labored) makes nonsense of it. In fact, in a later chapter he himself refers to the "hot August sun" in the days immediately preceding the battle.

Finally, in addition to these books, I cannot forbear to mention *The Ancient City*, by Peter Connolly and Hazel Dodge. In the absence of actual time travel, it is the next best thing. After studying the segment on Classical Athens, I felt as though I had been there.

With the exception of Callicles, all the fifth century B.C. Greeks named in this novel are historical. Themistocles is the only one for whom we have what is self-evidently an individual portrait—the Ostia bust—free of artistic conventions and idealization. Otherwise, I have had to use my imagination about personal appearance, aided by hints from sculpture (the baldness of Aeschylus) and names ("Miltiades," derived from the word for red ochre clay, was often bestowed on reddish-haired children).

The dualistic theology of Zoroastrianism is complex and fascinating, but I have not gone into it as it deserves. The Persian kings of the period in question were far from consistent in their practice of it, for their imperial policy was based on scrupulous (if insincere) respect for the innumerable gods of their various conquered peoples. Even among the Iranians themselves, Ahura Mazda was by tradition merely the chief god of a pantheon almost as inchoate as that of the Greeks, rather than the one uncreated God proclaimed by Zoroaster. The Persian Empire was not in any sense a Zoroastrian theocracy. But Darius I, one of the greatest masters of spin who has ever lived, used Zoroastrian imagery and terminology to justify his usurpation of the Persian throne. It was in this spirit that Datis used a distorted version of it as a propaganda tool as I have described. I have followed in his footsteps, albeit with even more outrageous distortion.

✠ ✠ ✠

In the matter of dialogue, I have permitted myself certain anachronisms in the interest of clarity.

The initial Persian conquerors of Ionia were Medes led by their General Harpagus, and since this was the Greeks' first contact with the Persian Empire they tended to refer to all the Persians as the "Medes," just as Near Easterners today call all Western Europeans "Feringhi," or Franks. In these pages the Persians are simply the Persians.

Conversely, the Greeks referred to themselves as "Hellenes," as in fact they still do. I have used the more familiar "Greeks," a name later applied to them by the Romans, who derived it from the Graeci, the inhabitants of the colony of Graeae in Italy. Interestingly, in light of the preceding paragraph, Near Eastern terms for the Greeks have always been some variation on "Ionians," the Greeks with whom the Near East was most directly in contact. (The Persian word was "Yauna"; in the Old Testament, one of the sons of Japheth, the son of Noah whose progeny peopled Europe, is "Javan.")

Likewise, I have used the well-known Latinized forms of Persian names rather than the originals. ("Cyrus," not "Kurush"; "Darius," not "Daryush.")

Whenever transliteration of Greek place-names is disputed, I cheerfully admit that I have simply picked whichever version struck my fancy, with a fine lack of that foolish consistency which as we all know is the bugbear of small minds. ("Mount Pentelikon," not "Mount Pentelicus"; "Phalerum," not "Phaleron.")

Grandpa's Box

Grandpa's Box

Retelling the Biblical Story of Redemption

STARR MEADE

ILLUSTRATED BY BRUCE VAN PATTER

PUBLISHING

P.O. BOX 817 • PHILLIPSBURG • NEW JERSEY 08865-0817

The base translation of *Grandpa's Box* is the New American Standard Bible, which is sometimes quoted exactly and sometimes paraphrased. The New American Standard Bible®. Copyright © 1960, 1962, 1963, 1968, 1971, 1972, 1973, 1975, 1977, 1995 by The Lockman Foundation. Used by permission.

Scripture verses appearing at the conclusion of chapters are from the English Standard Version. The Holy Bible, English Standard Version, copyright © 2001 by Crossway Bibles, a division of Good News Publishers. Used by permission. All rights reserved.

Page design and typesetting by Lakeside Design Plus.

Printed in the United States of America

Library of Congress Cataloging-in-Publication Data

Meade, Starr, 1956–
    Grandpa's Box : retelling the biblical story of redemption / Starr Meade ;
illustrated by Bruce Van Patter.
        p.   cm.
    ISBN-13: 978-0-087552-866-3
    ISBN-10: 0-87552-866-X (paper)
    1. Redemption—Christianity—Juvenile literature. I. Van Patter, Bruce.
II. Title.

BT775.M43 2005
220.9'505—dc22

                                                           2005047675

To one who is my main model for Grandpa,
my support in my writing, my advisor, and my very dearest
friend:
my husband, Paul.

Contents

The War

Amy slammed her locker door shut before the jumbled pile of books could fall out onto the floor. It was that most wonderful day of the month—the second Wednesday—when school was out early. That would give her a whole afternoon to spend at the "Trash to Treasure" secondhand shop. Who could tell what she might find? Of course, as he always did, the shop owner would let her explore it all she liked and use anything she found. That was because "Trash to Treasure"—part business, part hobby—belonged to Joe Maclusky, Amy's grandfather. Amy turned in to Grandpa's driveway and hurried past the battered blue pickup that he had used for his handyman service before retiring. She did not stop at the house, since Grandma went out shopping on Wednesdays. Instead, she headed straight for the brightly painted guesthouse at the back of the yard. She passed under the wooden sign reading "Trash to Treasure."

"I just picked up this typewriter last week," Grandpa was saying to a customer as Amy entered. "It needs a few repairs, but it's really a better typewriter than this other one."

"When could you have it ready?" the customer wanted to know.

"Check back on Monday and I'll have it working like new," Grandpa replied. Pleased, the customer left.

"Hi, Grandpa, how do these things work?" Amy said, all in one breath, pointing at the typewriters. Grandpa put a clean piece of paper into the typewriter that the customer had not chosen, and showed Amy how to type on the old machine.

"That's one of the things I like best about you, Amy John," Grandpa said. (Amy's middle name was really Jeanne, but Grandpa had called her Amy John as long as she could remember.) "You're always interested in new things." Amy beamed at Grandpa's praise and set to work. For quite some time she typed in silence except for the slow clack-clack-clacking of the typewriter keys. Finally she looked up and said, "Hey, Grandpa, what's Marc doing?"

"Let's go see," said Grandpa, stepping away from the plumbing parts that he had been separating into piles. Marc had not had to make a locker stop before leaving school, so he arrived at Grandpa's shop before Amy. He was busy by the back window, placing soldiers on a card table. Grandpa and Amy went to him and stood, watching.

Marc's dark brown eyes were narrowed into a thoughtful squint. Very carefully, so as not to disturb any of the other tiny wooden figures on the battlefield, he placed a Union soldier opposite a Confederate lieutenant who waited, sword drawn, to meet him. Marc leaned back, looking with satisfaction on the miniature Civil War scene he had created. "See," Marc said, pointing, "this cannon just shot off a ball into this group of soldiers here—that's why they're running every which way. And this horse just jumped over this wall." Marc lifted the horse over the wall. "But it got its foot caught and fell," and he lay the horse down on its side. "The rider's over there where he was thrown. And this officer here has rallied his men and is just about to lead a charge against the enemy." As though Marc himself were the officer, he waved with his own arm in a "Come on" gesture. Marc possessed a true fascination for war. He scorned the superheroes that so many of his friends admired. Marc was interested in real battles, and he read whatever he could find about any war in history. His reading had convinced him that military victory depended most of all on good strategy—careful planning that made the best use of men, weapons, the surrounding land, and the weather. Clever gadgets or superhuman abilities were fine for make-believe, but real war was not like that. Now, looking up from the miniature battlefield he had created, Marc asked, "Grandpa, were you ever in a war?"

"As a matter of fact, Marc, I'm in the middle of a war right now," Grandpa answered.

Surprised, Marc looked up quickly to see whether Grandpa was teasing him. "You are not," he said.

Amy jumped to Grandpa's defense. "Marc, don't be rude. Give him a chance to explain."

Marc was used to Amy's big-sister corrections. Most of the time she was nice enough about it, and she was usually right. He turned from her now and said, "Okay, Grandpa, what war are you in the middle of right now?"

Grandpa continued as though he had not heard Marc's objection or Amy's response. "It's a great and terrible war I'm in. It's not the kind in which people shoot and stab and blow each other up. Oh, no, it's much more serious than that. Think of all the wicked characters in all the war stories you've ever heard. Think of the strongest and cruelest villains, real or imagined. The enemy in this war is stronger and crueler than any of them."

Marc and Amy looked at Grandpa in surprise. How could their easygoing grandfather have an enemy as terrible as this?

Grandpa went on. "But the great thing about this war is that even though it's so hard and so long and even though the enemy is very powerful, this war is already won. Even the enemy knows that."

"An enemy that keeps fighting even when he knows he's lost? Why would he do that?" Marc asked.

"He's just that filled with hate and with the desire to do all the damage he can," Grandpa said. "He lost a long time ago, but he doesn't stop attacking. Sometimes it may look like he's winning, but he never really is."

"A good commander-in-chief has to see the big picture," Marc commented. "He can't just look at how one little skirmish turns out."

"Exactly," said Grandpa. "And this war is full of little skirmishes of all kinds, as well as the really important battles that could turn the tide of the whole war. You know, if you're interested, I'd be happy to tell you about some of the major battles. It might take a while because this war has been going on for centuries—"

This surprised even Amy. "Centuries?" she repeated.

"—but I could tell you a little bit each time you come to visit, and sooner or later you'd have a pretty good picture of this war."

"I'm game," Amy said. "I always like your stories, Grandpa. What about you, Marc?"

"I guess so," Marc agreed. "Grandpa *does* tell good stories. Are you sure these are stories about real battles?"

"Real battles," Grandpa nodded. "In fact, I've been making a collection of things that would remind me of those battles. Let me just go get my box." Grandpa went to the back part of his shop, the part where the things that were not yet for sale waited to be restored. There were brass pots that would be beautiful once they were polished, an antique clock missing an hour hand, drawers needing knobs, and chairs needing legs. This back part of the shop appeared hopelessly cluttered to most people, but not to Grandpa. He always knew just which pile contained what he wanted. Now he stepped over a once-elegant rocking horse that lay on its side, needing a new rocker and a coat of paint, and reached for a box, about the size of a fishing tackle box. He picked it up by the handles fastened on the sides.

Grandpa came back to the children and held the box up for them to see. It was a wooden box, simply made, and painted lemon yellow. Grandpa smiled. "Your dad made this for me up at camp one year, when he was about Amy's age," he said. He set the box down and lifted the simple hook that held the lid closed, allowing the children to see inside. "I guess you could call it my war chest," he added. As the children peered into the box, they saw many small figures—animals, people, and objects of all kinds. A number of them were carved from wood. Some were painted in great detail.

"Wow!" Marc breathed. "Where did you get all those?"

"Some I've collected from stores that sell miniatures," Grandpa replied. "Others I've carved myself out of wood. I work on them at night, after dinner. Your grandmother sits and reads then, but if I read at night, I go to sleep. So I carve."

"There are so many," Amy said. "And they're so detailed. How long has it taken you?"

Grandpa chuckled. "I really don't know. I've been working on these for years. I'm in no hurry, you know. It's just kind of a hobby." Amy shook her head. There was always something new to discover about Grandpa. He had so many different hobbies; many of them had to do with working with his hands. Now Grandpa selected two figures from his box and closed the lid. "Okay, we're ready to begin," he said.

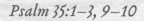
Psalm 35:1–3, 9–10

Contend, O Lord, with those who contend with me;
    fight against those who fight against me!
Take hold of shield and buckler
    and rise for my help!

Draw the spear and javelin
    against my pursuers!
Say to my soul,
    "I am your salvation!" . . .

Then my soul will rejoice in the LORD,
    exulting in his salvation.
All my bones shall say,
    "O LORD, who is like you,
delivering the poor
    from him who is too strong for him,
    the poor and needy from him who robs him?"

Sneak Attack

(Genesis 3)

"Do you remember the year before last when Grandma and I went with you and your parents to Pennsylvania? Do you remember going to Gettysburg together?" Grandpa asked. Marc and Amy both nodded.

"Do you remember how pretty it was as we drove along the battlefield there?" Grandpa continued.

"No," Marc answered bluntly. "I just remember that there were statues and war memorials *everywhere*."

"I remember," Amy said. "It was spring, so all the trees had flowers—pink and white and even lavender. I remember because I was thinking that it didn't seem at all like what I'd read about in my history book: three days of men dying and killing each other, by the hundreds. It seemed far too pretty and peaceful for that."

"That's exactly my point," Grandpa agreed. "A battle can take place in the most beautiful spot you'd ever want to see. By the time the battle's over, though, all sorts of horrible, ugly things will have happened. Sometimes the effects of that one battle will go on long after it's all over and done. That's how it was with the first battle in this war I'm going to tell you about. The battle took place in a garden more beautiful than anything you've ever seen in a world more perfect than the one you know. But something so horrible happened in this battle that, ever since, everywhere we look, we see scars from it."

Marc had begun to look suspicious. "Grandpa, are you getting ready to talk about Adam and Eve in the Garden of Eden?"

"You guessed it!" Grandpa answered. "But before you say, 'I already know this story—' " and Marc closed his mouth because that was exactly what he had been about to say—"stop and think about it as a battle and notice what an important victory was won there."

"Victory?" Amy asked, puzzled. "Adam and Eve *gave in* to Satan. How is that a victory?"

"Well, you listen, and when I get to the end, see if you can tell me how this was a victory. And Marc, you put your knowledge of warfare to use and see if you can tell us how the Commander-in-Chief was able to gain this victory." Both children nodded and settled down to listen.

"Did you know that one of the names the Bible gives to God is 'Lord of Hosts'?" Grandpa began. " 'Hosts' is another name for 'armies.' "

Marc perked up. "I didn't know that," he said.

Grandpa went on. "Lord of Hosts, Lord of Armies—God is the leader of all the armies of heaven. Now, who do you suppose are in those armies?"

"The angels?" Amy asked.

16

Grandpa nodded. "Yes, and before the first battle took place on earth, the war actually began in heaven, as a war between angels. One angel had been made by God to be especially beautiful and strong. He'd been given a very high position in heaven, but this angel wasn't content with that. This angel wanted not just to be high, but to be highest of all, higher even than God himself." Grandpa shook his head at the impossibility of such an idea. "So this angel won other angels to his side. When he thought his army was strong enough, he rose up and rebelled against God. He rebelled, even though it was God who had created him to be so beautiful and who'd given him everything he had.

"Well, I don't suppose it was much of a fight. God's angels defeated this angel and his allies and threw them out of heaven. Of course, you know who this angel is, don't you?" Marc and Amy nodded. "Satan," they answered together.

"Then, of course, God created the world. And he created it beautiful and perfect. The whole wonderful universe was one giant testimony to the greatness and glory of God. God also created a man and a woman. They were to have children and fill the world with people who would know and love God. People would worship and enjoy God. God would care for and delight in people. But then, before Adam and Eve had given birth to even one child, Satan attacked." Here Grandpa took one of the small objects he had removed from the yellow box and placed it on the closed lid, right in the center. The children saw that it was a little wooden snake, painted in brilliant colors, coiled and ready to strike.

"Marc," Grandpa asked, "in wartime, what is a traitor?"

Marc answered promptly, "A traitor is someone who was on one side, but then goes over to the other side to help the enemy."

"Precisely!" Grandpa said. "Satan needed a traitor. His plan was to get Adam and Eve to sin, because God is holy and hates sin. If Satan could get the first two human beings to rebel against God, as he'd done, God would become their enemy. Then people wouldn't be able to love and enjoy God, and God's plan would be ruined.

"So one day, when Eve was alone in the garden, Satan came to her in the form of a beautiful, talking serpent. Now, Marc, what is the most important thing a soldier can do?"

Marc thought for a moment. "Obey orders," he finally replied.

"Exactly," Grandpa agreed. "What if he doesn't like those orders? Or what if he thinks different orders might have been better?"

"Doesn't matter," Marc insisted. "A soldier has to obey orders."

"Adam and Eve were given these orders: eat fruit from any tree in the garden, *except* for the tree of the knowledge of good and evil. 'In the day you eat of that tree,' God told them, 'you will surely die.' Now, in the garden, alone with Eve, Satan said, 'You won't die! God knows that eating that fruit will make you like him; that's why he doesn't want you to eat it.'

"And Eve, not realizing what an important battle this was, began to doubt the orders she'd been given. She began to think they weren't good orders and they'd been given for a bad reason. She looked at the fruit on the tree—and it looked good to her. She listened to Satan's voice—and his argument sounded good to her. Then—" Grandpa paused for effect. He was pleased to see that Marc and Amy listened intently, as if they did not already know what would happen next. "Eve ignored the orders God had given her, and she ate the fruit. She gave some to Adam, and he disobeyed orders, too, and ate along with her.

"Right away, Adam and Eve understood that they'd lost a battle. They were ashamed and they were afraid. They didn't want to be on Satan's side after all, but it was too late. Satan, of course, must have been delighted! But—" and Grandpa raised one finger as though to warn his listeners not to jump to conclusions— "he hadn't really won, because no one can take God by surprise. God knew this would happen. Before ever making people, he'd already planned what to do when they rebelled against him.

"So God went to find Adam and Eve. They'd always loved God before, but now they were afraid of him and so they were hiding. God told them that pain and sorrow and death would be part of their world from now on because they'd disobeyed. But at the same time, he promised them that one day a woman would have a child. That child and Satan would carry on the war that Satan had begun. Satan would do all he could to hurt that child, but all he could do wouldn't be enough. The child would destroy him and his work. So, Amy, do you see how this was not a defeat for God but a victory?"

Amy nodded. "Sure. I see it now. Satan *did* manage to turn people against God, but God had already thought of a way to turn them back again."

Grandpa turned next to Marc, but before he could even ask the question, Marc spoke up. "The best military leaders always learn all they can about their enemy. If they can guess what the enemy might do, they know how to prepare for it. God didn't have to guess—he *knew* what was going to happen. His plan covered the enemy's sneak attack."

Grandpa removed the brightly colored serpent from the center of the box lid and laid it on its side. In its place, he set the other small figure he had taken from the box. It was a figure of a little baby. "So what Satan thought was his victory turned into his defeat." Grandpa chuckled. "That's a pattern you're going to see over and over in this war. There was nothing Satan could do but wait for the birth of the baby that would defeat him forever."

19

The Lord God said to the serpent,

"Because you have done this,
    cursed are you above all livestock
    and above all beasts of the field;
on your belly you shall go,
    and dust you shall eat
    all the days of your life.
I will put enmity between you and the woman,
    and between your offspring and her offspring;
he shall bruise your head,
    and you shall bruise his heel."

Enemy
Reinforcements

(Genesis 4:1–15, 25–26)

Grandpa rose from his chair and pulled a plain leather billfold from the back pocket of his jeans. He opened the billfold and worked at pulling loose two small snapshots. Grandpa held the pictures out for the children to see. "You carry our baby pictures in your wallet?" Amy asked.

"Sure do," Grandpa replied. "I was proud when my little Amy John and Marcus Lucius were born." (Grandpa had nicknames for everyone.) "Not as proud as your daddy was, though." Grandpa slid the photographs back into his billfold and returned it to his pocket.

"I watched your dad grow up," he told his grandchildren. "Lived with him for twenty years or so. I saw how proud he was of the paycheck he got from his first job. I saw how proud he was of his first car. But there was never anything like how proud he was on the day he held his firstborn child." Catching sight of Marc's face from the corner of his eye, Grandpa hurried to add, "The only other time I've seen him that proud was a few years later when a son, Marc, was born.

"Say," Grandpa asked, glancing at the cuckoo clock with the doors that faithfully opened every half hour even though the bird itself was missing. "Are you kids all ready to go when your mom gets here? She made me promise you'd be ready when she honks. Something about a soccer practice Marc can't miss."

Marc answered, "Is it okay if I leave my Civil War scene up until I come next time?" Grandpa nodded and Marc said, "Then I'm ready to go."

"Me, too," said Amy.

"Then let me go on with my story until your mom comes," Grandpa said. "*Your* dad was proud when you two were born, but think what it was like for Adam and Eve. Their little baby boy was not only the first child born to *them*; he was the first baby ever born in the world. Imagine them squeezing his chubby little arms and legs. Can't you just see his tiny little fingers wrapping around Adam's finger? Think of Eve gently touching his little bits of hair and whispering, 'His hair's so soft.' "

Amy smiled. She had never thought about Adam and Eve doing all those things with their baby, but now she could see just how it would have been. Marc, however, groaned, "Grandpa, please."

Grandpa turned abruptly to Marc and changed his tone. He became very matter-of-fact. "Okay, Marc, this is the first baby ever born, *and* he's Adam and Eve's first baby. There's another reason, though, that this birth would have been especially exciting to Adam and Eve. What did they expect this child to be when he grew up?"

"Maybe some kind of fighter," Marc suggested. "You know, because of that promise God made about crushing the serpent, back when they ate the fruit."

"I think you're right," Grandpa answered, "because they named this child Cain. Do you know what 'Cain' means?" Both Amy and Marc shook their heads. " 'Cain' means 'gotten one.' When he was born, Eve said, 'I have gotten a baby boy with the help of the Lord.' Sure sounds to me like she was thinking about that child God had promised.

"Adam and Eve would have wondered how their little Cain could crush the serpent's head, but they weren't worried about it. It was enough for them that God had made a promise about a baby—and now they had a baby. They waited and watched as Cain grew. Now he was holding things with his own hands. Now he was saying his first words. Now he was walking by himself. Were those little tiny feet the ones that would crush Satan's head? And what did it mean that Satan would bruise his heel?

"And now, here's another wonderful thing—God gave them a second little boy! They named this one Abel. They were so proud of big brother Cain, guarding his baby brother. When Abel was big enough, Cain taught him all the games he loved. As the boys grew, they wrestled each other, raced each other, swam together. Soon they weren't little boys playing anymore, but strong young men, who liked to flex their muscles and show off their strength." And Grandpa flexed his own arm muscle. "Now they were big enough to help Adam with all his work. It would have made sense to divide up the work that needed done, so Abel became a shepherd, working with animals, and Cain became a farmer, growing things to eat out in the fields.

"Now, you realize that Satan can't see the future. He didn't know exactly what God had in mind. All he knew was that God had promised a baby who would be his enemy and who would crush him. Now here are two babies who have grown to strong young manhood. What do you think, Amy John?" Grandpa asked, turning to her. "How do you think Satan was feeling about now?"

"*I* think he'd be feeling pretty nervous," Amy answered, nodding her head with certainty.

"And so he must have been," Grandpa agreed. "He began to look for a way to make sure that neither Cain nor Abel would ever fight against him in the war. Marc, what do you do in a war if you're getting nervous because you can see the enemy growing stronger?"

"You bring in reinforcements—other soldiers to make your army stronger," Marc answered.

"Satan had reinforcements," Grandpa said. "What do you think his reinforcements were?"

"The other bad angels you told us about?" Marc asked. He didn't think that sounded right, so he was not surprised when Grandpa answered, "No, not bad angels. Amy?" Amy shook her head. "I have no idea."

"Well, here's a hint," Grandpa said. "Satan got his reinforcements when Adam and Eve ate the fruit. What did they let into the world that would make it easier, from then on, for Satan to fight against God's people?"

"Oh, I know," both children cried together. "Sin!"

"Exactly," Grandpa replied. "Sin had come into the world and into people's hearts. Every person is born sinful, wanting to fight against God so that he can do things his own way. Cain and Abel were sinful, too. Satan could use that sin to try to get what he wanted.

"One day, Cain and Abel brought offerings to God, as Adam and Eve had taught them to do. Cain brought fruit and vegetables and grain he'd grown in his fields. Abel brought a lamb or a goat from his flock. The Bible tells us that the Lord accepted Abel's offering, but he didn't accept Cain's.

"Has it ever happened that something good happened to someone else, but it didn't happen to you, so you felt angry about it?" Amy shifted uncomfortably in her chair. She remembered the day last week when report cards had come out. Michelle had received straight A's—again—while Amy had brought home B's and C's. Michelle never studied for tests and never had homework. Amy had been so annoyed that she had not spoken to Michelle for three days. As for Marc, he would not meet Grandpa's eyes. He was thinking of the hundred dollars that his friend Garrett had received in birthday money. A hundred bucks—*and* the usual number of presents besides.

"When good things happen to other people and we get mad about it, it's called envy," Grandpa continued, "and envy is sin. Cain was full of envy. He told himself how unfair it was that Abel's offering should be accepted and not his. He thought of all the things he didn't like about Abel and all the ways that, really, he was better than Abel. He began to wish that something bad would happen to his brother. Finally, Cain began to think about how it would feel to *make* something bad happen to him.

"Now, Marc, if there's a war going on, and the commander learns there's a traitor in the camp who's planning harm to his soldiers, what does the commander do about it?"

Marc did not hesitate. "He arrests the traitor and locks him up—or maybe he even has him shot."

"Do you think the commander would sit down with a traitor and try to reason with him? Do you think he'd try to talk him out of being a traitor and give him a chance to do better?" Grandpa asked.

"Of course not," Marc answered. "If he wants to win the war, he can show no mercy."

"And yet," Grandpa said, "God showed mercy to Cain. He came to Cain and asked him, 'Why are you angry? Why are you so upset?' "

Now Grandpa turned to Amy. "Why did God need to ask Cain questions?" he asked. "Didn't he know what Cain was thinking?"

Amy thought for a minute. "When kids are in trouble at school, Mrs. Whittaker asks them questions, to get them to think about what they've done wrong," she said. "Maybe that's what God was doing with Cain."

"Good answer, Amy," Grandpa said. "God was giving Cain a chance to repent—to change his mind and do what was right. God went on to warn Cain that sin was waiting to destroy him but he mustn't let it. You see what an unusual Commander God is? He doesn't just destroy people who help the enemy. He offers them mercy. Now Cain had a clear choice—"

From outside, a car horn sounded. "Oh, my, is she here already?" Grandpa asked. "Well, I promised you'd be ready. Grab your stuff and scoot!"

"What about Cain?" Amy wanted to know.

"We'll have to finish his story next time," Grandpa said. "Remind me."

Romans 2:4

Or do you presume on the riches of his kindness and forbearance and patience, not knowing that God's kindness is meant to lead you to repentance?

Mercy for the Foe

(Genesis 6–8)

Grandpa always said that his shop was more of a hobby than a business. If that were true, it did not matter that the shop earned very little money. For Grandpa, it was payment enough to rescue something that someone was throwing away as junk, fix it up, and find just the person who would be delighted to have it. Marc and Amy enjoyed helping Grandpa with odd jobs on Saturday. He often paid them, but they liked helping at the store even when he did not. Today, Marc was trying to dig up the weeds in front of the store before the dark clouds overhead began to dump rain. Amy worked with a feather duster in the front part of Grandpa's shop, where things were for sale. After her first half hour, Amy had said, "I'm

27

warning you, Grandpa, this may take me all day. You have so much *stuff*!"

"Not to mention that you have to stop and examine every little thing before you dust it," Grandpa had teased in return. "But that's okay," he had hurried to add, when Amy was about to protest. "Curiosity is a good thing. It keeps us learning."

Glancing out the shop window now, Amy saw Grandma coming down the sidewalk from the house with a tray. "Mmm," she called to Grandpa, "I see cookies coming." Amy watched Grandma give the tray to Marc, then go back into the house to begin her Saturday cleaning. Marc brought the cookies into the shop, and the three sat down to munch.

For a few minutes, there was no sound but chewing. Then Amy's eye fell on Grandpa's yellow wooden story box with the figure of a baby still sitting on the lid from the last story Grandpa had told. "Oh, Grandpa, remember," she said. "You're supposed to finish your story about Cain and Abel. You were right at the part where God was giving Cain a warning."

Grandpa washed down his last bite of cookie with a gulp of milk. Then he said, "We can't know for sure, but Cain may well have thought about God's warning; maybe he even admitted to himself that it was wrong to envy his brother. Still, he kept thinking about how unfair it was that Abel's offering had been accepted and his had not. Then, when the two brothers were out in the field together, with no parents around, Cain killed Abel.

"Can you imagine what it must have been like for Adam and Eve when they found out? Two sons, both of them dearly loved—now one was dead and, even worse, the other one was a murderer. They'd thought Cain was the child who was going to crush Satan's head. Now Satan and Cain's own sin had crushed Cain. Cain was clearly not the child God had promised, after all. As for Abel, he was dead. What would happen to God's promise? Maybe it couldn't come true now." Grandpa removed the little figure of the baby from the top of his box.

"That's surely what Satan would have hoped," Grandpa continued, "but nothing can stop God. God gave Adam and Eve a third baby boy, Seth," and Grandpa once again placed the figure of the baby on the top of the box. "Of course, it turned out that Seth wasn't the promised baby either, but he *was* the one from whom the promised baby would come."

A loud crack of thunder rang out, causing both the children and Grandpa to jump. Then large raindrops began to pound against the shop's windows and roof. "Well, Marc, guess you'll have to give up on working outside for now," Grandpa said to Marc. "It should be easier to pull the weeds out, though, once the ground is good and soaked. For now, I guess you'll just have to sit back and listen to the story of the next battle. Have another cookie," he added, and passed the plate again. Then he went on.

"Adam lived to be almost a thousand years old," Grandpa said.

"Whoa," said Amy, "imagine how big a birthday cake he'd need for that many candles!"

"By the time he died," Grandpa went on, "Adam surely realized that the child God had promised wasn't going to be born in his lifetime. Since he lived such a long time, Adam was able to see his grandchildren and his great-grandchildren and his many-times-great-grandchildren. Children kept being born until the earth was full of people. The problem was that since every baby was born a sinner, the more people there were on earth, the more sin there was."

"More reinforcements for Satan," muttered Marc.

"Of course, there was still God's promise. People could be sorry about their sin. They could believe that God would do something about it, as he'd said he would. But what if no one did? What if all the people loved their sin so much that they all chose to fight against God and hang on to it? What if no one hoped for God to keep his promise?"

A lightning flash lit up the shop, grown dark on account of the storm. Another peal of thunder sounded at almost exactly the same instant. Marc jumped, splashing milk from the cup he held onto his jeans. Amy giggled.

Grandpa continued as though nothing had happened. "The Bible tells us that the wickedness of man was great on the earth and that every thought he had was only evil continually. Satan, no doubt, was thrilled to the depths of his evil being. One thing Satan knows from his own experience is that wickedness makes God angry. If all the people that God had made to love and enjoy him were wicked, God would have to punish them. If they refused to repent, maybe God would even destroy them. There would be no human beings left to be God's people. No baby would be born to crush Satan. Satan would have won. So you can imagine Satan's delight when God said, 'I will wipe mankind whom I have created from the face of the earth.' "

Grandpa rummaged through his box. He selected two new pieces. Keeping one hidden in his hand, he placed the other one on the center of the box top. The figure represented a small group of people. All the people had clenched fists. Some were waving their fists angrily in one another's faces. The others were shaking their fists at the sky, as if against God himself. Nothing was heard in the shop except the sound of the rain falling outside.

"God sent a flood to destroy the human race," said Grandpa. "This flood was big enough to cover the entire earth and destroy every living thing. It surely seemed that God had lost this battle. And that would mean that he'd lost the war. God didn't lose this battle, though. He won it, by making a very unusual move for a commander in wartime to make."

Marc perked up. Of course, he had heard the story of Noah and the flood countless times. He had never thought of it as a battle in a war, though, and now he was curious about this unusual battle plan.

"The flood was soon to begin," Grandpa continued. "Rain was going to pour from the sky for forty days and nights, with no letup.

God's wicked human enemies were cornered. There was no escape for them—the very mountaintops would soon be underwater. But before God's judgment fell, God made a way for people to escape his judgment. Did you ever hear of such a thing, Marc? A very decisive battle is about to begin, a battle that will finish off the rebels who keep making trouble. First, however, the attacking general not only allows the rebels a chance to escape, but actually gives them what they need to save themselves from him and the destruction he's bringing." Grandpa shook his head in wonder.

Amy could no longer keep still. "That's like Jesus, isn't it, Grandpa?" she said. "The ark's like Jesus. God judges people because they sin; but he gave us Jesus to save us from his judgment."

"Hooray for Amy John," Grandpa exclaimed. "Good thinking and good observing! God, by his great power, kept one man true to himself—and that man was—"

"Noah," the children answered together.

"The Bible tells us that Noah found favor in the eyes of the Lord. Through all the evil and violence of the world around him, he walked with God." Knowing how familiar the story was to his two grandchildren, Grandpa finished it by pausing for them to fill in the blanks. "God told Noah to build an . . ." ("Ark," the children said.) "and fill it with some of every kind of . . ." ("Animal," said the children.) "and go into it with his . . ." ("Family," they said.) "Then God closed the . . ." ("Door.") "And it began to . . ." ("Rain").

Grandpa removed the figure of the angry people from the box top and placed the other figure—a small ark—in its place. "To Satan's great disappointment, Noah was safe. God's plan was safe. The human race would begin again, and God's promise to crush Satan would be kept."

"And there is no other god besides me,
a righteous God and a Savior;
     there is none besides me.

"Turn to me and be saved,
     all the ends of the earth!
     For I am God, and there is no other.
By myself I have sworn;
     from my mouth has gone out in righteousness
     a word that shall not return:
'To me every knee shall bow,
     every tongue shall swear allegiance.'

"Only in the Lord, it shall be said of me,
     are righteousness and strength;
to him shall come and be ashamed
     all who were incensed against him."

Propaganda
and Resistance

(Genesis 12:1–9; 17:1–8)

As soon as the rain stopped, Marc went back outside to his work of pulling weeds. Just as Grandpa had predicted, it was much easier, with the ground well soaked. Amy went back to her dusting. Just as *she* had predicted, she never quite finished. There were too many fascinating things to examine as she worked.

As Marc was washing his hands after his yardwork and while Amy was still dusting, Grandma came out to the shop. "I'm going to need some hamburger buns for dinner," she announced.

"Hamburgers?" Grandpa said. "Are you two staying for dinner?" he asked Amy.

Amy nodded. "Yep. With Mom and Dad," she said.

"Good deal," said Grandpa. "Come on, let's go get buns."

Marc and Amy climbed into the bench seat of Grandpa's battered blue pickup truck. As they drove, they came upon a sign for a garage sale, and Grandpa stopped the truck. Grandpa always stopped for garage sales.

Grandpa and the children entered the garage, where they saw old furniture and piles of odds and ends, hastily brought inside earlier to protect them from the rain. Grandpa hurried through the piles until he came to some old lamps. He chose one, saying, "I'll take this one." Amy could not see why. The lamp had no light bulb and no lampshade. It was nothing but a metal stand. The metal was green, stained, and ugly. "Who's going to want that?" Marc wondered out loud.

"This is real brass," Grandpa answered. "Once I polish it and shine it up and stick a nice-looking lampshade on it, it will be a beautiful lamp. I'll show you when I get it done." Marc thought, *If you get it done*, but he did not say this out loud. Grandpa had a reputation for having too many projects. Some were half-finished, some scarcely begun, others not started at all. Yet he could never resist picking up just one more.

When they returned home, Grandma took the buns with a "thank you" and shook her head at the lamp. Dinner was not yet ready, so the three went out to the shop to find a place for the lamp. After setting it down in a corner next to four other lamps waiting for attention, Grandpa sat down with his yellow story box. "We have a few minutes," he said. "Let me tell you about the next battle in our war."

The children sat down and Grandpa began. "After the flood, God put a rainbow in the sky. Do you remember why?"

"It was there for a reminder," Marc said, "because God said he would never flood the whole world again."

"Right," said Grandpa. "So Satan had no hope of another world-wide disaster to wipe out mankind. He'd remember that every time he saw a rainbow. But if he couldn't do away with people altogether, maybe he could make them forget about God. After all, God had made people to know and enjoy him—what if no one did? God's promise was for those who believed he would keep it. What if no one believed the promise or even remembered it?

"Marc," Grandpa asked, turning to his grandson, "during World War II, how did Hitler get people to go along with his evil ideas?"

"He used propaganda," Marc replied.

"How do you know that word?" Amy interrupted. "I just learned it myself, in seventh-grade history."

"If it has anything to do with war," Grandpa chuckled, "Marc knows it."

"As I was saying," Marc continued, pleased to have impressed Amy with his vocabulary, "Hitler was always putting out information, like news stories or like books written by scientists that would say his ideas were right—even though they weren't. But people believed him."

"And of course, because Hitler was smart, he mixed into his false information enough truth to get people to believe it," said Grandpa. "Satan did something similar in our war. People would see something God had made and think it was wonderful—and it was! Satan, though, would suggest to them that, since that thing was so wonderful, the thing itself must be a god. The sun is warm and it gives light—what would we do without it? And people can't control it— it must be a god! Trees and rain and cattle and birds, even snakes— each one is so amazing when you stop and think of it—it must be a god.

"Such false ideas spread all over the world. Soon everyone was praying to the things God had made instead of worshiping the God who had made them." Grandpa raised the lid of his box and sorted through the pieces inside with his finger. He found the two pieces he wanted, and after closing the lid, he set one of them up on top of the box. Marc and Amy leaned forward to see what it was. It was a little figure of a sun, a moon, and two stars, representing the created things people made into false gods.

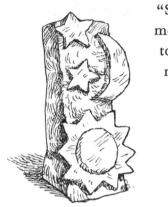

"Satan must have had another thrill of excitement," Grandpa continued. "Perhaps God's plan to have people who would know and love him was ruined. Everyone seemed to be worshiping other gods." Grandpa noticed that Marc and Amy were listening intently. He stopped and grinned, enjoying their suspense.

Amy saw the grin. "Well, go on, Grandpa," she urged. "Then what happened?"

"God spoke to a man named Abram, whom he'd already chosen for something important," Grandpa said. "God came to Abram and told him to leave three things. 'Leave your country, leave your relatives, and leave your father's house,' God said. Abram may have wondered where he was supposed to go if he left all those things, but God didn't tell him. He just said, 'Go to the land I'll show you.' That could have been anywhere! Then God *promised* Abram three things if he would go. God promised to give Abram the land he was going to show him. God promised to make a great nation from him. And he promised to bless him and to bless all the people of the world through him."

Marc interrupted. "Wasn't his name 'Abraham'?"

"It was later," Grandpa replied. "Later, God changed Abram's name to 'Abraham.' " Then Grandpa chuckled. "I'll bet Satan didn't like the part about all the people of the earth being blessed through Abram—what do you think, Amy? Wouldn't that have made Satan nervous?"

Amy was puzzled. "If you say so," she said, "but I'm not sure what that means."

Grandpa helped her. "What great nation would finally come from Abraham?"

"The nation of Israel," Amy answered.

"And who came from the nation of Israel and has turned out to be a blessing to the whole world?"

"Jesus," said Amy. She brightened. "Oh, I get it. God's promise to Abraham was the same as his promise to Adam and Eve—it was about Jesus coming someday."

"Bingo," said Grandpa. "Still, Satan might have thought it could never happen. After all, God was asking Abram to leave his family and his hometown of Ur—a big, modern, wealthy city—to go to a land that he hadn't even seen yet. Wherever it was, it wouldn't be anything like Ur. And there wouldn't be anyone there he knew. Plus, Abram's own family worshiped idols, just like everyone else did. Why would Abram obey God and leave home?

"To Satan's surprise, however, Abram packed up his wife, his servants, his possessions, and set off, with no idea of where he was going. Abram believed God, so he obeyed him. This wasn't because Abram was especially good. And it wasn't because he was any more righteous than anybody else. Abram obeyed God because God had chosen him. This afternoon, I chose a lamp. I didn't choose it because it was beautiful; it was just as ugly and beat up as all the other lamps. I chose it so that I could *make* it beautiful. God chose Abram, not because he was obedient, but so that God could *make* him obedient. I'll work on the lamp to make it beautiful. God worked in Abram's heart to cause him to believe and obey.

"So Abram went to the land that God showed him. All over that land, he built altars to the one true God who had led him there." With a flourish, Grandpa bumped the little figure of the

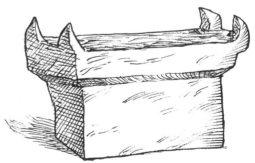

sun, moon, and stars off the box lid and replaced it with a miniature altar. "From Abram would come the Israelite nation. It would be Israel's task to show the idol-worshiping neighbors that there is only one true and living God."

Joshua 24:2–3

And Joshua said to all the people, "Thus says the LORD, the God of Israel, 'Long ago, your fathers lived beyond the Euphrates, Terah, the father of Abraham and of Nahor; and they served other gods. Then I took your father Abraham from beyond the River and led him through all the land of Canaan, and made his offspring many. I gave him Isaac."

A Lonely Battlefield

(Genesis 17:15–21; 21:1–7; 22:1–14)

Marc and Amy's mother appreciated the nearness of Grandpa's shop to the school that the children attended. They often walked to Grandpa's shop at the end of the school day and waited there until it was convenient for her to come for them. The rule was that they could not do anything at Grandpa's shop until all homework was finished.

On this particular afternoon, Marc's books and papers were still out on the table, but he himself was over in a corner setting up the Civil War soldiers. "Marc, did you finish all your assignments?" Grandpa called to him.

"Almost," Marc said, setting up one soldier, then replacing it with another as he tried to create the exact scene that was in his mind.

"If you're not done, you need to keep working," Grandpa admonished.

"I am working," Marc replied, positioning a last figure in his scene. "I'm working on my English assignment. We're supposed to write a paragraph telling a short story about anything we like."

"Let me guess," Amy called out from the corner where she was circling the answer to her last math problem. "You chose something about war."

"I saw this show on TV about a Civil War battle right here in Arizona," Marc said, "so that's what I wrote about. There were only a few soldiers from each side, just passing through, but they ran into each other along the way and had a fight. I was setting up the soldiers to see what it might have looked like." Marc went back to his papers and wrote rapidly for a few minutes. "There," he announced. "I'm done!"

Amy had already packed up her school things. She glanced at the little soldiers that Marc had set up. "It seems kind of funny that those soldiers had a fight about the Civil War way out here. It's a long way from where the rest of the action was."

"But they did, though," Marc answered. "Three soldiers even died in the battle. One of them is still buried there."

"What are you thinking?" asked Grandpa, who often knew what was on Amy's mind. "How lonely it would have felt, to fight and die so far from home and even from the rest of the war?" Amy nodded. Grandpa said, "Reminds me of a very lonely battle that Abram fought, all by himself, in our war story. Shall I try to fit in this next story before your mom gets here?" The children agreed, so Grandpa got his box. "By the time of this story, Abram's name had been changed to Abraham. Do you remember the three things God had promised to him?" Grandpa asked.

"Land, a great nation to come from him," Marc said, counting on two fingers. He stopped, then, not remembering the third promise.

"And that all the nations in the world would be blessed through him," Amy finished for him.

"By now, Abraham was living on the land God had promised, but what about the great nation? So far, God hadn't given him and his wife Sarah even one child. And now he was a hundred years old and Sarah was ninety." Grandpa laughed a little laugh. "That's even older than I am—too old for having babies! It looked like Abraham and Sarah would die childless. But—God had promised. And even though he had his moments of doubt, Abraham still believed that God could keep his promise. Finally, sure enough, when Sarah was ninety years old, she gave birth to a little baby boy. They named him Isaac—'laughter.' He filled their lives with just that—joy and laughter.

"Now imagine with me that at the end of a certain day, Abraham sat thinking about the day he'd just spent with Isaac. They'd gone from flock to flock and from herd to herd, checking on the animals. Abraham thought about all the different things Isaac would need to know. He'd have to know how to take care of flocks and herds, but he'd also have to know how to work with men. There were so many servants and herdsmen. And then, of course, there was the most important thing of all—Isaac would need to learn to love and obey the Lord. Because Abraham wasn't just passing on his wealth to this young man, but all of God's promises as well.

"As Abraham sat there thinking about Isaac's future, and maybe praying for his one dear son, he heard someone call his name. It was a voice Abraham didn't hear every day, but he'd heard it often enough that he recognized it when he heard it. It was the voice of God, calling, 'Abraham!' 'Here I am!' Abraham answered. Maybe he thought God was going to give him some more directions about Isaac.

"And, in fact, God began by saying, 'Take your son, your only son, whom you love, Isaac—' Abraham may have smiled to himself to think how well God knew him. Nothing was so dear to Abraham as

41

his son. He wasn't just 'his son.' He was his 'only son,' the son whom he loved, his own special Isaac. '—And go to the land of Moriah—' God continued.

" 'A three-day father–son trip!' Abraham may have thought, delighted. "But then God finished his directions for Isaac. '—And offer him there as a burnt offering on one of the mountains of which I will tell you.'

"Abraham couldn't believe he'd heard God correctly. God wouldn't ask for a *human* sacrifice. And God couldn't mean for Isaac to die. God had promised Abraham that his many descendants would come *through* Isaac. How could they come through Isaac if Isaac were dead? Or what about the blessing to all the nations? How would that happen if Isaac died? Abraham may have waited for more words from God, for further directions that would make more sense, but there was only silence.

"The Bible doesn't tell us whether or not Abraham slept that night," Grandpa continued. "Personally, I don't think he did. I've been a father and now I'm a grandfather, and if it had been me, I would have been far too troubled to sleep. Imagine the struggle taking place in Abraham's thoughts. Obeying God had always been the most important thing in Abraham's life. But Isaac was a very close second! How could Abraham possibly do this thing God was asking of him? Maybe he tried to imagine himself lifting the knife over his son the way he lifted it over an offering of a sheep, but he couldn't even stand to think about it. How could he kill his son, his only son, whom he loved, his Isaac? How could he, even for God?

"Early in the morning, Abraham woke Isaac and two servants. He saddled the donkey, gathered wood for the burnt offering, and set off to offer Isaac as an offering."

"How could he do that, Grandpa?" Amy breathed.

"I think he was still hoping God would somehow intervene," Grandpa answered. "He had three days; maybe those further directions were still coming. He knew God had promised him descendants and blessing through Isaac. He knew they wouldn't come from anywhere else. But he also knew God had told him to offer his son."

"Did Isaac know what was going on?" Marc wanted to know.

"He knew they were going to offer a sacrifice," Grandpa replied, "but he didn't realize the sacrifice was *him*. He asked where the lamb for the offering was. Abraham only said, 'God will provide for himself the lamb for the burnt offering, my son.'

"Finally, they came to a mountain called Mount Moriah and God showed Abraham that this was the place. The waiting was over. Abraham went on ahead with Isaac, leaving the servants behind. Somehow—through blinding tears, I'm sure—he explained to Isaac what had to happen. He tied up his beloved son and placed him on the wood on the altar." Here, Grandpa paused and placed the miniature altar he had used in the last story about Abraham on top of the yellow box. On the altar, he placed the figure of the baby that he had used in earlier stories.

"If Abraham obeyed God, he would kill the dearest person in all the world to him. He'd be destroying all hope for the future by killing the boy through whom the promise was to come. Abraham drew a deep breath. He couldn't look at Isaac as he raised his knife to drive it into Isaac's chest.

" 'Abraham!' called the voice that Abraham had been longing to hear.

" 'Here I am,' he answered, in what must have been no more than a shaky whisper.

" 'Don't harm the boy,' God said. 'For now I know that you fear God, since you have not withheld your son, your only son, from me.' Then Abraham saw a sheep in the bushes right by them. It was caught there by its horns. Abraham untied Isaac and helped him down from the altar. He picked up the sheep and put it in Isaac's place." Grandpa did the same, with his little figures. He removed the figure of the child from the little altar and put a small white sheep there instead.

"God taught Abraham and Isaac something about himself that day," Grandpa finished. "God provides more than just land and riches and prosperity. He provides an offering to die in our place. Abraham did not yet understand all that would come to mean. But he understood it well enough that he named that place 'The Lord Will Provide.' "

There was silence. Marc went back to his Civil War soldiers, but Amy remained where she was, thinking. Finally, she said, "Grandpa, all along God knew he was going to stop Abraham, right? He never meant for Abraham to really kill Isaac, right?"

"That's right," said Grandpa. "So you're wondering why God even put Abraham through such a hard test, is that it?"

Amy nodded. "Three days was a long time for him to think he was really going to have to kill his son," she said. "That must have been horrible."

"You have to remember that this war is bigger than what any one soldier, fighting bravely on his own battlefield, can see," Grandpa replied. "God is the Commander-in-Chief. He sees the big picture. He makes plans, and then he gives orders that will cause those plans to work out. Do you think those orders always make sense to each and every fighter at the time?"

"I guess not," Amy agreed, reluctantly.

"God's main purpose in this war," Grandpa went on, "is to have people who will be his people. God draws people to himself and makes them his own by showing them who he is and what he's like. Now, who else can you think of who had a son, an only son, a son whom he loved—who had to give him up to die?"

"Oh," said Amy, "God did."

"We all have people whom we love, so when we hear the story of Abraham and Isaac we can imagine how hard it would have been for Abraham to give up his son. We get a tiny idea of God's great love that would cause him to give up Jesus for us. Showing us his great

44

love is one of God's best ways to draw people to himself and make them his people."

Genesis 22:13–14

And Abraham lifted up his eyes and looked, and behold, behind him was a ram, caught in a thicket by his horns. And Abraham went and took the ram and offered it up as a burnt offering instead of his son. So Abraham called the name of that place, "The LORD will provide"; as it is said to this day, "On the mount of the LORD it shall be provided."

John 3:16

For God so loved the world, that he gave his only Son, that whoever believes in him should not perish but have eternal life.

The Choice of a Soldier

(Genesis 27–28)

Marc sat at the desk in his bedroom. His leg bounced up and down, up and down, the way it always did when he was thinking hard about something. In front of him, his Bible lay open to Genesis, where he had been reading. Left to himself, Marc might have chosen some other book of the Bible to read; Genesis didn't have very many battle stories. But he was working toward another patch for his shirt at Wednesday night Boys' Club. Finishing Genesis by the end of the month was one of the requirements.

Marc squinted at the model B-17 hanging from the ceiling. He did not see it, though, nor was he thinking about bombers at all. Instead, Marc was making up his mind that *he* liked Esau. Oh, sure, Jacob was always the hero of the Sunday school stories. He showed up in Genesis much more often than his twin brother, Esau. But Jacob was difficult to like. Besides, Esau was what a *soldier* ought to be. He was strong and used to living out-of-doors. He was skilled as a hunter. He was obedient and followed directions. If the stories in the Bible were all about one big war, why did Jacob—the dishonest mama's boy—play such an important part?

Mom's voice called that it was time for lights out and Marc, already dressed for bed, switched off the light and crawled between the sheets. He went to sleep thinking about how different the Jacob and Esau stories would have been if he had written them.

The next time Marc and Amy were in Grandpa's shop, Marc eyed the lemon-colored box. "Say, Grandpa," he said. "Do you have anything in that box for telling Esau stories?"

"Esau?" said Grandpa. "No, I don't believe I do."

"But I'll bet you have something in there for Jacob, huh?" Marc continued.

"Yes, that's right," Grandpa replied.

"Well, I don't think that's fair," said Marc. "I've been reading about Jacob and Esau. I think Esau was much more like a soldier than Jacob was. Not to mention that Jacob was a liar and a cheater. How come he gets all the glory in the stories?"

"Whoa, hold on," said Amy. "Marc, you've just been reading this stuff, but it's been awhile for me. Let Grandpa tell us the story first, and then argue all you want."

"Okay," said Marc. "You're going to see what I mean."

"Jacob and Esau were Isaac's twin sons," Grandpa began. "Esau was older because he was born first. But before the babies were born, God had told their mother, Rebekah, that he'd chosen the younger son. Jacob was the one through whom the promises and the blessings to Abraham would be passed on."

"See?" Marc muttered. "It starts out not fair, and it just keeps going like that."

"Marc thinks that Esau was more like a soldier because he liked *manly* things while he was growing up," Grandpa explained. "Esau liked to hunt and camp and stay out in the fields. He was a big, hairy outdoorsman."

"And all Jacob liked to do was to sit home with his mom and cook," said Marc.

"Marc, please," Amy protested. "Would you let *Grandpa* tell the story? He's really better at it than you are."

Grandpa smiled, took a miniature cooking pot from his box, and set it up on the closed lid. "That does seem to be what Jacob liked while he was growing up," he said. "Nonetheless, Jacob is the one God chose for the blessing. But now, what if Jacob turned out to be a scoundrel and someone who could never be pleasing to God? What if he did things that were so wicked that *everyone* would agree that he couldn't possibly receive God's blessing? In that case, it would seem certain that God's promise couldn't be kept and Satan would have won."

Grandpa paused and Amy spoke up again. "Oh, now I remember," she said. "Jacob cheated his brother, right?"

"It was his mother's idea," Grandpa said, "but that doesn't excuse Jacob. Jacob's mother came to him one day and told him what she'd just overheard. Isaac was old and thought he wouldn't live much longer, so he wanted to give his blessing to Esau. Rebekah had heard Isaac tell Esau to go hunting and come back with something to cook for him. After he ate it, the boys' father planned to give Esau his blessing. 'So here's what we're going to do,' Rebekah said. 'While Esau's out hunting, you bring me a young goat from our flock. I'll cook it for your father—I know just the way he likes it. He's too old to see well, so you take the food to him and pretend you're Esau. That way, your father will give the blessing to you instead of to your brother.' "

"That's really pretty mean," said Amy, "playing tricks on a blind man."

"Not to mention that the blind man was his own dad," said Marc.

"You're right," Grandpa agreed. "And Jacob was quite willing to go along with his mother's sneaky trick. His only worry was that he might get caught. 'What if my father reaches out and touches me?' he said to his mother. 'He'll be able to tell we're tricking him, because my brother's hairy and I'm not.'

" 'Don't worry,' Rebekah said. 'I'll put goat hair on your arms so that you'll feel hairy to the touch.' So Jacob agreed. Soon the food was ready, and Jacob took it in to his father.

" 'Who are you?' Isaac asked.

" 'I'm Esau, your firstborn,' Jacob answered. 'I've brought you the food you asked for.' "

Marc interrupted. "First lie," he said.

Grandpa continued. " 'How did you catch something so quickly?' Jacob's father wanted to know. 'God helped me,' Jacob replied."

"Second lie," said Marc just as Amy was saying, "Oh, brother."

"Just as Jacob had feared, his father wanted to feel him, and he asked him to come closer. When Isaac felt the goat hair on Jacob's arms, he said, 'It sounds like Jacob, but it feels like Esau. Are you really my son Esau?'

" 'I am,' said Jacob."

"Third lie," said Marc.

"And so Isaac ate the food and gave Jacob the blessing that should have gone to the oldest son," Grandpa continued. "No sooner had Jacob left his father than Esau came home and found out what had happened. He vowed that he would kill his brother. Jacob had to flee from home to escape." Grandpa removed the little figure of a pot from the box lid. "It would seem that God's promise had failed," he said. "God couldn't possibly pass the promise on through Jacob. Jacob was just too wicked.

"That may have been what Jacob was feeling, that first night away from home. That far from any town, it was pitch dark once the sun had set. There weren't even any houses around. Lonely, maybe scared, already homesick, Jacob lay down to try to sleep. He didn't even have anything for a pillow. He had to lay his head on a stone. He'd really made a mess of things! Surely God must have left him by now.

"Then Jacob went to sleep and had a dream. In his dream, he saw a ladder or a stairway. Angels were going up and down on these stairs, and at the very top he saw God. God spoke to Jacob in the dream. He made him all the same promises he'd made to Abraham."

Grandpa turned to Amy. "What were they again?"

"A great nation, land, and blessing," Amy answered promptly.

"Then God finished by promising Jacob, 'I will not leave you until I have done what I have promised.'" From his box, Grandpa took a small wooden model of a set of stairs. He placed it on the box lid, where the pot had been.

"When Jacob woke up, he said, 'Surely God is in this place and I didn't know it.' He set up a stone—remember the one he'd used for a pillow? The stone was a reminder of what he'd seen and heard. I'd like to tell you that Jacob went on from there to be honest and truthful all the rest of his life, but that's just not true. He still did some tricking and cheating. Yet God kept his promise and was with Jacob all his life. And even after Jacob died, through the rest of the Old Testament, God often called himself 'The God of Jacob.'"

Marc shook his head. "I just don't get it. Why would God stick with Jacob when Jacob was such a creep? Why not Esau? Why does Jacob get to be the hero?"

Before Grandpa could answer, Amy spoke up. "Think about it, Marc. What if God only picked people who were never going to mess up? Who do you know that never messes up? If God's going to have people for himself, which is what this war is all about, he's going to have to pick people and keep on loving them *in spite of* the things they do that are rotten. Don't you see, Marc? Jacob's not the hero of the story. God is."

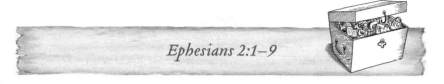

Ephesians 2:1–9

And you were dead in the trespasses and sins in which you once walked, following the course of this world, following the prince of the power of the air, the spirit that is now at work in the sons of disobedience—among whom we all once lived in the passions of our flesh, carrying out the desires of the body and the mind, and were by nature children of wrath, like the rest of mankind. But God, being rich in mercy, because of the great love with which he loved us, even when we were dead in our trespasses, made us alive together with Christ—by grace you have been saved—and raised us up with him and seated us with him in the heavenly places in Christ Jesus, so that in the coming ages he might show the immeasurable riches of his grace in kindness toward us in Christ Jesus. For by grace you have been saved through faith. And this is not your own doing; it is the gift of God, not a result of works, so that no one may boast.

A Failed Sabotage
Attempt

(Genesis 37, 39–50)

Amy held the glass to the light, admiring the rosy pink color. "I wonder what people did with this," she said. "You could serve ice cream in it or you could drink water out of it."

"I don't know how much ice cream was eaten out of that glass, at least back when it was first made," Grandpa replied. He left the lamp he was working on and came over to Amy, who had been searching with interest through his collection of old dishes. "That's a piece of Depression glass. Not many people had money to spend on ice cream during the Great Depression. They didn't even have money to spend on dishes. Pieces like this came free in the family oatmeal or flour or other food supplies they bought."

"We talked about the Great Depression in sixth grade," Amy said. "Wasn't that when the banks ran out of money and everyone suddenly became poor?"

"Well, it was a little more complicated than that, but yes, even people who had saved a lot of money lost it during the Depression." Grandpa began to rummage through a nearby stack of magazines. "People couldn't find jobs. Families lost their homes. People used newspapers for blankets and had a hard time even eating enough to stay alive."

"But people got beautiful dishes like this one free in their oatmeal," said Amy. "That must have made a bright little moment of encouragement in the middle of all the hard times."

Grandpa had found the magazine he was looking for. He opened it to a black-and-white photograph, then handed it to Amy. "This happened, too, and made things even worse. Times had already been tough for American farmers. Then the great Dust Bowl disaster hit. After years of little or no rain, the soil itself began to blow away, making it impossible to grow anything."

"You mean those huge black clouds in the picture are clouds of dirt?" asked Amy.

Grandpa nodded. "That's why it was called a Dust Bowl. Farmers gave up and moved away. If they hadn't, they wouldn't have been able to feed their families. There was a time like that in the story of our war—a tough time. No food and no way to grow any. May I tell you about it?"

"Sure," said Amy, and then called to her brother. Marc had been reading for almost an hour. Even though the book was about famous battles of World War I, he had been sitting in one place long enough and was ready to set the book aside. He came over to Grandpa and Amy, where he remained standing while Grandpa began.

Grandpa opened his box and removed several small figures. He held up the little staircase from the last story. "As you'd expect, God kept his promises to Jacob. He caused him to prosper and grow wealthy, which was a good thing, since God also gave Jacob a huge family. He had twelve sons, and who knows how many daughters. Jacob took his big family back home, to the land he'd run away from earlier. His family settled there and his sons grew up. Many of them married and had children of their own. So God's promise of many descendants to come from Abraham seemed finally to be coming true.

"But—what if the whole family were wiped out? What if they all died, leaving no survivors? Then God's promise of a baby to destroy Satan and his work couldn't come true. There came a time when Jacob's family *was* in danger of dying out. There'd been seven very good years for Jacob and his sons, in fact for everyone in the land. There'd been plenty of rain, the weather had been great, and the land had produced abundant crops. Jacob and his family, who were already rich, became used to having whatever they wanted whenever they wanted it.

"Then came the first year of famine. Nothing went right that year. The amounts of rain were all wrong. The weather wasn't good for raising crops or caring for animals. They had one trouble after another. Jacob wasn't worried, though. The past seven years had been very good. So he and his family lived on what they'd already stored up and waited for better growing conditions. But month after month went by, and soon there wasn't much left to live on. By the second year, things were getting desperate, and still the famine grew worse. Jacob began to worry that some in his large family would starve because of this famine. What he didn't know was that the famine was going to last for a total of seven long years. There was no way his family could survive a seven-year famine. So it seemed that there was no way God's promise could be kept."

Grandpa paused to place a figure on the lid of his yellow box. It was the figure of a cow. "Grandpa didn't make that cow right," Marc thought at first. Peering at it, he saw points sticking out all over it. Then he realized that it was the cow's bones he was seeing. "Of course," Marc thought. "It's because of the famine. It's how Jacob's cows must have looked."

"One day," Grandpa continued, "Jacob heard that there was grain to be bought in Egypt. So he sent his ten sons off to find out if that was true."

"I thought he had twelve sons," Amy interrupted.

"He did," Grandpa said. "But Jacob didn't want the youngest one to go all the way to Egypt. And another son, Joseph, was gone. Jacob thought Joseph was dead. That's because, one time, the ten other brothers had come back from the field with Joseph's coat, all torn and bloody. 'A wild beast has eaten him,' Jacob had cried, heartbroken, for Joseph was his favorite. 'He's surely been torn to pieces.'

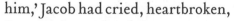

"So only ten of Jacob's sons set off for Egypt to try to find food. When the ten brothers arrived in Egypt, they met the ruler who was in charge of selling food to people. From the start, this ruler was suspicious of everything about them. 'You're not ten brothers here to buy food,' he said to them. 'You're spies.' And he locked them in jail. The brothers didn't know what to think. What would happen to them? And what would happen to their wives and children and their old father waiting for them at home?

"After three days, the Egyptian ruler came to them in prison. 'I've thought of a way to learn if your story is true,' he said. 'You say that you're ten brothers with the same father and that you have another younger brother at home. I'll sell you the grain you're asking for and let you go home. But I'll keep one of you here in prison. When the rest of you come back, bring your younger brother as proof of your story, and I'll let the prisoner go free.'

"It was then that the ten brothers began to talk among themselves about their guilty secret. Their other brother, Joseph, hadn't really been eaten by a wild animal." Grandpa winked at Marc and Amy. "But you knew that, didn't you?"

The children nodded. "His brothers sold him," Amy said.

"That's right," said Grandpa, "and that blood on his coat had been the blood of a sheep from the flock. Joseph's ten brothers had dipped his coat in the sheep's blood to trick their father. They'd hated Joseph because he was their father's favorite. So they'd sold him as a slave to get rid of him. The slave-traders who bought him took him far away—who knows where. Now that the brothers were having these terrible troubles, they remembered what they'd done and how guilty they were. They whispered among themselves that this was God's way of punishing them for being so cruel to their brother.

"So nine of them left one brother there in prison and went home to Jacob. They told him all about their trip and the suspicious ruler. Jacob said they would never take his youngest son to Egypt. He couldn't bear to lose him, too.

"But months went by, and finally all the grain they'd bought on their first trip was gone. There was no choice but to go back again and take their youngest brother with them. When they arrived in Egypt, the brothers were surprised to see that the ruler, who'd been so harsh to them before, was very generous with their younger brother. He piled gifts on him. Later on, they were even more surprised when that same ruler sent everyone but them out of the room and burst into tears in front of them. 'I'm Joseph!' he announced to them.

"Joseph told his brothers what had happened to him after they'd sold him. An army commander in Egypt bought him as a slave. Joseph had served the man well, but then he was sent to jail for something he hadn't done. While Joseph was in jail, God made Joseph able to explain dreams that two other prisoners dreamed. The dreams came true in every detail, just as Joseph had said. Later, when the pharaoh dreamed about skinny cows eating fat cows, Joseph explained that dream to him. Joseph said that God was warning the pharaoh about an upcoming famine. Pharaoh was so impressed with Joseph that he set him over all the land. Joseph's job was storing up food for the famine during the seven good years. Now that the seven years of famine were here, he was in charge of selling the stored-up food to all the people who needed it.

"Listening to all this, the brothers didn't think any of it was good news. They were terrified. The brother they had so cruelly sold was not only alive to tell on them, but he was a powerful ruler who could do whatever he wanted to them. All Joseph wanted to do, though, was to forgive them and send them home for their families. 'Don't be angry with yourselves for selling me here,' Joseph told them. 'It was God who was sending me ahead to save lives. There are still five years left of this famine. God sent me on ahead to preserve the family and keep us all alive. So it wasn't you who sent me here, but God. He has made me a ruler here over all this land. Hurry, go home, get your families and bring them here to Egypt so you can all survive this famine with plenty to eat.'

"So Jacob's family—and the promise—survived," Grandpa said, removing the skinny cow from the top of the box. He replaced it with a little figure in the shape of a basket overflowing with food. "God had won again."

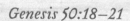

Genesis 50:18–21

His brothers also came and fell down before him and said, "Behold, we are your servants." But Joseph said to them, "Do not fear, for am I in the place of God? As for you, you meant evil against me, but God meant it for good, to bring it about that many people should be kept alive, as they are today. So do not fear; I will provide for you and your little ones." Thus he comforted them and spoke kindly to them.

Birth of a Deliverer

(Exodus 1:1–2:10)

Marc ran in the door of "Trash to Treasure." "Hey, Grandpa," he called, "look at my new patch from Boys' Club."

"Hi, Grandpa," said Amy, entering right behind Marc. "No homework today—yippee! Do you have anything you need done?"

After admiring Marc's patch, Grandpa answered, "As a matter of fact, Amy John, I set this box aside for you. It's full of picture frames. Some of them still have old pictures in them, and I need those taken out."

"Sure," said Amy, choosing a snack from the small refrigerator behind Grandpa's counter. She worked while she ate, and soon she had a whole stack of pictures beside her, most of them photographs of people. "I wonder who all these people were," she said, "what they were like, what they did. You know—what were their stories?"

Grandpa gave a last rub to the brass coffeepot he was polishing and set it down. "Well, they each had one, I'm sure of that," said Grandpa.

"Do you think any of these people were in our war?" Amy asked.

"Of course they were," said Grandpa. "No one's neutral in this war. Of course, some of the enemies are much more vicious than others. In our story's next couple of battles we'll see some kings who were determined to win their battles against God and his people."

"You're done with battles in Genesis, Grandpa, aren't you?" Marc asked. "I know because I got my badge for reading Genesis. Do you have war stories for the whole Bible?"

"Oh, yes," Grandpa replied. "In fact, in one sense, you could say that's just what the Bible is: the story of this war between God and Satan. It's the story of whether God would win and there would be a people of God, or whether Satan would win and there wouldn't be. Marc, when you read the book of Genesis, did you learn what the word 'Genesis' means?"

"Beginnings," Marc replied.

"Right," said Grandpa. "What kinds of things began in Genesis?

"The world," said Marc. "And sin. And all the bad things that go with it, like sickness and death and sadness."

"The people of God began, with the stories about Abraham," Amy added.

"Yep, all of those," Grandpa agreed. "And Genesis gives us the beginning of the war and the beginning of God's promise, both back there in Eden. So with all those things begun, we go on to the next part of the story, which we find in the book of Exodus. Do either of you know what 'Exodus' means?"

"A mass departure," Amy answered quickly. "We had that for a vocabulary word. It's whenever a whole bunch of people leave some-place at the same time."

"Oh, that's right," said Marc, "doesn't Exodus tell about the Israelites leaving Egypt?"

"Yes, it does," said Grandpa. "Where Genesis ends, God's promises are starting to come true, but there's more that has to happen. For instance, God had promised that Abraham's descendants would be a great nation. Do you know how many descendants there were when Genesis ended?"

"Oh, I remember reading this," said Marc. "There were—" he wrinkled his face, trying to remember—"I know, seventy!"

"Good remembering," said Grandpa. "Seventy makes a big family, but not a very big nation. Jacob's family lived in Egypt for several hundred years. While they were there, they had many, many children. Egypt became full of Abraham's descendants! So there we have it at last—our great nation from Abraham.

"Of course, I'm sure Satan didn't like what he was seeing. He'd hoped that famine would wipe out these people, so he wouldn't have to worry about a promised child coming from them. Now here they were, a great and mighty nation. The promised blessing to all other nations seemed right on track.

"Fortunately for Satan, he's always been able to find human allies to help him in his war against God and God's people. In this battle, the pharaoh was his ally. As the years went by, pharaohs died and new pharaohs took their place. Now there was a new pharaoh on the throne, a pharaoh who didn't know anything about Joseph or how he'd saved Egypt from famine. This pharaoh saw that his country was full of Hebrews (that's what the people who came from Abraham were called then)—"

"And those are the same as 'Israelites,' right?" Marc interrupted.

Grandpa nodded. "And they're also called 'Jews,' " Amy contributed.

Grandpa nodded again. "Hebrews, Israelites, Jews, all names for Abraham's descendants. Whatever you call them, Pharaoh was worried about them. He saw how strong they were. He began to worry that the day might come when there'd be more Hebrews than Egyptians. What if they rose up against the Egyptians and tried to take over?

"So the pharaoh said, 'We have to do something to keep the Hebrews from getting any stronger.' First, he tried to weaken them by turning them all into slaves." Grandpa reached for the yellow box that was always nearby when he told his stories. He found two pieces in the box, closed it and put one piece up on the lid. It was a miniature carving of a cruel-looking whip. "The Egyptians made the Israelites work hard, building whole cities for them. But this only made the Israelites stronger, and they had still more children.

" 'It isn't working,' thought Pharaoh (and maybe Satan). 'Something more drastic will have to be done.' So Pharaoh, already Satan's ally himself, tried to get the Hebrew midwives on Satan's side, too."

"What's a midwife again?" asked Marc. "I don't remember what that means."

"A midwife helps women when they give birth, kind of like a nurse, but a nurse only for women having babies," Grandpa answered. "Pharaoh ordered the Hebrew midwives, 'You can let baby girls live when they're born, but you're to kill baby boys.' "

"That's awful!" Amy said, shaking her head in disapproval.

Grandpa nodded. "Satan stoops pretty low in his war against God, doesn't he? What would happen to the Israelites if only girls survived and grew up?"

"Well, when all those girls grew up, there would be no Israelite husbands for them," said Marc. "So they wouldn't have any Israelite children, and eventually all the Israelites would die out."

"Exactly," said Grandpa. "I'm sure it seemed like a fine plan to Satan. Only problem was, the Hebrew midwives refused to cooperate. They didn't want to be allies of Satan or of Pharaoh in such a wicked scheme. They refused to kill the Hebrew boys.

"So Pharaoh commanded all the Egyptians. 'Daughters may live,' he told them, 'but every boy born to the Hebrews you're to cast into the River Nile.'"

"Drowning babies is about as evil as you can get!" Amy said.

"They probably wouldn't drown," said Marc, matter-of-factly. "They would probably get eaten by crocodiles first."

Grandpa pointed at the stack of photographs that Amy had removed from the picture frames. "Remember how you were wondering about their stories and which side they were on in our war?" Amy nodded. "There have always been countless people on God's side who have stories that most people will never know. Still, their stories play an important part in the one big story of the war. There were Hebrews like that living in Egypt during those four hundred years. These Hebrews faithfully passed on the knowledge of God to their children so that their children grew up trusting in God. Jochebed was just such a lady. She already had a little boy and a little girl. Now Jochebed had a newborn baby, and it was a boy. She refused to hand the baby over to the Egyptians, trusting God to help her do what was right. She hid the baby as long as she could, but babies grow, and soon he was too big and noisy to hide. So Jochebed prepared a little basket bed and painted it all over with pitch to make it waterproof. She put her baby in the basket and set the basket in the water plants at the edge of the river. Jochebed's daughter stayed nearby to see what would happen.

"Now, anything *could* have happened. Marc's perfectly right, a crocodile could have come along and snapped up the baby for his lunch. Or any one of many Egyptians could have come along, found the baby, and thought, 'Aha! A Hebrew,' and thrown the baby into the river as the pharaoh had ordered. Or nothing could have happened. The baby might have stayed there, stuck in the river plants, for days until he starved to death. But not only was the big sister watching over this baby, God was, too.

"As the sister watched, some ladies came to the riverbank to bathe. It was the pharaoh's grown daughter with her maids. Surely, except for the pharaoh himself, this was the worst possible person to find the basket with the baby inside. *Maybe she won't realize he's a Hebrew*, the sister may have hoped. The little girl could hardly watch when Pharaoh's daughter saw the basket and commanded her maids to bring it to her. Now she was opening the lid, now she was seeing the baby. His sister held her breath to see what the princess would say."

Amy realized that *she* was holding *her* breath and let it out slowly as Grandpa continued. "The sister heard the princess say, 'This is one of the Hebrews' children.' Oh, no! Discovered! But then the little girl realized that the woman was smiling tenderly at the baby. What a miracle! In spite of her father's order, God had prepared this woman's heart to pity this helpless baby with no one to care for it.

"Then the baby began to cry, just fussing at first, but louder and louder as he realized how hungry he was. This princess would have no way to feed a baby; what if she changed her mind and decided there was nothing she could do for him after all? The big sister knew she must be brave and act quickly. She stepped out in front of Pharaoh's daughter and said, 'Would you like me to get one of the Hebrew women who can feed the baby for you?'

"The princess nodded gratefully, and the little girl ran home to get her own mother. So it was that Moses—for that's what the princess named him—survived the pharaoh's evil order and was cared for by his own mother. When he was big enough, he went off to live in the palace with the pharaoh's daughter. But not before his mother and father had faithfully taught him what they knew to be true about God and his promises. Before Moses went off to live in enemy territory, he knew how God had protected him and he knew he would be on God's side, no matter what." Grandpa replaced the

figure of a whip with a figure of a little basket. From inside it, Marc and Amy could just see the face of a baby peeking out. "God's deliverance of his people was on its way."

Hebrews 11:23–27

By faith Moses, when he was born, was hidden for three months by his parents, because they saw that the child was beautiful, and they were not afraid of the king's edict. By faith Moses, when he was grown up, refused to be called the son of Pharaoh's daughter, choosing rather to be mistreated with the people of God than to enjoy the fleeting pleasures of sin. He considered the reproach of Christ greater wealth than the treasures of Egypt, for he was looking to the reward. By faith he left Egypt, not being afraid of the anger of the king, for he endured as seeing him who is invisible.

Commander-in-Chief

(Exodus 5–15)

Amy wiped the window cleaner from the last shop window. Sounds of spraying water came from around the corner, where Marc was cleaning window screens. "Marc," called Amy, moving toward him. "Hold out the hose for a minute." Marc did so and Amy held her cupped hands under the water, then splashed her face. "Whew!" she said, "it's *hot*! Even in the shade."

From nearby, where Grandpa was repairing a window frame, he answered, "For October, it *is* hot. Even for here in Phoenix. Seems to cool off later every year. I'm about done with this window. I'll go see if Grandma has something cold for us."

Soon Grandpa was back with frozen fruit bars for everyone. The children gratefully sank into the lawn chairs in the shade of the one large tree. They had been sitting for only a couple of minutes when Marc began slapping at tiny insects flying around his head. "More of those bugs!" he said. "They've been everywhere this week."

"We had a bunch of them in class yesterday," said Amy. "I think they came in on the new plant Mrs. Whittaker brought for the room."

"And your grandmother was complaining about them hanging around the fruit basket in the kitchen," said Grandpa. "Bugs," Grandpa continued. "I have a war story about bugs. Want to hear it while you eat those?" The children nodded. Grandpa, who had finished his fruit bar first, went into the shop and came right back out with his Bible and his yellow box.

"The battle in Egypt wasn't over just because one baby had been saved," he began, settling into his lawn chair. "This was going to be one of the biggest battles of the war. There would be attacks and counterattacks. As Moses grew up and saw how badly his people were being treated, he surely hoped that God would do *something* to help them. But Moses had no idea what God's strategy would really be. One day, Moses was out watching the slaves work. He saw an Egyptian beating a Hebrew. At first, maybe he only wondered why God allowed this to go on. Finally, though, as the beating continued, he couldn't stand it anymore, and he went after the Egyptian. He hit the Egyptian so hard that he killed him. Then Moses hid the body in the sand.

"But what Moses had done didn't stay hidden. Pharaoh found out about it and would have killed Moses for it, but Moses ran away from Egypt. He went to live in the desert with people who were shepherds. Moses got married, had children, and settled down to be a shepherd for the rest of his life. He may have thought sometimes about his past life in Egypt, but as the years went by, Egypt seemed farther and farther away. Memories of the Hebrews were like memories of another life altogether.

"But God remembered the Hebrews. And he knew how unhappy they were. The Bible says the Israelites cried to God for help because they were so miserable as slaves. God remembered his promises to Abraham, Isaac, and Jacob." Grandpa looked down at his Bible, open to the story he was telling. He read, " 'And God saw the sons of Israel, and God took notice of them.' One day, as Moses was taking care of sheep in the desert, he saw a most unusual sight. Do you know what it was?"

"It was a bush that was on fire, but it never burned up," Marc replied. Fire was another of Marc's interests, like war.

Grandpa nodded and went on. "God spoke to Moses from that bush. He told him that he was going to help his people, the Hebrews. First he would free them from the Egyptians, who were treating them so cruelly. Then he would lead them back to the land he'd promised to Abraham. And finally he would give them the land to live in.

"Of course, Moses thought this was wonderful news. Just as he was wondering exactly how God would do all this, God said to him, 'So come now, I'm sending you to Pharaoh so that you may bring my people out of Egypt.'

"Moses was more than just surprised—he was horrified! 'Me?' he exclaimed. And he began one argument after another to show God that he was not the man to send. 'Who am I, that I should be able to do such a thing? Pharaoh won't listen to me. The Israelites won't listen to me. How will they know you sent me? I never was a good speaker. I can't do this. Get someone else.'

"But God wanted Moses, and in the end Moses went. Now, the pharaoh from whom Moses had fled had died, but a new pharaoh ruled in his place. This pharaoh's heart was even harder. He was even more the ally of Satan than the last pharaoh had been.

"In fact, this pharaoh's response to God was even worse than Moses had feared. '*The* Lord says, "Let my people go?" cried Pharaoh. 'Who is the Lord, that *I* should obey him? I don't know the Lord, and I won't let Israel go!' Not only that, but then Pharaoh ordered an increase in the Hebrews' workload, which was already much too heavy.

"The people were in despair, and so was Moses. But God assured Moses that Pharaoh would find out who the Lord was. God promised that he would free the Israelites. He would take them to be his people, and he would be their God."

"There's that promise again," said Amy. "It just keeps popping up."

"And now the real battle began," Grandpa continued. "God attacked first by turning all the water in Egypt into blood. Pharaoh counterattacked by showing that his magicians could do the same kind of thing with their tricks. He wouldn't let Israel go.

"Seven days later, God attacked again. He filled Egypt with frogs. Frogs were everywhere—in the houses, between the sheets of the beds, in the ovens, on food in the dishes."

"Yuck!" Amy shuddered.

" 'Enough!' Pharaoh said. 'The people can go. Just get rid of these frogs.' The next day, all the frogs died. But Pharaoh hardened his heart and refused to let the people go.

"Next, God attacked the dust of the earth. He told Moses to stretch his rod out over the dust, and when Moses did, the dust turned to gnats."

"Like we have here, today," said Marc, brushing another small cloud of insects away from his head.

"Only much worse," said Grandpa. "Even Pharaoh's magicians said, '*We* can't do that. God's doing this!'—but Pharaoh refused to surrender. So God threatened swarms of more insects. This time, though, it would be different, God promised. In Goshen, the part of Egypt where the Hebrews lived, there would be no bugs. And so it happened. The swarms of insects were everywhere—except in Goshen. Pharaoh called for Moses, Moses prayed, and poof! the bugs were gone. Not one was left."

"That would be nice," Marc muttered, slapping his neck where he felt one of the tiny flies crawling.

"But of course, Pharaoh changed his mind. So God sent a sickness on the farm animals, and Egypt's livestock died. Pharaoh sent a servant to see how things were in Goshen. He learned that not one animal had died. Yet Pharaoh hardened his heart and refused to give up.

"Then came a plague of boils. Sores appeared on every human being and on every animal. Pharaoh's own servants couldn't come to work for him, they were so miserable. Still Pharaoh wouldn't admit defeat. 'Next it will be hail,' Moses warned. By this time, some of the Egyptians had come to see that everything God said through Moses always happened. These Egyptians were careful to stay inside and keep their animals in the barns. All who were outside when the hail began to fall were killed. The hail ruined plants and trees, too. Not, of course, in Goshen where the Hebrews lived. There was no hail there.

" 'Make the hail stop,' Pharaoh told Moses, 'and I'll let the people go.' The hail stopped, but the people went nowhere because, of course, Pharaoh hardened his heart one more time and didn't do what God commanded.

"Then God attacked with locusts for weapons. They flew in and ate any plants not already destroyed by the hail. At this point, Pharaoh's own people said to him, 'Egypt is being ruined! We won't have anything left! Let those people go!' But Pharaoh wouldn't. Next, God brought three days of intense darkness. Pharaoh still wouldn't give in. Finally, God struck down the oldest son in every Egyptian's family. At last, Pharaoh surrendered. He sent for Moses and begged him to take the Hebrews and go.

"Satan must have been watching this battle with great interest. He was surely disappointed to see the Hebrews leaving Egypt, rejoicing. But then Pharaoh changed his mind yet again. He took all the chariots of Egypt, hundreds of them, along with his entire army and set out after the Hebrews, who, of course, didn't have a single weapon with which to defend themselves. Pharaoh caught up with them by the sea. There were no boats, so the Hebrews were trapped.

"Satan must have been delighted. There was no escape for God's people. They would either be destroyed right here or be taken back to Egypt to be wiped out more slowly. Either way, no promised baby." Grandpa set the small model of a chariot up on the box top.

"But all the soldiers and chariots at Pharaoh's command were no match for God. God told Moses to stretch out his rod over the sea. When he did, the God who had commanded frogs and gnats, hail and darkness now commanded the sea. It divided right down the middle, allowing the Hebrews to walk across on dry land. When the Egyptians followed, God gave the waters another order and they returned to their place. The entire Egyptian army drowned."

Grandpa took away the chariot and replaced it with a little stick, like the rod Moses had used. "The Hebrews sang and danced. 'The LORD is a warrior,' they sang. They were right."

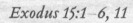

Exodus 15:1–6, 11

Then Moses and the people of Israel sang this song to the LORD, saying,

I will sing to the LORD, for he has triumphed gloriously;
    the horse and his rider he has thrown into the sea.

The LORD is my strength and my song,
    and he has become my salvation;
this is my God, and I will praise him,
    my father's God, and I will exalt him.
The LORD is a man of war;
    the LORD is his name.

Pharaoh's chariots and his host he cast into the sea,
and his chosen officers were sunk in the Red Sea.
The floods covered them;
    they went down into the depths like a stone.
Your right hand, O LORD, glorious in power,
your right hand, O LORD, shatters the enemy.
"Who is like you, O LORD, among the gods?
Who is like you, majestic in holiness,
awesome in glorious deeds, doing wonders?"

Issuing Orders

(Exodus 19–20)

"That's pathetic!" Marc said, shaking his head in disgust at what he was reading in his book of Civil War battles. His Civil War soldiers lay in confused piles on the table near him. "Grandpa, do you have any idea how bad some of the Union generals were?" he asked, looking up.

Grandpa had been making repairs on a small toaster. Now he plugged it into the wall and pushed down the lever to see if it would toast. "I've heard about that," he answered Marc.

"How bad could they have been?" Amy wondered. She was looking through Grandpa's random pieces of china, trying to decide which patterns and colors she liked best. "The North won, didn't it?"

"The North won," Marc agreed, "but it took a lot longer than it should have. For the first two years they didn't win a single battle, in spite of how many more soldiers they had. It was all because of the commanders. They gave lousy orders! Half the time, they gave no orders at all. And they would never listen to their men when their men knew all along what needed to be done. For instance, there was this one battle where the commander had already been doing absolutely everything wrong. Bunches of his men had already been slaughtered. And then a shell hit the house where he was staying and knocked him out. He stayed groggy the whole rest of the day—obviously unable to even think straight, but he wouldn't let anyone else give any orders. The battle turned out to be a Union disaster. Surprise, surprise."

"Imagine how the ordinary soldiers must have felt, or the junior officers who could have fought well if they'd been allowed to," Grandpa said. "What if you knew you were strong and brave and ready to fight, but you had no clear orders, so you didn't know what you were supposed to do? Soldiers have to have orders. They can't just decide for themselves what to do."

"That's just it," said Marc. "It doesn't matter how big or how good an army is; if there's no one in charge giving good commands, that army can't win."

"It's not like that with our Commander in our war," said Grandpa, unplugging the toaster, which was now working just fine. "Take a break from reading about depressing Civil War battles and I'll show you what I mean," he invited.

Marc closed his book and came to sit by Grandpa, who had picked up his story box. Amy set aside two more teacups, as ones she especially liked, and came to join them.

"When the Israelites left Egypt," Grandpa began, "they were a huge crowd of people of all ages. Think of the largest crowd you've ever seen, in real life or on TV; this crowd of Israelites was much larger. Think of how unruly such a crowd can be. It can turn into a mob in an instant! And then, how much did they know about God? Oh, sure, some of them—Moses' parents, for instance—had trusted God through all the hard years of slavery. But there were surely many others who didn't know much about the one true God. The only gods they knew about were the false ones that their Egyptian masters had worshiped. Satan surely hoped things would stay like this. Here was a situation he could work with! A large crowd of hard-to-rule people who didn't know much about God or about what he requires—he could corrupt them in no time, and make them just like all the other wicked, idol-worshiping nations.

"But of course, the people of God serve a Commander who knows what his people need. God knew that these people needed his law. So one of the first things he did, once he'd led them out of Egypt, was to take them to Mount Sinai. That's where he would issue their orders. The people set up their camp, and Moses went up the mountain. God told Moses to remind the people of all that God had done for them in rescuing them from the Egyptians. 'If you will obey my commands and trust my promises,' God said, 'then, of all the nations on earth, you will be my own people.' When Moses reported these words to the Israelites, they responded with great enthusiasm. 'We'll do everything the LORD says!' they promised.

"God told Moses that he would come down onto Mount Sinai in three days to give his laws to his people. They were to use the three days to get ready. They should wash themselves and their clothes. They were to set bounds all around the mountain. That was to keep anyone from touching it while God was on it.

"The people got ready, as God had said, and the third morning came. All the Israelites came out of their tents to see what would happen. This was exciting! What would they see? What would they hear? What they actually saw and heard turned out to be more than they were ready for!

"When God came down onto the mountain, he came in fire. So the whole mountain was covered with smoke. It looked like one huge furnace! The mountain itself was shaking violently. Even a mountain can be overwhelmed by God's presence! Loud thunder and flashes of lightning came from the top."

"That must have been something!" Marc interrupted. "You're talking about a fiery, smoking mountain—which sounds like a volcano. The mountain was shaking violently—that's an earthquake. And then there was a lot of thunder and lightning, and all of it real close. Imagine being in a violent lightning storm, in an earthquake, and right next to a volcano, all at the same time!"

"Was God *trying* to scare them?" Amy wanted to know.

Grandpa thought for a minute. "Well, part of the answer is that to creatures like us, the great and awesome Creator just *is* frightening. Not only that, but he's holy and we're sinners. God is tender, loving, and compassionate beyond what any of us can imagine, but he's also to be feared. Think of your principal at school. When he pops into your classroom for a visit, doesn't everyone sit up straighter and behave a little better? Even if you know the principal and really like him, you still feel like you want to be on your best behavior when he's around because you know what the consequences will be if you're not. Moses told the people that God had come to them in this way so they'd keep that sense of fear of him. It would help keep them from sinning.

"On that day, God spoke to his people. He gave them the words of what we now call 'the Ten Commandments.' The people listened, but they didn't like hearing God's voice. It scared them. At last, trembling, they said to Moses, 'You go up and talk with God. We'll do whatever he tells you. But don't let us hear his voice anymore; we're afraid we'll die!'

"So Moses went up the mountain alone, and God gave him two tablets of stone. God had written the Ten Commandments on them. Those Ten Commandments have been the marching orders not just for the Israelites, but for all of God's people ever since. They show us what our Commander-King is like. They let us know how we're to live under his rule. They guide us while we're in his great army so that we'll get along with our fellow soldiers. They show us how to think and act in a way that pleases him.

"It's a terrible thing for an army to have no orders at all. It's even worse if they have false orders, given by an enemy to trick them and lead them into a trap. That's what Satan would do to God's people if he could. It's a great thing that our Commander isn't silent. He's made his wishes very clear to us. And he's had them written down and kept for us in the Bible. Each new generation of soldiers can come to the Scriptures, where they can see for themselves what God's orders are."

Grandpa pointed at his box. "What do you see on top of the lid right now?" he asked.

"Nothing," the children answered together.

"When it comes to an understanding of what God wants, that's what Satan would like us to have—nothing. But instead of leaving us with nothing, God makes his will clearly known. He gives us his commands for our own good and for his glory." On the box top, Grandpa set a little wooden figure cut to look like the two stone tablets on which God had written the Ten Commandments.

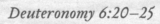

Deuteronomy 6:20–25

When your son asks you in time to come, "What is the meaning of the testimonies and the statutes and the rules that the LORD our God has commanded you?" then you shall say to your son, "We were Pharaoh's slaves in Egypt. And the Lord brought us out of Egypt with a mighty hand. And the Lord showed signs and wonders, great and grievous, against Egypt and against Pharaoh and all his household, before our eyes. And he brought us out from there, that he might bring us in and give us the land that he swore to give to our fathers. And the Lord commanded us to do all these statutes, to fear the Lord our God, for our good always, that he might preserve us alive, as we are this day. And it will be righteousness for us, if we are careful to do all this commandment before the Lord our God, as he has commanded us."

Provisions
for the March

(Exodus and Numbers)

"Hey, Grandpa, what do you have in the fridge?" Amy asked, tossing her backpack into the corner as she came through the shop door. "I'm starving! Lunch was those chicken sandwiches—again!"

"Second time this week," Marc added, coming in right behind her. "And we had them twice last week, too."

Grandpa came up from the back of the shop, where he had been trying to decide which of his many "fix-it" projects to start on next. "What's wrong with chicken sandwiches?" he asked.

"We have them all the time," Amy said. "Well, maybe not *all* the time, but twice last week, twice this week already—and the week's not over. How come we never get pizza anymore, or tacos?"

"But what's wrong with chicken sandwiches?" Grandpa repeated.

"Nothing's wrong with them, Grandpa," Marc explained. "We're just sick of them. We have them too much."

"What are you going to do if you're ever really in an army?" Grandpa asked. "Do you think they ask you what you want for lunch when you're out in the field? And how much variety do you think you get to have when you're really at war?"

Marc had no answer for this, so he wisely kept quiet. "At one point, people in our war almost went over to the other side because they got tired of their food," Grandpa said. "You two get a snack; I'll get my box; and I'll tell you while you eat."

After Grandpa had settled down next to the children with his box, he began. "It was a long way from Mount Sinai to the Promised Land. The wilderness in between makes our next battlefield. First of all, think of what's involved just in moving that many people from one place to another. Remember, this was in the days before cars and trains. How are you going to feed so many people on the trip? There were no convenience stores or big grocery stores along the way. And even if there had been, one store would never have held enough food for so many people. What about water? This was a desert. How could so many people find all the water they would need, not to mention the water they needed for all their animals? Yes, God's people ran into many problems on the way to the Promised Land. And any one of those problems could have done away with them for good.

"Take water, for instance," Grandpa said, holding up the glass of water he had been drinking. "One time, the people went for three days with no water. They couldn't have lasted much longer than that. On the third day, they finally found a place with water. You can imagine how desperate they all were for a drink by then. But

79

when the first people took a sip, they discovered it was bad water; they couldn't drink it. Can't you just feel the wave of despair that would have passed through that whole enormous crowd? Now what would they do? But when Moses prayed, God showed him a certain tree and said he should throw it into the water. When Moses did, God changed the bad water into water good for drinking. Two other times, the Israelites ran out of water in the desert. They could have died in the wilderness either time. But both times God brought water out of a rock for them, and they had all they needed.

"And then there was the problem of food. How do you provide food for an entire nation out in the desert? Marc, you know that's something a good general must always consider as he moves his army. Where will they get food? This crowd was larger than an army on the march. What would they eat? The first time they began to run low on food, the Israelites complained to Moses. 'This is great,' they said. 'We should have stayed in Egypt; at least there we had pots full of meat and all the bread we wanted. You've brought us out here to let us starve to death.' Satan would have been happy with that outcome! If all the people of God starved to death in the wilderness, there could be no promised baby to destroy him and his work.

"But of course, God's a better Commander that that. He knew all along how he was going to provide food for so many people. God told Moses that he would rain down bread from heaven. When the Israelites got up in the morning, all they'd have to do was step outside their tents and gather up the bread that had fallen in the night. Sure enough, in the morning, there was the bread. It lay all over the ground, just waiting to be picked up. The Israelites called the bread from heaven 'manna.' The Bible says it was white and flaky and tasted like wafers with honey."

Grandpa turned suddenly to Amy. "Think you would have liked manna?" he asked.

Amy nodded. "It sounds good," she said.

Grandpa looked at her for a moment, then at Marc. "Think you would have gotten tired of manna, if God served it twice in the same week?" he asked.

"Come on, Grandpa, that would be different," Marc protested.

"I don't know," Grandpa said, "it's human nature—sinful human nature, that is—to always find something to complain about. The Israelites liked the manna just fine at first. They understood that they were eating some very amazing food. Never in the history of the world had people received their daily food just by picking it up each morning after it had fallen from the sky the night before. But nevertheless, the Israelites got tired of it and started complaining.

" 'We're sick of this manna,' the Israelites moaned." Grandpa paused and peered over the top of his glasses at Marc, who squirmed uncomfortably, realizing that those were his very words about the chicken sandwiches.

"Then one of the Hebrews said, 'How come we never get fish anymore, like we had in Egypt, or cucumbers or melons?' " Now it was Amy's turn to feel uncomfortable, recognizing her own grumbling in the Israelite's complaint. Grandpa continued. "And another spoke up with, 'Or what about the leeks and the onions and the garlic?' 'Mmm-mm,' the Israelites said together. 'Who even *wants* to eat anymore?' someone else said. 'There's nothing to eat but this same old manna.' And there stood all the people of God in the doorways of their tents, miraculously provided for, and crying because they didn't like what God had provided.

"And that wasn't the only time the Israelites tempted God. They gave him plenty of chances to get angry with their wretched behavior and destroy them. This was actually their greatest danger. Sure, they were out in the middle of the desert with no water. And yes, they could have starved to death if God hadn't miraculously provided. There were even enemy nations who attacked them as they traveled. But the greatest danger the Israelites faced, and the one most to Satan's liking, was the danger of turning away from God.

Satan could always hope these people would be so wicked and stubborn that God would destroy them in his wrath. And there were several times when it seemed that Satan's hopes would be realized.

"For instance, you remember that the Israelites actually heard God's voice as he spoke the Ten Commandments. Can either of you remember the first two of the Ten Commandments?"

" 'You shall have no other gods before me,' " Marc answered promptly.

"And 'you shall not make for yourself an idol,' " Amy added.

"You remember how the Israelites asked Moses to go up on the mountain to talk with God because God's voice made them feel afraid?" The children nodded. "Well, while Moses was up there, the Israelites were down at the bottom of the mountain *making an idol*. They were doing what God had just told them not to do. Moses was furious when he found out! Rightly so. God was angry, too. He told Moses that he would destroy them, but Moses prayed for them and God forgave them.

"Another time, the Israelites rebelled and wouldn't go into the Promised Land when God told them to go. Then they rebelled and *tried* to go into the Promised Land when God told them to stay out. Over and over again, Satan must have felt so close to turning the people away from their God. He must have felt sure that it would be only a matter of time until God grew sick of their rebellion and gave up on them.

"One time, the people spoke against Moses *and* God, complaining about everything God had done for them. They were tired of the journey, they told Moses. 'Why did you even bring us out of Egypt?' they asked. 'You just want us to die in the desert. We have no food, we have no water, and we're sick of this miserable manna.'

"In response, God sent poisonous snakes. Many people were

bitten by the snakes, and many of them died. Satan was delighted. How perfect, he would have thought. Instead of a baby coming from the people of God and crushing the head of the serpent, the people of God would be destroyed by serpents, sent by God in anger." Here Grandpa stopped, fished about in his box, and drew out two figures. He kept one in his hand and placed the other one—a pile of snakes coiled together with their angry heads sticking up— on the lid. "The people cried out to Moses for help. Moses prayed, and God told him to make a snake out of bronze and place it on a pole, where every-one could see it. If anyone who had been bitten would just look at the bronze snake, he would be healed. So Moses made the snake and put it up on the pole. All the people who trusted God's word enough to look at that snake recovered from the snake bites and lived." Grandpa removed the little figure of angry snakes and replaced it with a carving of a pole with one snake on it.

"It took the people of God more than forty years to get to the Promised Land," Grandpa concluded. "Through many dangers and needs, God provided and kept them safe. It's absolutely amazing that these people would rebel against God so often! But it's even more amazing that God forgave them and put up with them just as often. On this battlefield, too, God's power and God's grace won the day."

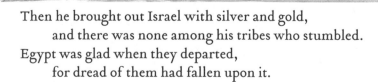

Psalm 105:37–43

Then he brought out Israel with silver and gold,
    and there was none among his tribes who stumbled.
Egypt was glad when they departed,
    for dread of them had fallen upon it.

He spread a cloud for a covering,
  and fire to give light by night.
They asked, and he brought quail,
  and gave them bread from heaven in abundance.
He opened the rock, and water gushed out;
  it flowed through the desert like a river.
For he remembered his holy promise,
  and Abraham, his servant.

So he brought his people out with joy,
  his chosen ones with singing.

Psalm 78:32, 36–38

In spite of all this, they still sinned;
  despite his wonders, they did not believe. . . .
But they flattered him with their mouths;
  they lied to him with their tongues.
Their heart was not steadfast toward him;
  they were not faithful to his covenant.
Yet he, being compassionate,
    atoned for their iniquity
    and did not destroy them;
he restrained his anger often
    and did not stir up all his wrath.

Captain of the Army

(Joshua 1, 6)

Both books would not fit into the overnight bag. Marc held one in each hand, considering which to pack and which to leave behind. He really liked the one about sea battles in World War II, but he had almost finished it. Perhaps he should take the one with short stories about famous generals, to be sure he had enough to read over the weekend. "Hurry, Marc, you'll be late for school," said his father. Marc decided. He set the naval-battle book on the chair and shoved *Famous Generals* into his bag. "Got everything?" his dad asked. Marc nodded.

"Got your toothbrush?" Amy checked.

Marc ran down the hall to the bathroom. "Guess not," Amy grinned.

"Isn't that just like Marc?" their father said. "Agonizing over which war book to take, but no toothbrush!"

It was the Friday before Columbus Day. After school, a three-day weekend awaited Marc and Amy. They would spend this weekend with Grandpa and Grandma because their parents were going away to celebrate their anniversary. Marc returned with the toothbrush. The children and their father headed for the car and off to school.

That evening, Marc sat on his sleeping bag on Grandpa's living-room couch, engrossed in his book about generals. When the children stayed at Grandpa and Grandma's, they took turns sleeping in the guest room. This weekend it was Amy's turn, so Marc had the couch. Grandpa came in. "Did you brush your teeth?" he asked. Marc nodded, without looking up from his book.

"Thanks to me," Amy said, from the rocking chair where she was flipping through one of Grandma's home-decorating magazines.

"Ten more minutes to read, then a story from me, and lights out," Grandpa said.

"I'm almost at the end of this chapter," Marc said, again without looking up.

When he had finished, he closed the book and said, "Grandpa, do you think generals ever get scared? All the ones I read about can't wait to become generals, and then they always seem so sure that they're going to do all the right things."

"Maybe that's because the people who write about them can see only what they do; they can't see what they think," said Grandpa. "I would think that good generals, the ones who are really brave, are anxious sometimes—even downright scared. Being brave doesn't mean you never feel frightened; it means you choose to do the right thing in spite of how you feel. I think the general in our next war story was a little scared, at least when he first became a general."

Amy closed her magazine and considered. "Let's see, the last story was about all sorts of problems in the wilderness," she said. "So, coming up would be . . . Grandpa, you don't mean Joshua, do you? Do you think he was scared?"

"Maybe, just maybe, a little bit," Grandpa said. "Let me show you why I think that." He went into another room and came back with his yellow box and his Bible.

"First of all, think about the task that Joshua had before him," Grandpa began. "Remember how difficult and rebellious the Israelites could be? And how would you like to be the next leader after someone as good and wise as Moses? Not only that, but Moses only had to move the people *to* the Promised Land. It would be Joshua's job to lead them into the land. He'd have to fight real battles to take away the land from the idol-worshipers who lived in it. He'd have to lead a group of untrained, inexperienced soldiers against strong warriors in fortified cities. You'd have to expect him to feel at least a little nervous!

"But mainly I think he was scared because of the things God said to him right in the beginning, when he'd just become the leader of the Israelites." Grandpa opened his Bible to the first chapter of Joshua. "Three times God told Joshua to be strong and courageous. Then God said, 'Don't tremble or be dismayed.' *We* don't know what Joshua was thinking, but God did. It sounds to me like God was answering the feelings of fear that he knew Joshua had.

"You must like the book of Joshua, Marc," Grandpa went on. "It's all battles and strategy. Sometimes the strategy is just what you'd expect in a war story—like when the Israelites attacked and conquered the cities in the middle of the land first, so their enemies in the north and in the south would be separated from each other. Other times, though, they did the strangest things in order to win battles. Sometimes Joshua gave orders that had no strategy at all. That's because he was a general in this war, but he wasn't the Commander-in-Chief. That title belonged to someone else. Even Joshua had orders to follow."

"You mean God, right?" Marc asked. Grandpa nodded and went on.

"Right before the very first battle, the real Commander-in-Chief appeared to Joshua. Joshua was camping with the Israelites by Jericho, the first city they were going to have to capture. The people in Jericho had heard about the Israelites and their God. They'd heard about the Jordan River parting down the middle and Joshua leading the Israelites across on dry land. They knew that all the people who'd attacked the Israelites along the way had always lost. So Jericho's gates were locked up tight. All its people were safely behind its high, fortified walls, and they had no intention of coming out! 'How will we get in?' Joshua may have been wondering as he walked by himself."

Grandpa opened the lid of his box and took out a little figure shaped to look like the face of a solid block wall. He set it on top of the box. "If they couldn't even get inside the walls, how could they take the city? How could God keep his promise to give them the land? So there was Joshua, pacing back and forth, deep in thought—and then, suddenly, he looked up and what did he see? A man who certainly hadn't been there a minute ago. Joshua didn't recognize him as being someone from the Israelite camp. No, he'd never seen this man before, and then Joshua noticed—and maybe his heart skipped a beat at this—the man held a drawn sword in his hand. Was this an assassin sent to kill him? The armed man made no move to attack, though, so Joshua spoke. 'Are you for us?' he asked, 'or for our enemies?'

" 'I come,' the man answered, 'as the Captain of the LORD's hosts.' Then Joshua understood. He, Joshua, was not responsible for God's army and for victories in these battles he faced. He was himself a soldier, following orders. God was the Commander. Joshua bowed down and worshiped.

"This is where the first strange strategy was given. Joshua made sure he understood it; then he faithfully carried out the orders God had given. He lined up all the fighting men with the priests behind them. Some of the priests carried the ark of the covenant—" Grandpa stopped. "Do you remember what that was?" he asked.

Marc thought for a minute. "It was a box," he said cautiously, "on poles. And it was covered with gold."

Grandpa nodded encouragement. "That's right."

"It had something in it," Amy added. "Was it the Ten Commandments?"

"That's right," said Grandpa. "And some of the manna. And Aaron's rod. That simple box stood for God being present with his people. So some of the priests carried that. Other priests carried trumpets. Joshua led the priests and all his soldiers as well to Jericho. The people inside the city watched. 'Here they come!' they cried, grabbing their weapons to defend themselves. But here's all they saw: the Israelites marched around their city once, with the priests blowing trumpets. That's all they did. Then they went back to their camp. Again the next day, the Israelites lined up, soldiers first, followed by priests with trumpets and with the ark of the covenant. Again they marched around the city once and went back to camp. 'What are they up to?' the people of Jericho wondered.

"They did it again on the third day, on the fourth day, the fifth, the sixth. By the seventh day, the people watching from Jericho were used to this. Maybe they didn't even bother to go for their weapons when they saw the Israelites coming one more time. But on that day, the Israelites acted differently. After marching around the city, they kept on marching and went around it again, then once more. They marched around it six times. Then, following God's strange orders to Joshua, the Israelites marched around Jericho one last time. This time, when the priests blew the trumpets, all the people shouted as loud as they could. The walls of the city—those great, thick, fortified walls—fell down at their shout. The Israelites charged straight ahead, into the city, and conquered the astonished people."

Marc shook his head. "That must have been something."

"Really!" said Amy. "When our class read about the Trojan War, we learned how thick city walls were in those days. They don't just fall down because people shout."

Grandpa chuckled. "Unless God orders them to," he said. He took the little wall from the box lid, opened the box, and dropped it inside. He took out another figure and set it in its place. It represented a miniature trumpet.

Joshua 23:1–3, 14

A long time afterward, when the LORD had given rest to Israel from all their surrounding enemies, and Joshua was old and well advanced in years, Joshua summoned all Israel, its elders and heads, its judges and officers, and said to them, "I am now old and well advanced in years. And you have seen all that the LORD your God has done to all these nations for your sake, for it is the LORD your God who has fought for you. . . . And now I am about to go the way of all the earth, and you know in your hearts and souls, all of you, that not one word has failed of all the good things that the LORD your God promised concerning you. All have come to pass for you; not one of them has failed."

Unlikely Weapons for Unlikely Soldiers

(Judges 6–7)

Amy woke to sunlight shining on her pillow and the sound of voices in the kitchen. She stretched with a happy little moan. There was nothing better than waking on Saturday morning and knowing that there was no need to get up today *and* that Monday was a day off as well. And was that Grandma's cinnamon-swirl French toast she smelled? Amy rose and dressed quickly, then went out to the kitchen.

"He knew they couldn't fight any longer. They were out of ammo. But he also knew he just couldn't let the enemy take that hill," Marc was telling Grandpa.

"Good morning, Amy," said Grandma, who was moving back to the stove with a spatula in her hand. "I was just about to call you. You do want some French toast, don't you?"

"Yes, please," Amy answered. "I love your French toast."

"Marc's telling me about someone he was reading about in his book this morning," Grandpa said. Amy shook her head in disbelief. How could even Marc be so interested in war that he would choose to read about it on Saturday morning instead of sleeping in? "What was the man's name again?" Grandpa asked, turning to Marc.

"Joshua Lawrence Chamberlain. He was a teacher," Marc explained to Amy. "But when the Civil War started, he signed up to fight for the North and ended up in charge of a regiment. I was telling Grandpa what he did at Gettysburg. He was supposed to guard a hill, and he'd been told not to lose it, no matter what. But the Confederates really wanted this hill, too, and they attacked and attacked and attacked. Chamberlain kept fighting them off, but he lost a bunch of his men and used up almost all the ammo.

"Now here's the cool part. Chamberlain's really not a soldier, right? He's a teacher. He doesn't know what to do without ammo, but his orders are, 'Don't give up the hill.' So he tells his guys, 'Fix bayonets!' " Here Marc set an imaginary gun on the ground and attached a pretend bayonet. He raised it to the level of his chest and stood poised to attack. "Then Chamberlain attacks the attackers. All the guys he has left go charging down the hill at the rebels with guns that are almost empty! And the rebels are so shocked that they turn and run! So he keeps his hill! Just by doing something crazy that was completely unexpected."

"And just because it *was* so unexpected, I'll bet he got a lot of praise for what he did," Grandpa said.

"He sure did," Marc replied. "The other officers kept saying things like, 'Well done, Chamberlain. I've never seen anything like it,' or 'Bayonets, huh? Amazing.' "

"Well, I've got a war story like that," Grandpa said. "We have a lot to do today, but Amy's just starting her French toast and I need another cup of coffee. Let me get my box."

Grandpa got his story box, poured coffee for himself and for Grandma, who was finally sitting down to her own breakfast, and returned to the table. "Whether it's a big game, or a big battle," Grandpa said, "whenever it seems impossible for someone to win but he wins anyway, he just gets all the more glory for it. There was every reason in the world to think that Gideon would *not* be a victorious leader in our war."

"Gideon?" said Amy. "What happened to Joshua? Weren't we just entering the Promised Land last night?"

"Oh, yes, there's a whole book in the Bible about Joshua and his battles to win the Promised Land. But of course, I'm not telling you every story in the whole Bible. For one thing, I don't have that many pieces for my box. And that would take a mighty big box!

"But you're right. Starting with Jericho, the book of Joshua is about God giving the Israelites the victories they needed to take the Promised Land. Then comes the book of Judges. In this book, the people were living in the land, but they weren't living in obedience to the God who had put them there. After Joshua died, the people started looking around at their neighbors. For some reason, the gods of their neighbors looked better to them than their own God. In spite of all the great things that God had done for them, His people began to worship silly statues that couldn't do anything.

"Whenever the Israelites turned to idols, God would bring other nations to raid and steal from them. They'd come capture people and take them away. They'd steal or burn crops. And the Israelites couldn't stop them because God wouldn't defend them. Whenever things got really bad, God's people would finally call out to him for help. Then God would raise up a leader to fight for them."

93

Amy held up her hand as if she were in class, to signal that she wanted to interrupt. "Weren't those leaders called 'judges'?" she asked. "And that's why the book is called 'Judges'?"

"That's right," Grandpa nodded. "God would use these judges to save his people. But every time, as soon as they were out of harm's way, the Israelites would turn their backs on God again and go back to idols. This happened over and over again.

"Surely Satan was happy about this. It must have seemed that his victory was right around the corner. The people of God weren't worshiping God. Their enemies were always defeating them. From Satan's perspective, what could be better? And things were especially gloomy in Gideon's day. The Midianites had been coming every year, with so many raiders that the Israelites were helpless. The Midianites would let the Israelites plant their crops and take care of them. Then right when it was time for harvest, the Midianites would come and steal what the Israelites had grown. They'd cover the land of Israel like locusts. Their camels alone were too many to count. When they'd eaten, taken, or destroyed absolutely everything the Israelites needed for food, they'd go home. Next harvest, they'd be back.

"Well, that would really stink!" Marc commented.

"You'd think the Israelites would get it and turn back to God," Amy added.

"After seven years of this, they finally did," Grandpa continued. "When God came to their rescue, he chose an unlikely man to lead an unimpressive army fighting with very unusual weapons. No one would have expected them to win!"

"Like a college professor leading a charge with nearly empty guns?" Marc asked.

"This fight was even more surprising than that one!" Grandpa replied. "Gideon himself thought he wasn't the man God should use. See, in those days, it was always *oldest* sons that were leaders. Gideon was the youngest son in the most unimportant family of his tribe. He wasn't particularly brave, either. But God made it very clear that Gideon was exactly the man God wanted to run the Midianites out of Israel.

"Thirty-two thousand soldiers came out to help Gideon. That *sounds* like a lot. But there were so many Midianites, you couldn't count them. Still, I'm sure Gideon was encouraged by those 32,000 men. The only thing was—God thought 32,000 was too many! He told Gideon, 'There are too many men with you. If they win, they'll think it's because they're such great warriors. Announce that anyone who's fearful should go home.' Imagine Gideon's dismay when more than two-thirds of his army disappeared. Twenty-two thousand men went home, leaving him an army of only ten thousand.

"Gideon must have thought, 'This is impossible. This is a tiny army. How can I possibly go against all those Midianites? How can I be expected to defend the people of God with an army like this?'

"But as far as God was concerned, this army was still too big. 'There are still too many,' God told Gideon. 'Take them to the stream to drink. Anyone who kneels down to drink goes home; those who lap the water like a dog stay.' Only three hundred lapped water. So suddenly Gideon found himself with an army of three hundred men."

Amy shook her head. "Even I can tell that's not much of an army," she said.

"That night, Gideon looked down into the valley and saw Midianite tents spread out for miles." On top of his box, Grandpa placed a figure that he had taken out. It was a carving of a row of tents, to represent the many rows of tents in the Midianite camp. " 'Go down to that camp and attack,' God commanded Gideon. 'I'll give you victory. But—' and here we see God's kindness to Gideon—'if you're afraid, take your servant and sneak down for a visit to their camp. What you hear will give you the courage you need.'

"Gideon *was* afraid, so he went down with his servant. There in the enemy camp, he heard a Midianite telling another man of a dream he'd dreamed. He said that he'd seen a loaf of bread roll into the camp, hit the tent, and knock it down flat. Sounds silly, doesn't it? But when the second man heard about this dream, he was terrified. 'That's the sword of Gideon,' he said. 'The Israelites' God has given our whole army into Gideon's hand.'

"Encouraged, Gideon went back to his three hundred men. He gave each one a trumpet and a pitcher with which to cover a lighted torch. That was it, Marc, all the weapons they had: trumpets, clay pitchers, and torches. The three hundred men were to go down in the dark and quietly position themselves at places all around the outside of the camp." Here Grandpa bent closer to the children and lowered his voice as if to be sneaky. "Once they were all in place, with the Midianites not suspecting a thing, Gideon gave the command. Together, all three hundred men broke their pitchers." Grandpa pantomimed breaking a pitcher, and his voice rose with excitement. "There was a crash, and then blazing lights as the torches shone out. Gideon's men blew their trumpets and shouted, 'A sword for the LORD and for Gideon!' That's all they did.

"But the enemy was so startled there in the darkness that they panicked. They drew their swords and began to fight. Of course, Gideon's men were *outside* the camp, so there was no one to fight with—except each other. In their panic, that's just what the enemy did; they fought each other. Then they began to run. Men were called from all over Israel to chase the Midianites. And the Midianites never returned to bother Israel again."

Grandpa removed the carving of the row of tents and replaced it with a little wooden carving of a flaming torch. "So an unlikely leader led the charge of a tiny army with ridiculous weapons against a huge host—and they won a great victory. And all the glory went to God alone, for who else could have done such a thing?"

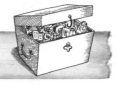

The king is not saved by his great army;
 a warrior is not delivered by his great strength.
The war horse is a false hope for salvation,
 and by its great might it cannot rescue.

Behold, the eye of the LORD is on those who fear him,
 on those who hope in his steadfast love,
that he may deliver their soul from death
 and keep them alive in famine.

Our soul waits for the LORD;
 he is our help and our shield.

A Foreigner Enlists

(Ruth)

"There," said Marc, setting a last flashlight on the shelf they had designated for useful household items. "I think we've got it all out on the shelves. Everything ready to sell is out where customers can see it."

"Wait," said Amy. "Let's see how it would look to a customer walking in." She went out the front door of the shop and came back in. After looking around the store, she moved a small clock to where it could be more easily seen, set a one-dollar vase farther from the five-dollar vases to prevent confusion, and rearranged the price tag on a stool to make it more visible. "Now I think we've got it," she said.

Grandpa had been busy. Over the past few weeks, he had worked hard at completing many of his half-finished fix-it projects. Amy and Marc had spent this morning helping Grandpa get some of these projects out onto the shelves. They had made room for more merchandise, written and stuck price tags, and set up displays. Now the store looked neater and even more inviting than usual.

"What are we doing after lunch, Grandpa?" Marc wanted to know.

"One thing always leads to another," Grandpa answered. "I got those things fixed and moved out of the back, but look at what was behind them." The children looked where Grandpa was pointing and saw a pile of boxes and trunks. "I'd forgotten about all this stuff," Grandpa said. "We need to go through those and see if there's anything we want for the store. We'll want to clean up the trunks. People are always coming in here, looking for trunks like those."

So after lunch, they attacked the pile. Amy and Grandpa emptied contents of boxes into stacks of "throw away," "fix up to sell," and "not sure yet." Marc wiped out the insides of trunks. After cleaning up several trunks, Marc opened another and said, "Hey, this one has stuff in it."

Amy went over to look and gave a cry of delight. "Look at that!" she said. "It's an old-time wedding dress." And she pulled out the delicate, lacy gown and held it up.

"It's not *that* old-time," Grandpa muttered, coming over to see. "There are some other things in there," he said, peering into the trunk.

Marc reached in, telling the contents of the trunk as he lifted each thing out. "Baby pictures," he said, taking out several in picture frames, "some official papers of some kind, and this funny black hat with the—what is this, a screen?"

"It's a veil on the hat," Amy answered.

"It looks like a hat that a lady might have worn to a funeral," Grandpa commented. "Oh, and here's a locket." He reached in and pulled out a necklace. He opened it.

Marc leaned over and looked into the locket. "What's inside?" he said. Then: "Someone's *hair*?"

"People used to keep locks of hair from people they cared about," Grandpa explained. "Or maybe someone who had died. This could almost be Naomi's trunk," he added, "one of the soldiers in our next battle."

"Finally! A story about a lady," Amy said.

"Hang the dress over there, Amy," Grandpa directed, "and let's go out to the picnic table for a lemonade break. I'll tell you about Naomi."

In three minutes' time, the children were sitting at the table in the shade, sipping lemonade, while Grandpa sorted through his box for the pieces he would need for this story. "Naomi lived in Bethlehem, during the time of the judges," he said.

"*The* Bethlehem?" Marc wanted to know. "The one where Jesus was born?"

"Same place exactly," Grandpa answered, "only that would be a lot later. Naomi had some happy times in Bethlehem. She loved and married a man named Elimelech. Together, they had two little sons. But the happy times didn't last. There was a famine in Israel, and Elimelech couldn't provide food for his little family."

"Maybe that was one of those times when the Israelites were being raided by enemies, like the Midianites," Amy suggested.

"Maybe so," said Grandpa. "Whatever the reason, there wasn't enough to eat in Bethlehem, so Elimelech told Naomi that they were going to move away. He'd heard that there was food in Moab, so that's where they would go.

"Naomi might not have been too sure about going to Moab. Moab wasn't part of the Promised Land. People didn't know God there; they worshiped idols. Maybe Naomi thought her husband shouldn't take them to Moab to live. Or maybe she understood that he didn't see any other choice if he wanted to feed his family. Maybe she wondered why God would allow things to get this bad. How could it be good to leave the land God had given them to go stay where idol-worshipers lived?

"Naomi and Elimelech and their sons lived in Moab a long time. Naomi's two little boys grew up and became young men, but her dear husband Elimelech died there in Moab. Now, you need to understand that in Bible times, it was more than just sad for a woman when her husband died. In Bible times, women didn't go out and get jobs. When there was no husband to earn money and take care of a wife, all she could look forward to was a life of poverty. Of course, if she had sons, they'd take care of her and provide what she needed. Sad as Naomi felt with her husband gone, at least she had two sons to help her out.

"By now, of course, Naomi's sons were young men, and as often happens when young men grow up, they wanted to get married." Listening, Marc made a face as if to say that no matter how grown up he became, he would never want to get married. "The only young women around, of course, were Moabite women. Now, God had clearly told the Israelites not to marry people from the neighboring nations. They were idol-worshipers. It would be all too easy for an idol-worshiping wife to get her husband to worship idols, too. Naomi may have been unhappy when her sons brought home Moabite wives. First, the family had left the land God had given them, and then Naomi's husband had died, leaving her a widow. Now her sons were doing what God had said not to do and were marrying women from families who didn't fear God.

"And things grew still worse for Naomi. Both her sons died, leaving her a widow *and* alone in a foreign land. Had God abandoned her? What else could go wrong? Of course, she had her two daughters-in-law, the women her sons had married. But they were both young enough to marry again and go start new families with new husbands. That was just what Naomi told them they should do. She herself, she said, would go back to her own land of Bethlehem. One daughter-in-law did as Naomi said and stayed there in Moab, hoping to remarry. The other daughter-in-law, Ruth, said that she would never leave Naomi. She would live in Naomi's land, with Naomi's people, and—most importantly—Naomi's God would be her God.

"So Ruth went with Naomi back to Bethlehem. When they got there, Ruth wanted to work to earn food for herself and Naomi. There was a law that when farmers gathered their crops at harvest, they were to leave little bits behind for poor people to gather. So Ruth went out to work in a rich man's field, gathering those little bits. At lunchtime, the rich man came to meet her. He spoke to her very kindly and made sure she was able to gather enough grain. When Ruth told Naomi about him later, Naomi wanted to know the man's name. 'I believe his name was Boaz,' Ruth answered.

" 'He's our relative,' Naomi said. 'He's a good man. Stay in his field and work. You'll be safe there.' And Naomi felt that, maybe, things were finally going to get better for her. Look at how God had led Ruth to just that man's field and no other.

"As Ruth went to work there day after day, Boaz began to admire this young woman. He realized that she was a Moabite woman and not an Israelite. But she had chosen to trust the true God to provide for her. And Boaz was impressed by the way Ruth took care of Naomi. As the days passed, Boaz's admiration for Ruth turned to love. As for Ruth, she was grateful for Boaz's kindness and for his generous gifts to her and Naomi. And so, on her part as the days passed, Ruth's gratitude toward Boaz also turned to love."

Grandpa glanced at his grandson and grinned. "What's the matter, Marc? Don't like this part?"

"I don't remember all this lovey-dovey stuff. Are you sure it's in there?" Marc replied.

"Well, I *am* making a bigger deal of it than the Bible does," Grandpa admitted, "but come on, all the best war stories have romance in them. Look at the tales of the Trojan War! Anyway," Grandpa went back to his Bible story, "Naomi could see what was happening. She knew that Ruth, being poor and a foreigner, would never let Boaz know she loved him. And Boaz was probably an older man. He might have thought Ruth wouldn't want a husband his age. Here were these two godly people who cared about each other, doing nothing about it. So Naomi told Ruth what to do to let Boaz know she would be willing to marry him if he wanted her. Ruth followed Naomi's directions, and Boaz was delighted! There was a law for relatives who had died, and Boaz carefully obeyed it. He gave Naomi money for Elimelech's land, like the law said, and he took Ruth as his bride. Together Ruth and Boaz had a little baby boy, Obed, the joy of Grandma Naomi's heart."

Grandpa set a figure of three little gravestones on the lid of his box. "Back in Moab, when she was so lonely and sad, Naomi must have felt that God had left her in enemy hands. Her husband, her sons, a way to provide for herself—all were gone. But Naomi learned that God is always at work in all the little circumstances of our everyday lives. He provides exactly what he knows will be best for us and for all concerned." Grandpa took away the gravestones and set a little carving of a woman—Ruth—holding a child—Obed—by the hand.

Amy looked doubtful. "But was it really okay for Boaz to marry Ruth, since she was a Moabite woman?" she asked. "I mean, if God's law said the Israelites weren't supposed to marry people from other countries . . ."

"It was never the 'other country' part that God didn't like," Grandpa explained. "It was always the idol worship. Naomi didn't know it at the time, but her dear little Obed grew up to have a grandson, too. His grandson was the great King David. And a great-great-great-grandson of David's would be the Lord Jesus, the promised

Savior. So God not only took care of Naomi, but also worked everything out so that Ruth, a Moabite woman, became an ancestor of the Lord Jesus Christ. God was showing us that he welcomes people from any nation when they come to him in faith."

Acts 10:34–35

So Peter opened his mouth and said: "Truly I understand that God shows no partiality, but in every nation anyone who fears him and does what is right is acceptable to him."

An Excellent Leader

(1 Samuel 8, 10, 13, 16)

"Are you sure you want to sleep out here?" Grandpa asked Marc. "Hard as we worked today, all I'm thinking about is my comfy bed. You sure you'll be okay on the ground?"

Marc had begged to be allowed to set up Grandpa's old camping tent in the backyard. Grandpa had sighed, being tired and knowing that Marc would need help. Still, good sport that he was, Grandpa had lent a hand, and now Marc was unrolling a sleeping bag on the tent floor.

"Oh, Marc's like Dad, Grandpa," said Amy, who had come out with Grandpa to watch Marc get settled in. "He can sleep anywhere."

Marc placed his pillow at the head of the sleeping bag, then set his book about famous generals and his flashlight beside the pillow.

At that, Grandpa admonished, "No staying up late either. We have church tomorrow."

"I'm just going to read one chapter," Marc promised. "Hey, can you tell us your next war story in here?"

"Let me get my box," said Grandpa in reply. When he came back, he was carrying not only his box, but a folding chair as well. "I'll tell the story in the tent," he said, "but I'm not sitting on the ground! These bones are too old!"

"I was thinking about that story you told us at breakfast, Marc," Grandpa began, "about that Chamberlain fellow leading the bayonet charge. Whoever put him in charge of that hill must have been awfully glad he did. One of the most critical things in any battle is having the right men in charge. Men will follow a good leader even when the odds seem impossible. So a commander-in-chief not only needs to know the terrain and what the enemy's doing. He also needs to know his men. He needs to know which leaders he can trust with his plans. Who's going to be faithful to do what he wants done? Why, without a good leader, an army's just an unruly mob.

"As the very best Commander-in-Chief, God knows that his people need a good leader. We talked about what happened after Joshua died. The people of God there in the Promised Land had no leader, and they all just did whatever they felt like doing—even when what they felt like doing was wrong. Here's what the book of Judges says about that time in Israel's history: 'In those days, there was no king in Israel; every man did what was right in his own eyes.' And when you get a whole bunch of sinners all doing whatever's right in their own eyes, it's not a pretty picture.

"The Israelites needed a leader who would lead them in following God's commands. But that's not what the Israelites thought. They thought they needed someone who would defeat all their enemies. You remember, they were having quite a time trying to defend themselves from the neighbors."

106

"Right," said Marc. "That's why Gideon had to rescue them from the Midianites."

"And Gideon was only one of several judges that God raised up to rescue them. But what happened every time a judge died?" Grandpa asked.

"The Israelites went right back to the same old idol worship that had gotten them in trouble in the first place," Amy answered.

"Exactly," said Grandpa. "So you see, their first need was for a king to lead them in obedience to God. But the people didn't understand this. So when they asked for a king, they didn't ask for a godly man. They asked for someone who could fight their battles.

"Sometimes the best way for God to show people that what they want really isn't good for them is by giving it to them. God gave the Israelites what they asked for. He gave them a big man who looked like a warrior. He stood a head and shoulders taller than everyone else. God gave Israel King Saul.

"Saul started off well. At first he was led by God's Spirit. But then there came a day when he showed what was really in his heart. A big battle was brewing between the Philistines and Israel. Saul had gathered six thousand soldiers. These men were eager to go and ready to fight. But then the Philistines showed up. They had six thousand horsemen alone, along with thirty thousand chariots and countless foot soldiers. As you might imagine, odds like these made the Israelites nervous.

"Saul wanted to attack right away, before his men had much time to think about how greatly they were outnumbered. The only problem was that God's prophet, Samuel, hadn't come yet. Samuel had told Saul to wait for him before he attacked. When Samuel came, he would offer sacrifices and ask God for victory. After all, if so small an army was going to win, it would have to be God's doing. But day after day went by, and Samuel didn't come. Saul's men grew more nervous every day. And then, one by one, they began to sneak away.

'I've got to keep my army together,' Saul must have thought. 'That's the most important thing I can do!' "

Grandpa peered at Marc in the deepening darkness. "Right, Marc?" he asked.

Marc considered. "Well, I want to say 'yes,' because the size of an army usually *is* at least *one* of the most important things in a battle. But this is a Bible story, and so I think I'm supposed to say, 'No, it's not that important here.' "

"*Usually* the size of an army is very important," Grandpa agreed. "But you're right, it wasn't as important here. And you're also right that this battle was different from most. That's because Israel in the Old Testament was the only country on earth to ever have God as its absolute ruler. When Israel fought, they were fighting for God, and God was fighting for them. So the most important thing any Israelite king could do was to be sure that he was carefully following God's orders.

"Saul knew this. But he ignored it. 'I've got to get on with this battle or I'm going to lose my whole army,' he thought. So he gave up on Samuel and offered the sacrifices himself. He was just finishing when Samuel showed up.

" 'What have you done?' Samuel asked. 'God would have kept you as king forever, with your sons as kings after you, if you had only obeyed. What's more important for a ruler of God's people than obeying God? You cannot remain as king. And your sons won't be kings either. God has found someone else to lead his people, someone who is a man after God's own heart.' "

Amy had been stirring restlessly in her chair, and now she protested. "I don't get it. Saul *did* pray and offer sacrifices. He just did it himself. What was wrong with that? Samuel shouldn't have been so late."

"You have to understand that not just anyone could offer a sacrifice to God," Grandpa explained. "It was only the priests, and in some cases certain prophets, whom God had chosen to offer sacrifices. God is holy, and people can't just go barging into his presence whenever and however they want to. They have to do it his way. And Saul didn't. From there on, it was downhill all the way for King Saul. He ended his life jealous, fearful, half insane, and given to violent outbursts of anger. By then, even the Israelites could see that this was not the man they needed for a king.

"Meanwhile, God sent Samuel to the house of a man named Jesse. One of Jesse's eight sons was the one God had chosen for the next king. When Samuel saw the oldest son, he was sure that he was the one! He was so tall and looked so strong. 'Not him,' God told him. 'I'm not looking at the outside. It's what's in a man's heart that will make him the king I'm looking for.' One by one, Samuel saw all of Jesse's sons, but it was the last, the youngest, whom God wanted for king. His name was David.

"What's the most famous David story there is?" Grandpa asked Amy. He turned in her direction, but he couldn't really see her. It had grown too dark. "David and Goliath," she answered immediately.

"In that story we see the difference between Saul and David," Grandpa said. "Here's the whole Israelite army, terrified of the huge Philistine warrior, Goliath. Every day, he comes marching out, demanding that they send someone to fight him, and no one's ever brave enough to go. Then along comes the boy David. He's not a soldier. He's had no training. He has no real weapons. And when they try to give him armor, he doesn't want it because he can't walk with it on. A huge, well-trained, well-armed warrior against a small, unarmed teenager. Terrible odds! But David understands that it's not about the odds. It's God who gives victory. So with complete confidence, knowing that God will fight for him, he goes out with those stones and that slingshot and kills himself a giant. And later when he becomes king and has a whole army at his command, David will still fight like that, trusting God for the victory."

Grandpa opened his box. "Shine your flashlight in the box, will you, Marc?" he said. Marc did so, and Grandpa rummaged until

109

he found a little crown. He set it up on top of the box. "The first king of Israel was a king that Satan could rejoice over. He wouldn't follow God's directions, so how could he lead God's people the way God wanted them led? So God removed him," and Grandpa removed the little crown.

"God knows his people's needs, and he always provides for them. He knew they didn't need just any king; they needed a *godly* king. So God gave them a godly king." Grandpa replaced the crown on the box lid. "And by doing so, he gave them a picture of what the promised child would grow up to be—the best of godly, faithful leaders for God's people."

Psalm 78:70–72

He chose David his servant
    and took him from the sheepfolds;
from following the nursing ewes he brought him
    to shepherd Jacob his people,
    Israel his inheritance.
With upright heart he shepherded them
    and guided them with his skillful hand.

Isaiah 9:6–7

For to us a child is born,
    to us a son is given;

and the government shall be upon his shoulder,
    and his name shall be called
Wonderful Counselor, Mighty God,
    Everlasting Father, Prince of Peace.
Of the increase of his government and of peace
    there will be no end,
on the throne of David and over his kingdom,
    to establish it and to uphold it
with justice and with righteousness
    from this time forth and forevermore.
The zeal of the Lord of hosts will do this.

A Fallen Leader

(2 Samuel 11–12; Psalm 51)

Amy joined Grandma and Grandpa at the breakfast table. "Where's Marc?" she asked. "Don't tell me I'm up before him. That never happens."

"I haven't seen him yet," Grandma replied. "Someone's going to have to go get him soon or he'll make us late for church."

Just then the back door opened and Marc stumbled in, rubbing his eyes. "Well, good morning," said Grandpa. "This is pretty late rising for you."

"It took me forever to get to sleep," Marc answered. "And then when I woke up, I was stiff all over."

"That's why I've outgrown sleeping on the ground in a tent!" said Grandpa. "I get stiff enough sleeping in a bed! I think even King

David, great outdoorsman that he was, came to feel the way I do about sleeping in tents. He always slept outside when he was a shepherd. And he slept outside with his army when he was fighting Philistines. And even for quite a while after becoming king, he always went to battle with his soldiers and slept out in the field with them. But there came a time when the army rode off to war and David stayed home. That turned out to be a bad choice. Because David was home in his comfortable palace when his soldiers were off in tents in the field, he got into some very serious trouble.

"I'll tell you about it while you eat," Grandpa said. Catching Grandma's warning look, he added, "But you two be sure to keep eating so you'll be ready for church on time." He got the yellow box, while Marc and Amy poured cereal and juice.

"Do you remember what God said about David that tells us why God wanted him to be king over his people?" Grandpa asked.

Amy's mouth was full, so she let Marc answer. "He was a man after God's own heart," Marc said.

Grandpa nodded. "And you remember why Saul's sons did not become kings after him?"

Amy swallowed her mouthful of cereal and replied, "It was because he didn't obey God's directions. So God took the kingdom away from his family."

Grandpa nodded again. "David turned out to be quite different from Saul. *He* was very loyal to God, the Commander-in-Chief. David took care of God's people the way he'd taken care of his father's sheep. He protected them from their enemies. He provided what they needed. He showed them what they should do. He corrected them when they did the wrong thing. And all the while, just like when he was a shepherd, he did what he did with an eye to pleasing God. David was *God's* choice of a king, and he was the model of what a godly leader should be.

"At one point in his reign, God made David a most wonderful promise. Now, listen and see if you can tell me how this promise to

113

David is one more promise about that child promised to Adam and Eve, the one who would destroy Satan and his work. Here's the promise: When David died, God would make his son king and give him a kingdom that would last forever."

Grandpa waited. "Do you hear it? Do you hear the promise about the coming child in there?"

Amy looked blank. "Wasn't he talking about Solomon?" she asked. "Wasn't Solomon David's son?"

"God must have been talking about Jesus," Marc said, "because he said his kingdom would last forever. No ordinary kingdom can last forever."

Amy's blank look disappeared. "Right," she said, "and Jesus was the Son of the son of the son of the son of David."

"So the promise about the child kept growing," Grandpa said. "Now people could expect a child to come from the nation of Israel *and* from the family of King David. And they knew this child would be king over God's people—a good king, like David, a king after God's own heart." Grandpa took from his box the same little crown he had used in the tent the night before and set it up on the box lid.

"Of course, Satan wanted to put a stop to all this!" Grandpa went on. "It shouldn't be too hard to get David to disobey God, as Saul had done. Then the kingdom would be taken away from David and his sons, just as it had been taken away from Saul and *his* sons. Of course, the best part of that would be—so Satan would have thought—that then there could be no promised child to rule God's people. And Satan's own rule would go on, undisturbed.

"So imagine Satan's delight when King David saw a woman who was married to one of David's soldiers and began to want *that* woman for himself. No other woman would do. It didn't matter that she already had a husband. No one would know what was going on. All the soldiers were away at war. So David took the soldier's wife for himself. Then, even worse, he sent a message to his commander at the battle. He gave orders to put the woman's husband in a spot

114

where the fighting was very heavy. The husband would be killed. David could marry the wife. And no one would ever find out.

"That's just the way it happened, and Satan must have been thrilled. Surely God would take the kingdom away from David and his descendants for behavior like that. Wouldn't you think so, Amy?" Grandpa turned to her and waited.

He did not have to wait long. Amy's strong sense of justice was outraged. "I think that's really low," she said indignantly. "Have your own soldier killed on purpose so you can take his wife! That doesn't sound like a good leader to me. I'm surprised that God *didn't* take the kingdom away from David. All Saul did wrong was offer sacrifices himself instead of waiting for Samuel. David murdered one of his own men!"

"And took his wife," Grandpa added. "It doesn't look like a promised child can come from this king." And he removed the little crown from the top of the box and sat in silence.

"*But—*" said Marc. "Come on, Grandpa, we know there's a *but—*. There always is."

Grandpa grinned. "*But—*God knew all about what David had done, *and—*he had known about it before it happened. He wasn't taken by surprise. God had known how badly David would sin back when he made the promise to David in the first place. And he'd known just what he was going to do about it. God sent Nathan the prophet to David with a story. 'There was a man,' Nathan told David, 'who had one little pet lamb that he had raised as a baby. He loved his little pet lamb. Another man was very rich and had large flocks of sheep and many goats and cattle. When the rich man had a visitor and wanted to prepare a meal for him, he didn't use any of his own animals. He took the poor man's one pet lamb, killed it, and cooked it for his guest.'

"David was furious—just as Amy would have been," Grandpa continued. " 'That man deserves to die!' David cried. And Nathan said to him, '*You* are that man.' At once David understood that, yes, he *was* that man. God had given him so much, while his faithful soldier had had only a simple home with a wife. David had taken that soldier's wife—and then he had killed the soldier. For months, David had been telling himself that what he had done was okay. All that was ended in a moment. God worked in David's heart to show him what a terrible thing he'd done. God filled David's heart with sorrow for his sin and with repentance.

"Like a bad army general, Satan is always underestimating his enemy. Here, he didn't stop to think that God loves to forgive sinners when they repent. And he hadn't considered that God can change a sinner's heart so that sinner *will* repent of even the most awful sins."

Grandpa replaced the crown on the box lid. "So the promise remained unbroken. The child would come to be a king, and he would come from David. And one thing more—the people of God, down through the years, would have a prayer they could use whenever they were feeling guilty over something they'd done wrong: Psalm 51. David wrote it after Nathan had spoken to him about his sin. Let me read it to you before we all go off to get ready for church." Grandpa opened his Bible.

Psalm 51

Have mercy on me, O God,
 according to your steadfast love;
according to your abundant mercy
 blot out my transgressions.
Wash me thoroughly from my iniquity,
 and cleanse me from my sin!

For I know my transgressions,
 and my sin is ever before me.
Against you, you only, have I sinned
 and done what is evil in your sight,
so that you may be justified in your words
 and blameless in your judgment.

Behold, I was brought forth in iniquity,
	and in sin did my mother conceive me.
Behold, you delight in truth in the inward being,
	and you teach me wisdom in the secret heart.

Purge me with hyssop, and I shall be clean;
	wash me, and I shall be whiter than snow.
Let me hear joy and gladness;
	let the bones that you have broken rejoice.
Hide your face from my sins,
	and blot out all my iniquities.
Create in me a clean heart, O God,
	and renew a right spirit within me.
Cast me not away from your presence,
	and take not your Holy Spirit from me.
Restore to me the joy of your salvation,
	and uphold me with a willing spirit.

Then I will teach transgressors your ways,
	and sinners will return to you.
Deliver me from bloodguiltiness, O God,
		O God of my salvation,
	and my tongue will sing aloud of your righteousness.
O Lord, open my lips,
	and my mouth will declare your praise.
For you will not delight in sacrifice, or I would give it;
	you will not be pleased with a burnt offering.
The sacrifices of God are a broken spirit;
	a broken and contrite heart, O God, you will not despise.

Do good to Zion in your good pleasure;
	build up the walls of Jerusalem;
then will you delight in right sacrifices,
		in burnt offerings and whole burnt offerings;
	then bulls will be offered on your altar.

Contest of Warriors

(1 Kings 18)

Marc and Amy dropped their life jackets into the back of the car, then hurried back to the edge of the lake to help Grandpa with the canoe. Together the three of them carried the old aluminum canoe to the car and lifted it onto the roof. With the children helping by holding the end of a bungee cord here and handing up another one there, Grandpa soon had the canoe secure. Marc ran to the picnic table where Grandma sat waiting with her book and the ice chest. "Did you have a nice canoe ride?" Grandma asked as Marc ran up, with Grandpa and Amy following behind.

"We sure did," Marc answered. "You should have come. It was pretty."

"Then who would have saved the picnic table?" Grandma said. "Holiday weekend, you know. Look, all the tables are taken. Besides,

I prefer to come here just with Grandpa and canoe under a full moon. It's more romantic."

Marc, never interested in romance, chose to ignore this last comment. "What's for lunch, Grandma? I'm starved!"

"Hot dogs," said Grandma, "and they'll be ready in a jiffy as soon as we get the grill going."

"My turn to light the grill," said Amy, arriving at the table with Grandpa.

"Get the matches," said Grandma, as Grandpa began dumping charcoal into the grill by the table. "They're in the bag with the cookie can and the chips."

Amy felt inside a bag; then, making a face, she said, "The pickle jar's in this bag, too, and it fell over. Some of the juice leaked out into the bottom. It stinks," said Amy, who didn't like pickles. She brought the matches to where Grandpa waited by the grill. "Ready?" she asked. When he nodded, she took out a match and scratched it along the side of the box. Nothing happened. She tried again. Still nothing.

"I can do it," Marc said.

"So can I," said Amy. "Just give me a minute." After a few more unsuccessful attempts, Amy returned the match to the box and chose another. It would not light either. "Let me see the matches," Grandpa said and examined the box. "It's the pickle juice," he announced. "It got on the matches, and they're too damp to work right." He thought for a minute. "I know. We can use the car's cigarette lighter." Grandpa went to the car and moved it close to the grill. He pushed in the car's cigarette lighter and waited until it popped out, the end glowing. Then he held the lighter to the end of a rolled napkin until the napkin caught fire. Cupping his hand to protect the little flame, he moved it carefully to the grill to light the charcoal.

"Matches too wet to start a fire," Grandpa said. "I have a war story about that sort of thing."

"But you don't have your box," Amy replied.

"Oh, yes, I do," Grandpa assured her. "I brought it just in case." He went to the trunk and pulled out his box. "That grill's got to heat for a few minutes. I'll have just enough time to tell it."

"This story happens some time after the stories about David," Grandpa began. "The kingdom David ruled had become two kingdoms. That's because David's son—remember who that was?"

"Solomon," both children answered together.

"Solomon had allowed his many wives to draw him into idol worship. So God had told Solomon that he would tear the kingdom away from him and his sons. Not completely, of course, since God had promised David there would always be a king from his family on the throne. But God said he would give most of Israel to someone else. And sure enough, that's what happened. As soon as Solomon died, most of the Israelites rebelled against Solomon's son, picked their own king, and started a whole new kingdom. This rebel kingdom kept the name 'Israel,' and the other smaller kingdom was called 'Judah.'

"The first king in Israel started right off by doing the worst thing he could possibly do. He set up two golden calves in his kingdom. He told the people that these were the gods who'd brought them out of Egypt. 'No need to go all the way to Jerusalem to worship God in the temple,' he told them. 'You can stay right here and worship one of these. It will be much easier for you.' That king—his name was Jeroboam—began something that continued as long as there was a rebel kingdom of Israel. From the first king to the last, every one of them led the people in idol worship.

"So today's story is about a battle between Israel's true God and one of the idols. It was King Ahab who introduced this idol to the Israelites. King Ahab was one of the worst kings the rebel kingdom ever had. And he was married to Jezebel. Think of the meanest stepmother or most wicked witch from any fairy tale and Jezebel was worse! She came from Sidon in neighboring Phoenicia, where people worshiped Baal. When Jezebel came to live with Ahab, she brought her favorite god along with her. It was Jezebel who paid priests and prophets of Baal to work there in Israel. Not only that. She wasn't content to have Baal worshiped *along with* God. No, she wanted *only* Baal worship as the official religion of the kingdom, so she set out to find the prophets of the true God and kill them."

Grandpa rose and went to the ice chest. He removed the package of hot dogs, opened it, and placed several hot dogs on the grill. When he returned, he took from his box an ugly little statue that he had carved from wood to represent Baal. He set it on the box lid. "It would seem that this part of the people of God, at least, were lost to God for good. But God wasn't ready to surrender these people to Satan yet! God had a faithful prophet who boldly stood up for God when things looked the worst. His name was Elijah.

"Elijah challenged the prophets of Baal to a contest. 'Meet me up on Mount Carmel, and we'll see whose god is really a god,' he said. One thing you have to know about Mount Carmel," Grandpa pointed out. "It's up at the very edge of the kingdom of Israel, right by Phoenicia. In ancient times, people believed that a god was strongest in his own land. This was one place in all Israel where Baal should be strong. It was like Elijah was giving Baal the home-court advantage! Baal's prophets must have felt pretty confident. The queen was on their side. The king was on their side. There were 450 of them—and Elijah? He was all alone. So the prophets of Baal were quite willing to come to Mount Carmel. The Israelites gathered, too, to watch the contest.

" 'How long are you going to go back and forth between two opinions?' Elijah challenged the people. 'If the Lord is God, follow him; if Baal is God, follow him.' Then Elijah explained the rules. An altar would be built for each god. Sacrifices would be placed on both altars, but neither sacrifice would be set on fire. Instead, the prophets would pray—Baal's prophets first, and then Elijah. Whichever god answered by sending fire from heaven to burn up the sacrifice was the true God. That sounded like a good idea to the Israelites, and they agreed."

"Do you think Baal's prophets really thought Baal could do that?" Amy wondered.

"I don't know, but they gave it their best shot," Grandpa replied. "What else could they do with everybody watching like that? So all morning Baal's prophets prayed to Baal. Nothing happened, so they began to dance and jump around the altar as well.

" 'Think that will get his attention?' Elijah teased them. 'Better shout louder. He must be busy or else he stepped away for a minute. Or I suppose he could be gone on a trip. I know, maybe he's asleep and you need to wake him.' "

"Now, *that's* trash talk!" said Marc, approvingly.

"So the prophets yelled louder. But the afternoon wore on, and still nothing happened. The Israelites were beginning to murmur. It didn't look to them like Baal was going to do anything. And they were tired of standing there waiting. Desperate for an answer, the prophets of Baal began to cut themselves with knives, trying to get Baal's attention. They kept it up until they had blood gushing all over the place—but, needless to say, still no answer.

"Finally, it was evening. The day was almost over, and it was Elijah's turn. Before he began to pray, though, he dug a ditch around God's altar. He called for water and poured it all over his offering and the wood underneath. He called for more water and poured it on the offering, too. He called for still more water and poured that out as well. By now, the sacrifice and the wood were soaked, and water was flowing off the altar and had filled the trench around it. You couldn't possibly set that on fire, could you, Amy?"

Amy shook her head "no," and Grandpa went on. "Elijah prayed. No dancing, no yelling, no gashing himself. He just prayed. And not over and over for hours, but just once. He prayed that God would show the Israelites that God alone is God and that he wanted the hearts of the people to be his again. One simple prayer. And as soon as it was over, fire fell from heaven. It completely burned the sacrifice and all the wood, it burned up the stones of the altar—"

"Whoa!" said Marc. "Stones don't burn!"

"—and it licked up all the water in the trench. Finally, the people were impressed. They fell on their faces on the ground, crying, 'The

LORD, he is God! The LORD, he is God!' " Grandpa removed the idol carving from the box lid, and in its place he put a little carved bonfire. "In any contest with the true God, Satan and his phony gods don't stand a chance."

He winked at the children. "And now, we'd better get those hot dogs or they'll be as burnt as the sacrifice."

Isaiah 46:3–7, 9

Listen to me, O house of Jacob,
    all the remnant of the house of Israel,
who have been borne by me from before your birth,
    carried from the womb;
even to your old age I am he,
    and to gray hairs I will carry you.
I have made, and I will bear;
    I will carry and will save.

To whom will you liken me and make me equal,
    and compare me, that we may be alike?
Those who lavish gold from the purse,
    and weigh out silver in the scales,
hire a goldsmith, and he makes it into a god;
    then they fall down and worship!
They lift it to their shoulders, they carry it,
    they set it in its place, and it stands there;
    it cannot move from its place.
If one cries to it, it does not answer
    or save him from his trouble. . . .

    remember the former things of old;
for I am God, and there is no other;
    I am God, and there is none like me. . . .

A Guided Missile

(1 Kings 22)

Amy held the black polished stone up to the sunlight coming in at the window. "I like the way you can see the light through these," she commented. "What did you say they were called, Grandpa?"

"Obsidian," Marc answered before Grandpa could reply.

"No, I don't mean the rock they come from," Amy said. "I mean when they're all polished like this, so you could use them for jewelry."

"They're called Apache tears," Grandpa said.

The children's weekend with their grandparents was almost over. Soon their parents would arrive to take them home. They were waiting out in the shop, which had been closed today. While she waited,

Amy had been picking through the bowls of items that Grandpa kept to sell to children who came in with money to spend. Three bowls held seashells and starfish and sand dollars that Grandpa had picked up on trips to California. A number of bowls, including the one Amy was looking through now, contained interesting rocks from the Arizona desert. There were even some Indian arrowheads in one bowl.

Marc joined Amy at the counter with the bowls and began examining the arrowheads. "Weapons sure have changed a lot!" Marc said.

"Those arrowheads would have been used for hunting, mostly," Grandpa replied. "But bows and arrows were used for war, too."

"In the old days lots of soldiers used bows and arrows," Marc said. "I think it'd be hard to fight with those. First you'd have to carry a whole bunch of arrows because once you shot one, it'd be gone. Then when you saw the enemy, you'd have to stop and get an arrow out and get all set up to shoot. And even if you were a really good shot, if the guy had armor on or if the city had a wall around it, your arrow would just bounce right off. How many arrows would you have to shoot to get even one hit? Compare that with weapons we have nowadays—like guided missiles, for instance."

"Unless the arrow's a *guided* arrow. Then it gets the job done," Grandpa said.

"I feel a story coming on," said Amy.

"Yep," said Grandpa, getting the yellow box and coming over by Marc and Amy. "Marc walked right into this one.

"This one's about a real battle. It was a battle between kings, like so many battles are. But from the point of view of our war, it was a battle between God and one king who tried to ignore God's word. All through the Old Testament, the Israelites kept wanting to worship idols, like the nations around them. God kept calling them back to worship him alone. God said that one way they could tell that he was the true God was this: whatever God said would happen always happened. The prophets of the false gods couldn't make that claim.

125

They could make all the predictions they wanted, but they were just guessing. Oh, every now and then maybe they'd get lucky and a prediction would come true, but most of the time, they'd turn out to be wrong. Not so with God. Whatever he said would happen always happened. Always.

"Why is that, anyway?" Grandpa asked, turning to Amy.

"Because God can see the future. He knows what's going to happen before it happens," Amy answered.

"Well, that's true, but there's more to it than that," Grandpa said. "Marc? Any ideas?"

Marc shook his head. "I would have said the same thing," he replied. "God knows what's going to happen in the future because he knows everything."

"It isn't just that he *knows* what will happen," Grandpa corrected. "He *knows* it will happen because he's the one who's going to *make* it happen. God is more than just the commander of one army or the leader of one nation. God's the king of the whole world and the ruler of all history. He makes his plans, sometimes he tells people what they are, and then he carries them out, just like he said. If ever someone could keep something from happening after God had said it was going to happen, then that someone would be stronger than God, wouldn't he?" The children nodded.

"In this story, King Ahab—you remember him, don't you?" Grandpa asked.

"The king with the evil wife," Marc said.

"Who wanted the Israelites to worship Baal instead of God," Amy added.

"Right," said Grandpa. "Well, in this story, King Ahab wanted to go to battle with the king of Aram, or Syria. It was about a city that Syria had taken from Israel. Ahab wanted it back. Ahab asked Jehoshaphat, the king down in the southern kingdom of Judah, to help him. Jehoshaphat said he would, but he added, 'First, we really should find out what God says about whether or not we'll win.'

"So Ahab summoned four hundred prophets. 'Should we go fight?' he asked them.

"These prophets sounded like so many cheerleaders! 'Oh, sure, go! No problem! You'll win. God will be on your side, and he'll give you victory.'

"King Jehoshaphat knew that Ahab had a tendency to worship false gods and to listen to false prophets. Jehoshaphat didn't trust this prophecy, even though it sounded so encouraging. 'Isn't there a prophet of *the Lord* that we can ask?' he said.

" 'Well, there's a prophet named Micaiah,' Ahab answered. 'But I hate him. He never prophesies anything good about me, only bad things.'

" 'Let's call him,' Jehoshaphat said.

"A servant went to get Micaiah. As they were going to where the two kings waited, the servant urged Micaiah to say the same kinds of things that all the other prophets had said. 'I'll say what the Lord tells me to say,' was Micaiah's answer.

"So King Ahab asked Micaiah to tell him the truth about what would happen, and Micaiah did. He prophesied that if the Israelites went to battle with the king of Syria, Ahab wouldn't come back alive. King Ahab may have been frightened. But if he was, he wasn't going to let anyone know it. He had Micaiah put in prison and ordered that he be given a diet of bread and water only. 'Keep him there until I'm safely home again,' Ahab ordered. It was his way of telling everyone—and maybe himself—'*I'm* not scared of God's prophecies. *I* don't believe they'll come true. *I'm* coming back, no matter what God says.'

"So the two kings ignored the word of the Lord from Micaiah and went to battle. Now, Marc, what does a commander always try to do about the other commander before a battle begins?"

Marc cocked his head and raised his eyebrow questioningly. "Well—he tries to find out his plans," Marc replied. "Is that what you mean?"

"That's exactly what I mean, and somehow King Ahab was able to do that," Grandpa said. "Or maybe he just guessed. But anyhow, the king of Aram told his captains, 'Don't worry about anyone else; just go after the king of Israel. I want him dead.' And Ahab knew that was the plan. So he made his own plans. He planned to disguise himself like a common soldier—a well-armored soldier, of course, because he wasn't going to take any chances, after that prophecy of Micaiah's. If he looked like an ordinary soldier, covered in armor, no one would recognize him as king. And to get the enemies even more off track, he told Jehoshaphat to be sure to wear all *his* royal clothing into the battle. That way, the enemies would go after Jehoshaphat instead of Ahab."

"Oh, that's real nice," said Amy. "With a friend like Ahab—"

"—who needs enemies?" finished Grandpa. "As you can see, Ahab was doing all he could to make sure Micaiah's prophecy didn't come true. He was out to prove that *he* was in control of things, not God and his word." Grandpa opened his box and pulled out a little man solidly covered in armor, which he set on top of the box. "But then, in the middle of the battle, a certain man drew his bow. We don't know who this man was or anything about him. But God had chosen this man and his arrow. The Bible says that the man just drew his bow at random. He wasn't even aiming at anything in particular! And the arrow that he shot 'just happened' to fly across the battlefield and through the one tiny chink in Ahab's armor. 'Take me out of the battle. I'm wounded,' Ahab cried to his chariot driver. So the chariot driver drove off to the side, out of the way of the fighting. The Israelites propped the king up in his chariot while the battle went on all day. As evening fell, King Ahab died, just as God had said."

Grandpa removed the little armed figure and replaced it with a little arrow. "Who moved that archer to use his bow just when he did?" Grandpa asked. "And who guided that arrow to just that one weak spot in the armor? What God says in his Word always happens because he's the one who makes it happen."

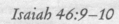
Isaiah 46:9–10

Remember the former things of old;
for I am God, and there is no other;
I am God, and there is none like me,
declaring the end from the beginning
and from ancient times things not yet done,
saying, "My counsel shall stand,
and I will accomplish all my purpose."

An Enemy
Changes Sides

(2 Kings 5)

Amy paused in the doorway of the school and looked out at the pouring rain. She shook out her umbrella, preparing to open it. "Hey, Amy!" She turned to see Marc running down the hall. "Would you take my stuff over to Grandpa's for me?" Amy hesitated. "Please. I have only two books, and they're not heavy. And you have an umbrella and I don't."

What was it about boys that made them never carry an umbrella? Amy thought.

"Okay," Amy agreed. "But now you owe me."

"Thanks," said Marc. "I'll beat you to Grandpa's 'cause I'm going to run. Anything you want me to do for you once I get there?"

"Heat some water for tea," Amy said. "I've been thinking about tea all day." Cool, rainy days like this one were unusual in Phoenix, so they always seemed like big events. Whenever they occurred, Amy liked to sip hot tea and savor the rare feeling of being inside and cozy while it was chilly and wet outdoors.

"It'll be ready when you get there," said Marc. "See ya," and he shot out the door.

When Amy arrived at "Trash to Treasure," she found Marc just taking her tea out of the microwave. She greeted Grandpa, leaned the wet umbrella in the corner and hung up her jacket, then hurried to get her cup from Marc. She was eager to settle in and start sipping while the tea was still hot. But when she grabbed the cup, tea sloshed out of it and onto her white blouse. "Oh, no!" she cried.

Right away, Grandpa, who had seen it all, asked, "Are you okay?"

"*I'm* okay," Amy answered. "It didn't get on *me*. But look at my blouse."

"Hurry and go rinse it out, while it's still wet," Grandpa advised. "It'll come right out."

"Are you sure?" Amy asked. "Look how dark it is. And it's right where it will show the most!"

"It'll come out. Trust me," Grandpa replied. "But you have to hurry before it dries."

Looking doubtful, Amy headed for the bathroom sink. She soon returned, her blouse wet but unstained. "Well, Grandpa," she said, "I'm happy to say that you were right. I didn't think it would come out. It looked so bad."

"Of course that reminds me of a story," Grandpa said.

"Of course," Amy answered.

"It's a story," Grandpa continued, "about a man who had tried everything to get clean. And when someone told him to try one more

131

thing, he didn't think it would work." Amy reheated her tea and sat down with Marc while Grandpa got his story box and came over to join them.

"After Ahab was killed by that 'random' arrow," Grandpa began, "first one of his sons and then a second one became kings in his place. But things weren't much better for Israel. The kings and the people still worshiped idols. And they still had trouble with the Syrians. Sometimes bands of Syrian raiders would come into Israel to steal things and to capture people for slaves.

"What a delightful state of affairs—from Satan's perspective. The so-called 'people of God' following other gods instead of their own; their enemies finding it easy to beat them in battle. *God's* idea was that other nations could look at his people and see that it's much better to worship the true God than to worship idols. But no one watching would have seen that now. It sure felt to Satan like he was winning.

"And it must have felt like that to one particular mom and dad in Israel. Their dear little daughter had been captured by one of those invading bands of Syrians, and who knew where she was now? How could God have allowed these wicked men to take their daughter? And what would happen to her? They might have been even more upset if they'd known that their daughter had been taken to the home of the one person who seemed most like Satan's ally in these battles. Who do you think that would be?"

Marc cocked his head and gazed thoughtfully at the ceiling. "The king of Syria?" he guessed.

Grandpa shook his head and looked at Amy, who set her teacup down on its saucer and pushed back in her rocking chair, also thinking. "A priest of one of the Syrian idols?" was her guess.

"The idols were nothing and the king would have been nothing without this man," Grandpa said. "The little girl went to work for the wife of Naaman, the captain of the Syrian king's army. Naaman was the man who gave the army and the country its strength. He was a great warrior who'd won battle after battle for his master, the king of Syria." Here Grandpa stopped to remove two figures from his box. He set one of them on the top. Leaning forward, the children saw that it was a little figure of a fierce-looking warrior, standing with his legs apart and his arms crossed. "The little girl from Israel hadn't worked in Naaman's house long before she discovered his one great weakness—he had leprosy. In those days, leprosy was a horrible disease—well, it still is, but in those days, there was no cure for it. A leper would be a leper as long as he lived. Leprosy would cause nasty-looking sores all over a person and even cause parts of his fingers or toes or nose or ears to rot away."

"Yuck!" Amy shuddered.

"Remember Elijah from a couple of stories ago?" Grandpa asked. The children nodded. "Well, he was no longer a prophet in Israel, but his student was."

"Oh, I know, Elisha," Amy said.

"I always get those two mixed up," said Marc.

"The little Israelite girl mentioned Elisha to Naaman's wife. 'I'm sure he could cure your husband's leprosy,' she said. No doubt Naaman had tried every doctor around and every cure he'd ever heard of. Nothing had helped. But Naaman told his master, the king of Syria, what the little girl had said, and the king sent Naaman to Israel with gifts, money, and a letter. The letter said: 'Dear King of Israel, I'm sending you my servant Naaman, so that you can cure him of his leprosy.' "

"He sent the letter to the wrong person," Amy protested.

"Yes," said Grandpa, "and the king of Israel thought he'd done it on purpose to pick a fight. He said, 'I can't cure this man's leprosy! Who do they think I am? But if I don't, the Syrian king will get mad and come fight us again. And we're not strong enough to fight right now. What am I going to do?'

"Elisha heard about the problem, so he also sent word to the king of Israel. 'Send Naaman to me,' Elisha said. 'Then he'll know there's a prophet of God in this country.' So Naaman came to Elisha's house.

But when Naaman knocked at his door, Elisha didn't even come out of his house to meet him. He sent a servant to the door with this message for Naaman: 'Go to the Jordan River and dip under the water seven times. Then your leprosy will be gone.' People were pretty superstitious in those days, especially idol-worshipers, but even Naaman thought a cure like that sounded ridiculous. How could dipping in a dirty old river help anything? And why hadn't Elisha come out to meet him? Didn't he realize how important Naaman was? What an insult! There was no way he would do this thing! And Naaman went away mad.

"But Naaman's servants mustered up all their courage and spoke to their angry master. 'If he'd told you to do some big thing, you'd have done it,' they said. 'This is nothing. What can it hurt to try?' So Naaman went to the Jordan River and dipped in it seven times, as God had told him to do through the prophet. When he came out of the river after the seventh time, his leprosy was gone. His skin was like new.

"It wasn't just Naaman's skin that became new and clean that day. God changed his heart as well. Naaman went back to Elisha's house to thank him. 'Now I know that there is no God in all the earth but the God of Israel,' he said. 'I will never again offer a sacrifice to any god but the LORD.' "

Grandpa removed the fierce-looking warrior from his box top and replaced it with another figure. This figure looked just like the same warrior, but now he was on his knees and his head was bowed. "God defeats some of his enemies by killing them in real battles, as he did with Ahab. But to capture an enemy fighter by changing his heart so that he wants to serve God—that's an even greater victory. And that's just what God does every time people turn from their old idols and put their trust in him."

Psalm 96:1–6

Oh sing to the Lord a new song;
    sing to the Lord, all the earth!
Sing to the Lord, bless his name;
    tell of his salvation from day to day.
Declare his glory among the nations,
    his marvelous works among all the peoples!
For great is the Lord, and greatly to be praised;
    he is to be feared above all gods.
For all the gods of the peoples are worthless idols,
    but the Lord made the heavens.
Splendor and majesty are before him;
    strength and beauty are in his sanctuary.

A Traitor's Plot Fails

(2 Kings 11)

Marc drew a line from star to star to star. When he had connected all the stars he meant to, he turned the worksheet this way, then that, then shook his head. "It doesn't look like a hero to me," he said. "It doesn't look like anything. It's just a crooked line with a straight line going off it."

Amy went to the table in Grandpa's shop where Marc was working on his science homework while they waited for their mother. Amy examined his drawing. "Hmm-mm," she agreed, "it *doesn't* look like much, does it? Who's it supposed to be?"

Marc turned back to his science book. "It's the Perseus constellation," he said, "whoever Perseus is. And these lines are supposed to be some girl—Andromeda—and this one's supposed to be Pegasus, the flying horse. I can kind of see the legs and maybe the heads for the girl and the horse, and I can see the wing of Pegasus. But as far as I'm concerned, Perseus is just a line. Who was he, anyway?"

"He's one of the Greek heroes," Amy replied. Her class had studied Greek mythology last year, and it had fascinated her. "He's the one who killed the Medusa."

"That lady with the snakes for hair?" Marc asked.

"Right," Amy answered. "And if you looked at her, you'd turn to stone. A king wanted to get rid of Perseus, so he sent him to kill the Medusa. And before that, Perseus's own grandfather tried to get rid of him. When he was just a baby, his grandfather put him and his mom in a chest and put the chest out into the sea."

"His own grandfather?" Marc asked, incredulously. "Did you hear that, Grandpa?" he called.

Grandpa looked up from where he was replacing the screws on the bottom of the music box he had been repairing. "The same thing happened in one of our war stories, only worse," Grandpa said. "When you finish your homework, I'll tell you about it."

"Oh, I'm done," Marc replied. "Perseus was the last constellation I had to find."

"I'm done, too," said Grandpa, tightening the music box's last screw. "Amy?"

"No homework tonight," Amy answered, as Grandpa picked up his story box and came to the table where the children sat.

"I don't remember a story about a grandfather trying to kill his grandson," Marc said, as Grandpa removed the two pieces he needed from the box.

"Actually," said Grandpa, "it wasn't a grandfather. It was a grand-*mother*. You remember that Israel had split into two kingdoms, right?" The children nodded. "What was the name of the one in the north, where Elijah and Elisha were?"

"Israel," the children answered together.

137

"Right," said Grandpa. "And so far, that's the only one we've talked about. But we did *mention* King Jehoshaphat, from the other kingdom, Judah. Do you remember him?"

The children didn't. Amy shook her head and Marc looked blank.

"Jehoshaphat from Judah was the one who made an alliance with Ahab from Israel." Grandpa reminded them. "They went to war together."

"Oh, that's right," said Marc. "Ahab told him to wear all his king's clothes into battle so that the enemy soldiers would shoot at Jehoshaphat instead of at Ahab."

"Now I remember," Amy said.

"Jehoshaphat was a good king for Judah," Grandpa continued. "He followed God, and he encouraged his people to do the same. But he did make one big mistake when he made that alliance with Ahab. And he took Ahab's daughter as a wife for his own son. The daughter's name was Athaliah, and she was every bit as wicked as her parents.

"Our story happens after Jehoshaphat had died. His son, the next king of Judah, had died, too, leaving Athaliah a widow. Athaliah's son Ahaziah was king. One day, Ahaziah left Judah on a trip and never came back. He was killed while he was away. Now, what would you expect a woman to do when she heard that her son had died?"

"Cry," said Marc.

Amy nodded. "And be sad," she agreed.

"What would you expect her to do with her grandchildren, if her son and their father were killed?"

Amy considered what her own grandmother would probably do. "She'd try to be brave for the grandchildren even if she didn't feel like it," she said. "She'd try to help them feel better."

"But not this grandmother," said Grandpa. "It seems that Athaliah wasn't sad at all to hear that her son had died. She was actually glad. She saw this as a fine opportunity for herself. If she acted quickly, she could step in and become queen. Which is just what she did.

"And we don't see her doing anything to comfort her fatherless grandchildren, either," Grandpa went on. "No, instead, she had other plans for them. Because after all, when the king dies, who's supposed to be the next king?"

"The king's oldest son," Marc replied.

"What if the king's oldest son dies, too?" asked Grandpa.

"Then the next oldest son," said Marc.

"And if the next son dies?" Grandpa continued. "And the next one? And the one after that until there's none left?"

"Well—" Marc hesitated, unsure. "Maybe the king's brother? Or his nephew?"

"Just what Athaliah was thinking," said Grandpa. "Everyone knew the king's son was to be the next king, but if there were no sons, people would need some time to figure out what to do. In that time, Athaliah could establish herself as queen. So Athaliah killed all of Ahaziah's sons."

"Her own grandsons!" Amy shook her head. "Bad as it is to think of a grandfather killing his grandchildren, it seems even worse when it's a grand*mother*."

"You're right," said Grandpa, "it's awful. But the worst thing wasn't that she was killing her own grandchildren. The worst thing was that she was trying to wipe out the whole royal family. What was especially bad about that?"

There was no answer from Amy or Marc. "Whose family was the royal family there in Judah?"

Still no answer. Then suddenly, Marc brightened. "Oh," he said. "David's."

"Right," Grandpa answered. "And what had God promised David?"

"Oh, I get it," Amy answered. "Someone from David's family was supposed to rule forever. So if Athaliah killed everyone from David's family, that promise couldn't come true."

139

"So Satan must have thought he'd finally won when Athaliah, thinking like Satan thought, destroyed David's family and made herself queen." Grandpa set the wooden figure of a queen on top of the box.

"But Satan wasn't the only one in this story who had a human ally," Grandpa said. "God had an ally, too, and it was Athaliah's own daughter. Her name was Jehosheba, and she loved and honored God. When Jehosheba understood that her mother was killing her own grandchildren—Jehosheba's nephews and nieces—she managed to rescue one. She rescued Joash, still just a little baby. Jehosheba had married a priest, Jehoiada. Together they raised little Joash."

"How did they keep him hidden?" Amy wondered, remembering what a problem hiding a baby had been for Moses' mother.

"They kept him hidden in the temple," Grandpa answered.

"That makes sense," Marc said. "Athaliah probably never went *there*."

"Joash's aunt and uncle hid him until he was seven years old. Then Jehoiada the priest decided it was time to act. He called Judah's soldiers together and showed them the little boy king. The soldiers surrounded Joash to protect him. Jehoiada placed a crown on his head and announced that he was king.

"Queen Athaliah heard the people shouting, 'Long live the king!' That brought her to the temple, you can be sure. 'Treason!' she shouted. But no one listened to her. Everyone knew she wasn't supposed to be the queen. She was arrested and taken away. They put her to death, and there was no one who felt sorry for her."

Grandpa removed the figure that represented Queen Athaliah and placed a little carving of a boy with a crown on his head in its place. "The royal family continued," said Grandpa.

140

"God's plans remained right on schedule. You just can't destroy those whom God has promised to preserve."

Psalm 89:3–6

You have said, "I have made a covenant with my chosen one;
    I have sworn to David my servant:
'I will establish your offspring forever,
    and build your throne for all generations.' "

Let the heavens praise your wonders, O LORD,
    your faithfulness in the assembly of the holy ones!
For who in the skies can be compared to the LORD?
    Who among the heavenly beings is like the LORD?

A Big Defeat
for a Big Enemy

(2 Kings 18–19; 2 Chronicles 32:1–23)

Marc peered over Amy's shoulder at the book she held. "Poetry?" he asked. "Why are you doing homework now? We have a four-day weekend." It was the Wednesday afternoon before Thanksgiving, and Marc and Amy were waiting at Trash and Treasure for their ride home. At the thought of four days of freedom, Marc was unable to hold in an excited "Wa-hoo!"

"Well, in the first place," Amy replied, "I don't like to wait till the last minute. I'll enjoy my four days off much more if I'm done with everything. And besides, I happen to like poetry."

"Well, you can have it," Marc replied.

Amy ignored him. "Grandpa, who's Sen-nach-er-ib?" she asked, trying to sound out the long name.

"Sennacherib?" Grandpa repeated. "He was a king in Assyria, in Bible times. Why?"

"I thought he must have something to do with Bible stories," Amy said. "I'm looking at this poem called 'The Destruction of Sennacherib,' and it's talking about Galilee and Gentiles and Baal and the Lord." She was quiet for a moment while she read a little of the poem. "I think it's about a battle," she added. "Grandpa, is this in one of our war stories?"

"As a matter of fact, it is," said Grandpa. "Want to hear it? Then the poem will make more sense."

"Yes, please," said Amy, and Grandpa came over with his story box.

"By the time this story takes place," Grandpa began, "the northern kingdom of Israel didn't exist anymore. The people in that kingdom never did stop worshiping idols, and their kings encouraged them to do it. God finally had enough. He sent the Assyrians to defeat them."

"We talked about the Assyrians when we studied ancient civilizations in history," Marc said. "The Assyrians could be pretty mean."

"My poem starts, 'The Assyrian came down like the wolf on the fold,' " said Amy. "That doesn't sound good."

"The Assyrians were famous for how mean they were," Grandpa agreed. "At the time of our story, they were the greatest world power on earth. Everyone was afraid of the Assyrians. So as you might expect, when the Assyrians took everyone captive from the northern kingdom, the people down in the little southern kingdom of Judah felt pretty nervous. What was to stop the Assyrians from coming after them as well? And sure enough, pretty soon Sennacherib, the Assyrian king, invaded Judah."

"And that's the Sennacherib in my poem?" Amy wanted to know.

"That's him," Grandpa replied. "In this battle, Sennacherib's the champion on Satan's side. On God's side, there's an Israelite king named Hezekiah, one of the very best kings ever to rule in Jerusalem. When Hezekiah became king, he worked hard at getting rid of idol worship. He taught the Jews to worship God again and obey him. Now, with Sennacherib coming at the head of the mighty Assyrian army, Hezekiah did the right thing again. He encouraged his people by telling them not to be afraid. Sure, Sennacherib was powerful, but not nearly as powerful as God. God would be with them. He'd help them and fight for them. The people listened to their king and felt braver.

"But then the Assyrian army showed up, with a nasty letter from their king. 'You can't fight us,' the letter said. 'You don't have horses; you can't ride. We've conquered one nation after another. There's no way you can resist.' It was hard to feel brave listening to words like that. And the letter didn't stop there. The commander of the Assyrian army said he had a message just for the common soldiers. 'You'd better surrender to my master, Sennacherib,' he called out to them. 'Don't listen to Hezekiah when he tells you that your God will fight for you. *All* the nations we defeated had gods. That didn't help *them*. No god has been able to save its people from our army, and your God won't be able to save you either.' "

Amy straightened in her chair. "But their gods were idols," she protested with indignation. "That's totally different!"

"Sennacherib wouldn't have understood the difference," Grandpa said. "But Satan surely did. But you know, Satan uses lies to fight his battles all the time. Like Sennacherib, Satan was probably feeling pretty sure of himself. Idol-worshipers had already conquered the kingdom of Israel because it had turned away from God. Only these few Israelites in Judah were left. If they became scared enough, maybe they'd give up their faith in God and turn away from him, too." Grandpa put a small scroll on the top of the box. "That letter from Sennacherib was quite a weapon. Satan used it to try to spread fear through God's people.

"Hezekiah knew just what to do with that letter, though. He took it to the temple and spread it out, as if to show it to God. Then he prayed. 'Listen to what they're saying,' Hezekiah told God. 'They're insulting you. They're saying that you're no different from the idols all the other nations serve. They're saying that you can't do any more than those gods can. Of course those gods can't do anything. They're made of wood and stone. But you're the real God. You made heaven and earth and everything there is. So please save us from Sennacherib. Then all the kingdoms on earth will know that you alone are God.'

"God answered Hezekiah with a promise. God promised that Sennacherib would never attack Jerusalem. He wouldn't come against it with a spear or an arrow or anything else. He wouldn't even get to Jerusalem. Instead, he was going to turn around and go home, back the same way he came."

"Really?" said Marc, leaning forward with curiosity. "How did that happen? When we studied the Assyrians in history, it didn't seem like they gave up too easily. If they wanted your city, they got it."

"Well, here's what happened," Grandpa explained. "God sent his angel to the Assyrian camp, and that angel, with no help from any army, killed 185,000 Assyrians—all their commanders, all their officers, all their mighty warriors—in one night."

"Here it is," Amy cried with excitement. Then she read from her poetry book:

> For the Angel of Death spread his wings on the blast,
> And breathed in the face of the foe as he passed;
> And the eyes of the sleepers waxed deadly and chill,
> And their hearts but once heaved, and for ever grew still!

Grandpa removed the little scroll that stood for Sennacherib's letter and replaced it with a carved figure of an angel holding an upraised sword.

"Was Sennacherib one of the 185,000 who died?" Marc wanted to know.

"No," Grandpa answered. "Remember, God said that he'd go back home by the same way he came. The Bible says he returned in shame to his own land."

"I guess so," said Amy. "How would he explain what had happened to his army?"

"The last line of your poem gives a great explanation for what happened to his army and all its famous strength," said Grandpa. "Read it to us."

"It says it 'hath melted like snow in the glance of the Lord,' " Amy read. Looking up in surprise, she said, "Grandpa, how did you know it said that? Do you know this poem?"

Grandpa nodded. "Sure do," he answered. "It's one of my favorites."

Marc shook his head unbelievingly. There was always something new to learn about Grandpa. This was almost too much—Grandpa *liked* poetry.

"That's not the end of Sennacherib's story, though," Grandpa added. "He didn't die with his army, but the Bible tells us how he did die. His own sons killed him. And guess where he was and what he was doing when they did it?"

The children shook their heads. They had no idea.

"He was in the temple of his god, Nisroch, and he was in the very act of worshiping that god," Grandpa said.

"Wow!" Marc exclaimed. "And he was the one who said the real God couldn't protect his people. Guess we see whose god really couldn't protect!"

All of them are put to shame and confounded;
    the makers of idols go in confusion together.
But Israel is saved by the LORD
    with everlasting salvation;
you shall not be put to shame or confounded
    to all eternity.

For thus says the LORD, who created the heavens
    (he is God!),
who formed the earth and made it
    (he established it;
he did not create it empty,
    he formed it to be inhabited!):
"I am the LORD, and there is no other."

War against the Word

(Jeremiah 36)

Marc stabbed the last mouthful of pie with his fork. "This is going to be the straw that broke the camel's back," he announced, then lifted the pie to his mouth and ate it. "That did it!" said Marc. He fell off his chair and onto the floor. He lay still for a brief but dramatic moment, then rose and returned to his seat.

Amy pushed her plate, with pie still on it, away from her. "I can't even finish mine," she said. "It's great pie, Grandma, as always. But I'm *stuffed*. I'll finish it later."

Thanksgiving Day was nearly over. The usual enormous feast had been enjoyed, the kitchen had been cleaned, and games had been played. Dessert had been delayed in hopes of making more room in overloaded tummies, but now it was finished as well.

"Marc and Amy, you should gather up your things," their mother said. "We'll be leaving soon."

"But we haven't had a single story from Grandpa this whole day," Amy pointed out. "Can't we have just one story before we leave?"

"I'm going to help Grandma with these last dessert dishes," their mother answered. "So you two get your things together first, and then you can listen to a story. That is, if Grandpa doesn't mind."

"Grandpa never minds," Marc said. "He loves telling stories. Don't you, Grandpa?"

For reply, Grandpa went off to find the story box. When Marc and Amy were ready to leave, they came and sat by Grandpa.

"Before we start this story, let's review a little bit, to see where this story fits in the big story," Grandpa suggested. "Amy, when did God first say there would be a war between Satan and his people?"

"In the Garden of Eden," Amy answered promptly. "And that's also where he made the first promise of a child who would destroy Satan and his work."

"Good," said Grandpa. "Marc, where did the people of God come from?"

"Egypt," Marc answered, just as promptly. "They were slaves there, and God sent Moses to get them out."

"True enough," Grandpa answered. "But how did they end up in Egypt in the first place? Maybe I should have said, *who* did the people of God come from?"

"Oh, they came from Abraham," Marc said. "And they were in Egypt because of a famine. Joseph had saved up food in Egypt, so his family came to live there to have enough to eat."

"Amy, you always have the answer to this one, but I haven't asked you for a while: what three things did God promise to Abraham? Do you remember?"

"Yep," Amy nodded with confidence. "A great nation, land, and blessing for all the nations."

"So God's Old Testament people were Abraham's descendants. They left Egypt and went to the Promised Land—what was life there like at first?" was Grandpa's next question. "Did they have good leaders? Did they follow God?"

"No and no," Marc answered. "They kept getting in trouble because they kept worshiping idols."

"Until—what?" asked Grandpa.

"Until they got a king," said Marc.

"But their first king was Saul, and he wasn't a good king," Amy added. "Then God gave them David."

"And what promise did God make to David?" Grandpa asked.

"There would always be someone from his family on the throne," Amy said just as Marc was saying, "A son of his would be king forever."

"Good, good," Grandpa beamed. "And that was a promise about—"

"Jesus," the children answered in unison.

"What happened to Israel right after Solomon died?" Grandpa continued.

"It split into two kingdoms," Marc said. "Israel and Judah."

"One of those kingdoms always worshiped idols and never had a good king," Grandpa said. "Which one was it?"

"Israel," Amy answered.

"And so what happened to the kingdom of Israel?"

"The Assyrians conquered it and took the people prisoner," said Marc.

"What about Judah? Did the Assyrians conquer it?"

"Nope," said Amy. "Like my poem said, Sennacherib's army was wiped out when he tried it."

"Okay, good, let's go on," said Grandpa. "So Judah was still around, but this story takes place in Judah's final days. Israel had set a lousy example, and unfortunately, Judah followed it. The people in Judah and many of its kings chose to ignore God's commands and worship idols. Over and over, God sent prophets to call the Jews back to himself, but they wouldn't listen. Finally, it was too late. Judgment was coming. Not the Assyrians, but another world power began to threaten God's people. And this time, God would let Judah's enemies win."

"Was it Greece, Grandpa?" Marc wanted to know. Grandpa shook his head. "Persia?"

"Close," Grandpa answered. "It was the world power that came along right before Persia. It was Babylon. God's prophet of the day was Jeremiah. No one liked Jeremiah because no one liked his message. 'It's too late now; judgment has come.' That was Jeremiah's message. 'God will let the Babylonians destroy your city because of your sin. Stop fighting, surrender, and go off to Babylon. And while you're there, turn back to God. Serve him again, and eventually he'll bring you back to your land.'

"Marc, when a country is at war and someone inside the country encourages the people to surrender, what happens to him?" Grandpa asked.

"He's called a traitor," Marc answered. "And he probably gets killed—or at least put in jail—so no one can hear his message."

"And that's just what happened to Jeremiah," said Grandpa. "The rulers of Judah put him in jail to keep him quiet. They also locked him in stocks, beat him, made fun of him; once they even put him down into an old abandoned well, and he sank into the mud at the bottom all the way up to his waist."

"Yuck!" said Amy, making a face.

"And all because they didn't like his message. But the thing was, it wasn't his message; it was God's message. When the people tried to silence Jeremiah, they were really trying to silence the Word of God. And that can't be done. That's been a big part of our war story down through the centuries. There's always someone who's trying to silence the Word of God. There's always someone who doesn't want people to have God's Word or who wants to prove that there's nothing to it. Satan's special forces have been out to destroy God's Word ever since God first gave it.

"In tonight's story, God told Jeremiah to write on a scroll everything God had ever given him to say. By this time, that was a lot of writing. Jeremiah had been prophesying for years. 'If they hear how great my anger is because of their sin,' God told Jeremiah, 'maybe they'll repent and pray to me.' So Jeremiah called his scribe, Baruch. A scribe is like a secretary," Grandpa explained. "Jeremiah told Baruch what to write, and Baruch wrote it all down. Then God told Jeremiah to have Baruch take the scroll to the temple and read it to the people.

"When Baruch read the scroll, some of those who heard it were troubled by what it said. 'The king needs to hear this,' they said. So they took the scroll to the king to read God's Word to him. The king at that time was Jehoiakim, one of the last kings to reign in Jerusalem. It happened to be wintertime when the people brought him Jeremiah's scroll, and Jehoiakim was sitting by a fire. The king listened to the first part of God's Word from the scroll; then he stopped the reader. Those who'd brought him the scroll wondered what was coming next. Was he frightened to hear how angry God was, as they'd been? Would he tear his rich king's clothing to show that he was sorry for his sin? They watched as King Jehoiakim got up and walked over to the reader. They saw him take out a little knife and cut off the piece of scroll he'd just heard. Then they watched as he carried it to the fire and tossed it in."

Amy gasped. Grandpa opened his box and took out a miniature fire. He placed it on top of his box.

"As the piece of God's Word burned, King Jehoiakim said,

'Keep reading.' He listened to the next section, cut that one off, and threw it into the fire. Piece by piece, King Jehoiakim heard—and then burned—the entire scroll. He destroyed all that God had told Jeremiah to say and write down. And when the king was done, he gave orders to arrest Jeremiah and Baruch the scribe. He wasn't just going to destroy the Word of God that Jeremiah had spoken so far. He was going to make sure that no further Word of God came through Jeremiah.

"But it's just not that easy to get rid of God's Word. God hid Jeremiah and Baruch, so the king's men couldn't find them. And God gave Jeremiah all the same prophecies again and told him to have them written down once more. So even though King Jehoiakim burned that whole scroll, we still have the words that God gave to Jeremiah. It's in the book Jeremiah in our Bibles. God made sure that it would get written down, and he protected it through the centuries down to our time—just like the rest of the Bible. Of all the people who've tried to silence the Word of God, not one has ever been able to do it."

Grandpa removed the fire from his box top and placed a small carving of an open Bible in its place. "And King Jehoiakim—what happened to him?" Marc wanted to know.

"He was punished, just as God's Word to Jeremiah said he would be. King Nebuchadnezzar came from Babylon to invade Jerusalem. He locked Jehoiakim in chains and took him away. Jehoiakim died a prisoner in Babylon. Satan and his allies never learn. They've gone right on making war on God's Word ever since, and they've gone right on losing. God's Word remains forever."

"And," Amy added, "since it *is* Thanksgiving Day, that's something we should add to our list of things to be thankful for. God hasn't just given us his Word; he's protected it all these centuries, so we can still read it."

"Amen to that!" Grandpa agreed.

153

A voice says, "Cry!"
> And I said, "What shall I cry?"
All flesh is grass,
> and all its beauty is like the flower of the field.
The grass withers, the flower fades
> when the breath of the Lord blows on it;
> surely the people are grass.
The grass withers, the flower fades,
> but the word of our God will stand forever.

Victory on Enemy Ground

(Daniel 2–3)

Marc set the child's rocker down by the front door. In his other hand, he held a tall lampstand with no shade. He opened the door with his free hand and found the light switch inside. Light spilled out through the doorway, and Marc picked up the rocker and stepped into the shop. Amy followed with a box full of dishes. Behind her came Grandpa. With one hand, he pulled a wagon filled with tools, toys, and small appliances. With his other hand, he pulled a bicycle.

Amy set her box on the table inside the shop and rubbed her arms. "Brr-rr!" she said. "It's cold in here!" The children had spent the

Saturday after Thanksgiving shopping garage sales with Grandpa, and the store had not been opened all day.

"Grandpa, can we make a fire?" Marc asked eagerly.

"It *is* pretty chilly," Grandpa agreed. "But not a very big fire. We won't be out here very long."

Marc got wood from the wood box, opened the door to the small wood-burning stove, and stacked it in the way Grandpa had taught him to do. Soon a cheery fire popped and crackled in the stove. "I'm just going to sit here for a minute and warm up before I help you put stuff away," said Amy. "Is that okay?"

"Sure," said Grandpa. "We'll join you. And I'll tell a story because the next one's about a stove anyway—well, a furnace."

"Oh, I know what this story's going to be," said Marc.

"I'm sure you do," said Grandpa, "but have you thought about how it's the story of a battle in our ongoing war story? Listen and I'll show you what I mean.

"In the last story we had, King Jehoiakim cut up Jeremiah's scroll and burned it because he didn't like what it said. But that didn't keep the words in the scroll from coming true. Just as God had said, the Babylonians came. They destroyed Jerusalem and broke down its walls. They burned the temple. And they carried away most of God's people as prisoners into Babylon.

"Boy, did it look like Satan was winning the war now. He'd always wanted to keep that promised baby from being born. If there was anything he could do to harm the people who were called God's people, he'd do it. If there were no people of God, then that baby couldn't come from them after all. And now, what a great chance he had to wipe them out—or so it seemed to him.

"In the first place, God didn't seem to be taking very good care of his people. They'd lost everything to the Babylonians. Didn't that mean that Babylon's gods were stronger than their God?"

156

"Of course not." Amy sat up straight and protested. "It just means that the Israelites had been disobedient and God wasn't fighting for them anymore."

"*We* know that," Grandpa agreed, "and Satan knew that, too. But remember, he lies. He puts bits and pieces of truth together with things that aren't true so that people will swallow the whole package. It didn't *look* like God was very strong. He hadn't even been able to defend his own temple. It was gone. Hardly anyone had remained true to him.

"But God had a battle or two for his own glory that he wanted fought in Babylon. He had his own soldiers who would be faithful to him, even when outnumbered and in enemy territory. One of them was Daniel. God gave Daniel a mission. Daniel was to encourage God's defeated people while they were captives in Babylon. God wanted them to know that he was still the greatest ruler of all, no matter what it looked like at the moment. And while he was at it, God wanted the people of Babylon to see that as well. So God gave King Nebuchadnezzar a dream. The dream was about a statue. It had a gold head, a silver chest and arms, a bronze tummy and thighs, and iron legs. In Nebuchadnezzar's dream, a stone that hadn't been cut out with human hands crashed into the statue's feet. The feet broke and the statue fell down."

Marc laughed. "It sounds like bowling," he said.

"Kind of," said Grandpa, "but then the whole statue broke into tiny pieces and the pieces blew away in the wind. But the stone that knocked down the statue grew until it was bigger than the biggest mountain. It got so big, it filled up the whole world. Well, Nebuchadnezzar was dying to know what this dream meant. But no one could tell him. Except Daniel. Daniel prayed that God would show him the meaning of the dream, and God did. The statue represented the kingdoms of the earth, Daniel told the king. Babylon was the gold head. But it wasn't going to last. It was going to be replaced by another kingdom. That's what the silver chest and arms meant.

Marc, which kingdom replaced Babylon? You told me this the other day."

"That would be Persia," said Marc, pleased to be able to offer this fact.

"The bronze part of the statue stood for—"

"No, no, no, let me say it!" Marc interrupted. "Let's see, after Persia came—Greece!"

"And the last one would be Rome," Amy added. "I remember that from studying mythology."

"Well, I'm happy to know that you two get something out of going to school," said Grandpa. "What would the stone be, then? It was a kingdom that came during the time of the Romans, and it would never end."

"Was it Jesus?" Marc asked.

"That's it!" Grandpa nodded. "The stone was the kingdom of God that Jesus would bring. God wanted his people—and Nebuchadnezzar—to know that no matter what it looked like now or how it might look in the future, God's kingdom would triumph once and for all. His kingdom was the only one that would last.

" 'Well, that's all very well and good,' Satan might have thought. 'But that's all in the future.' If he could scare God's people enough now with the power of an enemy king, they might not be around in the future. And then how could that kingdom ever come?

"And so maybe Nebuchadnezzar's great idea was from Satan himself. Nebuchadnezzar's great idea was to build a giant statue, just like the one in his dream. Only this statue was made entirely of gold. That's because Nebuchadnezzar didn't like the idea of his kingdom being replaced by another one. He set his all-gold statue up in the middle of a great plain there in Babylon, and he called all his workers and officials and servants to come and worship it."

There was a scraping noise as Amy dragged her chair back away from the stove. "Yikes," she said, "that fire's getting hot."

"Like the furnace Nebuchadnezzar built," said Grandpa. "He had a huge furnace built, and he said that anyone who wouldn't worship his statue would be burned alive."

Amy, whose leg was hot and itching from having been so close to the stove, thought how unpleasant that would be.

"Daniel doesn't seem to have been there that day," Grandpa continued. "I don't know why, but he's not mentioned in the story. But his three friends were, Shadrach, Meshach, and Abednego. They were among the few faithful soldiers God had left, and they weren't about to disobey their commanding officer. They knew God's law. They knew they weren't to bow to anything but God. So when the order was given to bow and worship, they remained standing."

"I guess that must have really stood out," Marc said. "When everyone else bows, it's pretty easy to see three guys standing up."

"Exactly," Grandpa agreed. "And Nebuchadnezzar was furious. He wasn't used to being ignored. He brought those three young men to him and said, 'You have one more chance, and that's it! You can bow or you can go into the furnace; it's up to you.' Then the king added, 'And what god is there who can save you then?'"

"He's going to find out," Amy murmured.

"Of course, you know how this story goes," said Grandpa. "Those three said that maybe God would save them and maybe he wouldn't. But whether he did or not, they weren't going to bow. And that made the king even angrier. He ordered that the furnace be heated seven times hotter than it normally was and that the three young men be thrown in." By way of emphasis, Grandpa opened the stove door and added another log. The fire blazed up, and both Marc and Amy moved their chairs back from the heat. "It was so hot that the guards who took Shadrach, Meshach, and Abednego to the door to throw them in died from the heat themselves." Grandpa opened the box that sat near him and took out a small figure of a furnace.

"But it wasn't long before Nebuchadnezzar noticed that the three men were walking around inside the furnace as though it weren't

159

hot at all. The only thing the fire seemed to have burned were the ropes they'd been tied with. 'And who's that other one in there?' Nebuchadnezzar asked. 'We put only three men in the furnace, but there are four now. And the fourth one looks like the son of a god.' Now Nebuchadnezzar hurried to bring the men back out of the furnace. Tell me, Amy, how do *you* smell after we've roasted marshmallows around a campfire?"

"Smoky," Amy answered, wrinkling her nose in distaste. "That's the one thing I don't like about camping. I always come home smelling like the campfire."

Unnoticed, Marc shook his head. *Girls!* he thought, but he didn't say it.

"Well, these three didn't even smell like smoke—not their hair, not their clothes, nothing," said Grandpa, removing the furnace from the box top and setting a group of three men in its place. "On that day, God's people and the idol-worshiping king clearly saw that God is greater than any earthly kings. And he never stops taking care of his people."

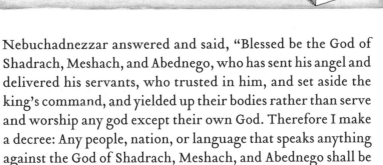

Daniel 3:28–29

Nebuchadnezzar answered and said, "Blessed be the God of Shadrach, Meshach, and Abednego, who has sent his angel and delivered his servants, who trusted in him, and set aside the king's command, and yielded up their bodies rather than serve and worship any god except their own God. Therefore I make a decree: Any people, nation, or language that speaks anything against the God of Shadrach, Meshach, and Abednego shall be torn limb from limb, and their houses laid in ruins, for there is no other god who is able to rescue in this way."

Mission Accomplished, Right on Schedule

(Ezra 1:1–4; Ezra 4; Haggai 1; Ezra 5–6)

Marc and Amy waved to their mother and ran down the sidewalk and into Grandpa's shop. "What are you doing here so early?" Grandpa asked Marc as he came in.

"Don't you remember?" Marc said. "Mom has to go to the dentist before work, and it's too early for school. So we're here till school starts."

"Don't *you* remember?" Grandpa grinned in reply. "I forget things as soon as I hear them. Good morning, Anna," he called to Amy.

Marc looked around to see who else was in the shop. When he saw only Amy, he said, "Now, Grandpa, don't tell me you forgot her name. It's Amy, not Anna."

161

"And don't tell me *you* forgot that I'm Anna in the Christmas play tonight," Amy said to Marc. "That's what you're talking about, huh, Grandpa?"

Grandpa nodded. "That's right. Can't wait to hear my Amy John singing the part of Anna." The solo parts in the church Christmas play always went to the junior-high students. At last Amy was in junior high, and she had been thrilled to finally have a solo part. As for Marc, he was not yet old enough for a solo part, which suited him just fine. Once again, he would be an anonymous member of a group of shepherds, and he could not have been happier.

"But Grandpa," Amy was saying, "I've been wondering about something. When I do the part of Anna, I'm supposed to be seeing the baby Jesus being brought into the temple. And I'm supposed to be an old lady who's been in the temple for years and years where I pray and serve God."

"Right," said Grandpa, nodding.

"Well, where'd the temple come from? And how come Jews were living in Jerusalem when Jesus was born, anyway? Because in the stories you've been telling us, the Jews were taken away from Jerusalem to Babylon. And the Babylonians had torn down the temple and burned it, so how could Jesus be taken to it?"

"Pull up a chair by the stove and I'll tell you," Grandpa replied, hurrying off. When he came back, he was carrying two boxes. One was the yellow box he always used when he told his war stories. The other was a box of doughnuts, which he passed to Marc and Amy.

"Of course, the Jews couldn't stay in Babylon forever," Grandpa began. "God had made too many promises for that to happen. By the time the Babylonians came, God had already promised that the child who was coming would be born in Bethlehem. He'd also promised that the people living in Galilee would see him. Those are both places in Israel. So the people of God had to be back in the Promised Land by the time Jesus was born. Plus, God had specifically promised his people that they'd be captives in Babylon for seventy years and no longer. After that, God would bring them back to their land.

"Satan may have thought, 'Fat chance of that!' " Grandpa paused. "Speaking of fat—Are there any doughnuts left in that box?" Marc passed him the box. Grandpa selected a doughnut and took a bite. He swallowed, then continued. "How were a few pitiful little Israelites going to escape from a great world power like Babylon and go home? No, it seemed that they were stuck for good. God's promises about where the child would be born and where he would live just couldn't come true.

"But the Commander-in-Chief of *our* army has all authority. Even over the other side! God's the one who decides who's going to rule what kingdom and how powerful it's going to get. So when God had done all he meant to do through Babylon, he brought Babylon to an end and set up another kingdom in its place."

"Persia!" Marc interjected, still feeling good about knowing these things.

"Persia it was," said Grandpa. "But that didn't necessarily help anything. Persians didn't worship God any more than Babylonians did. And the Persian ruler, Cyrus, didn't know or serve God. Satan may have thought he was still safe, and the Jews still couldn't go home. But the Bible says that God can turn the hearts of kings any which way he wants to, whether they know him or not. God put it into Cyrus's heart that there should be a temple to God in Jerusalem again. Maybe he wanted as many different peoples with as many different gods as possible to be praying for him, just in case any of those gods were real. Whatever the reason was, Cyrus sent a decree out into his kingdom. This decree said that any of God's people who wanted to go back to Jerusalem and build a temple for God were free to go. Cyrus even provided the money and the other things the Jews needed for rebuilding.

"Okay, I see," said Amy. She was over by Grandpa's mini-refrigerator, pouring herself a glass of milk. "So that's how there could be a temple where Anna saw the baby Jesus. Anyone else want milk?"

Amy asked. Marc shook his head no, and Grandpa held up his mug to show that he was still drinking coffee. Amy came back with her milk.

"But hold on a minute. It wasn't that easy," Grandpa cautioned. "A group of Jews did go back to Jerusalem. First thing, they started building a new temple, because that was the most important thing to them. But as soon as one of Satan's schemes doesn't work, he always comes up with a new one.

"So Satan sent the neighbors to offer help. The other people living in the area came to the Jews at Jerusalem and said, 'Let us build with you.' "

Marc looked puzzled. "How was that a problem?" he asked. "I'd think the Jews would have been glad for the help."

"It was a problem because these people didn't know the true God. Oh, they offered sacrifices to him, all right, but they offered sacrifices to all kinds of gods. The true God was just one more to them. Satan may have hoped the Jews would become friends with these people. If they started doing religious things together, in no time the Jews would be right back into idol worship again and they'd be on God's bad side once more. But this plan of Satan's didn't work either. God gave his people the wisdom and the courage to say, 'No, thank you; we'll build by ourselves.'

"Back to the drawing board for Satan. If he couldn't trap God's people with *friendly* neighbors, he'd fight them with *enemy* neighbors. So now the neighboring peoples began making up lies about the Jews. They wrote to the king—not Cyrus anymore—and told him that the Jews were planning rebellion. That's why they were rebuilding, their letter told the king. It was so that the Jews could be strong enough to fight against the king. So the king issued an order saying that all temple-building had to stop.

"And how do you think the Jews felt about that?" Grandpa asked, turning to Amy.

Amy wiped off her milk mustache with a napkin and answered, "They must have been sad."

164

"That's what you'd think, huh?" Grandpa agreed. "But that wasn't really the case. Satan had been busy, not just with the neighbors but with the Israelites as well. It seems they were all too happy to stop building the temple because now they'd have more time for building their own houses. So they got busy working for themselves. They built and then they decorated and then they added on and then they remodeled. They never seemed to run out of things to do to make their own houses nice and comfy, while God's house sat half-begun." On the top of his box, Grandpa placed a little figure he had carved. It was a roofless, unfinished building.

"A fine state of affairs—from Satan's viewpoint. As if the people had never learned they were to do God's will first of all. As if they still didn't realize that it was more important for them to have God than to have anything else. It looked like they'd go right back to ignoring God in no time, and they could be taken off into captivity again—maybe for good this time. Satan could always hope.

"And then God sent prophets: Haggai and Zechariah. One came to scold the people because they hadn't honored God by finishing his temple. The other came to encourage them to work and do their best until it was done. Satan wasn't worried. These people had a reputation for not listening to God's prophets. But this time, they did listen. God worked in the hearts of the Jews in Jerusalem, and when they heard the words of Haggai and Zechariah, the people wanted to obey God. They went back to work on the temple. This time when the neighbors sent a letter to the king—King Darius now—he wrote back, saying, 'Leave those Jews alone. Let them build their temple. And *you* find the money to pay for it!'

"So the prophets prophesied to encourage them and the people built—and the enemies paid for the whole thing! And at last they finished the temple." Grandpa replaced his figure of a half-finished building with another carving, this time in the shape of the completed temple. "Exactly seventy years had gone by, just as God had promised. Eventually, this temple, too, would be destroyed. One more temple

would be built before Jesus came, and that, Amy, would be the one Anna was in. But God's people were safely settled back in the land he'd given them, and there they would stay. They would be there when the promised child came."

Marc, wiping the last bits of doughnut crumbs from his mouth with his shirtsleeve, caught sight of his watch.

"Oops. We'd better go, Grandpa. It's almost time for school," he said, rising and picking up his backpack.

"Okay. I'll see you tonight at the play. Sing pretty, both of you," Grandpa said. "And Amy, I'll be coming backstage afterwards to get your autograph. That is, if I can fight my way through the crowd of adoring fans."

"Oh, Grandpa," said Amy.

Jeremiah 29:10–14

For thus says the LORD: When seventy years are completed for Babylon, I will visit you, and I will fulfill to you my promise and bring you back to this place. For I know the plans I have for you, declares the LORD, plans for wholeness and not for evil, to give you a future and a hope. Then you will call upon me and come and pray to me, and I will hear you. You will seek me and find me. When you seek me with all your heart, I will be found by you, declares the LORD, and I will restore your fortunes and gather you from all the nations and all the places where I have driven you, declares the LORD, and I will bring you back to the place from which I sent you into exile.

Every Little Detail

(Esther)

"Grandpa, Grandpa, I won!" Marc began hollering while he was still running up the sidewalk. He burst through the door of "Trash to Treasure," still hollering.

"Congratulations!" Grandpa said, coming to meet Marc. "I knew you could do it." And he held out his hand to shake Marc's.

Marc hurried to set down his school things so that he could receive Grandpa's handshake. "First place!" he said. "I'll get a trophy *and* I'll get to go out for pizza during class time." Marc paused, calming himself just a little. "Thanks for praying for me, Grandpa," he added.

"I pray for you every day," Grandpa answered.

"But did you really pray about the chess tournament?" Amy asked. "Marc's winning a chess tournament doesn't seem like a very important thing to pray about. No offense, Marc, but there are wars and people starving to death—you know, big stuff."

"Well, to tell you the truth, I did pray about the chess tournament, but not exactly that Marc would win," Grandpa explained. "I prayed that he would do his best for God's glory and that God would help him to grow through it, whether he won or lost. But it would be wrong to think that God doesn't care about the little tiny details of life. God not only cares about them, he ordains them."

"What does 'ordain' mean?" Marc wanted to know.

"It means that God determines what will happen and how it will happen. It's really very amazing when you think about it. God's not only working out how everything will turn out in the end. He's also working right now through each little detail in every ordinary life to bring good to his people and glory to himself." Grandpa chuckled. "Which is why, in our war story, we know for sure that God's side will win. You're too excited about the tournament to do homework right now anyway, so let me tell you a war story that shows what I mean. Grab a snack while I go get my box."

Amy chose pretzels and grapes and Marc got the crackers and cheese while Grandpa was off getting the story box. Once they were all seated, Grandpa began. "Do you know that there's a book in the Bible that never mentions God once?"

"Let me guess," said Amy, "Song of Solomon, right?" Grandpa shook his head. "No?" said Amy. She thought again. "Then what is it?"

"It's the book of Esther," Grandpa answered.

"Really?" said Marc. "Then why is it in the Bible?"

"Because even though it never mentions God, you can see him all through the story. He works out all sorts of ordinary, everyday details to accomplish his plans.

"This story is the last of our war stories in the Old Testament. That means it was getting very close to the time that the promised child was to be born. So of course Satan was beginning to feel desperate. This is the story of one more attempt to wipe out the whole Israelite nation, so that the promised baby couldn't be born. Who was Esther?" Grandpa asked, turning to Amy.

Amy swallowed her bite of pretzel and said, "A Jewish girl who became queen."

"Queen of what?" Grandpa turned to Marc, since he was always eager to supply answers about the early civilizations he had studied last year in fourth grade.

"Persia, right?" Marc answered.

"Yes, and how did a Jewish girl get to be the queen of Persia?" Grandpa asked.

"Oh, I remember that part," Amy said. "The king got mad at his queen because she wouldn't come when he told her to, so he wouldn't let her be queen anymore, and he had to get a new one. So he had this big—well, it was kind of like a beauty contest. Esther was one of the girls who came and the king liked her best, so he made her queen."

"Good," said Grandpa. "Now, did you ever stop to think about *why* the first queen and the king had their falling-out? Or who it was who made Esther so beautiful? Or how it happened that, of all those girls, the king preferred Esther? Ordinary, everyday details—a quarreling couple, the way somebody looks, the likes and dislikes of a king—all arranged by God to do what he knew needed to be done.

"And here comes another ordinary detail. Esther's cousin, Mordecai, had raised her because her parents had died. Mordecai worked for the king. He just happened to be standing near two of the king's guards one night and overheard their conversation. These guards didn't like the king, and Mordecai heard them planning to assassinate him! Mordecai told Esther about it, and she told the king. So Mordecai saved the king's life, just because he happened to be in the right place at the right time. Who caused *that* to happen? This little incident was written down in the king's history book. Now, you two remember that history book. It's going to be important later.

169

"Also in the palace of the Persian king was a nobleman named Haman. Haman had the second-highest position in all the land. He expected everyone to honor him by bowing down to him. And everyone did—except Mordecai. Whenever Haman walked by, Mordecai was the only person who remained standing. And it made Haman furious! You'd think Haman would be happy with all the honor he had, instead of demanding more—does that remind you of anyone, by the way? Can you think of anyone else in this war who had highest honors but couldn't be happy unless he had more?"

"Oh, it's like Satan in heaven, back at the beginning of the story," Marc answered.

"That's right," said Grandpa. "And that's not the only way Haman was like Satan. Because he was mad at Mordecai and Mordecai was an Israelite, Haman decided that he hated *all* Israelites. Getting rid of Mordecai wouldn't be enough for him. He would destroy every last one of the people of God—an idea that must have come from Satan himself." Grandpa stopped. "By the way," he said, "are you two remembering that history book, where the king wrote that Mordecai had saved his life? Don't forget it.

"So then, Haman went to the Persian king—whom history knows as Xerxes I, by the way—" Grandpa added, for Marc's sake. Marc nodded, not really sure whether that was a Persian king he had studied in school or not. "Haman went to Xerxes and offered the king money if the king would let him get rid of all the Jews. Xerxes didn't care. Haman was his friend, and what were a few foreigners more or less? So the king issued a decree that on a certain day all the Israelites, young and old, in all places of his kingdom were to be killed."

Grandpa opened his box and took out a green plastic sword, the kind sometimes used to hold appetizers together. He placed the sword on the box lid.

"This is where Esther saves the day," Amy said, raising her arm and making a fist in a sign of victory. "I love it when girls are the heroes!"

"Don't get ahead of my story," Grandpa pretended to scold. "First she had to struggle with that a little. At first, Esther didn't know that any of this was going on. Mordecai sent her a message about it and begged her to go to the king to talk him out of it. 'I can't do that!' Esther sent the message back. 'I haven't been invited. I haven't seen the king for thirty days.'"

"He was her husband, for crying out loud," Amy protested.

"*But* he was the king of Persia," Marc replied. "You couldn't go see him whenever you felt like it. You had to have an invitation or you couldn't go. No matter who you were."

"Wasn't there something about a scepter?" Amy asked. "If the king held it out to you, it was okay, but if not, you were dead?"

"That's right," Grandpa said. "So Esther didn't want to go. But Mordecai understood how God works out ordinary details to get his plans done. It was God who'd placed a Jewish girl on the Persian throne right before the king gave this terrible order. 'Maybe you've become queen for just such a time as this,' he told Esther. So Esther, scared to death, went to see the king. Without an invitation. What if the king were in a bad mood? She had no way of knowing. She just went, hoping God would work out the ordinary detail of what mood the king was in. And God did. When the king saw Esther, he was delighted. He held out his scepter and asked her what she wanted. 'I'll give you half my kingdom!' he told her.

"'Just come to a special dinner I'm making for you,' was Esther's answer, 'and bring Haman with you.'" Grandpa stopped again. "You're still remembering that history book, aren't you?" he asked. The children nodded.

"At dinner, Esther only asked that Haman and King Xerxes come again to another banquet the next night," Grandpa continued. "She promised she'd tell the king then what she really wanted. Haman

171

left Esther's banquet walking on air. He was the king's favorite, he must be the queen's favorite—everything was perfect for him! But then he saw Mordecai, and guess what he was doing?"

"Not bowing," Marc answered.

Grandpa nodded. "Haman went home almost in tears. 'I don't care how much I have or how much I'm honored,' he complained to his wife. 'How can I possibly enjoy it when that Mordecai will never bow to me?'

" 'Don't be silly,' his wife said. 'Just get rid of him. Do it now. Build yourself a gallows; then, first thing in the morning, go ask the king to let you hang Mordecai on it. You know the king will do whatever you want.'

"Happy again, Haman built his gallows and went to bed. That same night, King Xerxes couldn't sleep. He tossed and turned, but it was no use." Grandpa pretended to think. "Who is it that gives people a good night's sleep, I wonder," he said.

"God, of course," said Amy.

"Well, God didn't let Xerxes sleep that night. So Xerxes called for someone to read something that would put him to sleep—what book do you think he asked for?"

"I know, I know," Marc cried. "It was that history book, wasn't it? That's why you wouldn't let us forget it."

Grandpa nodded. "And the reader just happened to read the story of how Mordecai had saved the king's life. An ordinary, everyday occurrence—choosing which story to read. That story reminded Xerxes that nothing had been done to reward Mordecai. So, just as the sun was coming up and Haman was coming in to ask for permission to hang Mordecai, Xerxes saw him and asked how he should honor someone who deserved a great reward. 'Who could he possibly be thinking of but me?' Haman thought, so he gave the king many wonderful ideas of how to honor this person. 'Great!' said the king. 'Go do all that you've just said—to Mordecai!'

"Haman was horrified, but he had to do it. And he couldn't ask to hang Mordecai now. And that night, at Esther's banquet, Haman was even more horrified to learn that Queen Esther was a Jew, one of the people he was planning to kill. When the king learned from Esther how evil Haman was, he wanted him killed immediately. 'There's a gallows out there,' one of the servants said.

" 'Hang Haman on it!' the king roared. So Haman was hung on the very gallows he'd built for Mordecai. As for Mordecai, he was given all Haman's riches and was promoted to fill his old position. And of course, the people of God were *not* wiped out after all. That's because God is the one directing all the ordinary details of everyday life so that what he wants to be done happens." Grandpa removed the sword and put a little figure of a queen in its place.

Psalm 33:10–12

The LORD brings the counsel of the nations to nothing;
    he frustrates the plans of the peoples.
The counsel of the LORD stands forever,
    the plans of his heart to all generations.
Blessed is the nation whose God is the LORD,
    the people whom he has chosen as his heritage!

The Champion Arrives

(Luke 1:26–38; 2:1–7; Matthew 2)

Amy stepped back and examined the little Christmas tree from a distance. In her hand she held one last ornament, a glittering silver star. Where should it go? She found a bare spot and hung the star in it, then stepped back to look again. Marc plugged in the tree lights. "See, look, Grandpa, don't you think the shop looks better now?" Marc asked.

Grandma had decorated the house for Christmas as soon as Thanksgiving was over. Grandpa's shop, however, had continued to look no different from the way it always did. Grandpa enjoyed many activities, but decorating for holidays was not one of them. Now, with Christmas vacation having begun and Christmas Day just around the corner, Amy had asked if she and Marc could decorate the shop. Grandpa had agreed. So Marc and Amy had asked their mother and grandmother for leftover decorations. Then they had used the garlands, the ornaments, the lights, and the three-foot artificial tree they had received to dress up the shop for the holidays.

"That does look nice," Grandpa agreed, impressed in spite of himself.

"Let's turn off everything but the Christmas lights and sit by the stove and enjoy it!" Amy suggested.

"Good idea," said Marc. "Grandpa, you can tell us a war story."

"Well, I'm always ready to tell another story," Grandpa replied, flicking the switch so that the shop was illuminated only by Christmas lights. "And at this time of year and sitting here in the middle of all this Christmas cheer you've made, you know what story it has to be." And he picked up his story box and settled in a chair by the stove.

"The birth of Jesus, right?" asked Marc, pulling a chair from the table and moving it next to Grandpa. "Angels and babies and sheep— I don't usually think of this as a war story."

"Oh, but there are soldiers in this story!" Grandpa answered. "And kings at war with each other. You'll remember all that when you hear it. Now think all the way back to the garden where this war began," Grandpa said. "Who started it?"

"Satan did," Marc answered promptly. "He got Eve to eat the apple."

"Yes, Satan started it. But then who promised that the war would go on?" Grandpa asked.

"God did," said Amy. "He said a woman would have a child and there'd always be war between the child and the serpent."

"Think about other war stories you've heard," Grandpa said. "Can you think of some champions in war—you know, soldiers that were such good fighters that the people on their side couldn't lose while they were fighting?"

"Achilles at the Battle of Troy," Amy answered immediately, always delighted to bring up Greek mythology. "And on the Trojan side, Hector—but Achilles killed Hector, so Achilles was more of a champion."

"Goliath in the Bible story—until David came along," Marc contributed. "And the Red Baron was Germany's hero for a while in World War I."

"In our war," Grandpa continued, "the promised child would be the champion for God and his people. Victory over Satan depended on him. And the promise wasn't just that Satan would lose; the promise was that he would be crushed. That's why Satan had been doing everything he could to keep that child from being born. You've seen that in many of the stories we've had so far. But of course, Satan was going to a lot of trouble for nothing. At just the right time, on the exact day God had set aside, in the very place where God had announced it would happen—the child was born.

"Now, God had made many promises about this baby, right?" Grandpa asked. The children nodded. "And we've talked about only a few of them. The Old Testament is *full* of promises, hundreds of them, about this baby. So God's people, who knew his Word, understood that when this baby finally came, he was going to be something special. But they had no idea just *how* special he would be. There was probably no one who expected this baby to be the very Son of God himself. So in order to get the message out that his Son had been born, God sent some unusual messengers. You already mentioned one set of messengers, Marc—who were they?"

"Angels," Marc answered. "To the shepherds. Grandpa, can I put some more wood in the stove?"

Grandpa, intent on his story, had failed to notice how low the fire was burning. He nodded, and Marc rose from his chair, opened the stove door, and added more wood.

"Lots of people send birth announcements," Grandpa went on, "but there aren't too many babies whose births are announced by angels! What was the other unusual way God announced this baby's birth, Amy?"

Amy slipped out of her sweater and scooted her chair back just a little. Marc's added wood had caused the fire to blaze up in a fresh burst of heat. "The star," she said, "to the wise men."

"That's right," Grandpa said. "Magi from the east—we call them wise men—who studied the stars saw an unusual one and went looking for the King of the Jews. They didn't know where to look because they didn't have the Scriptures. Now, Marc, if you were one of the magi and you were looking for the King of the Jews, where would you expect to find him?"

"In Jerusalem, because that was the capital city of the Jews," Marc answered. "And now I know what you're going to say about soldiers and kings."

"Told you you'd remember," Grandpa said. "Jerusalem was just where they went. And once they got there, they began asking everyone they found, 'Where's the new baby king? We saw his star and we've come to worship him.' When Herod, the king in Jerusalem, heard that another king might have been born, he was worried. 'But maybe it's just a rumor,' he may have thought. So he called for the men in Jerusalem who would know the most about God's Word and its prophecies. 'Is a king supposed to be born?' he asked. 'And if so, where?'

"The scribes and the priests—those were the people doing the king's research—showed the king words that the prophet Micah had written centuries before. The prophecy said that a ruler would come from Bethlehem. Now Herod was more than worried. Another ruler besides him? That couldn't be! There wasn't room for two! He'd have to get rid of this new one. You can see how perfectly Herod's thinking fit in with what Satan wanted. Herod decided to find this new baby and make sure he never grew up to be a king."

Grandpa opened his box and removed a figure of a king holding up a sword. He placed it on top of his box. "How could Herod find

this baby without raising any suspicions? After all, if the magi or if the baby's relatives knew what Herod was thinking, they might help the baby escape. So Herod tricked the wise men. He told them, 'Go look in Bethlehem. I think that's where you'll find him. And after you've found him, please, come back and tell me exactly where he is. I want to worship him, too.' The wise men appreciated Herod's help. They didn't realize what evil he was planning, so they promised they'd be back with the information he wanted. Then they set out for Bethlehem.

"As you know, the magi did find the baby and they did worship him. What they didn't do was go back to Herod. God sent an angel to the wise men in a dream, warning them not to return to the king, so they went home by a different way. Back in Jerusalem, King Herod waited—and waited—and waited. Finally he realized he'd been tricked. 'How dare they?' he fumed."

"Of course, he'd tricked them in the first place," Marc pointed out.

"Yes, and if tricks weren't going to work, Herod would take more drastic action," Grandpa continued. "The baby wasn't out of danger yet. Once Herod realized he'd never see the magi again, he came up with a horrible plan. 'If I don't know which baby boy in Bethlehem to kill, I'll kill them all!' he said. So he sent soldiers to Bethlehem. On King Herod's orders, the soldiers killed every boy in Bethlehem, two years old and younger. And Herod thought he'd taken care of any newborn king."

Grandpa paused. "That's awful!" Amy exclaimed. "How could he make his soldiers kill *babies*?"

"Not only that," Marc added, "*God* was the one sending the baby. Trying to kill the baby was fighting against God."

"That's right," Grandpa said. "But Herod couldn't keep God's promise from coming true. Before the soldiers got to Bethlehem,

Joseph had a dream. In it, an angel told him, 'Hurry! Get up! Take the baby and his mother and flee to Egypt. Herod's looking for the child. He'll destroy him if he finds him.' So Joseph, Mary, and Jesus left town that very night. They went to Egypt and stayed there until Herod died. When the soldiers arrived in Bethlehem, Jesus wasn't there."

Grandpa removed the figure of the king and his sword and dropped it back into the box. In its place, he set a miniature Egyptian pyramid. "So in spite of centuries of Satan's hatred and his attacks, God won a tremendous victory in this story. The child he'd promised had been born and was safely alive, hidden away in Egypt. The champion of God's people had come. Satan's defeat could be only a matter of time."

Isaiah 9:6–7

For to us a child is born,
    to us a son is given;
and the government shall be upon his shoulder,
    and his name shall be called
Wonderful Counselor, Mighty God,
    Everlasting Father, Prince of Peace.
Of the increase of his government and of peace
    there will be no end,
on the throne of David and over his kingdom,
    to establish it and to uphold it
with justice and with righteousness
    from this time forth and forevermore.
The zeal of the LORD of hosts will do this.

Winning a Lost Battle

(Matthew 4:1–11; Luke 4:1–13)

Marc turned slightly sideways to ease his body past the rock in his way on one side of the path without letting his jeans brush against the cactus on the other side. Once he was safely past these obstacles, he glanced at his watch. "One o'clock?" he exclaimed. "No wonder I'm so hungry! When are we going to eat?"

"My fault," said Grandpa. "If we'd gotten away earlier, we'd have been back at the car by noon. But when Mrs. Clark said she had to get rid of her grandfather clock right away and I could have it if I'd come get it, well, what could I do? How could I pass up an opportunity like that?" "Trash to Treasure" was always more demanding right after Christmas. Many people were tossing out old "trash" to make room for new "treasures" they had received as gifts. Today, the last Saturday of Christmas vacation, Grandpa had wanted a break away from the shop, so he had invited Marc and Amy to join him for a hike on South Mountain.

"Too bad you can't eat rocks!" Amy said in an unsuccessful attempt to cheer Marc. "There are plenty of those around!"

"We're almost back to the car," said Grandpa. "Then we'll eat lunch there at the overlook. Ten more minutes at the most." Marc brightened immediately.

The three walked on for several more minutes under the warm sun. They came around a corner and through a dip in the road, and finally the parking lot was in view. Arriving back at the car, they took out their lunches and went to sit on a pile of rocks near the edge. The city of Phoenix glittered right below them at the foot of the mountain.

"That wind this morning made it nice and clear," Grandpa commented, taking sandwiches and apples out of an old backpack. "The view's great! Hey, guess what? There are granola bars in here, too! Of course, I don't know how *long* they've been in here! I'm not guaranteeing how good they'll be. You know," he continued, distributing the lunch items as he spoke, "this view and Amy's comment about eating rocks reminds me of our next war story. I'll tell you while we eat. But before we start this story, it's important that you understand what a representative is. What are some ways you've heard that word used?"

The children thought. Amy spoke up. "Oh, I know," she said. "Jill's the seventh-grade class representative to student council."

"Good," said Grandpa. "The whole seventh grade can't go to the student-council meetings, so Jill goes as their representative. She votes in the place of all the other seventh-graders. If there's a debate about something, Jill argues in the place of the other seventh-graders."

181

"People in Congress are called state representatives, and they meet in the House of Representatives," Marc offered. "But I'm not exactly sure what that means."

"They're the people who make the laws for our country," Grandpa explained. "Imagine if, every time a new law were made, every single citizen in the whole United States got together to vote on it. It would be impossible, wouldn't it? So each state chooses representatives who are supposed to know how the people in their state would feel about certain laws. When they vote on a law, they're representing their state. When a representative votes, it's as if his or her state has voted.

"The very first human representative was Adam. God chose him, back in Eden, to represent every person who would ever be born. Whatever Adam chose to do about Satan's temptation would count as though every other human being had done it, too. So when Adam sinned and fell away from God, all mankind sinned and fell away from God.

"Jesus came to be a new and better representative for his people. So the first thing he had to do was face Satan and his temptations. The first battle he had to win was the one Adam and Eve had lost."

Here, Grandpa reached into his shirt pocket and drew out a little wooden snake. It was the same figure, painted in bright colors and coiled ready to strike, that Grandpa had used in the very first story he had told. Grandpa saw surprise on his grandchildren's faces. He grinned, a little embarrassed. "Well, I just brought them along in case. I thought there might be a chance for a story. You never know." He set the snake on a boulder.

Grandpa continued his story. "Now, Satan certainly understood what was at stake here. He knew that Jesus couldn't do anything to help sinners if he were a sinner himself. If Satan could get Jesus to sin—just once—Jesus himself would need a Savior. So Satan made Jesus' temptations harder than the one Adam and Eve had faced. Adam and Eve were in a garden, full of trees covered with delicious

182

things to eat. There was only one fruit they couldn't have. Jesus, however, was in a desert—it probably looked a lot like this. And he hadn't eaten anything for forty days. Marc, you think *you* were hungry!"

Marc, now contentedly munching his apple, turned his back on the city below and looked out over the desert landscape in the other direction. All he saw were sky, rocks, cactus, and an occasional scrubby bush—it didn't look like a very hopeful place to find food. "So Satan's first temptation seemed reasonable enough," Grandpa continued. "He simply invited Jesus to do something he could easily have done. 'If you're the Son of God,' Satan said, 'command these stones to become bread.' "

"What would have been wrong with that?" Amy wanted to know. "It *had* been forty days. And he needed food."

"Jesus was supposed to use his power for the works *God* had given him to do, not to take care of his own needs," Grandpa explained. "Jesus was to trust *God* to give him what he needed, including his food. Adam and Eve's problem was *not* trusting God for what they needed. They didn't trust him to tell them what was good and what was evil; they wanted to know for themselves, so they ate the fruit. Unlike them, Jesus won his battle with Satan. He answered Satan by quoting Scripture. 'Man shall not live on bread alone,' he said, 'but on every word that comes from the mouth of God.'

"Satan turned right around and attacked again. This time, he took Jesus to the top of a high mountain. They could see cities and kingdoms from up there."

"Like we can see Phoenix from here," Marc said, shading his eyes against the sun. "Look, there's the ballpark!"

"We can see more than Phoenix," Amy added, pointing off into the distance. "There's Camelback Mountain, so that's Scottsdale over there."

"But Satan's mountain was different from any mountain we'll ever be on," Grandpa continued. "Because the Bible says he was able to show Jesus all the kingdoms of the world in one instant. 'I can give you all these kingdoms and their glory,' Satan told Jesus. 'It's all been given to me, and I give it to whomever I wish.' "

"Wait a minute! Is that right?" Amy interrupted. "I thought God was the one who decides who rules when. Isn't that what the story about Daniel and Nebuchadnezzar was all about?"

"It's right and it's not right," Grandpa answered. "Remember, Satan uses half-truths in his war against God. Propaganda. False stuff mixed in with true to try to trick people. Satan *has* been given control in the earth for the time being, in the sense that God allows him to tempt people and get them on his side to fight against God. But he can do that only as God allows. When God says that a kingdom ruled by one of Satan's allies must come to an end, it always does. And even while a ruler who is on Satan's side is in power, God uses the things that ruler does to bring about God's own purposes. Satan has tricked many rulers into thinking they can resist God and do things their way. Of course, Jesus wasn't fooled for a minute.

"Satan's offer to Jesus was, 'I'll give you all these kingdoms and their glory if you'll just bow down to me.'

"Jesus answered him with Scripture again. 'You shall worship the Lord your God and serve him only,' he said. A second victory! But still Satan didn't leave the battlefield.

"This time, he took Jesus to one of the highest points of the temple. 'If you're really the Son of God, you should jump off,' he said. And then, Satan himself quoted the Bible. He does that, you know. His propaganda is most powerful when he uses Scripture to back it up. Of course, he twists it to mean things that it doesn't really mean."

"Well, how would you know?" Marc asked. "I don't mean Jesus, but an ordinary person. Like me. If I hear someone quoting Scripture, I'm not going to argue with it. How would I know if they're using it to mean something that it doesn't really mean?"

"You might have to wait until you get a chance to look it up for yourself," Grandpa said. "Then you could check to see if the person was using it as it was meant to be used. But the very best thing you can do is to get to know your Bible really well. Study it—a lot! Read it—a lot! Satan will have a hard time tricking you if you know God's Word for yourself."

"You should pick up one of those little guides for reading through the Bible in a year," Amy suggested to Marc. "I got one from church. I may not get all the way through in a year, but I'll make it sooner or later." Marc nodded. "Now, Grandpa, go on with the story."

"So there Satan was, with Jesus up on the temple roof," Grandpa continued. "And he told Jesus to jump. 'Because,' Satan said, 'the Bible says that God will have his angels protect you; you won't even hurt your foot on a rock!' That would prove to everyone that Jesus really was the Son of God, wouldn't it? If he could jump from the temple and not get hurt at all?

"But Jesus knew that wasn't God's way. He wasn't supposed to prove who he was by doing stunts. And the people weren't to follow him because they saw stunts; they were to have faith. So Jesus answered Satan's misused Scripture with another Scripture: 'You shall not put the Lord your God to the test.'

"At that point, Satan gave up—for the time being, anyway. There would be plenty of other times when he would come back to tempt Jesus, but none of them would be any more successful than this one. For now, Satan retreated and the victory belonged to Jesus. And to us. Because whenever Jesus obeyed God, it was as the representative of his people. Every time he did something that pleased God, it was as if his people had done something pleasing to God. You often hear that Jesus died in the place of his people. And he did. His people had earned God's judgment, but Jesus took their place and God judged him instead. But Jesus also *lived* in place of his people. They couldn't please God because of their sin. So Jesus lived a life of perfect obedience in their place." Grandpa removed the brightly colored snake from the boulder where it sat, dropping it back into his pocket. He replaced it with the little carving of an open Bible that

185

he had used in another story. This time, it symbolized Jesus' powerful weapon.

Hebrews 2:17–18

Therefore he had to be made like his brothers in every respect, so that he might become a merciful and faithful high priest in the service of God, to make propitiation for the sins of the people. For because he himself has suffered when tempted, he is able to help those who are being tempted

Romans 5:19

For as by the one man's disobedience the many were made sinners, so by the one man's obedience the many will be made righteous.

Rescuing a Prisoner of War

(Mark 5:1–20)

Amy looked up from her book with the feeling that she was being watched. Sure enough, Marc, seated at Grandpa's table and surrounded by books and papers, was staring intently at her. Amy scowled slightly. She was about to ask, "What are you looking at?" (and her tone might have been a little cross) when she realized that Marc was not staring *at* her. He was staring *through* her. He was clearly not seeing her at all. She waved her hand through Marc's line of sight and he straightened, focusing his eyes on her.

"What are you working on over there?" Amy asked. "You're sure lost in thought."

"Oh, it's a history report," Marc answered.

Amy stretched. She had been sitting long enough. She rose and came over to Marc at the table. Glancing at his material, she asked, "What's it about? Let me guess—it has something to do with war, right?"

Marc grinned. "Of course. It's about a rescue in World War II. There were some American and British POWs in a camp in the Philippines, and some U.S. Army Rangers went in to get them out."

Grandpa looked up from where he was rubbing polish on a brass kettle. "Oh, I just read a book about that," he said. "The prisoners were the survivors of the Bataan Death March, right?" Marc nodded. "Those men went through some horrible things as prisoners of war," Grandpa said, shaking his head.

Amy's face lit up with a sudden thought. "Hey, Grandpa, are there any prisoners of war in our war stories?" she asked.

"Hmm-mm," Grandpa said, thinking. Then: "Yes, I guess you could say there are."

"Why don't you tell us a story about one?" Amy asked. "I don't know about Marc, but I'm tired of sitting."

Grandpa hesitated. "I don't know. Marc seemed pretty absorbed in what he was doing. I wouldn't want to distract him."

"Actually, I was done," Marc said. "Anyway, I've finished the rough draft."

"You're done?" Amy asked, remembering how he had been staring at her without seeing her. "Then what were you thinking so hard about?"

Marc grinned, embarrassed. "I was just imagining what it would be like to be a Ranger."

"Oho!" Amy said. "You weren't thinking. You were daydreaming."

"They're kind of cool, Rangers," Marc continued. "I like how they always try to get all their own guys back out of dangerous places. Like this rescue my report's about."

"Okay, Grandpa," said Amy, "we need a story of someone going back in to rescue a prisoner, like the rescue in Marc's report. Can you do it?"

Grandpa set down the kettle and the polishing rag, got up, and came to take a seat at Marc's table. "Well, one way we could think about all of God's people," he said, "would be as prisoners of war. Satan captured us, so to speak. He had us doing all kinds of things we wouldn't have done if we were still the way God made us to be. People are sinners who love to do evil. They can't get along with each other. They're always doing things to harm themselves. None of this was God's intention when he made us. Left to ourselves, we're prisoners and we can't escape."

Amy pulled one of the chairs from the table, turned it around backwards, and straddled it. "People need to be rescued, like Marc's guys in—where were they?" she said.

"The Philippines," Marc answered. "And Grandpa, you're going to say that Jesus is the one who rescues us, right?"

"Of course," said Grandpa. "And then I'm going to tell you a war story that shows us Jesus rescuing one very tortured, tormented prisoner of war. Because it's a great picture of what he does for every one of his people.

"Jesus had been teaching by the Sea of Galilee. He got into a boat with his disciples and crossed over to the other side. When he got there, he was met by a very interesting kind of guy. The kind of guy you would steer clear of if you saw him coming down the sidewalk someday. In the first place, the man was wearing no clothes."

"Whoa! *I'd* turn around and go the other way!" Amy said.

"He had chains on his ankles and wrists, but they were broken. That was because people kept trying to chain him up to keep him from hurting himself or anyone else. But this man had superhuman strength, and he always broke whatever chains they put on him. Now, fortunately for the neighbors, this man didn't have a lot to do with other people. They couldn't keep him in a house. He insisted on living in the tombs, with the dead bodies."

"Creepy," Marc muttered.

"So, Jesus and the disciples had just landed on the shore. They were getting out of the boat, when this man, wearing nothing but broken chains, came running to meet them. And that wasn't all. As the man ran toward the boat, he was yelling—not necessarily saying anything, just making a lot of racket. He always did that. And as he yelled, he hit himself hard with stones that he was carrying. He hit himself over and over, cutting and gashing himself and making himself bleed. Okay, Amy John, you're good with your imagination. Use it right now to imagine you're a disciple watching all this. Tell me—what are you thinking?"

"Well, I don't feel very good about this," Amy replied, closing her eyes and trying to imagine herself in the scene. "I really wish he wouldn't come over here. The guy's crazy, and no one can stop him. Look what he's doing with those stones. What if he comes after one of us?"

"Well," Marc contributed, "at least there's strength in numbers. There are twelve of us, plus Jesus, and only one of him. And besides, if we had to, we could always jump back in the boat and row like crazy. I don't care how strong he is; sooner or later he'd get tired of following us."

"Those are probably just the kinds of things the disciples were thinking," Grandpa agreed. "But Jesus had a whole different way of seeing. When Jesus saw this naked wild man screaming and cutting himself, he saw the ugliness of what had been done to his Father's creation. God hadn't made this man like this. He had created him in the image of God. This was just the wreck of a man. It was the work of Satan and his demons." Grandpa rose and went to the nearby countertop where his yellow box sat. He opened the lid to remove two figures and brought them to the table. Keeping one hidden in his hand, he set the other one on the table. It was a figure of a man, looking as much like a beast as a man. Broken chains hung from his wrists, and his face and body were twisted with rage.

"Right away, Jesus began to command the demons that were living inside this poor man to come out of him. The demons were stronger than the man, and they made him stronger than anyone who ever tried to control him, but they were no match at all for Jesus. As the man came closer, he was crying out, 'Jesus, Son of the Most High God, please, I beg you, don't torment me!' You see, the demons knew good and well who Jesus was, and they knew he had all authority, even over them.

"When Jesus asked, 'What's your name?' the demons answered, 'Legion.'" Grandpa turned to Marc. "Marc, what's a legion?"

"It was a division of the Roman army," Marc answered. "Kind of like a regiment."

"How many soldiers?" Grandpa asked next.

"Well, that depends on when you're talking about," Marc answered. "But always thousands. Sometimes three thousand, other times as many as six thousand."

Amy shook her head in amazement. "Is there anything about war you *don't* know?" she asked.

Grandpa continued without waiting for Marc to answer her. "So a legion is a lot! And that's what the demons said. The name was 'Legion, because,' they said, 'we are many.' Now, these demons knew they had to leave the man. Jesus had commanded them to. They had no choice. So they begged him to let them go into a herd of pigs that was feeding up on a nearby hill. Jesus gave them permission, and they went into the pigs. Right away, the pigs charged for the cliff's edge, ran off it into the sea, and drowned."

"Wow!" Amy said. "I'll bet that was quite a shock to the people taking care of the pigs."

Grandpa said, "Those people ran back to town as fast as they could to tell everyone else. A whole crowd came out of the city to see what had happened. And you know what they found?"

"No pigs!" Marc replied.

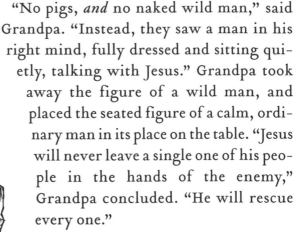

"No pigs, *and* no naked wild man," said Grandpa. "Instead, they saw a man in his right mind, fully dressed and sitting quietly, talking with Jesus." Grandpa took away the figure of a wild man, and placed the seated figure of a calm, ordinary man in its place on the table. "Jesus will never leave a single one of his people in the hands of the enemy," Grandpa concluded. "He will rescue every one."

There was silence for a moment. Then Amy asked, "But, Grandpa, what about April's dad? You know how we keep praying for him at church because he drinks so much. For a while it'll look like God answered our prayers and he'll do really well, and then there he goes, drinking again. And April thinks he really is a Christian. What about him? Why doesn't Jesus rescue him from the enemy?"

"Well, remember, none of us are all the way rescued yet," Grandpa answered. "A Christian is someone whose heart has been changed and who wants to follow Jesus, but no Christian is perfect. We will be, someday, in heaven. God has promised. Until then, we still sin. Satan can still tempt us, and sometimes we give in. But the day will come when the enemy doesn't have even the tiniest little bit of power over us at all." Grandpa chuckled. "Maybe in heaven we'll be like ex-prisoners of war, sitting around swapping stories about our wonderful rescues."

He has delivered us from the domain of darkness and transferred us to the kingdom of his beloved Son, in whom we have redemption, the forgiveness of sins.... And you, who once were alienated and hostile in mind, doing evil deeds, he has now reconciled in his body of flesh by his death, in order to present you holy and blameless and above reproach before him.

Safe in Enemy Territory

(John 1–8)

Seconds after the bell rang, the doors of the school flew open and students began pouring out. Marc was in the first wave of students to exit the building. He looked for his mother's car and was surprised to see, instead, his grandmother standing near the sidewalk. He hurried over to her. "What are you doing here, Grandma?" he asked.

"Your mom called to say that she couldn't get to the school right on time and you're supposed to come over to our house for a few minutes instead," Grandma explained, just as Amy walked up to them. "Sounds like your mom's having one of those days," Grandma said, with a sympathetic grin. "You two will have to be extra nice to her when she does pick you up."

"We're always extra nice, Grandma," Amy assured her grandmother confidently. "Do you have anything good to eat at your house? I'm starving!"

"As a matter of fact, I made caramel apples today," Grandma answered. "You can test them for me."

"Yum!" the children cried together, and the three set out for Grandma and Grandpa's house. Grandma's caramel was much runnier than the caramel on store-bought caramel apples, and you always ended up eating some of it with a spoon, but it tasted much better than what you could buy in any store. Grandma made caramel apples only once a year, and for the children, it was an eagerly awaited event.

In Grandma's kitchen, Marc and Amy each chose an apple, being careful to scoop from the plate all the caramel that had run off into little puddles. Grandma gave them an apple to take to Grandpa, out in his shop. When they entered the shop, Marc called out, "Hi, Grandpa," while Amy cried, "Break time! Time for caramel apples!"

"Grandma said you'd be dropping in for a few minutes," Grandpa said, as he set down the rag he had been using to wipe wood stain onto a child's chair. "And I'm ready for a break. Thanks for bringing the apple."

For the first few bites of apple, nothing could be heard in the shop except munching and an occasional "Mmm-mm." Then Marc said, "Grandpa, since we're here for only a few minutes and don't have time to really get started on anything else, could you tell us the next war story?"

"I'd love to," Grandpa replied, and he went off for his box. When he returned, he said, "Now, what I'm going to do today is to squeeze a whole bunch of stories into just one telling, because all these stories would make the same point we made in our last story. You remember the last story, right?"

"The guy with the demons," Amy answered.

"Right. Now, what's the most important thing you would know about Jesus if you'd been there and seen Jesus cast all those demons out of that man?" Grandpa asked.

"That Jesus has the most power," Marc replied. "There was a legion of demons and just one Jesus, but the demons did what he said. They were even afraid of him."

Grandpa continued to quiz the children. "And who is the only one who could have more power than demons?"

"God," they replied in unison.

"And so the people watching all this should have figured out that Jesus is—"

"God," the children said again.

"Exactly. And that was the reason Jesus did all the amazing things he did," Grandpa said. "In fact, when John wrote about Jesus, he didn't even call those amazing things 'miracles.' John always called them 'signs.' A sign points to something else. All Jesus' miracles pointed to who he was and what he came to do. You tell me—what were some of those signs?"

"He healed a lot of people," Amy said.

"What kinds of things did he heal them from?" Grandpa asked.

"Blindness, for one thing," Amy said. "And leprosy." And she took another bite of apple.

"Yes, and if Jesus could heal a blind man or a leper with a touch or even with just a word, wouldn't he have to be God? Who else could do that? And if he could make blind eyes see, couldn't he open spiritually blind eyes as well? If he could remove the leprosy from a body, couldn't he make a soul clean and free from sin?

"What other signs did Jesus do, Marc?" Grandpa asked, turning to his grandson.

Marc thought for a minute. Then, "Oh, I know!" he said. "He fed five thousand people with two pieces of fish and five pieces of bread."

"Good!" said Grandpa. "Does that remind you of any story we had in the past, about crowds of hungry people far from stores needing bread and getting it in a miraculous way?"

"The Israelites," Marc answered, "in the wilderness. God gave them manna from heaven."

"Right," said Grandpa. "And in the whole history of the world, the only one who's ever given people food from heaven is God. So if you'd been part of that crowd of five thousand men (*plus* women and children) who ate bread that hadn't been there before, but then it was, what should you have realized about Jesus?"

"That he must be God," said Marc.

"He calmed storms, too," Grandpa continued. "Remember?" The children nodded. "His own disciples said, 'Who is this, that even the winds and the waves obey him?' "

"Seems kind of obvious, doesn't it?" Amy asked, getting up to throw away her apple core. "Want me to take yours for you, Grandpa?" she offered.

"Yes, please—but hang on to the sticks," Grandpa cautioned. "Grandma will wash them and use them again. It may seem obvious to us who Jesus was," Grandpa replied. "But we have the rest of the New Testament to explain it to us. And you have to remember how important it was to the Jews of Jesus' day to hold on to the idea that there's only one God. Jesus couldn't be a human being like they were *and* be God. That would be impossible—or so they thought. And besides, if Jesus were God, wouldn't that make two gods? They didn't realize that God is a Trinity—Father, Son, and Holy Spirit, but still only one God. Even the twelve disciples had a hard time understanding how Jesus could be a man, as he clearly was, *and* do things that only God could do.

"And then, making it even harder, you have to remember how badly things are messed up because of Adam and Eve's sin. When it comes to the truth about God, people just don't get it. They can't. Their eyes are blinded by their sin. And not just sin blinds people. The Bible says the god of this world blinds people's minds too, so they can't see the light of the gospel. Who would that be—the god of this world?"

"Satan," Amy answered, remembering the story in which Satan had told Jesus that all the kingdoms of the world were his to give to whom he pleased.

"And so, in many cases, the more signs Jesus did, the more miracles he performed, the more hardened his enemies became," Grandpa went on. "And of course, they were jealous of him besides! He attracted bigger crowds. He was more popular. The people said that his teaching had more authority than theirs. So every day, Jesus' enemies became more convinced that they had to get rid of him.

"King Herod wasn't the only person during Jesus' lifetime who tried to kill him. And just as Satan would have been delighted if Herod had succeeded, Satan also would have loved it if any of these other assassination attempts had worked out. Of course, Jesus was going to die anyway—that's what he had come to do. But it had to be at the right time and in a certain way. Otherwise, his death would have been like anybody else's. It wouldn't have bought salvation for sinners and it wouldn't have defeated Satan and undone his work.

"So we can probably figure that Satan was busy stirring up jealousy and anger in people, trying to make them mad enough to kill Jesus before his time. For instance, twice Jesus claimed to be equal with God. The Jews who heard that picked up rocks to stone him to death." Grandpa opened his box and removed two items. The one he set up on the lid first was not a carving or a figure at all, but just a small pebble from the yard. Marc and Amy understood that it represented the stones that Jesus' enemies picked up to throw at him. "But they didn't stone him. In both cases, they really wanted to kill him, but somehow he just slipped away. It wasn't time yet.

"Then, another time, when Jesus said that God didn't care only about Jewish people, but about others as well, a whole crowd of angry people took Jesus to the top of a hill, where they planned to throw him over the edge!"

"Really?" said Marc.

"Oh, yes," said Grandpa. "But again, he just passed right through the middle of them and went on his way."

"How could he keep doing that?" Amy wanted to know.

"I don't know," Grandpa replied. "Was he able to make himself unrecognizable, like a good spy can do in wartime? Or was he able to make all his enemies completely powerless for a time, like a powerful general during an invasion of enemy territory? I don't know, but however it happened, Jesus stayed alive to carry out his mission. He would disarm and destroy Satan, as God had promised. Jesus wouldn't die until he died on the cross." Grandpa removed the stone from the box lid and replaced it with a little wooden cross.

John 7:28–30

So Jesus proclaimed, as he taught in the temple, "You know me, and you know where I come from? But I have not come of my own accord. He who sent me is true, and him you do not know. I know him, for I come from him, and he sent me." So they were seeking to arrest him, but no one laid a hand on him, because his hour had not yet come.

199

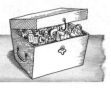

John 8:19–20

They said to him therefore, "Where is your Father?" Jesus answered, "You know neither me nor my Father. If you knew me, you would know my Father also." These words he spoke in the treasury, as he taught in the temple; but no one arrested him, because his hour had not yet come.

John 10:37–39

"If I am not doing the works of my Father, then do not believe me; but if I do them, even though you do not believe me, believe the works, that you may know and understand that the Father is in me and I am in the Father." Again they sought to arrest him, but he escaped from their hands.

Most Dreaded Enemy Conquered

(John 11)

"Got it?" Grandpa asked.

Marc nodded, holding tightly to his side of the old desk. Together Marc and Grandpa lifted the desk and began to inch it into the space they had cleared for it against the wall. Just then the shop door flew open and Amy ran in. "There's a dead baby bird out in the yard!" she announced.

"Okay, Marc, that's good," Grandpa nodded at Marc. "Set your end down there, and then we'll push it in the rest of the way." As Marc was following Grandpa's instructions, Marc said to Amy, "Where?"

"By the table under the tree," Amy replied. "There must be a nest in the tree and the bird fell out."

Dead birds didn't bother Marc. "I'll take care of it," he offered and headed out to the yard.

"Wait! What are you going to do with it?" Amy wanted to know.

"Throw it out, of course," Marc replied.

"In the trash can?"

"What else?"

"No, I think we should bury it," Amy said. "Grandpa, can I bury it?"

Before Grandpa could answer, Marc responded with, "What's the big deal? It's just a bird."

"I know," said Amy, "but it just looks so little and sad, all still on the ground."

"Now, you know," Marc lectured, "death is perfectly natural. It's a necessary part of the cycle of life."

Amy stared at Marc. "You sound like one of those nature shows on TV," she said, "and I don't care. It's still sad."

Grandpa joined the conversation. "Death is something we all try to get used to, Marc, because sooner or later every living thing dies. But it's really *not* natural. It's not the way things should be. God didn't create death to be a part of life. Death is an ugly spot on God's creation. And everyone who's had to bury someone they love knows just how ugly it is. Death is one of the enemies in our war. And it's one of Satan's most effective weapons." He turned to Amy. "You'll find the shovel just inside the door of the shed. You can make a little hole for the bird in the very corner of Grandma's rose bed. Then come back in and let me tell you a war story about Death."

Amy went out for the shovel. Marc went with her to help dig the hole, although he felt the need to mutter something about funerals for birds being silly as he went. When they came back in, Grandpa had them wash their hands while he got the story box.

"One day, Jesus received a message from some of his very best friends, two sisters in the town of Bethany," Grandpa began.

"I know who they were," said Amy. "Mary and Martha."

Marc, not to be outdone, added, "And their brother was Lazarus, the guy who—oh! I know what this story's about!"

"Me, too, but let Grandpa tell it," said Amy.

Ignoring the interruptions, Grandpa continued. "The message said simply, 'Lord, the one you love is sick.' "

"That sounds like something girls would say," said Marc. " 'The one you love'—why didn't they just say, 'Lazarus is sick'?"

"Well, I think they might have been reminding *themselves* that Jesus really did love their brother," said Grandpa. "This was a pretty serious illness, and they were worried about what might happen to Lazarus. But they knew that Jesus could work miracles, and they knew that he loved Lazarus. They were sure that if he just knew their brother was sick, he'd come heal him. So Jesus got their message. Then do you know what he did?"

"He went there," said Marc, "only he was too late and Lazarus was already dead."

"But what did he do *before* he went there?" Grandpa asked.

Marc didn't answer because he didn't know.

"He stayed where he was for two more days," said Grandpa.

"Was he busy or something? Or didn't he realize how serious Lazarus's sickness was?" Amy asked.

"He waited on purpose," Grandpa said, "*because* Lazarus was so sick."

"Did he want Lazarus to die?" Marc asked.

Grandpa didn't answer, but went on with his story. "Imagine how Mary and Martha felt while they waited for Jesus to come. They saw their brother grow weaker and weaker. They'd seen Jesus heal blind and lame people. They'd seen him cast out demons. It would be easy for Jesus to heal their brother. Why didn't he come? Didn't he love

203

him after all? Didn't he love *them*? But Jesus didn't come, and Lazarus died.

"Four dreadful days went by. Every morning, Martha would wake up, happy for one short moment before she remembered that Lazarus was dead. And then her next thought would be, 'And Jesus didn't come to help us.' And a new day of misery would start. She'd get up and get ready to meet the many people who came every day to grieve with her and her sister. And all day she'd be thinking, 'If Jesus had come, Lazarus wouldn't have died.'

"One day, someone slipped into the house, past all the visitors, and whispered to Martha, 'Jesus is coming.' She quickly left the house and started down the path. Soon, sure enough, there was Jesus coming toward her. When she met him, she just couldn't help it. The first thing out of her mouth was, 'Lord, if you'd been here, my brother wouldn't have died.' She didn't say, 'Why didn't you come? Why didn't you help us?' but everyone knew that's what she was thinking.

" 'Your brother will rise again,' Jesus told her.

" 'I know he'll rise again at the resurrection at the end of time,' Martha answered.

" 'I am the resurrection and the life,' Jesus answered her. Then Jesus asked for Mary, so Martha sent someone back to get her. As Mary left the house, a crowd of weeping visitors followed her. When Mary saw Jesus, she fell at his feet in a new outburst of tears. Just like Martha, Mary said, 'Lord, if you'd been here, my brother wouldn't have died.' Jesus asked where they'd buried Lazarus, so they led him to the tomb to see. And then there it is: that famous shortest verse in the Bible—"

" 'Jesus wept,' " said both children at once.

"Now, why do you think Jesus wept?" Grandpa asked. "He knew the end of this story. He knew he was about to raise Lazarus from the dead. Why would he have been sad?"

"He felt sorry for Mary and Martha?" Amy suggested.

"Yes, he did, and I'm sure that's part of it," Grandpa said. "Jesus shares his people's hurts and sorrows, even though he knows just what he's going to do to make everything better at last. But there was more to it than that. The Bible says here," and Grandpa peered into his open Bible to find the exact words, "that he was deeply moved in his spirit and was troubled."

"Did he feel bad because he hadn't come sooner?" Marc asked.

"No, he waited on purpose," Grandpa replied. "Here's what I think made Jesus so upset. I think that Jesus could see, in this dear family he loved, what a mess Satan had made of his Father's beautiful creation. The way God made families in the first place, they never would have been all torn apart by someone dying. God created man in his own image, to show God's glory. But dead and dying people don't look very glorious. Every time someone died, Satan could be proud of the damage he'd done to God's best creation. And Jesus didn't like that." Grandpa took from his box a figure that looked like a rock with another smaller rock in front of it for a door. "You remember this is what graves looked like in Jesus' day," he explained. "They were caves where bodies were laid, and then a rock would go in the doorway to close up the entrance." And Grandpa set the little figure on top of his box.

"Jesus gave a command to open the tomb. Martha said, 'Oh, no, don't do that. He's been dead four days.' What if we left that baby bird lying out in the yard for four days, Marc? What would happen to it?" Grandpa asked.

"It would start to rot. By four days, it would stink," Marc answered matter-of-factly.

"And that's what Martha was worrying about. That's what had happened to Lazarus's body by now. But that's exactly why Jesus had waited so long. He wanted people—and Satan!—to know that he can do more than just *keep* people from dying. He can even do more than bring people who have just died back to life again. Jesus has such power over death that he can even *turn back* the decaying process. He could make Lazarus alive and whole and good as new, even if he *had* been dead four days. So they opened the tomb and Jesus called in a loud voice, 'Lazarus, come out!' " Grandpa paused.

Amy imagined what it would have been like to stand by an open tomb and wait to see if anything would come out. She felt the prickle of goose bumps just thinking about it. Grandpa chuckled. "I can imagine it was very, very quiet around that tomb that day. Every-one watched to see what would happen. They didn't have to wait long. The man who had been dead heard Jesus' command and came shuffling out of the tomb, shuffling because he was all wrapped up in the cloths that people wrapped around dead bodies. 'Unbind him, and let him go,' Jesus said."

Grandpa removed the stone door from his little figure of a tomb and showed the children the inside. There was nothing there. He set the empty tomb on the box, and said, "Even Satan's most powerful weapon is useless when Jesus is on the battlefield."

1 Corinthians 15:55–57

O death, where is your victory?
O death, where is your sting?

The sting of death is sin, and the power of sin is the law. But thanks be to God, who gives us the victory through our Lord Jesus Christ.

32

Victory from Defeat

(Matthew 27; Mark 15; Luke 23; John 19)

Marc paused by the table where Amy was drawing. "What's the map?" he asked her.

Amy finished shading a section of her map with green and set down the colored pencil. "France," she replied. "It's for my oral country report. We need to have visuals, including a map."

"Where's Normandy on here?" Marc asked, peering at her map. "I was just reading about Normandy."

Looking back and forth from the map on the page in her book to the map she was drawing, Amy found Normandy and pointed it out to Marc. "There must be some important battle or something that happened there," she said, "or you wouldn't have been reading about it."

"Don't tell me you've never heard of the invasion of Normandy in World War II," Marc answered. "It's the story of D-Day." And to himself, Marc thought, *She's in the seventh grade, for goodness' sake; where has she been?* But he was gracious enough not to say it.

"Oh." Amy searched her memory. "Yes, I've *heard* of it, but I don't remember what I've heard. Tell me about it. Maybe I can use it in my report. And what does 'D-Day' mean again?"

" 'D-Day' is what they call the day when any really important military operation is going to happen. In this case," Marc explained, "the Allied soldiers were trying to get France back from the Nazis, who'd taken it over. So the Allies planned to invade France secretly with so many soldiers and so much equipment that the Nazis wouldn't stand a chance. Trick was—how to get all those soldiers and all that stuff into France secretly. They decided to come across the English Channel from Britain—here," and Marc pointed out the English Channel to Amy on her map. "So they had to try to *sneak* 175,000 soldiers—and 50,000 motorcycles, tanks, and bulldozers—all across the English Channel without being seen. They needed five thousand ships and eleven thousand airplanes to do it. And the English Channel is sixty miles long—that's a long way to have to sneak. And they had to do all that in one night."

"Wow." Amy was impressed. "So I take it they did it—that's why it's famous, right?"

"They did it, all right," Marc answered. "But they lost a lot of soldiers doing it. It was really, really risky. They knew that before they started, but they figured they had to do it or the war might never end."

Grandpa came into the shop just then, carrying the toolbox from his pickup truck. "Which war are you talking about?" he asked, hearing only Marc's last sentence.

"World War II," Marc replied. "I was telling Amy about the invasion of Normandy. Grandpa, you went to France once. Did you go to Normandy?"

Grandpa shook his head. "No, but I'd like to sometime," he said. "That *was* a risky business," he agreed. "Did you know that when General Eisenhower told the young paratroopers good-bye that day, he waited till their planes were in the air and then began to cry? He'd been told that perhaps as many as seventy-five percent of them might be killed. A very costly battle—but a very important one for winning the war." Grandpa set down the toolbox. "I have a story about a costlier battle that was even more important for how our war turned out. Want to hear it?"

"Sure," Marc and Amy said together. Then Amy added, "Mind if I keep coloring my France map at the same time? I can still listen."

"No problem," said Grandpa. "I'll leave this toolbox and go get my war box," and he went off to pick up the box and his Bible.

When he came back, he settled into a chair at the table next to Amy. Marc took another one. "I'm sure you know what story this is," Grandpa began. "You already know which battle in our war was the costliest, and you know it's the battle that won the war. It's the story of Jesus going to the cross.

"Satan's very clever, but he can't see the future. He can make some good guesses, but he isn't all-knowing, like God is. He didn't really know *how* God planned to undo the damage Satan had caused. He just knew that Jesus had something to do with it. So he wanted to get Jesus out of the way, either by causing him to sin or by destroying him.

"People were jealous of Jesus, and it was easy for Satan to turn that jealousy into hatred. Every time the religious leaders turned around, it seemed like Jesus was more popular than he'd been the day before. People listened to them less and less, but more and more to Jesus. And of course, Jesus didn't follow the rules these leaders wanted him to follow. He was always criticizing them. He was always telling them that their rules weren't really God's rules. With Jesus being so popular, maybe other people would start ignoring

209

their rules, too. Something had to be done! But what? Because Jesus *was* so popular, they'd have to be careful.

"Then one day Satan gave Jesus' enemies just what they needed so that they could do what Satan wanted. One of Jesus' twelve disciples came to them, a man named Judas Iscariot. Judas said he'd help them arrest Jesus secretly, if they gave him enough money. The Bible says that Satan entered into Judas to get him to do this. Judas had become angry with Jesus, and Judas had always loved money. So Judas was an easy target for Satan. Jesus' enemies promised Judas thirty pieces of silver if he'd lead them to Jesus when they could arrest him without a crowd around. So one night, Judas led a band of soldiers to a garden where Jesus liked to go to be alone and pray. The soldiers arrested Jesus and took him away.

"The next step was a trial. Of course, that was a little harder because Jesus hadn't done anything wrong, and everyone knew it. Jesus' enemies tried paying people to lie about him, but their stories didn't agree with each other, so that didn't work. Satan was frustrated, and so was the high priest. The high priest finally said to Jesus, 'Are you the Son of the Most High God?'

"If Jesus had just kept quiet, they couldn't have done anything to him. But he didn't keep quiet; he answered. 'Yes,' Jesus answered, 'I am.'

" 'Aha!' Satan may have thought. 'This is too easy!'

"The high priest cried, 'We don't need any more witnesses! This man's making himself out to be God! That's blasphemy! He deserves to die.'

"But then Satan and his allies hit another obstacle. The Roman authorities didn't allow Jews to sentence a prisoner to death. Only the Roman governor in Jerusalem was allowed to do that. So they took Jesus to Pilate, the governor. It was obvious to Pilate, too, that Jesus hadn't done anything wrong. But while Pilate was trying to decide what to do, Jesus' enemies—and Satan—were working the crowd. They were stirring up the people who'd gathered. They wanted the crowd to demand Jesus' death."

"Wait a sec," Amy said, looking up from coloring her map. "I thought the crowd was on Jesus' side."

"It was on some days," Grandpa replied. "But crowds are fickle. They can change in a moment. That's how it was with this crowd. When Pilate stepped outside, a mob of angry Jews met him, yelling, 'Crucify him! Crucify him!' Pilate still didn't want to condemn an innocent man to death, but then Satan gave Jesus' enemies a great idea. One of them said to Pilate, 'Jesus says he's a king. That means he's against Caesar. You wouldn't want word to get back to Caesar that you're against him, would you?' And Pilate, afraid of getting in trouble with Caesar, gave the order for Jesus to be put to death.

"You know the rest of the story," Grandpa said. "It's a grim story, and crucifixion was a grim way to die. Very slow, very painful—and in Jesus' case, a crowd of people gathered round to make fun of him as he died. Satan must have had several very happy hours. The one who was supposed to destroy his work was hanging on a cross, like a criminal, being tortured to death. Nothing to fear from him now."

Grandpa fished something out of his box. Marc peered closely at Grandpa's hand and was surprised to see that he had taken out only one figure this time, not two. Grandpa set up on top of the box the same wooden cross he had used once before. "Jesus was dying. Surely Satan had won.

"But then, all at once, a couple of surprising things happened. When someone dies a long, painful death, especially after twenty-four hours of sleeplessness and beatings, such as Jesus had just endured, they might moan, they might sigh, but they die quietly. Exhausted. Jesus, on the other hand, shouted." Grandpa looked at his Bible. "It says he cried out with a loud voice. I believe it was a victory shout. And at that minute, Satan may have begun to realize that he'd played right into Jesus' hand. 'It is finished!' Jesus said. And then he died—but I want you to know that none of the four writers telling this story in the Bible say, 'Jesus died.' Two of them say that he breathed his last, and two of them say that he gave up his spirit. That's because death didn't just happen to Jesus, the way it does to everybody else. Jesus didn't *have* to die because he wasn't a sinner like the rest of us are. Jesus chose to die as a sacrifice for his people.

"The other interesting thing that happened when Jesus died was this: the huge, thick curtain in the temple, which kept people out of the Most Holy Place where God was, split in half from the top to the bottom. God was announcing that Jesus' death had paid for the sins of his people and had taken them out of the way. God's people were free to come into his presence again. The contest between God and Satan about whether God would have a people for himself had been decided. Satan had lost, once and for all."

Grandpa stopped. The children waited. Then Amy said, "But Grandpa, you forgot to put something else on top of your box, to show that God had won."

"That's because the same thing Satan thought would destroy Jesus was the very thing Jesus used to destroy *him*—the cross," Grandpa explained. "So the cross, which seemed to be the symbol of Jesus' defeat, came to be the symbol of his greatest victory."

Colossians 2:13–15

And you, who were dead in your trespasses and the uncircumcision of your flesh, God made alive together with him, having forgiven us all our trespasses, by canceling the record of debt that stood against us with its legal demands. This he set aside, nailing it to the cross. He disarmed the rulers and authorities and put them to open shame, by triumphing over them in him.

Deadliest Weapon
Made Useless

(John 20)

Amy pushed the colored pencils, her books, and the map of France to the center of the table. She scooted her chair back to see Grandpa better. "You know you can't stop there, Grandpa," she said. "You really have to go on and tell us the next part of the story."

"Go on, Grandpa, tell us the next part," Marc agreed. "Mom's not here yet, and we're done with our assignments for now. We can't go home with Jesus still dead on the cross!"

So Grandpa put the little cross back in the box, took some other items out, and began again. "We've celebrated so many Easters that it's easy for us to take Jesus' resurrection for granted," he said. "We all know that Jesus didn't stay dead. We haven't lived for a single minute believing that Jesus is dead. But imagine how Jesus' friends felt *after* watching him die and *before* finding the empty tomb. Imagine what gloomy thoughts they must have had! They'd been sure that Jesus was the one whom God had promised. They'd seen him perform miracles. They'd heard him teach about God in a way no one else had ever done. They might not have understood all he came to do, but they were certain that he was the Son of God.

"But then he died. Just like everybody else dies. Only worse, because it was a horrible, painful death and he was surrounded by mocking enemies. His friends, standing there at the foot of the cross, must have prayed for a miracle. They heard his enemies call out, 'If you're really the Son of God, come down from the cross.' And they thought, 'You *are* the Son of God. Come down!' But nothing happened. The minutes just kept dragging by, with Jesus' suffering growing worse and worse. Finally, his friends must have wished he *would* die, just so that his pain would stop. Just so that it would be over with. And then he did; he died. It was over. And with the end of his life, all their hopes ended, too.

"They buried him and went home. What else could they do? They kept the doors locked because not only were they very sad, they were also afraid. What if Jesus' enemies came after them as well? That Friday and Saturday must have seemed to go on forever to Jesus' friends. Peter and John and his other followers puzzled over it all, again and again. How could this have happened? Jesus had prevented the deaths of so many other people, and he'd even raised people from the dead; how could he himself have died? Jesus had calmed storms and commanded demons. If he wasn't God, how could he have done that? But if he was God, how could he have died? Nothing made sense, and life didn't seem worth living. And for Peter, there was an added heartache. Because when Jesus was all alone and on trial, when he was being mocked and beaten and needed a friend, Peter was so afraid that he'd said he didn't even know him."

Grandpa paused. The room was silent. Marc and Amy were caught up in his story, imagining the sorrow and despair of the disciples while Jesus lay in the tomb. Grandpa had taken from his box the same little model of a tomb he had used for the Lazarus story. This time he placed inside a little figure of a body wrapped in graveclothes. He put the stone in the way for the door and set the tomb on top of his box. "To the disciples, it certainly seemed that Death and Satan had won.

"Then, early Sunday morning, while it was still dark, Peter was startled by a loud banging at the door. When he opened it, one of Jesus' friends named Mary was at the door, nearly frantic. 'They've taken Jesus' body out of the tomb, and we don't know where they've laid him.' Maybe Peter became angry, wondering why Jesus' enemies couldn't leave him alone, at least now that he was dead. He and John set out for Jesus' tomb to see what had happened. They ran all the way. As the men drew near the tomb, they saw what Mary meant. The stone that closed up the doorway had been pushed aside, and the tomb stood open. Now, tell me, Amy, if Marc and I were to run somewhere, who do you think would get there first?"

"Definitely Marc," Amy replied promptly.

"I'll bet Grandpa could run pretty fast," Marc said generously.

"Not for very long I couldn't," said Grandpa. "John was young—not quite as young as Marc is, but young—so John could run faster than Peter. John got to the tomb first, but he was a little shy about walking in, so he stopped at the opening. But not Peter. Once he got there, he blew past John and went right on in. John followed him then, and what do you think they saw?"

"Nothing," Marc answered. "Jesus was gone."

"They didn't see Jesus, but they did see something," Grandpa said. "They saw the cloths that had been wrapped around him. Now, those wrappings were long strips of linen that were wrapped around and around the body. In between the layers were lots of spices, weighing maybe a hundred pounds. And some of the spices were sticky, making those strips of linen cloth stick together and harden. If someone had taken Jesus' body, why would they have gone to all the trouble of removing those wrappings? Why wouldn't they have just taken the body, wrappings and all? Plus, Peter and John saw the cloth that had covered Jesus' face rolled up by itself in a separate place. Why would a graverobber take the time to do that? Maybe Jesus hadn't been moved by someone else. Maybe he'd never really been dead. Maybe he'd revived and walked out on his own."

"No, that couldn't be," said Marc. "Because even if he hadn't really died, he would have at least *almost* died. He would have been way too weak to work his way out from under all those tight wrappings and heavy spices you're talking about. Plus, how could he have moved such a big stone all by himself, as weak as he would have been?"

"Good thinking," Grandpa approved.

Amy had been wriggling in her chair, eager to add her part. "And if Jesus was just unconscious and then woke up, it wouldn't make any more sense for him to take time to roll up the face cloth and set it neatly out of the way than it would for thieves to do it."

"So," Grandpa continued, "when Peter and John saw what they saw—the graveclothes still there, with no Jesus inside them and the face cloth lying by itself—the Bible says they 'saw and believed.' They weren't sure what had happened or how, but they began to think that something wonderful had taken place. And then, of course, that evening they actually saw Jesus. He was alive and well. Not just revived and weak and recovering, but risen from the dead, never to die again.

"Now, I want you to think with me for a moment about what was at stake here. What if Jesus had *stayed* in the tomb? What if he *hadn't* risen from the dead? Would it matter?"

Amy suggested, hesitantly, "Well, death was one of the worst things that happened because of sin. You said that in the Lazarus story. So if Jesus had stayed dead, that's one part of Satan's work that Jesus wouldn't have changed."

"Right," said Grandpa. "If Jesus hadn't come back from the dead first, then no one else would ever rise from the dead. But there's something else."

The children sat quietly, thinking. "Do you remember that Jesus had prophesied his death, *and* his resurrection, several times? What if he hadn't risen from the dead?"

"He would have been wrong," Marc said simply.

"And if he'd been wrong about that, what about all the other claims he'd made for himself? If he'd said that he was the Son of God *and* that he would rise again, but then he didn't rise, could you believe he was the Son of God?"

Marc and Amy shook their heads "no." Grandpa flipped quickly through the pages of his Bible. He found what he was looking for, then said, "This is what Paul says about Jesus in the book of Romans." He adjusted his glasses and read: " 'who was declared with power to be the Son of God by the resurrection from the dead.' The resurrection proves that Jesus is God. And if he hadn't been God, would his death have saved anyone?" Grandpa paused, letting Marc and Amy consider this. "The only reason Jesus' death was worth enough to pay for all the sins of all his people was that it was the Son of God who died, not just some ordinary human.

"The resurrection is the most important thing in the whole Christian faith," Grandpa said. "Take away the resurrection, leave Jesus dead in the tomb, and the whole thing falls apart." Grandpa removed the little figure from the tomb. "But as Paul said and as they sing in Handel's *Messiah*, 'But now has Christ risen!' He appeared to more than five hundred people over the next forty days. If he *hadn't* risen, there was plenty of time and plenty of opportunity for his enemies to come up with the dead body, but they never did because it just

217

wasn't there. Then Jesus went up into heaven, with the promise to come again. Now, tell me, Marc, what often happens to great war heroes when they're done fighting?"

"They receive medals and honors," Marc replied.

"Yes," said Grandpa, "and there in heaven, like the champion warrior that he is in this all-important war, Jesus received the greatest honors. But what do war heroes often go on to do later? Think of Washington and Grant and Eisenhower."

"Oh, I know," Amy spoke up before Marc could. "They become leaders of their country. Those guys were all elected president."

"Right," Grandpa said again. "And that's what happened with Jesus, too. God made him the head of his people, the church. And God put him over all things for the rest of history. He's ruling the affairs of the whole world and making sure that everything that happens is for the good of God's people and for the glory of God.

"What a champion!" Grandpa shook his head admiringly. "Satan, sin, death—all defeated in three days' time, *and* by means of his own death. What a wonderful Savior we have."

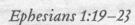 

Ephesians 1:19–23

And what is the immeasurable greatness of his power toward us who believe, according to the working of his great might that he worked in Christ when he raised him from the dead and seated him at his right hand in the heavenly places, far above all rule and authority and power and dominion, and above every name that is named, not only in this age but also in the one to come. And he put all things under his feet and gave him as head over all things to the church, which is his body, the fullness of him who fills all in all.

Equipping the Soldiers

(Acts 2)

"Roman soldiers must have been in great shape!" Amy said to no one in particular, as she leafed through one of the used books that Grandpa had for sale.

"Has Marc gotten to you?" Grandpa teased. "Are you reading books about war now, too?"

"Oh, no," Amy answered. "I was just checking to see if you had anything on Greek or Roman mythology in all these used books. And you don't, but there is this book about the ancient Romans." Amy held up a book with a picture of a statue of a Roman emperor on the front.

With determination, Marc ignored Amy's comments while he worked out the last of his assigned math problems. He finished calculating, wrote down the answer and circled it, and closed the math book. Then Marc jumped into the conversation. "So why do you say Roman soldiers had to be in such great shape?" he asked.

"Well, look at all this stuff they had to carry around everywhere," Amy answered, holding up a picture of a Roman soldier with his equipment. "Breastplate, helmet, shield—all those things must have been heavy. But that's just the armor. Then there are the weapons— a dagger, a sword, and look how long that spear is! How could you even walk without that getting in your way? And then they had packs with all this stuff inside: food, dishes, cooking pots, and there's a hammer and a shovel and an ax—what are those for? Hobbies in their spare time?"

"No," answered Marc, who, of course, knew all about these things. "They needed weapons *and* tools. It was the Roman soldiers who built all those great Roman roads. They marched all over Europe conquering things, right? Well, they had to have something to march *on*. If there wasn't a road, they built one themselves. And if they decided to stop and stay somewhere for a while—maybe to spend the winter, or maybe to make sure that certain conquered people didn't rebel—they had to have tools to build their forts."

"See what I mean? Carry all that *and* march *and* build things! They must have been in great shape!" Amy said. "Still, I'll bet sometimes they wanted to *accidentally* forget some of this stuff and leave it behind so that they wouldn't have so much to carry."

"Oh, no," Grandpa said. He gave one last polish to the antique picture frame in his hand. Then he held it out at arm's length to see whether it met his approval. Setting it down, he continued. "A soldier knows he needs his equipment. Cruelest thing a commanding officer could do would be to send his soldiers off into battle without enough of the right equipment. It's a pain to carry all that stuff, but a soldier wouldn't want to be without it when he needs it."

"So, Grandpa," Amy said, closing the book on ancient Rome. "Do you have a war story about equipment?"

"As a matter of fact, I think I do," Grandpa said, reaching for his yellow wooden box and his worn Bible.

"Well, imagine that," said Marc, in mock surprise. Then he added, "Grandpa, you have a war story for everything."

"Well," Grandpa replied, "there are a lot of them. And I'm not even telling you half of them! There are tons of stories we're skipping. Now, this story starts with Jesus going back into heaven. Right before he left, he gathered his disciples together one last time and issued their orders. 'Tell everyone everywhere who I am and what I've done,' he told them. 'Teach everyone you come across all the things I've taught you. Baptize and make disciples of people from every nation.'

"Now imagine that you're Peter or James or John and you're listening to Jesus tell you this. Has it ever happened to you that someone expects you to do something and you don't have a clue how to go about it?"

Amy chuckled. "I remember the first time I ever babysat. It was for little Laura Coleman. Mrs. Coleman was actually walking out the door when she said, 'Oh, and she probably needs her diaper changed,' and then, bam, the door closed and she was gone. I'd never changed a diaper in my life! I had no idea what to do!"

"So what did you do?" Marc wanted to know.

"I called Mom and followed her instructions, step by step," Amy said.

"But before you thought of that, I'll bet you felt a little lost, didn't you?" asked Grandpa. "A little overwhelmed?"

Amy nodded. "And that's how the disciples felt, only much more so," said Grandpa, continuing his war story. "Peter and James and John weren't preachers or public speakers—they were fishermen! They hadn't even gone very far in school. And think of all the things Jesus had taught them. How would they remember it all? Or what if they got it wrong and ended up telling people things that Jesus hadn't really meant? And who would believe them anyway? There

221

were plenty of times when people didn't even believe Jesus, and *he* could work miracles."

"*And*," Marc interrupted, "there was the 'fear factor,' too."

"What's that?" Amy asked.

"Well, think about it," said Marc. "When it was dangerous to know Jesus, Peter had said that he *didn't* know him. And where did Jesus find the disciples after he rose from the dead? Hiding in a locked room because they were scared. I would think, besides all those other things you're talking about, Grandpa, they'd be just plain scared to do what Jesus told them. Especially since he was leaving them to go back to heaven."

"Good point." Grandpa nodded. "So we could say that these soldiers were seriously *un*equipped to go into battle and do what their Commander was telling them to do." From inside the yellow box, Grandpa removed a figure of a plain fisherman, holding a fishing net. "Doesn't look like much of a soldier, does he?" he asked. "But of course, the Commander knew they didn't have what they needed to obey him. That's why he told them not to go anywhere and not to do anything until they'd been given what God had promised to give."

"Aha! Their equipment!" Amy said.

"Jesus told his followers they'd be his witnesses in Jerusalem, in Judea, in Samaria, and in the remotest part of the earth—but not yet," Grandpa continued. "For now they were to wait. I imagine they were relieved to think that they didn't have to jump right into this overwhelming task. So they went back to Jerusalem and waited for God to equip them. And he did—on the day of Pentecost."

"Oh! I know what the equipment was!" cried Marc, just as Amy was saying, "I know what happened on Pentecost."

222

"Yes, but do you know what the day of Pentecost was in the first place?" Grandpa asked them both. "It was already a special day before this story happened."

The two children looked blank. "It was some kind of Jewish holy day," Marc ventured.

"That's right," said Grandpa. "It was a celebration of the harvest. It was a day for thanking God for blessing the seeds the people had planted and for making their crops grow and give fruit. Which makes it the perfect day for what happens in this story. The disciples were gathered together when, suddenly, God kept his promise and sent the Holy Spirit to fill them all. From now on, all who put their faith in the Lord Jesus would have the Holy Spirit living inside them. That was how they'd find the strength and the courage and the wisdom to do the things Jesus gave them to do. Now, can you *see* the Holy Spirit?"

The children shook their heads.

"Can you hear him with your ears?"

They shook their heads again.

"Since this was brand-new, and so that everyone would understand that this wonderful thing was happening now, God sent a strong wind to fill the house and little tongues of flame along with the Holy Spirit. And another special thing happened, too. All these simple Jewish people were able to speak in foreign languages they'd never studied."

"That must have been wonderful," murmured Amy, who struggled with Spanish in school.

"It *was* wonderful," Grandpa agreed, "because the city was filled with foreigners from all over the world who were there to celebrate Pentecost. Jesus' followers were able to go out into the streets and talk to all these different people in their own languages about who Jesus was and what he'd done.

"Well, of course, people were amazed. And they wanted to know what was going on and how all this could be possible. So Peter, now fully equipped to carry out Jesus' command, began to explain. He preached a sermon to all those gathered around. He spoke out for Jesus boldly, showing how he had fulfilled so many prophecies. Peter told the crowd that Jesus was the one whom God had been promising to send. He bravely insisted that Jesus had risen from the dead, and he ended with this really courageous statement." Grandpa peered into his Bible to be sure he said it correctly. "Peter said, 'Let all the house of Israel know for certain that God has made him both Lord and Christ—this Jesus whom you crucified.' That's pretty bold, don't you think?

"Amy just gave us a list of that Roman soldier's equipment," said Grandpa. "Let's list what God has given his soldiers by giving them the Holy Spirit," said Grandpa.

"Peter sure wasn't afraid anymore," Amy volunteered.

"And he was able to talk about prophecies and about Jesus, even though he'd never preached before," added Marc, who always hated giving oral reports in school. "In fact, all of Jesus' followers were doing that."

"Yes," said Grandpa, "and Jesus had promised that the Holy Spirit would make the twelve disciples able to remember correctly the things Jesus had taught them. Then there's one more important piece of equipment the Holy Spirit provides. Remember, the disciples might have worried about whether anyone would believe them. After all, they weren't supposed to just *talk* about Jesus; he'd told them to 'make disciples.' How could they make people believe what they said? Well, they couldn't, of course, but the Holy Spirit could.

"You'd expect that after Peter ended his sermon with such a strong accusation—'you've crucified God's promised Savior!'—his audience would have been furious and come after him in a rage. But you know what really happened?" Grandpa peered into his Bible again. "They were pierced to the heart—they had guilty consciences! They cried out to Peter, 'What do we do?' Why were they so different now? It was because the Holy Spirit had worked in their hearts to change them. He caused them to see their sin. So when Peter told them to repent and be baptized in the name of the Lord Jesus, they did it—three thousand of them! That's why Pentecost was the perfect day for all this. Peter planted the seed of God's Word with his sermon. The Holy Spirit blessed that seed and produced a harvest in people's hearts. Now Peter and the others knew they had all they needed to make disciples." Beside the fisherman figure, Grandpa placed a small dove, to represent the Holy Spirit.

"A bird?" Marc asked.

"It's the Holy Spirit dove," Amy told him. "Remember? When Jesus was baptized, the Holy Spirit came down on him like a dove."

"Jesus had equipped his followers with all they needed," Grandpa repeated. "They had the good news about Jesus. And they had the gift of the Holy Spirit."

Acts 2:16–18, 21

But this is what was uttered through the prophet Joel:

"And in the last days it shall be, God declares,
that I will pour out my Spirit on all flesh,
    and your sons and your daughters shall prophesy,
and your young men shall see visions,
    and your old men shall dream dreams;
even on my male servants and female servants
    in those days I will pour out my Spirit, and they shall
        prophesy. . . .
And it shall come to pass that everyone who calls upon the name
    of the Lord shall be saved."

Resist!

(Acts 3–5)

Amy worked patiently at the tangled chain in her hand. Surely if she could just loosen this bit here and then pull that piece through it, the knot would be undone and she would have untangled one more necklace. Then just as she thought she had it, the whole knot seemed to move between her fingers and it was just as tight as ever. She sighed and began again. The cross on the end of the gold chain was unlike any cross she had ever seen. Its unusual shape fascinated her. She had been able to untangle all the other pieces of used jewelry, and now they hung on a little wooden stand, ready for sale. She liked this necklace the best, but the knot in the chain was proving very stubborn.

The door to the shop opened and Grandpa entered. "Thanks for minding the phone. Any calls?" Amy shook her head and kept working at the chain. Then Grandpa noticed Amy's rack of untangled jewelry. "You've really made progress there," he said.

"Yes, but I can't undo this one knot," Amy said, still working. She stopped and held up the necklace. "Look at this cross. Isn't it pretty?"

Grandpa looked at the cross that Amy was holding up for his inspection. "Oh, that's a Huguenot cross from France," he explained. He pronounced it *hugh-guh-naht.* "See how it's made from four flower petals? They're the petals of a lily, a symbol for France, because Huguenots wanted people to realize that they were loyal to their country. There's a fleur-de-lis (*flur-duh-lee*) in between each petal; that's another symbol of France. And then look, the empty space left where each fleur-de-lis touches a flower petal is in the shape of a heart. And you have the Holy Spirit dove suspended from the bottom of the cross."

"What *is* a Huguenot?" Amy wanted to know.

"Huguenots were the Protestants in France, back when it was illegal to be a Protestant in France," Grandpa explained. "Huguenot pastors weren't allowed to preach. Huguenot Christians weren't allowed to get together for worship. They did it anyway, of course, and sometimes suffered for it. When we were in France, we visited a town that had a tower in it. In the top of the tower was a room— not a very big room, either. A Huguenot woman had been locked in that tower for decades. You could see on the tower wall where she or one of her Huguenot friends had scratched the word 'resist' in the wall with a hairpin or a fingernail or something."

Amy sighed. "Why do so many people hate Christians?" she asked.

"It's because of the war in our story," Grandpa answered. "You know what God told the serpent in Eden—the one who would come from the woman and those who were on Satan's side would always be enemies. Even though he's already lost the war, Satan and his allies will still do all they can to hurt God's people. Our next story shows exactly that," Grandpa said. "How about if I tell it to you while you work on that chain?"

"Okay," Amy said, nodding without looking up from the tangle.

Marc set down a map that he had been examining. It showed the progress of World War II in the Pacific. "I can save this for later," he said, and came to sit near Amy. Grandpa went to the counter for his yellow box. Amy continued to work on the knot.

"I'm sure Peter was quite encouraged with the results of his first sermon," Grandpa began. "Imagine three thousand people turning to Christ from just one sermon. But not all the results of his preaching would be so happy. One day, he and John were going to the temple to pray and they saw a lame man, sitting by the temple gate, begging. Peter stopped in front of the man and told him, 'I don't have any money to give you, but I'll give you what I have.' Then he said, 'In the name of Jesus of Nazareth, get up and walk.' And he grabbed the man's hand and pulled him to his feet. John may have wondered what in the world Peter was up to—but there the man stood, on feet that were now perfectly fine. He began to walk and jump. He went right into the temple with them, on his own two feet, praising God. Now, this man had been at that same temple gate every day, begging, so everybody knew him. It caused quite a commotion when people saw him walking. In no time at all, there was a crowd around Peter and John, wanting to know what this was all about.

"So Peter preached another sermon. First he made it clear that *he* didn't have the power to heal lame men; it was Jesus working through him who had done it. Then he went on to explain that Jesus was the one God had promised who would come to set his people free, the one who fulfilled all the prophecies about the Messiah. Peter told his audience that Jesus had risen from the dead. Then he said that each one of them must turn from their sin and believe in Jesus. If they did, God would forgive them and bless them. That was as far as Peter got, when along came the priests and some of the soldiers from the temple guard. They arrested Peter and John and took them off to jail."

"But they weren't doing anything wrong," said Amy, still not looking up from the knot. "In fact, they helped that man."

"They were teaching that Jesus had risen from the dead," Grandpa replied. "Jesus' enemies hated that story! They'd killed Jesus to get rid of him, but that story about him rising from the dead made him more popular than ever. The priests and Jewish leaders were still losing followers. They had to stop that story from spreading!

"So Peter and John spent their first night in jail. In the morning they would face Jesus' enemies, the rulers and elders of the Jewish people. What they didn't know, as the night passed in the dark prison cell, was that God had used Peter's preaching again. The Holy Spirit had worked in people's hearts once more, causing them to repent and believe. Now there were five thousand men alone who believed in Jesus, without counting women and children."

This time Amy did look up. "Well, *how many* women and children?" she wanted to know.

"It doesn't say," Grandpa answered. "You could probably figure at least one woman and one child for each man."

"That would make fifteen thousand Christians," Marc said. "They've come a long way from the five hundred who first saw Jesus after the resurrection."

"Jesus was taking captives right and left," Grandpa agreed. He chuckled. "The thing that's different about this Commander is that when he takes people captive, that's when they really become free. When morning came, Peter and John appeared before a very unfriendly audience. But thanks to the Holy Spirit inside him, Peter wasn't afraid. He said, 'You killed Jesus, but God raised him; you rejected him, but God has chosen him; and he's the only way of salvation God has given.'

"The religious leaders didn't like that one bit! But as Amy said, Peter and John really hadn't done anything wrong. A lame man had been healed, and all Jerusalem knew about it. So Jesus' enemies had to let Peter and John go free. First, though, they warned them not to speak or teach at all in Jesus' name, and threatened them with what would happen if they did. Peter and John, still bold because of the Holy Spirit, told them, 'You decide whether we should obey God or you; as far as we're concerned, we *can't* stop telling what we've seen and heard.'

"Peter and John knew how vicious these people could be. They'd seen what the same leaders had done to Jesus. So as soon as they were free, Peter and John met with the other believers to pray. They didn't ask God to keep them safe; they asked him to keep them brave, so that they would continue to tell the good news about Jesus. When they were done praying, God answered. He caused the house they were in to shake, and he filled them all with great boldness so that all of them could tell others about Jesus.

"As the days went by, the new church grew. It grew in understanding of who Jesus is and what he requires of his followers, and it grew by crowds of people joining it every day. And the jealousy of Jesus' enemies grew, too. Finally, the high priest and his pals couldn't stand it anymore. Once again they arrested the apostles and put them in jail. But prison bars mean nothing to our Commander. In the night, God sent an angel to open the doors of the jail. The angel told the apostles to go preach in the temple, and they obeyed. In the morning, the high priest sent officers to the jail, to bring Peter and his companions to trial. But the officers came back, saying, 'The doors are still locked and the guards are still guarding, but the prisoners aren't there.' As the high priest puzzled over what was going on and what to do about it, someone stepped into the meeting and said, 'Hey! The men you're looking for are in the temple, teaching the people.'"

Marc grinned. "I'll bet the high priest felt silly."

"Once the high priest and his men finally had the apostles in front of them," Grandpa continued, "they said, 'We gave you strict orders not to teach in Jesus' name, but you've filled the whole city with your teaching.'

" 'That's because we have to obey God before men,' Peter answered, speaking for them all. 'You killed him, but God raised him and has seated him at his own right hand. God has made him a prince and the only Savior of Israel.'

"Of course, that made these men mad! They liked to think of *themselves* as princes in Israel. They liked to make the people think *they* were their saviors. In fact, the chief priest and elders were so angry that they decided then and there to kill Peter and the others. Just as they'd killed Jesus. And they would have done it except for one man who spoke up and told them to calm down; this would all blow over soon. So the apostles weren't killed, but they were beaten and ordered again not to speak in Jesus' name.

"No one wants to spend time in jail. No one wants to be beaten. And no one wants to live his life in fear of powerful enemies, always wondering what they'll do to him next. The priests and leaders and Satan were counting on all these things to stop Jesus' followers. They were hoping to scare them so that they'd be quiet and stop spreading the good news of Jesus." Grandpa put two small items on the top of his box. One was a little carving of a barred window, like one would see in a prison. The other was the cruel-looking whip from an earlier story.

"But they couldn't stop Jesus and his army. Satan's forces had fear and torture and prison as their weapons. But God had given his soldiers the gospel to preach." Grandpa removed the barred window and replaced it with the small open Bible that he had used twice before. "He'd given them the Holy Spirit so that their preaching had the power to change hearts." Grandpa removed the whip and replaced it with the little Holy Spirit dove from his last story. "In spite of all of the enemy's best efforts, the Bible tells us that the Word of God kept spreading. The number of disciples kept growing, and growing quickly. *And*—now, get this—even a great many of the priests believed and came to obey Jesus."

"Cool!" said Marc, just as Amy gave a cry of triumph. "I got it!" she said, holding up the Huguenot cross on the end of an untangled chain.

"Good job!" said Grandpa. "And I want you to keep that cross, since you worked so hard at getting the knots out."

"Thanks, Grandpa," said Amy, and she fastened the chain around her neck.

Acts 5:29–32, 41–42

But Peter and the apostles answered, "We must obey God rather than men. The God of our fathers raised Jesus, whom you killed by hanging him on a tree. God exalted him at his right hand as Leader and Savior, to give repentance to Israel and forgiveness of sins. And we are witnesses to these things, and so is the Holy Spirit, whom God has given to those who obey him." . . . Then they left the presence of the council, rejoicing that they were counted worthy to suffer dishonor for the name. And every day, in the temple and from house to house, they did not cease teaching and preaching Jesus as the Christ.

The Army Moves Out

(Acts 6:1–8:4)

"Your new necklace looks very nice with that sweater," said Grandpa. Amy reached up and fingered the Huguenot cross that Grandpa had given her. "Thanks," she said. "I wear it all the time. I really like it. Grandpa, do you know any more about that lady you told us about, the Huguenot lady in the tower?"

Grandpa pulled out a chair and sat at the table where Amy was having an after-school snack of juice and pretzels. "Well, let's see," he said, trying to remember. "The name of the town we were in was Aigues-Mortes"—Grandpa pronounced this *ayg mort*—"let me write that down for you; it's French, so you don't spell it the way it sounds." He scrawled the name on a used envelope that he pulled from his shirt pocket. "And if I remember correctly, the lady's name was Marie Durand. But you should check with your grandmother to see if that's how she remembers it, too." And Grandpa wrote the woman's name on the envelope as well.

"Thanks, Grandpa. I'm going to go in the house and use the computer, if Grandma's not on it. I want to see if I can find out anything more about Marie Durand on the Internet." Amy popped the last pretzel into her mouth, washed it down with the rest of her juice, and set the glass in the sink. Then she left the shop.

When Amy returned half an hour later, she found Marc on the floor, surrounded by piles of magazines. "What are you doing?" she asked.

"Putting all these in order for Grandpa," Marc said. "I've got all the same kinds together, and now I'm arranging them by year and by month."

Grandpa's face lit up. "You've already gotten that far?" he asked. "That is such a big help! I keep thinking I need to do that, but I never get around to it. Thank you so much!" Grandpa turned to Amy. "How did your research go? Did you learn anything more about the lady in the tower?"

Amy nodded, and a shadow came over her face. "It's really pretty sad," she said. "You were right; her name was Marie Durand. And she was only fifteen when they locked her in that tower. Only fifteen! And she stayed in it for thirty-eight years. So she was fifty-three when they finally let her out. All those years in one room in a tower. Never going anywhere. Never seeing anyone—except the handful of other people locked in there with her. It was the women's prison for that area, so some of the other women were Huguenots, too, but there were also women who were really criminals. There wasn't any heating or cooling. Marie Durand was never able to get married or have children. *And* she hadn't seen her mother since she was four, which was when her mom got arrested for holding a church meeting in her house. Her dad was arrested two years before she was, and they hung her brother for being a Protestant pastor. Grandpa—" Amy's troubled eyes searched Grandpa's face. "Why did God let all that happen to her? In the last story you told us, an angel came and got Peter and the apostles out of jail. Why couldn't God have done something like that for Marie Durand?"

"God *could* have done that for her—" Grandpa began.

"Well, I know he *could* have," Amy interrupted. "I guess I mean why didn't he?"

"That's just it," said Grandpa. "We don't always know why God does things the way he does, or why he doesn't do the things we wish he would. In fact, more often than not, we *don't* know why. But God lets us see why sometimes, so that when we can't see why, we'll trust him anyway. Sit down and let me get my box. Our next war story is a good example of one of those times when we wish God would do something different, but then he lets us see why he did it the way he did."

Amy sat on the floor next to Marc, who continued sorting magazines into piles. Grandpa stepped away and came back with his box. Then he began.

"Marie Durand and her family were martyrs for their faith in Jesus. That means they chose to suffer and even die rather than turn away from following Christ. There have been many martyrs in the history of the church. Every now and then, God miraculously rescues martyrs from their enemies, but most of the time he doesn't. And like you, surely the people who love them wonder *why* he doesn't. Today's war story is about the first martyr in the Christian church. His name was Stephen.

"Stephen was a man who knew the Scriptures. He trusted in Jesus and was full of the Holy Spirit. When the people in the early church needed someone responsible to put in charge of something important, they turned to Stephen. In the church were widows who had no money and needed help. The whole church voted on those to put in charge of giving these women food to eat every day, and Stephen was one of the men they picked.

"Not only that, God gave Stephen the power to perform miracles. The Bible doesn't tell us what the miracles were, but it seems likely that he was able to heal sick people who came to him. And God made Stephen an excellent speaker. He spoke with such wisdom that even the best-educated men who argued with him about whether Jesus was the Messiah always lost their arguments. Stephen was a valuable man to the early church.

"So when Stephen's friends heard that he'd suddenly been arrested, they were terribly upset. How could he have been arrested? He wouldn't do anything to break the law. It was because those men who argued with Stephen turned out to be sore losers. They couldn't out-argue him, so they got people to make up lies about him, just as had happened with Jesus. So, using false accusations, they arrested Stephen and hauled him off to a trial.

"The high priest—the one that was always getting the apostles in trouble for preaching about Jesus—asked Stephen what he had to say for himself. Stephen began a speech—a long speech that was really kind of a sermon about Jesus. Maybe his church friends who were watching the trial relaxed then. Stephen was always a good speaker. He'd get out of this okay."

Marc looked up from his sorting. "That's what they think," he said. "His speech is just going to make everything worse."

"Ah-ah-ah," said Grandpa, "no fair getting ahead of me. Stephen's speech went on for quite a while! In it, he tried to help Jesus' enemies see that they were following the same pattern with Jesus that their ancestors had followed when God sent messengers to them. Joseph, Moses, the prophets—they'd all been rejected. When Stephen got to the part where he called Jesus 'the Righteous One' and said they'd betrayed and murdered him, all his enemies had heard enough! The Bible says they began to gnash their teeth at him."

"What's that mean?" Marc asked.

"It's kind of like grinding your teeth together and biting with nothing in your mouth," Grandpa replied.

Marc tried this. "That hurts!" he said.

"Well, that's just how mad they were," Grandpa replied. "Now, do you remember what happened when Peter preached to Jesus' enemies?"

"They felt really bad about killing Jesus, and a whole bunch of them repented and believed in him," Amy said. "That's just what I mean—how come that didn't happen in this story?"

"Hold on, I'm getting there," Grandpa said. "In this story, when Stephen preached, the people who heard *him* became really upset, too—but angry-upset, not guilty-upset. That's when they began the teeth-gnashing. God didn't give Stephen several thousand converts as he'd given to Peter. And he didn't rescue Stephen the way he'd rescued Peter from jail. But he did open Stephen's eyes to be able to see something that hardly anyone ever gets to see. Stephen looked up into heaven and saw the glory of God and Jesus himself. When Stephen said, 'I see the heavens opened up and the Son of Man standing at the right hand of God,' it was the final straw. How dare he suggest that Jesus, the one they hated so much, was sharing God's glory? Stephen's enemies began to shout, covering their ears so that they wouldn't have to listen to the things he was saying. Instantly, they were an unreasonable, angry mob. They rushed at Stephen and dragged him out of the city.

"His friends were horrified. Things had gotten out of control so fast. There was nothing they could do but watch all this happen. Surely many of them prayed that God would stop this crowd and somehow rescue Stephen. But God didn't. Once they got him out of the city, the mob picked up stones and began to throw them at him. They threw stone after stone, hitting him again and again. And he died.

"Like Amy, Stephen's friends must have wondered how God could stand by and let this happen to Stephen. Why didn't he stop it? And that wasn't the end of it. Watching Stephen die, Satan's allies were encouraged. They'd stopped Stephen from preaching! If they were just tough enough, they could stop all the other preachers from talking about Jesus, too. On that very day, persecution against the whole church began. Christians all over the city began to be dragged away to prison. Others, not just Stephen, were put to death. To escape, Christians had to leave town, leaving behind their homes, their businesses, their friends. The church was broken up and scattered everywhere, with people moving to many different towns and cities to get away." From his box, Grandpa took a little figure of an angry man with a stone in his upraised fist. He set it on top of his box; then he sat back, as though he were finished. "And there you have it. That's why."

"*What's* why?" Amy asked.

Marc stopped his sorting. "Did I miss something?" he asked.

"That's why, in this case, God allowed Stephen to be stoned to death," Grandpa explained, "and that's why he allowed persecution to break out against the whole church as a result. So that the church would be scattered."

"How was that a good thing?" Amy asked.

"Do you remember the orders that Jesus, the Commander, gave to his forces just before he went back into heaven?" Grandpa asked.

"They were supposed to tell everyone about him, and baptize people, and make disciples," Marc replied.

"But *where* were they to do that?" Grandpa persisted.

Amy's face lit up, as though she had just realized something. She had. "Oh, I know," she said. "It was in one of our memory verses for Girls' Club. 'In Jerusalem, in all Judea and Samaria, and in the remotest parts of the earth,' " she recited.

"They hadn't taken the message of Jesus *anywhere*," Grandpa said. "They were perfectly happy to stay right there in Jerusalem. The church was growing. The apostles were preaching. Miracles were taking place. It was a great place to be. It would have been hard to leave all that. But the church needed to grow beyond Jerusalem. The gospel needed to spread into the whole world. Listen to what happened when Christians left Jerusalem because they were being persecuted." Grandpa opened his Bible, found the place he wanted, and read, " 'They were all scattered throughout the regions of Judea and Samaria . . . therefore, those who had been scattered went about preaching the word.' "

Grandpa removed the angry figure with the stone and replaced it with a little figure of a man carrying a pack in one hand and a scroll in the other. The children guessed that the scroll was a Bible. "God took a horrible thing—Stephen's murder and persecution against the church—and used it to send his gospel out into the world. That way, the church would grow as it was supposed to do."

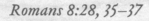

Romans 8:28, 35–37

And we know that for those who love God all things work together for good, for those who are called according to his purpose. . . . Who shall separate us from the love of Christ? Shall tribulation, or distress, or persecution, or famine, or nakedness, or danger, or sword? As it is written,

"For your sake we are being killed all the day long;
    we are regarded as sheep to be slaughtered."

No, in all these things we are more than conquerors through him who loved us.

A Powerful Foe
Is Vanquished

(Acts 8:1–3; 9:1–31)

Amy opened and closed drawers hopefully. The old wooden desk had more things that could open than she had ever seen in one piece of furniture. The desk was new to Grandpa's shop, and Amy was checking to see whether anything interesting had been left in it. Grandpa stood at the table, sorting through a box of books to decide which ones to put up for sale on his shelf and which ones to discard. Marc sat by himself, leafing through the pages of a book. From his corner came occasional whispers of "Wow," and "Oh, brother."

Finally, Grandpa and Amy heard him mumble, "People should really follow the rules. It's not fair when they don't."

Grandpa could contain his curiosity no longer. "What are you looking at, Marc?" he asked. "Some kind of sports thing?"

"Marc doesn't look at sports things; he looks at war things." Amy's muffled voice came from inside one of the desk's cabinets, where she had thrust her head.

Marc did not hear her. "No," he answered Grandpa, "I was looking at some stuff about prison camps. There are all kinds of rules about how countries are to treat each other when they take prisoners of war, but the rules sure get broken a lot."

Amy pulled her head out of the cabinet. "See?" she said to Grandpa. "It's always about war with Marc."

Marc ignored her. "The Allied prisoners in the Philippines during World War II were treated just awful. Like, for instance, the guards would make the prisoners dig graves for themselves, and then they'd blindfold them and make them kneel in the graves like they were going to be shot. But then the guards would just shoot a blank and laugh and say, 'Wasn't that a great joke?' Or like in our own country, Andersonville, during the Civil War. No houses or shelters of any kind, any time of the year! There was one month when a hundred prisoners in that prison camp died every day because the nutrition and disease were so bad. In fact, it says here that the commander of Andersonville was hung after the war, for the way he ran that prison."

"I guess it's always been like that," Grandpa said. "In Bible times, too, conquering armies were pretty harsh in the way they treated those they conquered. The Assyrians would skin people alive—"

"Yuck!" said Amy.

"—and drag prisoners away by hooks in their noses. The Romans, too, if they found someone who even looked like he was trying to rebel against their rule, would crucify him. That's one of the most painful deaths ever invented."

241

Disappointed with the desk, all of whose drawers and cabinets proved to be empty, Amy turned her attention to the conversation. "What about our war, Grandpa?" she asked. "Does our side ever take prisoners? What happens to them when we do?"

"Oho, I'm glad you asked," said Grandpa, pushing the box of books yet to be sorted to the back of the table and reaching for his yellow box. "When our Commander, the Lord Jesus Christ, conquers enemies, he treats them in a most unusual way. Marc, are you done looking at that for now? Want to come over here and hear my prisoner-of-war story?"

"Sure," said Marc, closing the book and leaving it on his chair.

"Not counting Satan himself, of course, who do you think was the very worst enemy of the early church?" Grandpa asked.

"The high priest?" asked Marc. Grandpa shook his head.

"Herod?" asked Amy. Grandpa shook his head again.

"This enemy honestly thought that fighting against Jesus was the best thing he could do for God," Grandpa began.

"Oh, it's Saul!" cried Amy as Marc said, "I know, it's Paul."

Grandpa nodded. "It is Saul," he said, "who later went by the name of Paul. Saul grew up being taught in schools whose teachers were all Pharisees. What do you know about Pharisees from the stories about Jesus?"

"They're the ones who were always arguing with Jesus, and jealous of him," Amy answered.

Grandpa nodded again. "So of course, Saul thought Jesus was an evil man who made himself out to be the Son of God and said things about himself and about God that just weren't true. When Jesus was crucified in Jerusalem, Saul must have rejoiced. 'Serves him right!' he would have thought. Then he heard the rumor that Jesus hadn't stayed dead. That made him furious. Those disciples of Jesus had no business spreading lies like that. And how dare they tell everyone that Jesus was the Savior whom God had provided for Israel! They must be silenced.

242

"Saul decided to devote his life to stamping out Jesus' followers and their stories. Whatever it took to stop them was okay with Saul. When Stephen was stoned to death, Saul held the cloaks of all the stone-throwers. He thought being stoned to death is just what *should* happen to someone who claims that an ordinary human is God.

"In fact, Saul was probably behind the persecution that began the day Stephen died. He didn't even give Stephen's friends a chance to mourn him. Right away he started breaking into Christians' houses and dragging them away to prison, both men and women. That's why so many Christians fled Jerusalem. Not good enough for Saul. He didn't want just *Jerusalem* free of Jesus' followers and their stories. He wanted the whole world free of these blasphemers. Saul was sure that was what God would want. So Saul chased them, going to all kinds of trouble to follow them to other cities, arresting them and taking them back to Jerusalem to be punished."

In his box, Grandpa found two figures and removed them. Grandpa set the first one on top of the box. It showed an angry little man with his arm upraised to heaven, as if to shake his fist against Jesus. "Now, if an ordinary human general had an enemy this powerful and this dangerous, what would he do about it?" Grandpa asked, turning his gaze to Marc.

"He'd probably try to kill him if he possibly could," said Marc.

"Would he try to take him alive?" Grandpa asked.

Marc considered. "Well, maybe, if he thought he could get some good information out of him," he said. "But if he couldn't be taken alive, most commanders wouldn't hesitate to have him killed, when he's doing that much damage."

"Well, let's just say that an enemy this serious about fighting was taken alive," Grandpa suggested. "Think he'd cooperate much?"

Marc shook his head emphatically. "Of course not!" he said.

243

"Think the commander of the side he'd fought against would give him a really important mission to carry out? Think he'd trust him with that?" Grandpa pressed.

"Even I realize that would be crazy," said Amy.

Grandpa smiled; then he went on with his story. "Saul was in the very act of fighting against Jesus when Jesus captured him," he said. "It was a move that Jesus had been planning all along. Jesus had something in mind for this enemy of his. And it didn't matter how hard this enemy fought or how strong he was or how much he didn't want Jesus' plan—Jesus is an irresistible conqueror. He always conquers what he sets out to conquer.

"He conquered Saul in the middle of the road, when Saul was on his way to a town called Damascus to find more Christians to take back to Jerusalem to be punished. Saul was almost to Damascus, planning how he would catch those Christians and what he'd do to them once he had them. His heart was as full of hatred against Jesus as it had ever been. Suddenly, a very bright light flashed from heaven all around Saul. He fell to the ground and heard a voice saying, 'Saul, Saul, why are you persecuting me?'

" 'Who are you?' Saul asked. Then the voice said, 'I am Jesus, whom you're persecuting.' Jesus? The voice belonged to Jesus? Then he really wasn't dead? The disciples' story about his resurrection was true? But Saul didn't have long to think about any of these things, because the voice went on to tell him to get up and go on to Damascus. 'There,' said the voice, 'it will be told you what you must do.' "

Grandpa chuckled. "How do you like that?" he said, looking from one grandchild to the other. "Not 'what I'd like you to do,' or 'what you can do if you want,' but 'what you *must* do.' No choice about it. Jesus had conquered, and this man who had been his worst enemy would now become his servant.

"When Saul got up off the ground where he'd fallen when the light first hit him, he couldn't see a thing. Even with his eyes open, he was blind as a bat. People had to lead him by the hand to get him to Damascus. There in Damascus he stayed alone for three days. He didn't eat; he didn't drink. I imagine Saul had a lot to think about. On the third day, God sent a believer named Ananias to Saul. When Ananias prayed for Saul and baptized him in the name of the Lord Jesus, Saul's eyes were able to see again. And Saul himself could finally see the truth that he'd fought so hard for so long.

"Now listen to the mission that Jesus gave Saul. Jesus said he was sending him to the Gentiles, the people who weren't Jews, so that their eyes could be opened to see the truth as well. Jesus said he wanted to take captives among the Gentiles, too—he was going to turn them from Satan's rule and place them under God's, just as he'd done with Saul. Saul was to be Jesus' instrument to do this.

"Saul went on to take the gospel of Jesus to Gentiles all over the Roman empire. He became the Apostle Paul, the one human being who did more than any other to establish Christ's church." Grandpa removed the angry, fist-shaking figure and replaced it with a small model sailing ship.

"Anytime the commander from one side disarms the worst enemy from the other side, it's considered quite a victory," Grandpa concluded. "But our Commander conquered his enemy, Saul, by so changing his heart that he became one of his most faithful servants ever!"

2 Corinthians 5:14–15, 18–20

For the love of Christ controls us, because we have concluded this: that one has died for all, therefore all have died; and he died for all, that those who live might no longer live for themselves but for him who for their sake died and was raised. . . . All this is from God, who through Christ reconciled us to himself and gave us the ministry of reconciliation; that is, in Christ God was reconciling the world to himself, not counting their trespasses against them, and entrusting to us the message of reconciliation. Therefore, we are ambassadors for Christ, God making his appeal through us. We implore you on behalf of Christ, be reconciled to God.

Out to Conquer the World!

(Acts 10)

"Did you find that book in the batch of used books I just got?" Grandpa asked Marc. Marc nodded.

"*Myths and Legends. Stories of Alexander the Great,*" Amy read aloud from the front of Marc's book. "Oh, I remember learning about him," she said. "Wasn't he the guy with the horse? Bucephalus was its name."

Marc nodded again. "He named a bunch of towns after that horse," he said. "One of the greatest military geniuses ever. He conquered most of the known world. He would have kept going, but once he got to India, his soldiers were just too worn out to want to go on any more. It says here that he set up twelve altars to Greek gods at the easternmost boundary of his empire, then headed for home"—Marc struck a dramatic pose as he read—" 'with despair in his heart.' I wonder if he could have conquered the whole world with a more willing army."

Grandpa set down the book he had selected from the same box. "But that's part of being a military genius," he pointed out. "No matter how much you know about military strategy, you're only as good as your army. If, at any point, you can't motivate your army, your strategy's wasted. Military commanders have used all kinds of things to motivate their armies," he added, "money, honor, love." Then Grandpa began to laugh.

"What's so funny?" Amy wanted to know.

"I was just thinking of a time in one of the stories from our war when God used something most unusual to get his followers to move on and win the next battle," said Grandpa. "It's really kind of funny."

"Well, let's hear it," said Amy just as Marc was saying, "Tell it to us."

Grandpa reached for his box and began.

"Do you remember God's promises to Abraham, way back toward the beginning of this war?" Grandpa asked.

"He promised him land," Marc began, "and a bunch of descendants who would be the nation that would fill the land—"

"And blessings!" Amy chimed in.

"Blessings for whom?" Grandpa asked.

"All the nations of the earth," said Amy. "They would all be blessed through Abraham."

"And remember the story of Ruth? Where was she from?" Grandpa asked.

"I don't remember where she was from," Marc answered, "but she wasn't from Israel."

"And yet God brought her to himself, and she became the grandmother of David, which made her the great-great-great-great-grandmother of Jesus himself," said Grandpa. "You can see that it was always God's intention to conquer the world. He wanted people who would be *his* people from every nation on earth.

"But God chose to start with the Israelite nation. He told the Israelites to keep themselves pure from the idol worship of the nations around them. So the Jews got the idea that God cared *only* about their nation. They thought the only people who could ever be right with God were Jews. So even at this point in our war story, when so many people were coming over to Jesus' side, it never occurred to the Jewish Christians that the gospel might be for Gentiles, too.

"You know, Marc, another detail about Alexander the Great's failure to conquer the world: his first soldiers were Greeks. As he conquered other countries, he tried to bring in their soldiers and make them equal with his Greeks. The Greeks didn't like that at all. The Jewish Christians were kind of like those Greek soldiers. *Jews* were God's people, not Gentiles. Jesus was *their* Savior and Lord; he wasn't for the Gentiles. The gospel was about *Jews* being forgiven by God, not about Gentiles. If it had been left up to the 'army' of the early church, Jesus would never have conquered the world. The gospel would never have gotten out of Israel. God's promise to Abraham about blessing for all the nations would have gone unfulfilled."

Grandpa stopped and rummaged in his yellow box. He pulled out what had been a wooden rectangular block, into which he had carved out valleys, leaving parts sticking up for mountains. He had painted an area blue for the sea, and, with a fine-tipped brush, had lettered the word "Israel" and several other place names as well. The children leaned forward. "Wow! It's a map!" said Amy.

"Of Israel," Marc added.

"This just couldn't go on! God's people had to understand that the gospel was for everyone. Somehow God had to convince them

249

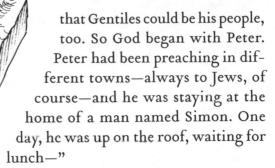

that Gentiles could be his people, too. So God began with Peter. Peter had been preaching in different towns—always to Jews, of course—and he was staying at the home of a man named Simon. One day, he was up on the roof, waiting for lunch—"

Marc looked puzzled. "On the roof?" he asked. "Why was he waiting for lunch on the roof?"

"Homes in Israel had flat roofs," Grandpa explained. "People made them into little areas like patios. Sometimes they'd sleep up there in the summer because it was cooler. Peter had been praying, but he was hungry and his mind kind of drifted off, and before he knew it he was half asleep. That's when God gave him an odd vision. In the vision, Peter was still on the housetop, thinking about food, when a sheet full of animals came down from the sky. All kinds of animals were on this sheet, not just the kinds that were considered 'clean' or okay for Jews to eat. There were birds on it, too, and crawling things—"

"Crawling things? Like what?" Amy asked with a shudder.

"Snakes," said Marc with relish. "And big, ugly spiders. And slimy worms and centipedes."

"Disgusting!" Amy said.

"That's what Peter thought," said Grandpa. "He'd always carefully observed the Jewish rules for eating, which allowed only certain kinds of birds and animals for food. But here were all kinds. And then a voice he recognized said, 'Arise, Peter, kill and eat.'

" 'No way, Lord,' Peter protested. 'I've never eaten anything unclean.'

"The same voice spoke again. 'What God has cleansed, no longer consider unclean,' it said.

"Then the whole vision was repeated again. And then once more."

"I guess Peter got the point," Amy said.

"Well, he got the point that he wasn't to call things unclean if God said they were clean," Grandpa agreed, "but he had no idea what this was all about. Surely not animals and food. But just as Peter was sitting up on the roof puzzling over what in the world the Lord was trying to tell him, there was a knock at the door below. The Holy Spirit told him then, 'There are three men at the door, and they're looking for you. It's okay to go with them because I sent them myself.'

"It was a good thing God told him this, because when Peter went down, he found three Gentile men. Their master, a Roman centurion, had sent them to ask Peter to come to his house. Now, Jews didn't go to Gentiles' houses. They thought it would make them unclean. But Peter knew that if Jesus wanted him to go there, it would be fine. When he got to the home of the Roman centurion, a man named Cornelius, Peter found that the whole household, family, servants, and all, had been gathered to meet him. 'Why have you sent for me?' Peter asked.

" 'I was praying in my house four days ago,' Cornelius explained. 'An angel came and told me I should invite a man called Peter to come see me. He said that Peter was staying with a friend by the sea. So I sent for you right away, and you've been kind enough to come. We're all here to learn what God wants you to tell us.'

"Peter was amazed. Not just at how all this had happened, but, even more, that God wanted Gentiles to hear the gospel. So Peter began to preach. He told about Jesus and his life—things that Cornelius was aware of. Then he explained that Jesus had risen from the dead. He told about the prophecies in Scripture and explained that Jesus was the one whom God had promised. Just as Peter was saying that the way to be forgiven for sin was by believing in Jesus, and before he'd even finished his sermon, the Holy Spirit came upon Cornelius and all the others who were listening to this message.

"Peter and the Jewish Christians who were with him were dumbfounded. Even the Holy Spirit was for Gentiles? Whoever would have thought it? But there they were, speaking in other tongues and praising God, just as the Jewish Christians had done when the Holy Spirit was first given to them. 'We've got to baptize them,' Peter said. 'We've got to treat them like Christians. How can we not, when God has given them the Holy Spirit, just as he did to us?' Peter baptized them, and they became the first group of non-Jewish Christians.

"It certainly wasn't smooth sailing from there on out. Peter got in trouble with Jewish Christians at first for going to a Gentile's house, but once they heard his story they calmed down. Their reaction was like Peter's: 'Well, isn't that incredible? God has given *Gentiles* the repentance that leads to faith!' Later on, they had to work through things, such as how much of the Jewish law Gentiles had to follow. Which parts of the Bible were for everyone, and which parts were just for Jews before the Savior came. There were even some pretty hot arguments about those issues from time to time. But the important thing was that Jesus' loving conquest of the world by the gospel had begun." Grandpa put his carving of a map back into the box and set a miniature globe in its place.

Isaiah 49:5–7

And now the LORD says,
    he who formed me from the womb to be his servant,
to bring Jacob back to him;
    and that Israel might be gathered to him—
for I am honored in the eyes of the LORD,
    and my God has become my strength—
he says:
"It is too light a thing that you should be my servant
    to raise up the tribes of Jacob
    and to bring back the preserved of Israel;
I will make you as a light for the nations,
    that my salvation may reach to the end of the earth."

Thus says the LORD,
      the Redeemer of Israel and his Holy One,
to one deeply despised, abhorred by the nation,
      the servant of rulers:
"Kings shall see and arise;
      princes, and they shall prostrate themselves;
because of the LORD, who is faithful,
      the Holy One of Israel, who has chosen you."

Not Even the "Big Guns" Can Help

(Acts 12)

Amy screamed and dropped the apple. It fell to the floor with a thud. Marc and Grandpa ran to her, both asking, "What's wrong?"

"There was a worm in my apple!" Amy said with a shudder. "I saw it wiggling around. And I'd already taken two bites!"

Marc picked up the apple and set it gently on the table. He moved very carefully so as not to frighten the worm, which he hoped would show itself again. Sure enough, in a small dark spot in the apple, the very end of a worm, alive and moving, could be seen.

"Yuck!" said Amy. "I'll never eat another apple as long as I live!"

"Look on the bright side," said Marc. "At least you didn't find half a worm."

Amy looked at him blankly. " 'Cause that would mean you'd *eaten* the other half!" Marc laughed.

"Oh, that's sick," Amy answered. Then, "Grandpa, what are you thinking?" she asked. "You've got that story look on your face. Don't tell me you have a war story about wormy apples."

Grandpa shook his head. "No, not wormy apples, but it does have worms in it. I'd forgotten all about it until you found that one. Want to hear it?"

The children nodded. "But what about this apple?" Amy asked.

"I'll throw it away in the outside trash can for you," Marc offered gallantly.

"And why don't you go get an orange instead," Grandpa suggested to Amy. "Sometimes oranges grow green fuzz, but I don't think they ever have worms."

Marc disposed of the apple, Amy found an orange, and Grandpa brought his story box. Then he began.

"Marc," he asked, "when a commander isn't getting to the enemy the way he'd hoped to, what can he do? Besides bringing in more troops."

Marc considered the question. "Well, he could bring in more fire-power. Bring in more or bigger guns."

"Just what I hoped you'd say," said Grandpa. "Satan had lost the war, which was bad enough. But he also wasn't making much progress in discouraging the other side. So far, though, he'd been working only with Pharisees, synagogue leaders, and a high priest. So he decided it was time to bring in the big guns. What if he got a king involved in fighting against God's people? Kings have more power than other people. They can do more to hurt you if they're against you. So Satan put King Herod, the king over the Jews, to work for his side."

"Is that the same Herod that tried to kill Jesus when he was a baby?" Amy asked.

"No," Marc answered. "Because the way Jesus' family knew it was time to leave Egypt was when that Herod died."

"Then who is this Herod?" Amy asked.

"This Herod is that Herod's grandson," Grandpa replied. "But the whole bunch of Herods were cruel tyrants. In between the Herod from the Christmas story and the Herod in today's story, there was the Herod who beheaded John the Baptist."

"Oh, that's right," said Marc, remembering.

"Anyway," Grandpa continued, "Satan decided it was time to bring a cruel king back into the picture. Maybe with his power and his tortures, he could scare the Christians into keeping quiet and the gospel wouldn't spread. It was easy for Satan to get Herod on his side. That's because the two things that mattered most to Herod were popularity and praise from other people. Satan showed Herod how popular he could be with the Jews if he took their side against Jesus' followers. From then on, Herod was completely on Satan's side in the fight against Christians." On the yellow box top, Grandpa placed a small crown.

"The Bible says that the first thing Herod did was to 'lay hands on some who belonged to the church, in order to mistreat them.' It doesn't tell us exactly what he did, but it sounds like he hurt them physically. One thing we do know is that he killed James. This was John's brother—remember how in the stories of Jesus there are always the three: Peter, James, and John? That's the James Herod killed. He was the first of the twelve disciples to die for Jesus.

"Right away, Herod's popularity in the opinion polls of the day skyrocketed. The Jews were delighted with what Herod had done. So Herod decided to kill Peter, too. He arrested Peter and threw him in jail. He planned to put him to death the next day. Until then, he ordered sixteen guards to watch him. He had Peter's hands chained to a guard on each side. Then he locked Peter up behind two guarded gates."

"That's a little extreme," said Marc. "Peter's just a guy. What's he going to do? Call in the Marines and a helicopter to get him out?"

"Well, remember, Peter had a bit of a reputation," Grandpa said. "He was the one who'd been safely locked up one minute and then suddenly standing somewhere else the next. Herod felt he couldn't be too careful." Grandpa smiled mysteriously.

Amy saw the smile and said, "There's a surprise coming, isn't there?"

"So, it was the middle of the night," Grandpa continued. "The church was gathered in the house of one of its members, praying desperately for Peter. Peter, however, was asleep between his two guards."

"Asleep?" Amy asked, incredulous. "How could he be asleep? Wasn't he worried?"

"Well, in any case, Peter was asleep," Grandpa affirmed. "So asleep, in fact, that the angel who came had to hit him on the side to wake him up."

"Another angel?" asked Marc.

Grandpa nodded. "The angel told Peter to get up and get dressed. As he said that, Peter's chains fell off. 'Now follow me,' the angel said. Peter thought he was dreaming, but he did as he was told. They walked by all the guards, out of the locked prison, and to the city gate—which opened for them, all by itself. At that point, Peter realized he wasn't dreaming. Then the angel left."

"What about all those guards?" Marc asked. "They didn't notice any of this?"

257

"Evidently not," said Grandpa. "I guess they were really sound asleep."

"If they were, God was making them sleep," said Marc, "because Roman guards didn't sleep through guard duty. If anything happened to what they were guarding, they were put to death."

"That's right," Grandpa nodded, "and these guards *were* executed, the next day. Peter, once he understood that he really was free and wasn't going to be killed, went to the house where he knew people were praying for him. Now here comes the funny part—anyway, I think this is funny.

"Picture this: Peter knocks at the door and a servant girl comes to see who's there. She looks out, she sees Peter, and she's so excited, she forgets to open the door. She runs back in to the prayer meeting. 'Oh, please help Peter,' everyone's praying. 'Send a miracle. Free him from prison. Let him escape and not be put to death tomorrow.' The girl, whose name is Rhoda, hates to break up the prayer meeting, but she's got to say something. 'Peter's at the gate, right outside,' she announces. And what do you think all the Christians do? Do they begin praising God for answering their prayers? Do they thank the Lord for giving them just what they'd asked for? No, they figure it can't be true. 'You're crazy,' they tell Rhoda. 'No, he's really there and he's knocking,' she insists.

"Well, then everyone gets real quiet to listen, and sure enough, they hear knocking. Do they believe yet that God has answered their prayers? Nope. Now they tell each other, 'Well, it must be his angel.' Meanwhile, Peter, wondering what's the holdup, just keeps knocking. Finally, someone opens the door and lets him in. He tells them all that had happened and leaves for another place, where Herod won't be looking for him.

"The Bible says that there was no small disturbance in the morning when Peter couldn't be found," said Grandpa.

"That's got to be an understatement!" Amy commented.

"Herod searched for him, but couldn't find him. He had to be thinking, 'How'd he *do* that?' That's when he had the guards executed, and he himself headed for another town." Grandpa paused.

"Where are the worms?" Marc asked. "You said there were worms."

"That's next," Grandpa assured him. "Remember, popularity and praise were what Herod valued most. They're what Satan used to win him over. Herod went to another city, where the people really wanted to make him happy. So as he stood there, finely dressed in his royal robes giving a speech, the people began to chant, 'The voice of a god, and not a man. The voice of a god, and not a man.' Did Herod say, 'Oh, you shouldn't say that; I'm not God'? Of course not. He just ate it up. He soaked up their praise and accepted it all as if he really deserved it.

"Immediately, the Bible says, an angel of the Lord struck him down because he didn't give God the glory. He was eaten by worms and died."

"That's gross!" said Amy. "What does that mean?"

"I don't know for sure," said Grandpa, "but it doesn't sound very pleasant, does it?" Grandpa removed the crown from the box top. The children leaned forward to see the figure he put in its place. It was the body of a man with a crown on his head, lying as if prepared for burial.

" 'But,' the Bible says, 'the word of the Lord'—which Herod had tried to stop—'continued to grow and to be multiplied.' A king's not such a big gun, is he, when the fight is against the King of kings?"

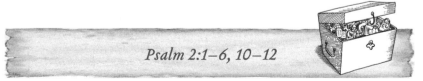

Psalm 2:1–6, 10–12

Why do the nations rage
and the peoples plot in vain?

The kings of the earth set themselves,
    and the rulers take counsel together,
    against the Lord and against his anointed, saying,
"Let us burst their bonds apart
    and cast away their cords from us." . . .

He who sits in the heavens laughs;
    the Lord holds them in derision.
Then he will speak to them in his wrath,
    and terrify them in his fury, saying,
"As for me, I have set my King
    on Zion, my holy hill."

Dr. Luke, War Correspondent

(Acts 13–14, 16)

"Marc, have you ever heard of Ernie Pyle?" Amy asked, as the two children neared Grandpa's store one day after school. "Tim Jamison did an oral book report about his biography today."

Marc shook his head. "No. Who's that?"

Amy brightened. "Yes!" she breathed. "At last! I know a war trivia fact that my brother, Marc-Know-All-There-Is-To-Know-About-War Maclusky, doesn't know! Woo-hoo!"

"All right already," Marc grumbled, secretly pleased, as he always was, when Amy made a big deal about how much he knew. "So who *is* Ernie Pyle?"

"Who *was* Ernie Pyle?" Amy answered. "Tim says he died on a little island in the Pacific Ocean, toward the end of World War II."

"A soldier?" asked Marc, wondering how he could have missed hearing about a famous soldier.

"No, a war correspondent," Amy replied. "You know, one of those reporter guys who travel with the army and send back stories for the papers. But even if he wasn't a soldier, he went absolutely everywhere the soldiers went, facing all the same dangers. The soldiers really liked him because, supposedly, he told their stories the way they wanted them told. And of course, without him, people at home wouldn't have known their stories at all. They wouldn't have known all the awful things the soldiers were going through to try to keep people free at home."

"I've always thought those war-correspondent guys were pretty cool," Marc said. "They end up in some pretty dangerous places, not because they have orders to go, like soldiers, but because they choose to go, so that they can send back stories for people at home. So this guy died in one of the battles, huh?"

"Actually not," said Amy. "Tim said it was getting close to the end of the war, and Ernie Pyle was riding down a road in a jeep when enemy soldiers opened fire. Hey, I wonder what Grandpa would come up with if we asked him to tell us something about a war correspondent from his story box."

"Hey, Grandpa," the children called out as they came through the shop door and set their school things in the corner. "Do you have any stories about war correspondents?"

Grandpa laughed. He had been painting a large discolored picture frame. Now he said, "War correspondents? Where'd you get that idea?" Grandpa stopped to think, his paintbrush poised in midair. "Yes," he said finally, "I think I could come up with a story that has a war correspondent."

"I knew it," said Marc, and he shook his head admiringly. "You can think of one of your war stories for everything. Well, neither of us has any homework, so we're ready when you are."

Grandpa applied the last few strokes of paint, closed the paint can, and went to the sink to rinse his brush and wash his hands. Then he picked up his box and went to join the children. "From here on out, most of the war stories in the New Testament are going to be about Paul. From the time Peter escaped from prison on, most of Acts is about Paul's missionary journeys. Which, of course, are stories of the gospel going into all the world. That makes them stories about Jesus rescuing people from Satan's rule and bringing them under his own. That makes them war stories. And there was someone who wrote many of these stories down so that the rest of the church could know about Jesus' victories."

"Sure, the person who wrote Acts," Amy said, realizing that this must be what Grandpa meant.

"Right. And who was that?" asked Grandpa.

The children looked at each other, then back at Grandpa, shaking their heads. "It was Luke," said Grandpa, "not really a writer or a reporter, but a doctor."

"Is that the same Luke who wrote 'Luke'?" asked Marc.

Grandpa nodded.

"But is that really a war correspondent?" Amy asked, skeptically. "War correspondents are actually there at the battles."

"Oh, well, Luke was," Grandpa assured her. "At least, he was there for many of them. Some of the stories eyewitnesses had to tell him—and Luke always made a point of getting information only from eyewitnesses, like any good reporter—but he often went along with Paul on his trips. So he saw many of the things he wrote about.

"Everywhere the gospel went," Grandpa said, settling into his storytelling, "Paul and his companions found opposition. But they

263

also saw plenty of examples of Jesus' power overcoming that opposition. The battles were hard. But the victories were grand!"

Grandpa looked through his box. "This is going to cover more than one battle, so I need a lot of pieces," he said, selecting several. He closed the lid. "One of the first battles was on an island. Paul was telling the Roman ruler there about the gospel, and he was very interested. But there was a magician who lived on the island. His magic tricks had made him famous, and people listened to him. Now this magician was trying to convince the Roman ruler not to listen to Paul." Grandpa set his first piece down on the box top. It was just a little stick. "I know, it doesn't look like much," he admitted. "Pretend it's a magic wand and it represents all the times that forces of magic or demons tried to oppose the gospel.

"Finally, Paul spoke directly to this magician. He told him that he was a son of the devil and an enemy of righteousness. He told him that he'd be blind for a time, and immediately the magician couldn't see. The Roman ruler was amazed and believed Paul's message.

"In another city, when Paul was with his friend Barnabas, God worked through Paul to heal a lame man. Right away, all the people who lived there wanted to offer sacrifices to them."

"To Paul and Barnabas?" Marc asked. "Why?"

"The people were Greeks," Grandpa explained. "They worshiped many gods." On the box top next to the magic wand, Grandpa set a figure on a throne with a lightning bolt in his hand.

Amy leaned forward. "Zeus," she said.

"The Greeks had a story about two of their gods, Zeus and Hermes, who disguised themselves as men and came down to visit a certain town," Grandpa continued. "None of the people in the town invited the gods in, which made the gods angry."

"Oh, I remember this story," Amy cried. "There was one poor married couple who invited them in, right?" she asked.

Grandpa nodded. "Yes, and *they* were rewarded, but what happened to all their neighbors?"

"Zeus sent a flood and wiped out everything they had," Amy answered.

Grandpa nodded again. "So when the Greek people in our war story saw two strangers heal a lame man, they figured it must be *their* turn for a visit from the gods, and they didn't want to make the same mistake. They hurried to sacrifice a bull to Paul and Barnabas. Of course, Paul seized the opportunity to preach a sermon about the true God and the Savior he had sent.

"Then things took an ugly turn. Enemies from a nearby town, where Paul had already preached, came looking for him. They were Jewish religious leaders who were jealous of Paul. Too many people had come to hear Paul preach, more than usually came to hear *them*, and they didn't like that. They had run Paul out of their town, but then they heard he was in this neighboring town and came after him. These enemies stirred up the crowds 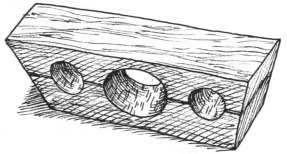 and got them to stone Paul. They threw rocks at him until they thought he was dead, and they dragged him outside the city and left him." Grandpa set the stone that he had used in a story about Jesus next to the other two figures.

"And there was the time when Paul cast a demon out of a slave girl. That made her masters mad because she used to tell fortunes for money, and now she couldn't do it. So they had Paul arrested, along with his friend Silas, and had them put in stocks in the jail."

"Are stocks those things like boards with holes in them?" Marc asked. "They lock your feet in the holes and leave you there, right?"

"Right," Grandpa said. "I have one right here that I made." And he set a little piece of wood, into which he'd carved two holes, by all the other pieces. "But at midnight, there was an earthquake. All the prisoners' chains fell off and all the prison doors opened. As a result, the jailer and his whole household heard the gospel from Paul and they were all baptized.

"War story after war story—and Luke wrote about them all. There were shipwrecks." Grandpa placed the little ship from a previous story on its side next to the growing line of little pieces on his box top. "Paul wrote that he was beaten with sticks three times and with a whip five times." Grandpa added the whip from an earlier story to his collection. "But none of this opposition stopped Paul. God gave him the strength he needed to keep on advancing against the enemy. And captive after captive was taken from Satan's side and brought to God's side."

With a swish of his hand, Grandpa knocked all the pieces from the box top: magic wand, idol, stone, stocks, overturned ship, and whip. In their place he set a single small figure. Marc and Amy peered at it, then at Grandpa, puzzled. "Feet?" they said together.

"Paul talked about feet in one of his letters," Grandpa said. "He quoted a verse from Isaiah about how beautiful the feet are that carry the good news of the gospel. You'd have to say, God gave Paul beautiful feet!" A car horn sounded from the driveway. "Uh-oh. There's your mom. We'll have to save the rest of Luke's war correspondence for tomorrow—are you coming over tomorrow?"

"Yes," Amy answered as the children gathered up their school things.

"There's more?" asked Marc.

"Oh, yes, the last part of Acts is very dramatic, and Luke was there for it all. See you tomorrow!" Grandpa waved as the children ran out the door.

How beautiful upon the mountains
    are the feet of him who brings good news,
who publishes peace, who brings good news of happiness,
    who publishes salvation,
    who says to Zion, "Your God reigns." . . .
The Lord has bared his holy arm
    before the eyes of all the nations,
and all the ends of the earth shall see
    the salvation of our God.

Still Advancing

(Acts 20:16–28:31)

"So, Grandpa," Marc asked, as he rummaged in his backpack for the snack he had left over from school, "if today you're going to tell us about the end of Acts, does that mean your war stories are almost finished? Because after Acts, there aren't any more books in the New Testament with stories."

"You're right, my war stories are about done," Grandpa agreed. "Which is to say that I've used up almost all the story reminders I have in my war chest. It's not to say that you've heard all the stories there are about this war between God and Satan. There are many, many more, both in the Bible and in the history that comes after Bible times. And every day, all over the world, the war continues, so the stories keep growing."

"But the war's already won, right?" Amy asked.

"And it's hopeless for Satan, right, Grandpa?" Marc double-checked.

"Yes and yes," said Grandpa. "Every battle just brings greater victory and more honor for our Commander. Listen to how hard Satan tried in this story. This is the story that Luke ends his book with."

Grandpa took two items from his box, and the children settled comfortably in their chairs to listen. "As Paul traveled, he took up a collection in every church to help needy Christians in Jerusalem. He took this money to Jerusalem, along with Luke and several other companions. Some of these companions, like Luke himself, were Gentiles. Remember that, because it's going to be important."

"Got it," said Marc.

"When Paul got to Jerusalem, he learned that there were many Jews there who'd heard about him. They'd heard that he preached to Gentiles, but they'd misunderstood what he taught. What Paul really taught was that a person is made right with God by faith in Jesus and not by keeping the law. What the Jews thought he'd said was that it's fine to ignore God's laws. So before he even got there, there was a city full of people who were mad at him.

"One day, some of these people saw Paul in the temple. Only Jews were allowed in the temple. Gentiles couldn't go in. When these already angry Jews saw Paul in the temple, they jumped to the conclusion that he'd brought his Gentile traveling companions in with him—which he hadn't. A whole crowd of these angry people came together and physically dragged Paul out of the temple. They would have killed him for sure, if it hadn't been for the commander of the Roman fort there in Jerusalem. His job was to keep the peace, so when he heard about the mob, he ran to see what was happening. He brought a bunch of soldiers with him, which was a good thing, because this mob was violent. They stopped beating Paul only because they saw the soldiers coming.

"The Roman commander put Paul in chains and asked what he'd done wrong. The crowd was shouting all kinds of different things, so the commander decided to take Paul into the barracks and question him. Paul's enemies were afraid that they were going to lose him. The soldiers actually had to carry Paul up the stairs of the barracks because the mob was so intent on getting their hands on him again."

Amy shook her head. "Wow," she said. "Paul's got to be feeling a little beat up by now!"

Grandpa nodded. "And once he got into the barracks, the commander ordered that Paul should be whipped until he told what he'd done to make the crowd so angry."

"Why didn't he just ask him?" Amy asked.

"That's not the way Romans did things," said Marc.

"At least it wasn't the way they did things with non-Romans," Grandpa corrected. "Thing is, Paul *was* a Roman citizen; he'd been born a Roman citizen, so it was illegal to beat him when he hadn't even had a trial. Paul was quick to point this out to the man with the whip, who passed it on to the commander. Right away, the Romans lightened up on their treatment of Paul.

"The next day the commander ordered the Jewish council to assemble. He brought Paul to the assembly, still hoping to learn what terrible crime he'd committed. Paul knew he wouldn't get a fair trial from this group. So to outsmart them, he cried out that he'd grown up a Pharisee. Now, the council was made up of Pharisees and their rivals, the Sadducees. And just as Paul had hoped, the Pharisees began to defend him while the Sadducees tried to get their hands on him. Their argument grew so fierce that the commander was afraid the two groups would tear Paul to pieces. Once more he rescued Paul and took him back to the barracks."

"You've got to feel sorry for that commander," said Amy. "He's not doing very well at getting to the bottom of things."

"By now," Grandpa continued, "Paul must have been wondering how all this would end. Would he ever be able to get back to his work of preaching the gospel? That night, the Lord Jesus himself appeared to Paul. 'Take courage,' he told him. 'You've been a faithful witness for me here in Jerusalem, and you must do the same in Rome.'

"The very next day, Paul's enemies took a vow, which was a very serious thing to a Jew. They vowed not to eat and drink again until they'd killed Paul."

"Whoa," said Marc. "That's serious."

"Here was their plan. They'd ask the commander to send Paul to them again for a trial. As he was being brought to the trial, the forty men who'd taken the vow intended to ambush him and kill him. Now, Paul's nephew lived in Jerusalem. And somehow he found out about this evil plan and warned the commander. So the commander got together a guard for Paul of two hundred soldiers, seventy horsemen, and two hundred spearmen. Under cover of darkness, he sent Paul, with this guard, to the nearby port city of Caesarea. The commander sent the Roman governor Felix a letter to explain the situation and asked Felix to take charge of his prisoner.

"When Paul reached Caesarea, Felix put him in prison there and did nothing to decide his case. While Paul sat in jail in Caesarea for two years, Luke traveled to the nearby towns, where Jesus had lived and taught. That way, Luke could gather eyewitness information for his gospel. He probably wrote the gospel we call Luke during those two years.

"Paul might have been stuck in jail there forever if Felix hadn't been replaced by a new governor named Festus. Festus suggested that Paul go back to Jerusalem for a trial. But Paul knew that the Jews there would kill him if he went back. So he used his legal rights as a Roman citizen to appeal to Caesar. That meant his case would go all the way to Rome for Caesar to decide."

"I don't know if that was such a good idea," Marc commented. "You wouldn't want some of those Caesars to get *their* hands on you either!"

"Well, it was Nero who was one of the worst, but he hadn't done anything against Christians yet. So Paul was handed over to a Roman centurion named Julius, along with some other prisoners, and they all set sail for Italy." Grandpa opened his Bible to the map section in the back so that he could show the children the route they would have taken from Caesarea to Rome.

"Was Luke on the boat with them?" Amy asked.

"Yes," said Grandpa. "And he ended up with some pretty exciting things to write about. For instance, they got caught in a terrible storm. The wind was so violent, they couldn't steer the ship. They had to just let it blow them wherever it would. This storm went on for fourteen days. There was no sun, no stars—they had no idea where they were. Even the sailors gave up hope of surviving. Finally, they saw an island and tried to land the ship. But it got stuck on a reef, where two seas met. So there sat the boat, unable to move, while opposite seas beat against it from both sides. The ship began to break in pieces. Everyone who could swim struck out for the island, and those who couldn't grabbed pieces broken off the boat and hung on for dear life. Amazingly, no one was drowned.

"Then, on the island, Paul was helping to gather wood for a fire to dry off. A poisonous snake crept out from under some wood and attached itself to his arm. Everyone thought he was a goner for sure, but he just shook it off and wasn't harmed at all. That's when the people who lived on the island decided that Paul must be a god. Those who were sick came to him and were healed. I'm sure Paul explained the gospel to them as well.

"Finally, months after they had set out from Caesarea, they arrived in Rome. No speedy trial and freedom ahead, though. The book of Acts ends by telling us that Paul was kept in Rome for two more years. It was probably during those two years that Luke wrote

Acts. He ended his book right there, with Paul still a prisoner in Rome, because Luke didn't know what would happen next.

"Now what do you think?" Grandpa asked, looking at each of his grandchildren. "Hadn't Satan done a great job? Using angry Jews, lazy Roman officers, and storms, he had set aside the church's greatest spokesman and most effective missionary. Wouldn't other Christians be discouraged from preaching the gospel, seeing what had happened to Paul? Wouldn't Paul himself be useless in the war effort, sitting in one prison location after another?"

Grandpa set little chains, ending in wrist cuffs, on the top of his box and waited for an answer.

"Well, yes, that's how it would *seem*—" Marc began.

"—but we know enough about your stories to know that's not really what happened," Amy finished.

"Of course it's not," Grandpa agreed. "Luke tells us that Paul was allowed to stay in his own rented house during his time in Rome. He had a guard, but anyone could come and see him. Individual people came to see him there, and crowds came, too. Paul preached the gospel to them all. In one of Paul's letters, he wrote that the whole Praetorian guard—Roman soldiers—heard the gospel. If Paul had guards night and day, what do you think he talked about with them during all that time? In that same letter, Paul mentioned the Christians in Caesar's household, so the gospel had even gotten inside the emperor's palace. Paul said that instead of Christians being discouraged from preaching because of what had happened to him, they were actually made bolder by his example. So in spite of Satan's attempts to keep Paul from preaching, the gospel just kept advancing. The victories were always the Lord's. Luke ended his writing of Acts by saying that Paul was still 'preaching the kingdom of God, and teaching concerning the Lord Jesus Christ, with all openness, unhindered.' "

Grandpa left the little chains on top of his box, but placed a little house next to them. "A house?" asked Amy. "Why a house?"

"This stands for the house that Paul rented while he was a prisoner," Grandpa explained. "The gospel went out powerfully from that little house, winning allies to Christ even in Rome, the capital of the world."

Romans 16:25–27

Now to him who is able to strengthen you according to my gospel and the preaching of Jesus Christ, according to the revelation of the mystery that was kept secret for long ages but has now been disclosed and through the prophetic writings has been made known to all nations, according to the command of the eternal God, to bring about the obedience of faith—to the only wise God be glory forevermore through Jesus Christ! Amen.

Victory at Last!

(Revelation)

The next time that Amy and Marc walked to Grandpa's shop after school, Amy asked, first thing, for Grandpa's box. She did not stop to find a snack, which was her usual habit. She did not even set her backpack down. "Is it okay if I look through your box?" she asked.

"Sure," said Grandpa, handing it to her. "Looking for anything in particular?"

"Just wondering if there were any pieces left that we hadn't seen," said Amy, sorting through the figures.

"You've seen most of them," he assured her.

Amy lit up. "Most? Not *all*?"

Grandpa held up two fingers. "Two pieces left," he said, "for my last story."

"So there *is* one more story!" Amy cried. "I knew there had to be! Because what was happening where you stopped and what I see when I look around me don't seem to match up."

Grandpa could see that Amy was troubled. "What do you mean?" he asked gently.

"The way you tell it, the war's already won, and Jesus just keeps taking captives right and left," Amy said. "No matter what Satan comes up with, God's people always overcome him. The gospel keeps spreading, the church keeps growing—but here we are a long time after all that happened with Paul, and it doesn't seem like the war's been won at all. Every time I have to get a current event ready for school, I go flipping through the newspaper and see one horrible story after another. War and terrorists and murder and people starving—it doesn't *look* like Satan's works have been destroyed. And it seems like God's people always *lose*—at least, they lose more than they win. Seems like we're always hearing about new laws that move *away* from what God wants. Are you *sure* the war's already been won? Has Satan really been defeated?"

"My last story is just for you," Grandpa said. "May I?" and he reached for the box she held. She gave it up, and he quickly found the two pieces he had not yet used. "Marc!" he called. "Last story from the war chest."

Marc hurried in, saying, "I certainly don't want to miss the last story!"

"It's kind of a story," Grandpa said, "but it's really a vision that God gave someone. God knew that his people would have the kind of questions Amy's having. He knew they might get discouraged. So he gave this vision to the Apostle John and commanded him to write it down.

"Now, in our last story, Paul was still a prisoner in Rome," said Grandpa. "He was finally released, and not long after that, there was a huge fire in Rome."

"Oh, I remember this," cried Marc. "Some people said Nero started it."

"And Nero was—?" asked Grandpa.

"The emperor of Rome," Marc replied. "*He* said the Christians started the fire."

"Nero was an evil man," Grandpa continued. "Many people didn't like him. So to get attention off himself, he said that Christians had started the fire in Rome. This is where really bad persecution began. Christianity became illegal and it became Roman policy to persecute Christians. Nero was the one who started feeding Christians to wild animals in the Colosseum. Tradition has it that both Peter and Paul were killed during Nero's persecution. Then after Nero, under the next couple of emperors, persecution was on again, off again.

"Then came the emperor Domitian, who was cruel in his persecutions, too. Rome seemed determined to stamp out Christianity and Christians. People were killed, tortured, driven from their homes by the thousands. John, of course, faithfully continued to preach the gospel, and for his trouble, he was exiled to an island by the name of Patmos." Grandpa stopped. "You know what 'exiled' means, right?"

"It's when they kick you out of your own country and make you live somewhere else," said Marc.

"That's right," said Grandpa. "If it looks to *you* like Satan's winning, Amy, imagine how it seemed to the Christians living then."

"Right," said Amy, nodding. "That's exactly what I mean."

"The Lord Jesus knew how hard this was for his people," Grandpa continued. "He wanted them to understand why this was happening and how it would all turn out. He wanted to remind them that he would be victorious at last, and that they would be victorious with him. So he appeared to John on the island and gave him a 'revelation,' showing him how things really were and how they were going to turn out. Jesus told John to write it down so that people then and people right down to our own time could be encouraged by it."

"Is that the book of Revelation?" Amy asked.

"It is," said Grandpa. "Revelation is kind of like pulling back the curtain at a play to reveal or show what's going on backstage. What *we* see are all the horrible things that go on in the world, especially in times of extreme persecution like John's day. God's people need to see what's *really* going on. Why do these things happen? And will Jesus really conquer? John saw many strange and amazing things in his vision—"

"I'll say," Marc agreed. "I've read some of it, and it's pretty weird. Mountains that fall into the sea and change the water into blood. And locusts that sting people like scorpions. And horses that breathe out fire and smoke. It's pretty strange stuff."

"That's because it's full of symbols, things that stand for other things," Grandpa explained. "But there are some main points that keep coming out. For one thing, Jesus made it clear in his revelation that all these things we don't like happen because of the war between him and Satan. In one part of the vision, John saw an ugly dragon crouched by a woman who was about to have a baby. The dragon was waiting for the baby to be born so that he could devour it. But when the baby was born, it was caught up to God and escaped. Remind you of any of our war stories?"

"It's kind of like Herod and the baby Jesus," Amy said.

"It's also like all the times that people tried to destroy God's people before Jesus came," Marc added.

"In the vision," Grandpa went on, "the dragon became very angry because he couldn't destroy the baby. So he went off to make war against those who obey God and hold to Jesus by faith. With this vision of the dragon and the woman, Jesus was showing John and

all of us why this war goes on and why its battles are so tough. Satan is furious because
he couldn't destroy Jesus, so he goes
after his followers. But he knows he's
going to lose." Here Grandpa set a
figure of a small, fierce dragon on
the box top.

"In his vision, John also saw
many of the things that make it
hard for Christians to trust God. He
saw the souls of Christians in heaven
who've died for their faith. He saw godly Christian leaders get killed
by the church's enemies while people rejoiced. He saw Satan produce false prophets who taught the opposite of the gospel, while the
whole world seemed to listen to them. Like Amy said, it sure didn't
look like Satan was losing. But through it all, Jesus let John see behind
the curtain, so to speak, into heaven. He showed him how Jesus was
still ordering everything exactly according to his will. He saw that
none of it was taking Jesus by surprise. All of the Lord's plans were
right on schedule.

"Another main idea in John's vision was the idea of evil getting
punished at last. The things you were talking about, Marc, were pictures of judgment—the stinging locusts and the bloody water. Those
things were a reminder that Jesus calls people to repent. If they don't
repent, they will face his judgment. The evil rulers—the Neros and
Domitians—of this world won't get away with their cruelties forever. John even saw Satan himself finally thrown into a lake of fire
at the end of time.

"The best part of the revelation, though, is that Jesus is indeed
Lord, and will triumph at last. In one of John's visions, he saw Jesus
ride out on a white horse to do battle against all his enemies. Thousands gathered against him—but they were all defeated as soon as
he showed up! John saw scene after scene of angels and people in
heaven, praising Jesus as the Victor and the one who would rule for-

ever. Remember the Hallelujah chorus, from Handel's *Messiah*? This is where it comes from, Revelation." And Grandpa, who had a nice singing voice, sang a few lines:

> And he shall reign forever and ever,
> Hallelujah, hallelujah,
> King of kings,
> And Lord of lords,
> Hallelujah, hallelujah.

Grandpa removed the dragon from his box top and placed the figure of a rider on a white charger, outfitted for battle, in its place.

"Then John saw what will happen when God wins the war. He will get what he was fighting for all along. He will have a people who will be his people. They will be with him forever, and he will be their God.

"Be patient, Amy," Grandpa said, slipping his arm around her shoulders. "What you see now isn't all there is to it. Satan and all his work will someday be gone forever. Jesus will rule the universe with no one to fight against him. And all his soldiers, however hard their battles were, will finally be home from the war. The peace that begins on that day will never end."

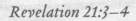

Revelation 21:3–4

And I heard a loud voice from the throne saying, "Behold, the dwelling place of God is with man. He will dwell with them, and they will be his people, and God himself will be with them as their God. He will wipe away every tear from their eyes, and death shall be no more, neither shall there be mourning nor crying nor pain anymore, for the former things have passed away."

Note to Parents

When so many books retelling Bible stories for children already line the shelves of bookstores, why would I write yet another one? What did I hope to offer in *Grandpa's Box* that the other books do not? Bible storytellers usually take one of three approaches. After they tell the story, they may draw a moral from it, much like Aesop did with his fables. Or they may focus on the human "hero" of the story (or, in some cases, the "villain"), encouraging children to follow (or avoid) the example that character sets. Or the teller of Bible stories may just present the story as a fact of Bible history and go on to the next one. I believe that God had the same primary intention in giving us Bible stories as he had in giving us the rest of his Word— he intended to reveal himself to us. Anyone can plainly see that God exists because his creative works surround us. None of us, however, could have any clear concept of what he is like had he not revealed himself to us in his written Word.

I once heard it said that the Bible is like a museum and every part of it shows us another aspect of the wonder of its author. We move through its pages from one exhibit to the next, marveling at how each new passage adds to our understanding of our great God. This is as true of biblical narrative as it is of any other Scripture passage. Every time we read any Bible story, we should ask ourselves, "What is *God* doing in this story? What does this story show me about *God*?" I wrote *Grandpa's Box* wanting children to see that the main character of every Bible story is, always, God. Every story in Scripture shows us something about God that he wants us to know.

I chose only forty-one stories, but I chose them from both Old and New Testaments and set them down in chronological order, pointing out that all the stories tell the one story of God's purpose to have a people for himself. All of the stories give us glimpses of God working out that purpose, beginning in the Garden of Eden and ending with John on Patmos. This overview emphasizes another aspect of Bible stories that people of all ages sometimes forget: the Bible stories really comprise one story. The Bible story describes God's work of redemption accomplished for and in his people. In this story of redemption, God reveals himself to us.

Although *Grandpa's Box* can be read by children on their own, may I encourage you, their parents, to encourage them in their reading and discuss the various stories with them. Especially help them to see what each story shows us about God. A few discussion questions for each chapter can be found online at P&R Publishing's website (www.prpbooks.com/grandpasbox). A list of references for the stories themselves follows this note, in case you would like to see the stories in their biblical context or would like to read them straight from the Bible. May you and your child come to see the power, the grace, and the sovereignty of the God of glory in these stories of his victories.

Outline of Bible Stories

1. Introduction to the War

Old Testament

2. The fall   Genesis 3
God wisely planned for a Redeemer from sin.

3. Cain and Abel   Genesis 4:1–15, 25–26
God calls people to repentance; God provides one from whom the promised Seed would come.

4. Noah and the flood   Genesis 6–8
God judges sin and destroys evil; God provides a refuge from his judgment.

5. God calls Abraham   Genesis 12:1–9; 17:1–8
God chooses some by grace to save, working in their hearts so they will respond to him, and delivers them from their idolatry.

6. Birth, sacrifice of Isaac   Genesis 17:15–21; 21:1–7; 22:1–14
God is able to keep his promises; God provides a substitute.

7. Jacob and his vision at Bethel   Genesis 27–28
God is a God of grace, blessing in spite of a person's lack of deserving.

8. Joseph and his brothers   Genesis 37, 39–50
God sovereignly uses evil to accomplish his purposes.

9. The baby Moses preserved   Exodus 1:1–2:10
God provides a deliverer for his people.

10. The exodus from Egypt   Exodus 5–15
God commands the forces of nature and is greater than world rulers and armies.

11. The giving of the Law   Exodus 19–20
God reveals his moral law.

12. Miracles in the wilderness   Exodus and Numbers
God is faithful to his people even when they are unfaithful.

13. Joshua and Jericho   Joshua 1, 6
By his great power, God fulfills his promises to his people.

14. Gideon   Judges 6–7
For his own glory, God uses the most unlikely means to accomplish his purposes.

15. Ruth   Ruth
In his grace, God reaches out to those who have worshiped other gods and are not his people.

16. Saul and David   1 Samuel 8, 10, 13, 16
God provides the righteous king his people need.

17. David's sin and repentance   2 Samuel 11–12; Psalm 51
God works in his people to bring them to repentance and forgives their sin.

18. Elijah on Mt. Carmel   1 Kings 18
The Lord alone is God.

19. Micaiah's prophecy and Ahab's death   1 Kings 22
God works all things to accomplish what he has said will come to pass.

20. Healing of Namaan   2 Kings 5
God often conquers his enemies through mercy and grace, using the faithful witness of his people.

21. Athaliah and Joash   2 Kings 11
God preserved a descendant of David because he is faithful to his promises.

22. Hezekiah and Sennacharib   2 Kings 18–19; 2 Chronicles 32:1–23
God has all power over all rulers and armies; God answers the prayers of his people.

23. Jeremiah's scroll   Jeremiah 36
God preserves his word from his enemies' attempts to destroy it.

24. Nebuchadnezzar's dream; the fiery furnace   Daniel 2–3
God's kingdom is over all kingdoms and alone will last.

25. Rebuilding of the temple   Ezra 1:1–4; Ezra 4; Haggai 1; Ezra 5–6

God faithfully keeps his word to his people; God accomplishes his purposes through directing the will of rulers, calling his people by his servants, giving his people a will to work.

26. Esther   Esther
God ordains everyday details to the end that he may protect and preserve his people, and accomplish his purposes for them.

New Testament

27. Birth of Christ, escape from Herod   Luke 1:26–38; 2:1–7;
Matthew 2
God brings his word to pass; God gives a Savior; God preserves the Messiah from enemies.

28. The temptation of Christ   Matthew 4:1–11; Luke 4:1–13
God gives a "second Adam," able to remain obedient to God under temptation.

29. Healing a demoniac   Mark 5:1–20
In Christ, God demonstrates his rule and power over demons.

30. Jesus' miracles and claims; the Jews' opposition   John 1–8
God provides a Savior, giving evidences of his authenticity, and preserves him from enemies.

31. Raising of Lazarus   John 11
In Christ, God demonstrates his power over death.

32. The crucifixion   Matthew 27, Mark 15, Luke 23, John 19
In Christ, God saves us from our sin and from his wrath at our sin.

33. The resurrection   John 20
In Christ, God triumphs over the grave; God gives all authority to Christ, who rules all things for the good of the church and for the glory of God.

34. The coming of the Holy Spirit   Acts 2
God gives to his people what they need to do the work he has given them of making disciples of all nations.

35. The disciples refuse to be intimidated by persecution Acts 3–5
God enables his people to remain faithful to him in the face of opposition.

36. Stoning of Stephen   Acts 6:1–8:4
God sovereignly uses evil to accomplish his purposes.

37. Saul's conversion   Acts 8:1-3; 9:1-31
    God often conquers his enemies by so changing their hearts that they become his most faithful servants.

38. Conversion of Cornelius and his household   Acts 10
    God provides salvation for those outside of his Jewish people too.

39. Peter freed from prison by an angel   Acts 12
    God's word and purpose triumph over the plans of earthly rulers.

40. Paul's missionary journeys   Acts 13–14, 16
    God sends out his people as his messengers and as "conquerors"; God's power is greater than all opposition.

41. Paul's imprisonment and trip to Rome   Acts 20:16–28:31
    God continues to advance the gospel, in spite of worsening opposition, sending it into the very seat of the greatest earthly power (Rome).

42. John's exile and vision on Patmos   Revelation
    God comforts his people in their suffering on his behalf by showing them that victory is his, that they will be with him forever, and that Satan will be destroyed at last.

Starr Meade served for ten years as the director of children's ministries in a local church and has taught Bible and Latin classes in Christian schools. She lives in Mesa, Arizona, where she is currently teaching classes to homeschoolers.